Andy McNab joined the infantry as a boy soldier. In 1984 he was 'badged' as a member of 22 SAS Regiment and was involved in both covert and overt special operations worldwide.

During the Gulf War he commanded Bravo Two Zero, a patrol that, in the words of his commanding officer, 'will remain in regimental history for ever'. Awarded both the Distinguished Conduct Medal (DCM) and the Military Medal (MM) during his military career, McNab was the British Army's most highly decorated serving soldier when he finally left the SAS in February 1993. He wrote about his experiences in two phenomenal bestsellers, *Bravo Two Zero*, which was filmed in 1998 starring Sean Bean, and *Immediate Action*.

He is also the author of the bestselling novels *Remote Control*, *Crisis Four*, *Firewall*, *Last Light*, *Liberation Day*, *Dark Winter* and *Deep Black*. Besides his writing work, he lectures to security and intelligence agencies in both the USA and the UK.

www.**booksattransworld**.co.uk

AGGRESSOR

Andy McNab

BANTAM PRESS

LONDON • TORONTO • SYDNEY • AUCKLAND • JOHANNESBURG

TRANSWORLD PUBLISHERS
61–63 Uxbridge Road, London W5 5SA
a division of The Random House Group Ltd

RANDOM HOUSE AUSTRALIA (PTY) LTD
20 Alfred Street, Milsons Point, Sydney,
New South Wales 2061, Australia

RANDOM HOUSE NEW ZEALAND LTD
18 Poland Road, Glenfield, Auckland 10, New Zealand

RANDOM HOUSE SOUTH AFRICA (PTY) LTD
Isle of Houghton, Corner of Boundary Road and Carse O'Gowrie,
Houghton 2198, South Africa

Published 2005 by Bantam Press
a division of Transworld Publishers

A catalogue record for this book is available from the British Library.
ISBN 978 0593 050316 (cased) (from Jan 2007)
ISBN 0593 050312 (cased)
ISBN 978 0593 050323 (tpb) (from Jan 2007)
ISBN 0593 050320 (tpb)

Typeset in 11/13½pt Palatino by
Falcon Oast Graphic Art Ltd

Printed in Great Britain by
Mackays of Chatham plc, Chatham, Kent

7 9 10 8 6

Papers used by Transworld Publishers are natural, recyclable products made from
wood grown in sustainable forests. The manufacturing processes conform to the
environmental regulations of the country of origin.

PART ONE

1

Monday, 5 April 1993

The three of us clung to the top of the Bradley armoured fighting vehicle as it bucked and lurched over the churned-up ground. Exhaust fumes streamed from its rear grille and made us choke, but at least they were warm. The days out here might be hot, but the nights were freezing.

My right hand was clenched round an ice-cold grab handle near the turret. My left gripped the shoulder strap of my day sack. We'd flown three thousand miles to use this gear, and there was nothing to replace it if it got damaged. The whole job would have to be aborted and I would be severely in the shit.

Nightsun searchlights mounted on the four AFVs strafed the front of the target buildings. The other three were decoys; ours was the only one transporting a three-man SAS team. That was if we could all keep a grip on the thing.

As our driver took a sharp left towards the rear of the target, our Nightsun sliced a path across the night sky like a scene from the Blitz.

Charlie was team leader on this one, and wore a headset and boom mike to prove it. Connected to the comms box outside the AFV, it meant he could talk to the crew. His mouth was moving but I didn't have a clue what he was saying. The roar of the engine and the clatter of the tracks put paid to that. He finished, pulled off the headset, and lobbed it onto the grille. He gave Half Arse and me a slap and the shout to stand by.

Seconds later, the AFV slowed, then came to a halt: our cue to jump. We scrambled down the sides, taking care our day sacks didn't strike anything on the way.

The vehicle swivelled on its own axis, mud cascading from its tracks, then headed back the way we'd come.

I joined Charlie and Half Arse behind a couple of cars. They were obvious cover, but we'd only be here a few seconds, and if the Nightsuns had done their job, anybody watching from the building would have lost their night vision anyway.

We hugged the ground, looking, listening, tuning in.

Our AFV was now grinding along the other side of the building with its mates, Nightsuns working the front of the target. And now that they were a safe distance from our eardrums, the loudspeakers mounted on each vehicle began to broadcast a horrible, high-pitched noise like baby rabbits being slaughtered. They'd been doing that for days. I didn't know how it was affecting the people inside the target, but it certainly made me crazy.

We were about fifty metres from the rear of the target. I checked Baby-G: about six hours till first light. I checked the gaffer tape holding my earpiece, and that the two throat-mike sensors were still in place.

Charlie was sorting out his own comms. When he'd finished taping his earpiece, he thumbed the pressle hanging from a wire attached to the lapel of his black corduroy bomber jacket, and spoke low and slow. 'This is Team Alpha. We clear to move yet? Over.' Brits found his thick Yorkshire accent hard enough to understand; fuck knows what the Americans at the other end would make of it.

He was talking to a P3 aircraft circling some twenty-five thousand feet above our heads. Bristling with thermal imaging

8

equipment to warn us of any impending threat while we were on the job, it also carried an immensely powerful infrared torch. I checked that my one-inch square of luminous tape was still stuck on my shoulder. The aircraft's IR beam was invisible to the naked eye, but the reflections off our squares would stick out like sore thumbs on their camera. If we were compromised and bodies poured out of the target to take us on, at least P3 would be able to direct the QRF [Quick Reaction Force] to the right place.

The reply from the P3 came to my earpiece too. 'Yep, that's a free zone, Team Alpha, free zone.'

Charlie didn't bother to voice a reply; he just gave two clicks on the pressle. Then he came alongside me and put his mouth right against my ear. 'If I don't make it, will you do something for me?'

I looked at him and nodded, then mouthed the question, 'What?'

I felt the warmth of his breath on the side of my face. 'Make sure Hazel gets that three quid you owe me. It's part of my estate.'

He gave me the kind of grin that would have won him an audition with the Black and White Minstrels. It had been years since he'd subbed me for that fucking bacon sandwich, but the way he went on about it you'd have thought he'd paid off my mortgage.

He rolled away and began to crawl. He'd know that I was second in line, with Half Arse bringing up the rear. Half Arse also had personal comms, but his earpiece was just shoved into his jacket pocket. He was going to be the eyes and ears while Charlie and I worked on target.

The crawl was wet and muddy and my jeans and fleece were quickly soaked. I was beginning to wish I'd worn gloves and a couple of extra layers.

Like the other two, I kept my eyes on those parts of the target behind which the P3 couldn't penetrate: the windows. The rabbit noise and searchlights should keep the occupants' attention on the front of the target until we were done, but we'd freeze at the slightest movement, and hope we hadn't been seen or heard.

'You've got thirty to target, Team Alpha.' P3 were trying to be helpful.

Torchlight flickered behind a curtain on the first-floor window. It was directed inwards, not out at us. It wasn't a threat.

We carried on, and six minutes of slow crawling later we were where we needed to be.

2

The flaky white, weather-boarded exterior was only the first of three layers. The building plans showed there were likely to be another two behind it. One was tarpaper to prevent damp and help with insulation, and then there'd be the interior stud wall, which would have a finishing coat of either paint or paper, or both. None of which should be a problem for the sophisticated gear we were carrying.

As planned, we'd crawled to a point between two ground-floor windows. A utility box the size of a coal bunker was set against the wall. It was an ideal location for the stuff we were going to leave behind.

Fingers shielding the lens of his mini-Maglite, Charlie opened the utility box with a square lug key and had a quick look inside.

Half Arse had his pistol out; he kept his eyes on the windows and his ears everywhere else. He'd had a buttock shot away during an op a few years back, and right now I wondered if it meant his arse was only half as cold as mine. His wife wanted him to have an implant so he didn't scare the kids when he took them swimming, but they weren't available on the NHS, and he refused to go private. 'I'm too tight-arsed' was his standard joke. 'Or rather, tight half-arsed . . .' Nobody ever laughed. It wasn't very funny, and nor was he.

We knew that everyone in the various Pods [tactical operations] would be watching the thermal and IR imagery of us at work, beamed down to them by the P3. We wanted to make sure it was a job well done; don't mess with the best was the message we wanted to transmit – though right now it was the last thing any of us was worried about; personally, I just wanted to do the business and get away alive. This was my last job before I left the Regiment. It would be the mother of all ironies if I got dropped or injured now.

I eased my day sack off my back. A distant voice inside the building shouted out something but we ignored him. We'd only react if someone was actually shouting that they'd spotted us; otherwise, we'd be stopping and starting every five minutes. You just have to get on with it until you know there is a definite drama. That was what Half Arse was here for.

Charlie had worked out where he wanted to fix the device. He pressed a thumbnail into the wood at almost ground level and gave me a nod. I brought out a pyramid from my day sack, seven inches high and made of alloy. Instead of a peak, it had a hole, and at each of the four corners was a fixing lug.

Guided by the beam from Charlie's Maglite, I positioned the pyramid so the hole was directly over his nail mark, and held it there while he put a battery-powered screwdriver to the first lug. Very slowly, very deliberately, the shaft of the screwdriver rotated. It took the best part of two minutes to screw it in tight. By the time the first three were in, my hands were almost numb.

A different voice shouted from inside. It was closer, but it wasn't talking about us. He was complaining about the rabbit noise, and I couldn't blame him.

The sweat on my back was starting to cool and I could feel fingers of wind fighting their way down my neck. At last,

Charlie fixed the last lug and I gave the structure a wiggle left and right to test it was stable. He was the mechanic; I was the oily rag. The rest was up to him now.

He retrieved a drill bit half a metre long and seven milli-metres in diameter from his day sack and threaded it carefully into the pyramid hole, oblivious to everything else that was going on.

He blew on his fingers to warm them, then eased the drill in further until it just touched the wood of the exterior wall. This kit couldn't be worked by any old knuckle-dragger, which ruled me out. It called for a delicate touch and a steady hand. Charlie was the best of the best; he always said that if he hadn't gone into this line of work, he'd have taken up brain surgery. Maybe he wasn't joking; I saw him settle a bet once by turning one five-pound note into two with a razor blade. Back in Hereford, they called him the CEO of MOE [method of entry]. There wasn't a security system in existence that he couldn't defeat. And if there was, he wouldn't lose any sleep over it. He'd get me to blow it up instead.

Next out was the power cable, connected to a lithium battery inside his day sack. Charlie plugged it into the pyramid. There was a moment's delay as jaws inside the pyramid clamped round the bit, and then it began to turn, so slowly it almost seemed not to be moving. The only sound was a barely audible, low-frequency hum.

There was nothing we could do now but wait as it started to work its way quietly, slowly, methodically through an inch of wood, a sheet of tarpaper, and about half a centimetre of plasterboard. I moved against the wall to make myself as small a target as possible if anyone looked out of a window. My right hand lifted my fleece and rested on the grip of the pistol pancake-holstered on my jean belt. My left pulled the zipped-up front over my nose for warmth.

This kit worked on the same technology they used in neuro-surgery; if you're drilling through a skull it helps to be doing so with something that stops when it senses it's about to hit the cranial membrane. Our one behaved the same way when it was just about to break through the final layer of paint or paper. And – so it left no sign – it automatically collected the debris and dust as it went.

Charlie disconnected the power and pulled out the bit, then took out a fibre-optic rod with a light on the end. He moved it down through the pyramid, just to make sure he wasn't about to break through the stud wall. Everything seemed to be fine. He removed the fibre optic, reinserted the drill, and re-connected the power. The gentle hum resumed.

It moved quicker as it hit the tarpaper, then slowed again as it encountered the plasterboard. Charlie stopped it again and repeated the operation with the fibre optic.

I looked over at Half Arse. He was lying on his back with his feet nearest the wall, his pistol resting on his chest, pointing up at the first-floor windows. He must have been freezing his arse off – or what was left of it. I thought about the Americans in the Pods, drinking coffee and smoking cigars while they watched our progress. Most of them were probably wondering why the fuck we didn't get a move on.

It took nearly an hour before the drill stopped turning for the third and final time. Charlie did his trick with the fibre optic again and gave us a thumbs-up. He removed the drill bit, put the screwdriver to the first lug, and began to turn it anticlockwise.

When he'd removed the pyramid, Charlie dug out the microphone. It too was attached to a fibre-optic cable, so it could be put into position correctly.

I stowed the gear carefully, bit by bit, in my day sack. No point rushing it and making noise.

With a flourish, Charlie connected the microphone to the lithium battery and laid a metre-long wire antenna on the ground.

As soon as the power was switched on, there was squelch in

my earpiece. The signal was beamed to the Pods and then bounced back to us. We didn't want to have to get on the net to check that we'd done the business.

I heard the microphone rustle as Charlie fed it gently into the freshly drilled hole. He stopped now and again, eased it back a fraction, then pushed it through a bit more. As it got closer to the membrane, I could hear a woman murmuring to her children, and a man moaning in agony. It must have been the one who'd taken a round in the stomach during the first attack.

It was almost time to leave. Charlie closed and relocked the utilities box as I dug the wire into the earth and smoothed it over. He did a quick final sweep of the area with his shielded Maglite, and we got rid of a couple of footprints. Then we started to crawl back to RV with the Bradley.

Voices echoed in my earpiece as we went; a man mumbled passages from the Bible; a child whimpered and pleaded for a drink of water.

We had done our bit.

Now it was time to hand our toys over to the Americans.

3

Two weeks later

The baby rabbits screamed all night long. It was close to impossible for us to sleep – and we were six hundred metres from the action. Fuck knows what it must have been like for the hundred-odd men, women and children on the receiving end of their relentless squeals, taped on a loop and amplified a thousand times through the AFVs' loudspeakers.

It was still dark. I unzipped my sleeping bag just enough to slide my arm out into the cold. I tilted my wrist close to my face and pressed the illumination button on Baby-G. It was 5.38am.

'Day fifty-one of the siege of Mount Carmel.' I kicked the bag next to me. 'Welcome to another day in paradise.'

Anthony stirred. 'They still playing the same bloody record?' It was strange hearing him swear in perfect Oxford English.

'Why, mate? You got any requests?'

'Yes.' His head emerged. 'Bloody get me out of here.'

'I don't think I know that one.'

It didn't get a laugh.

'What time is it?'

'Half-five, mate. Brew?'

He groaned as he adjusted position. Tony wasn't used to sleeping hard. He belonged in a freshly starched white coat, back at his lab, twiddling test tubes over Bunsen burners, not roughing it alongside guys like me, teeth unbrushed so long they'd grown fur, and socks the consistency of cardboard.

'The papers were calling it the siege of Mount Apocalypse yesterday,' Anthony said. 'Lambs to the slaughter, more like.' It came from the heart. He wasn't at all happy about what was happening here.

Once we'd fixed the listening devices, nobody was interested in the Brits who'd been sent to Waco to 'observe and advise'. We were surplus to requirements. After a three-day consultation with Hereford, who'd had a consultation with the FCO, who'd spoken to the embassy in Washington, who'd spoken to whoever, Charlie and Half Arse had flown back to the UK. I was told to stay and keep an eye on Tony. The Americans might still want to use the box of tricks he'd brought along.

I rolled over and fired up our small camping gas stove, then reached for the kettle. When it came to home comforts, that was pretty much it. There wasn't a toothbrush in sight, which probably explained why the Yanks kept their distance.

I looked through one of the bullet holes in the side of the cattle trailer that had been our home for the last five days. The darkness of the Texas prairie was criss-crossed by search-light beams. The AFVs circled the target buildings like Indians around a wagon train, Nightsuns bouncing wildly. The psyops guys were still making life a living hell for those trapped inside. The media had got it right. We were trapped on the set of *Apocalypse Now*.

The compound, as the Feds were calling the Branch Davidians' hangout, comprised a mishmash of wooden-framed buildings, two three-storey blocks and a large rectangular water tower. In anyone else's language, it would

17

have been described as a religious community, but that wouldn't have suited the FBI. The last thing they wanted was for this operation to smack of persecution, so compound it was.

There's a ten-day rule when it comes to sieges; if you've not resolved the situation by then, the shit has really hit the fan. And we were pushing the envelope five times over. Something had to happen soon. The administration wasn't looking too clever as it was; with every new day that passed, things just got a whole lot worse.

The ear-piercing, gut-wrenching screams suddenly stopped. The silence was deafening. I peered through the bullet hole. Three or four AFVs were clustered near the car park. Intelligence from ex-members of the cult had suggested that since storage space inside the buildings was at a premium, a lot of them kept their belongings in the boots of their vehicles.

The first AFV lurched forward, ploughed through the fence and kept straight on going. I gave Tony another nudge. 'Fucking hell, look at this.'

Tony sat up.

'They're crushing all the cars and buses.'

'What the hell are they trying to do?'

'Make friends and influence people, I guess.'

We watched the demolition derby while the water boiled.

4

As soon as the last vehicle was flattened, the AFVs spread out again. They started to circle, the Davidians' fresh laundry embedded in their tracks. Almost immediately, the screams of the animals boomed out again from their loudspeakers.

People were on the move outside our trailer, making their way to and from the array of shower cubicles, toilets and food wagons that had sprung up on our patch of the seventy-seven-acre tented city. An army may march on its stomach, but US law enforcement drives there in a stretch limo and gets paid overtime.

There was no shortage of bodies to be catered for. SWAT teams, FBI hostage rescue teams, federal marshals, local sheriffs; the place was teeming with them. No fewer than four Pods were sprinkled around the compound. Alpha Pod was right next door to our trailer; the other three had their own command set-up, and, as far as we could make out, were doing their own thing. There were more chiefs than Indians on this prairie, that was for sure, and nobody seemed to be in overall charge. To make matters worse, they all wanted to be, and every man and his dog was clearly itching to fire up the biggest and ugliest military toys they could get their hands on.

This operation had all the makings of a weapons-grade gangfuck, and there was a rock-festival-sized audience gathering to witness it. Hordes of shiny, aluminium-skinned Airstreams, clapped-out Winnebagos and bog-standard pick-ups lined the road the far side of the cordon. The rubberneckers were coming from miles around for a good day out, sitting on their roofs, clutching their binos, enjoying the fun. There was even a fun-fair, and stall upon stall selling everything from hotdogs and camping gas stoves to *Davidians: 4, ATF: 0* emblazoned T-shirts [Alcohol, Tobacco and Firearms, Bureau of].

This was certainly cowboy country, in more ways than one. Waco was about a hundred miles south of Dallas, and home to the Texas Rangers' museum. Everybody I'd seen at the funfair seemed to be wearing a Stetson. Everybody apart from the Ku Klux Klan, that is. They'd turned up three days ago, offering the FBI their help getting in there and killing all them drug-taking, cult-loving child molesters.

Tony and I sank back down and finished off our brews while I got the kettle on for the next round. It was the highlight of the day.

Muffled speech and laughter came and went along the out-side of the trailer. I smelled cigarette smoke. The cocking of weapons and ripping of body-armour Velcro signalled the change of shift. By my reckoning there were at least three hundred police officers on-site, with vehicles to match. Most of them were in BDUs [United States Army battledress], and carrying enough weaponry to see off a small invasion.

I also knew that the Combat Applications Group – Delta Force – had a team here somewhere. Delta had been modelled on the same squadron and doctrine set-up as the Special Air Service in the 1970s. They were probably doing much the same as we were, stuck at one of the Pods, being told jack shit about what was going on and sleeping rough in a trailer. I hoped so, anyway.

We all knew that it was illegal for the military to act against US citizens. The Posse Comitatus Act banned it from domestic law enforcement, and 'domestic' included a three-mile stretch of territorial water. There was only one exception to the rule: President Clinton had signed a waiver allowing law officers on drugs interdiction operations to use military vehicles and personnel to combat the forces ranged against them. In other words, the ATF and FBI had a Get Out Of Jail Free card, and judging by the Abrams tank parked up across the way, it looked like they intended to play it at the first available opportunity.

David Koresh and his fellow Bible-bashers couldn't have known what they were letting themselves in for when they resisted the original attack by the ATF almost two months earlier.

5

The water boiled. I tipped Nescafé into two mugs and poured. You couldn't move for catering wagons round here, but I didn't fancy joining the breakfast queue now the night shift was over. Apart from anything else, it meant venturing out into the cold, and I liked to put that off until the sun came up.

I hung on to Tony's brew as he faffed about, trying to unzip. He rubbed his eyes and groped around for his glasses in the glow from the stove. He was all right, I supposed. He was thirty-something, with the kind of nose that made it look like his forefathers came from Easter Island. His hair was brown, and style-wise he'd gone for mad professor. Either he didn't have any idea what he looked like or, more likely, he just didn't care; because he was one, his head so full of chemical formulae he didn't seem to know what day it was.

There were nine thousand or so eggheads employed by DERA [Defence Evaluation and Research Agency], and Tony was one of them. You didn't ask these guys at exactly which of the eighty or so establishments up and down the UK they worked, but I was pretty sure, given why he was here, that he wouldn't be a complete stranger to the germ warfare laboratories at Porton Down in Wiltshire.

I'd looked after boffins like him before, holding their hand in hostile environments, or escorting them into premises neither of us should really have been in, and I tended to just let them get on with whatever they had to do. The less I knew, the less shit I could be in if things went pear-shaped. These sorts of jobs always tended to come back and kick you in the bollocks. But one thing always puzzled me: Tony and his mates had brains the size of hot-air balloons, and spent their whole lives grappling with the secrets of the universe – so how come they couldn't even get a decent brew on?

The RAF had flown a big container in with us to Fort Hood, then had it trucked on-site, and Tony carried the keys. He seemed pretty much a pacifist, so maybe it just contained enough fairy dust to make everybody dance out of the building, but I doubted it. The FBI had been pretty keen to have access to Charlie's siege surveillance devices, but the inside of Tony's head was what they really wanted. His business was advanced gases; he seemed to be on first-name terms with every molecule on the planet. What's more, he knew how to mix them so precisely that they killed, immobilized, or merely incapacitated you to the point where you were still able to crawl.

A flurry of shouted instructions belted out of Alpha Pod's command tent. Special Agent Jim D. 'Call Me Buster' Bastendorf was tuning up for his morning gobbing-off session to the new shift commanders, and as usual making everything sound like a bollocking.

Bastendorf really did like everyone to call him Buster, but it took us no time at all to christen him Deaf Bastard, then, because it was less of a mouthful, Bastard for short.

Bastard was a Texan and that meant everything – his shoulders, arms, hands and, most of all, his stomach – was bigger than it needed to be. It would have done him no harm

23

at all to stay away from the two-pound T-bones after Christmas. He had a severe crew cut and a heavily waxed Kaiser Wilhelm moustache. He kept on curling the ends, as if letting them droop would be a sign of weakness. Yessirree, Jim D. Bastendorf knew exactly what his mission was: to kick ass, bust heads, solve the problem.

Everything was a battle for this man; every minute of every day was a fight he had to win. His jaws worked non-stop on chewing tobacco. Every quarter of an hour he'd gob a mouthful of thick, black, saliva-covered crap into a polystyrene cup, trawl out another wad from a tin in his back pocket, and start the whole process again.

His problem with us began with Tony's accent. Whenever Tony asked a question or tried to offer some input, he just looked blank, and took to referring to him as 'that Limey fag in the trailer' who 'don't know shit from Shinola'. I was this other Brit waste of space who kept asking damn-fool questions: 'What about this? What about that? Do you really think that keeping these guys awake 24/7 is going to get them to come out?'

When it came down to it, he didn't have a clue what we were doing here. Our brief was short and to the point. So long as we kept out of his way, had the correct little blue passes hanging from our necks at all times, and shared his view that we'd all been floundering helplessly till he rode over the hill like the Fifth Cavalry, we could stay here for ever, for all he cared – which was just fine by me, because I didn't care much either. If Bastard didn't want to listen, it wasn't my problem. The Davidians' water supply had been fucked up, and sooner or later they'd get hungry or thirsty or bored. They'd come out eventually, so I'd just keep getting the kettle on for Tony and me until the white flags started appearing.

Bastard roared with laughter. People were shouting instructions to get over to the command post. Something was happening.

24

'Shut the fuck up!' Bastard boomed. 'Check this out – show-time!'

I unzipped my bag and got to my feet. There was another sound above the scream of rabbits and screech of tank tracks. Bastard had thrown a switch so that his mates could listen in on the conversation between the negotiators and the Bible-bashers.

A child of no more than five was on the phone inside the compound. I could hear muffled crying in the background. 'Are you going to kill me?' her small voice asked.

6

The negotiator was on a US Air Force base miles away – another bad tactic. He spoke gently, as Bastard's boys in the command tent shrieked and whistled. 'No, honey, no one is coming to kill you.'

'You sure? The tanks are still outside . . .'

'The tanks won't hurt you, honey.'

Another, male voice took over in the compound. 'Why are you letting your guys drop their pants at our women?' He was going apeshit. 'These are decent women in here; you know that's not the way to go. Why should we trust you?'

Bastard roared, 'About time them bitches saw some prime ass!'

From the sound of it, this got his boys' vote. I bet they were mooning at the speaker.

I exchanged a glance with Tony, who'd been staring at his coffee. We both listened as the negotiator tried to come back with a reasonable response. 'You know what these guys are like; you know the ones who fly the helicopters or drive the tanks, they haven't got the same mindset as us. I'll try and do something about it, OK?'

Bastard guffawed. 'Fuck that, and fuck you too, Mr Mindset! You just keep on talking; leave the ass-kicking to the big boys.'

There was a fresh burst of applause. I could picture the big boys shrugging off their pants again, waving their arses at the speaker.

I took a sip of my brew. Whatever the negotiator said, it didn't look good for Koresh and his crew. The ATF had ignored his invitation to come in and inspect the place for illegal weapons and whatever else they thought the Davidians had up their sleeves, and instead had mounted a full-scale armed operation.

Maybe it was a coincidence, but it just so happened that the ATF were losing credibility in Washington right now, and it was budget time. They clearly wanted to put on a bit of a display – they'd invited the media along, and given them ringside seats. They'd even got their own cameras rolling, in case the newshounds missed any of the action.

The Branch Davidians must have known something was up when they clocked the film crews setting up shop. Their suspicions would have been confirmed when helicopters started swooping round the rear of the compound, partly to draw their attention away from the cattle trailers full of armed ATF agents headed for the front door, partly so the US public could see their tax dollars on the screen.

The Davidians returned fire, as they were entitled to do under American law. They even called 911 to tell the police they were being attacked, and begged for help.

The gun battle lasted for an hour, the longest in American law enforcement history. At the end of it, four ATF agents lay dead, with another sixteen wounded. When little brother gets his arse kicked, big brother comes to sort it out. The FBI took over. From that moment on, the Branch Davidians were doomed. This was one movie that wasn't going to have a happy ending.

Tony took a sip of coffee and looked at me sadly as he listened to the conversation that followed.

The Davidians wanted water . . .

The negotiators said they wanted to help out, but they just couldn't oblige. Their hands were tied.

People were starting to die of thirst here . . .

It was possible the FBI might be able to do something if some of the Davidians came out and gave themselves up, as a token of good will. How did that sound?

Tony was totally out of his depth here. He didn't like the sound of the AFVs, and he didn't like the shouting that came as part of the law enforcement package. He particularly didn't like being so near things that went bang. He'd have given anything right now to be tucked away in that lab of his, feeding laughing gas to Roland Rat or whatever the fuck it was they did there. He gave me a brave smile. 'Another day, another dollar, eh?'

'Easier said than done, mate.' I tried to sound upbeat for him. 'Best not to worry about what you can't change. It'll give you a headache.'

Tony looked away, staring sightlessly through the side of the trailer as Bastendorf's audience got right on with enjoying the show.

7

I didn't particularly care which way this thing panned out. I was just looking forward to getting back to Hereford and the squadron. I was out of the Regiment in a couple of months' time and needed to sort a few things. Not that I had much to organize. The Firm [Secret Intelligence Service] were going to do everything for me, sort out bank accounts, take control of my life.

Islamic fundamentalists had been on a slaughtering frenzy in Algeria ever since the army seized power in 1992. They'd unleashed a fierce terrorist campaign against a broad spectrum of civilian targets, including secular opposition leaders, journalists, artists, academics, and foreigners – especially oil industry foreigners.

A job looking after oilmen and rigs came up; the wages were three times what I was on, so there wasn't much thinking involved. Why get out of the Regiment in five years' time and start doing the same job? Why not start right away? I was out in five years anyway, whether I liked it or not. The army had wiped my arse for me ever since I'd joined at sixteen. They'd only used three sheets at a time – one up, one down, one to shine – but I'd still been wondering what it would be like to have to stand on my own two feet. And now I didn't have to worry.

I handed in my notice and got approached by the Firm a week later. I still wasn't sure why, but it didn't matter. It meant not having to fill in tax forms or pay rent. And I'd find out what they wanted me for soon enough.

I was just about to suggest a stroll to the canteen to see if the queue had gone down when a series of loud crashes came from the compound.

'What are you doing? You're attacking the children, what about the children?'

The negotiator went straight into monotone. Bastard and his crew quit their banter to listen. 'Do not open fire. This is not an assault. We will not be entering the building. I repeat, do not open fire. This is not an assault.'

The line went dead. Almost at once, the loudspeakers on the armoured vehicles began to blare, in the same monotone as the negotiator, 'This stand-off is over, do not fire any weapons. This is not an assault. This is not an assault, do not fire any weapons.'

Tony and I put down our brews and ran to the back of the cattle trailer to get a better view. Three combat engineer vehicles, tracked, armoured monsters with big battering rams out in front, were rumbling around the compound. One pushed straight through the wall like a finger through wet paper.

Searchlights and Nightsuns jerked around the target. Another CEV forced its ram into the far corner of the building and stopped.

'Oh my God, oh my God . . .' Tony couldn't get the words out quickly enough. The searchlights were still dancing like dervishes as the third CEV half disappeared through a wall.

'This is not an attack,' the loudspeakers barked. 'Do not open fire.'

Tony couldn't believe what he was seeing. 'If this isn't an attack, then what the hell is it? Look, Nick, look . . .'

I was looking, along with close on two hundred law enforcers standing on the roof of every vehicle, trying to get a better view. Some of them even had their flash cameras out, getting a few snaps for the folks back home.

Tony scrambled over the trailer gate like an uncoordinated child. He hit the ground and started running towards Alpha Pod.

I followed. The structure was kept upright by air forced through inflatable tubes in the frames. A generator chugged away just outside. This being an American command post, there was also air conditioning. Warm air hit our faces. There was a strong smell of coffee. It was a smoke-free area, and there were signs up to say so. Health and safety initiatives in a war zone were always good to see.

Every table was groaning with TV monitors and computers. Cables trailed across the floor. Radio operators were hunched speechlessly over their sets. Everyone had their eyes glued to the screens.

The monitors showed all elevations of the target, apart from the rear. The two screens that had been covering the back were now just black and flickering. Two screens displayed aerial views from P3 cameras still circling at twenty-five thousand feet. The IR and thermal images looked like black and white negatives. Bright white light showed the heat coming from the exhaust of the CEV at the back of the building, then white flames as the driver changed gear before ramming into it.

Bastard stood in front of the screens, and he liked what he saw. 'Get some!' he yelled at the screen. He muttered a few asides to his cronies and gobbed baccy juice into his cup. The crew around him added their cheers.

'Yo, Momma!'

Thirty seconds later, the vehicle reversed.

'Hey, Koresh, how you like that new air freshener?'

'Y'all find that tank's ass stinks more than ours!'

I looked at Tony. 'Gas?'

'They're injecting like mosquitoes.'

The FBI's patience had run out. They'd gas them and then round them up as they staggered out, coughing and spluttering, fluids dribbling from every orifice. Next stop would be the back of a wagon or an ambulance, and downtown to the ER before they got arrested.

'Good news.' I grinned at Tony. 'That's you and me on a plane home.'

But Tony wasn't smiling. He strode up to Bastard. 'What gas are you using?'

Bastard just kept on staring at the screens. He shrugged his shoulders. 'Dunno, old bean. Just gas, I guess.'

Tony was flapping, looking around at the room for some kind of moral support. He didn't receive it. A couple of Bastendorf's men started to smirk, sensing fun. Tony pointed to the monitors as another CEV crashed into the compound. 'Have they got respirators in there? What about the children? In those confined spaces you're going to kill them! Why aren't they already coming out?'

Bastard ignored him. Outside, the symphony of slaughtered animals returned and another CEV embedded itself in the building. It stayed put for about twenty seconds and then pulled out. Another mosquito injecting its poison.

Bastard just stood there, glued to the screens.

Tony grabbed his shoulder and spun him round so their faces were only inches apart. 'This is going to kill them, do you not understand?' His voice was choked with emotion. 'They're all going to die!'

Bastard sneered. 'Not your party, son. Get out of my face, I got work to do.'

No one else spoke.

I was standing in the doorway. First light was just cracking; visibility had improved.

A cheer went up from the onlookers at the edge of the cordon.

I scanned the perimeter, and the penny dropped.

Where were the ambulances to treat the casualties? Where were the reception parties to process the prisoners? Where were the wagons to take them away? Why were all these guys watching the attack, rather than being part of it?

8

I turned back. Bastard had reached breaking point. 'Get the fuck outta here, faggot! What the fuck you Brits doing here anyway?'

Bastard lifted his spade-sized right hand and pushed against Tony's face. Tony wasn't made for hard sleeping, and he wasn't built to take a slapping either. He reeled back and toppled onto one of the radio operators. The guy stood up but he wasn't going to help. This was the boss's business.

I took three quick strides and got in between them. The command tent fell silent and the rabbits and the rumble of the CEVs filled the space. Bastard didn't have to say anything. His intentions were written all over his face. Tony was spread across the radio operator's table and was sliding towards the ground.

'I'll take him away. I'm sorry, he's not used to seeing this sort of thing. I'll get him out of the way for you.' I raised my hand in conciliation.

But Bastard was feeling too feisty to back off. He poked me in the chest. 'Who the fuck are you anyway? Another fag Brit?'

I was here to look after the talent. I stood my ground.

Tony's shoulders rubbed against my legs as he tried to get up.

I put out my hand and touched Bastard's jacket. His chest was rigid; the fucker had body armour on. I glanced right and left to see if I could sense how much support he'd be getting. The answer seemed to be plenty.

There was no way I could win this. Bastard was a big old boy, and his mates would pile in the moment anything kicked off. If the two of us had a day of reckoning, it wasn't today.

'We'll go now.' My eyes were locked on his. 'This isn't his thing.'

One of the guys in the tent came up and put his hand on Bastard's shoulder. 'It's not worth it, Buster. These guys were sent here to help. Special relationship, right . . .'

Bastard's jaw jutted as he returned my stare, weighing his options. His eyes never left mine. Then, without a word, he turned on his heel.

I guided Tony out of the tent but he didn't come willingly. He still wanted answers.

The light was good enough to see the US flag fluttering from the antenna of one of the CEVs as it manoeuvred round the compound. It wasn't the only Stars and Stripes flying. I wondered if any of them had noticed the much bigger one hanging from the Davidians' own pole.

The armoured vehicles had churned up the ground so much round the target it looked like the Somme. Litter from crushed wheelie bins was scattered by the strengthening wind.

I had my arm round Tony's shoulder, guiding him back to the trailer. But he didn't want to go. 'I've got to check something.'

'What can we do? There's—'

Tony pulled free and started to run. The steel container flown in by the RAF was about two hundred metres away.

I set off after him. It wouldn't hurt. If nothing else, it took him two hundred metres further away from Alpha Pod.

As we approached the container, I could see it had sunk an

inch or two into the ground under its own weight. When we got closer, I could see the two back doors had carved an arc in the soft ground where they'd been pulled open. The padlock had been cut.

Tony was almost hyperventilating with rage. 'They had no right, Nick. You know the deal. They were only to take it after consultation. In the name of God, Nick, what are they doing?'

I looked inside. Several of the half-size oil drums were missing. The gas inside was under such pressure, Tony had told me, that it was solid. When the seals were removed, it degraded into fine particles, which could then be pumped into a building under pressure.

He leaned against the container as if he'd taken a punch in the gut. I hadn't noticed until then, but the animal screams had stopped. The only sounds were the rattling of tank tracks and Nancy Sinatra singing, 'These Boots Are Made For Walking'.

Wind gusted off the prairie as I shut the container doors.

Another roar of approval went up from the spectators. Tony's eyes followed a flurry of activity alongside several 4x4s on the track to the outer cordon. Binos raised, the thrill-seekers were pulsating with excitement as they munched on their fresh breakfast muffins. In an hour or two the funfair would start up again, and the novelty stalls would churn out more *Davidians: 4, ATF: 0* T-shirts. But by then the scoreline would be well out of date.

I leaned against the container with Tony. Police in body armour, M16s over the shoulder, milled around with cups of coffee and egg rolls, eager to get a good view.

Tony shook his head in disbelief. His eyes welled with tears. 'They're going to die in there, Nick. They won't be coming out. Some of the children are probably dead already. We must stop it. Who do we see? Who do we call? This is madness!'

I turned my head. 'We're not going to stop anything, mate. Look at this lot.' The BDU-clad bodies took more pictures and cheered Nancy's every word. 'You're flogging a dead horse, mate.'

The tears started to roll down his cheek. 'What? What are you talking about?'

'What the fuck do you think is happening? Look at those wagons.' I pointed at the CEVs rampaging round the compound. 'And fuck knows what's going on round the back. Why do you think the lines have been cut? There's an agenda, mate. They want the fuckers dead.'

His jaw dropped. Tony didn't share the Rambo mindset of those in the helicopters and tanks. He invented toys for them to play with, but I could see he wasn't used to joining in the game.

'Look, the people on the ground here aren't the decision-makers. That's way above their pay scale. They're just having fun doing it. They got the go from way up, mate. And you can bet your bottom dollar they wouldn't touch this gas of yours unless the UK said they could. They've just fucked you off the plan now they've got your gear.'

'But it's women and children in there. They're killing them! Someone must do something!'

I put my hand on his shoulder to stop him from bouncing up and down. I also wanted to make sure he wasn't going to run off again and try to do something that I wouldn't be able to reverse him out of. 'Listen. Ever since this thing kicked off, Koresh and the rest of them have been made to sound like the devil's disciples. Think of it in Bastard's terms. It's a black and white world, and these are the bad guys.'

Tony's head was in his hands, and his shoulders had started to shake.

'I'll go and get a brew on.' I let go and patted his shoulder. 'Coffee?'

What else was there to say?

9

By eleven o'clock it was getting pretty hot on my vantage point on top of the cattle trailer. I'd fetched Tony several brews, but last time I looked he hadn't touched any of them. He still had his arse planted in the mud and his back slumped against the container.

I took off my jacket and pulled up the sleeves of my sweat-shirt. The wind had picked up, blowing tumbleweed across the heat haze between us and the target. The way things were going round here, it wouldn't have surprised me to see Clint Eastwood ride into shot.

Still no one had come out of the buildings. Either they'd all been killed by the gas, or they'd killed themselves rather than surrender, or were being kept inside by Koresh. I wondered what had been going on round the back. I hadn't seen any-thing, but I knew automatic gunfire when I heard it. Our guys, their guys, or both? Who knew? At this stage of the day, if they wanted to drop each other it was up to them. I just wanted this to be over and done with so we could pack up and go home. Maybe I'd buy myself a T-shirt on the way out.

I looked back towards the container to check on Tony. He

was still there, and still very much in his own little world. The urgent roar of a CEV engine pulled me back towards the compound. It was making another entry into the building, and this time the monotone had replaced Nancy Sinatra. 'This is not an attack. Do not open fire.' They seemed to think that if they repeated the message often enough, we'd all start to believe it.

The police and federal marshals' day shift had clocked on hours ago, but the overnight guys had hung around to watch the finale and they were starting to get a little bored now. If Tony was right, most of the Davidians were dead. So why weren't the FBI masking up teams and sending them in to look for survivors? I didn't have much sympathy for the adults, but the kids hadn't asked to be there.

An angry yell came from near the command tent. I jumped to my feet to get a better view.

Tony and Bastard were squaring up to each other. Tony was almost jumping up at Bastard's face, pushing him back with his hands as the FBI man tried to pass. A group had gathered. But I knew none of them was going to intervene. Bastard's body language said he was going to take care of this piece of business himself.

10

I jumped off the trailer and ran towards them. Tony was certainly making me earn my money today. I barged though the gathering crowd.

'Tony, calm down, mate. It's all right.'

His head didn't move. His eyes, red and swollen, were still fixed on Bastard.

'It's not all right.' He jerked a finger over at the buildings. 'Do you know what's gone on over there? *Do you?*'

I was about to answer when I realized it wasn't me he was talking to. 'They will have died horrendously. That gas is the same stuff they use on death row. Did you know that?'

Bastard couldn't be bothered to answer, but Tony wasn't going to give him the chance. 'Do you know why they strap men down before they press the button?'

There wasn't a flicker in Bastard's eyes. But everybody else's looked at Tony for the answer.

'Because it makes the muscles contract so violently they break every bone in the victim's body. *And that's what's happening to the women and children in there!*'

Bastard stared blankly into Tony's eyes. 'Hey, we're all just here to get the job done. What's your fucking problem?'

Tony took a step closer. 'I'll tell you what my problem is. The space is too confined. You're killing them!'

Bastard no longer bothered to put the brakes on the smile that was spreading across his face. He just turned to me, and when he spoke it was so calm it was scary. 'Tell your fag friend that we are dealing with some very bad people here. They are religious fanatics who've stockpiled—'

'Fanatics? The little girl we heard couldn't have been more than five years old!' Flecks of spittle flew from Tony's mouth. 'What are you doing? What is going on? This is madness! This is murder!'

Bastard stared down at him as he wiped his face. 'Murder? Well, chew on this, fag. It's your goddam gas, so I guess that makes you an accessory.'

Tony stepped back, stunned.

Bastard revelled in the sight. 'Kinda catches in the back of your throat, don't it?' He looked up to share the moment with the crowd. 'Hey, just like that gas of yours.'

That did it for Tony. He pulled his hand back and bunched it, but Bastard was too quick for him. His own fist connected with Tony's chest. As he pulled back for another punch, I moved behind him, grabbed his arm and pulled, adding momentum to the swing. He did a 180 on the spot.

Bastard was quick to square up to me as I stood my ground instead of following through with some punches to put him down. It was the right thing to do; he hadn't attacked me, after all. He had lost face, and needed to reassert; that was OK, I understood that, I couldn't let that happen. He was a big man, and if one of those fists made contact I was going to need one of those non-existent ambulances. But it was too late for me to worry about that now.

Bastard started towards me, just as a shout went up from one of the vehicles, half in shock, half in celebration. 'Fire! Fire!'

Bastard turned his head. I grabbed Tony. 'Get the kit together, we're fucking off!'

Four or five columns of smoke started to rise from the compound as we ran. Even if there had been a fire crew in place, the combination of the heat of the day, the wind and the gas – that would now have dried to a fine powder – made the chances of putting it out next to zero.

As if on cue, a policeman jumped down from his wagon, ran a few metres towards the compound, then turned back to face the crowd. He unfurled an ATF flag for all to see. 'It's a pot-bellied stove!' he half shouted, half laughed. 'Open it up, let the fuckers burn!'

He waved the flag and scores of men hooted and hollered. In the background, I heard a barrel organ. The fairground was sparking up.

PART TWO

1

Noosa, Queensland
Thursday, 21 April 2005

The sun had been char-grilling the top of my foot, but it took me a long time to notice. The sand I was gazing at was just too blindingly white, the sea too dazzlingly blue.

I pulled it back under the table, and leaned forward to suck up the last of my milkshake. I always made a gurgling noise when I got to the dregs, on principle. Not that anyone at the Surfers' Club seemed to mind. They were too busy surfing-and-turfing their way through the kind of mammoth lunches Silky and I had just put away.

While I waited for her to come back with a couple of ice creams, I had one last slurp and got back to admiring the view. Sun, sea, sand, and thousands of miles of bush behind me; coming here had definitely been the right call.

She returned with two cones, the contents of which were already dripping down her hands. I got the chocolate one.

'I cannot believe you were going to go round America instead.' Silky licked tutti-frutti off her free hand and sat down. 'I just saw George Bush on TV. He says Iran and Syria are next on the list. I do not understand that man. What is the matter with him?'

She came from Berlin. I had known her for three months, and her accent still reminded me of the black-and-white war films I used to watch as a kid.

'I mean, why doesn't he just talk to them?' She hooked her shoulder-length blond hair behind her ear so it didn't fall across her face, before bending down to give some serious attention to her cone. 'I have been to Syria – they're nice people.'

'Your fault for looking at the TV.' I sat up. 'I don't even read the newspapers now. It's all bullshit. And when you've got a view like that,' I nodded in the direction of the incoming waves, 'what more do you need?'

Her head tilted sharply and her blue eyes speared me over the top of her sunglasses. 'After last night, you still have to ask this?'

I grinned. 'The ocean will still be here tomorrow. But will Silky? One can never tell with you hippies.'

She arched an eyebrow. 'Just because George Bush keeps adding to his list, Nick, doesn't mean that you have to keep cutting from yours . . .'

'That's me. Hand luggage only.'

Silky nodded thoughtfully, dumped the rest of the cone on her plate and wiped her hands.

'Bush can live his dream.' I looked back at the sea. A line of surfers rode a perfect wave. 'I'll have mine.'

And I did. Bumming round Australia in a camper van, freefall rig in the back, a backpacker along for the ride. The only bit of pressure each day was deciding whether to risk looking like a dickhead on a surfboard, or to do something I was pretty good at, jumping out of aeroplanes. Only dress code, T-shirt, shorts and flip-flops – and the collection of friendship bracelets I'd accumulated over the last few months around my wrist. Money wasn't a problem. When I ran short, I just drove to another boogie [freefall parachute meet] and packed rigs. I didn't regret for a moment dumping Plan A, to

46

buy a bike and tour the States. One look at the CNN weather forecast for November back in Washington had been enough.

Silky checked her watch. 'Better hit the road if we're going to make it by tonight.'

'You still want to come?'

'Of course. I want to meet your friends.' She stood up and adjusted her cut-off Levi's. 'And we hippies never turn down a free bed.'

It felt pretty good to see all the men turn as she brushed her hand across her long, tanned thighs as we walked to the car park. She'd taken my lectures about sand discipline to heart. I liked to keep the stuff on the beach, where it belonged, and not in vehicles and tents.

The sun was fierce on my shoulders and head, and I knew what was coming. It was hot as an oven inside the 1980s, box-shaped, mustard-coloured VW combi. The guy who'd sold it to me in Sydney had thrown in the corrugated tinfoil window screen for free, but I never remembered to put it up.

Silky made a final check that she wasn't bringing any sand in with her and threw a beach towel over the burningly hot PVC.

'It'll feel cooler once we get moving,' I said.

'What will?' She pouted. 'The van, or us?'

The air-cooled wagon chugged slowly out of the car park and through the busy streets of the little resort. It looked as if it had been around the planet a couple of times, let alone a continent. I hoped it wasn't going to finally throw in the towel before I got back to Sydney, cleaned the thick layers of bug kill off the windscreen, and sold it to some other sucker.

We hit the highway south to Brisbane and I was soon on autopilot, elbows on the steering wheel as I stared at the long straight ribbon of tarmac and through the shimmering heat haze. Silky sorted out a cassette from the shoebox between us. There weren't many still intact; she'd left the box on the seat one afternoon and most of them had melted so badly they looked as if they belonged on a Salvador Dalí canvas.

The Libertines sparked up through the crackly door speakers and were soon competing with the rush of wind through the side windows.

Silky settled back in her seat, her sandalled feet resting on the dashboard. A few songs in, she turned to me and said, 'We're a good fit, no?'

I didn't know where that had come from, but she was right. Coming to this place and meeting her had been one of the best things I'd ever done.

It hadn't been a tough decision, binning George. I never got to find out which department of the CIA or the Pentagon he worked for, and really didn't give a shit any more.

I just got up one morning, packed everything I owned into two cheap holdalls and a day sack, and went to the office. I told George the truth. I'd had enough; I was mentally fucked. I sat across the desk from him, waiting for one of his habitually scathing replies. 'I need you until you're killed or I find some-body better, and you aren't dead yet.' But it didn't happen. Instead I got, 'Be gone by tomorrow, son.' The war would go on without me.

As I walked out of the building for the last time, en route to pick up my bags from an apartment I was never going back to, I felt nothing but relief. Then I thought, fuck it; George could have tried a little harder to keep me.

There was a noise like a drunken hod carrier tap-dancing on the roof and I slowed down; I knew exactly what it was. Silky jumped out and stood on the running board. Her surfboard was coming unstrapped again; the wind was getting hold of it. It didn't matter how many extra bungees I bought her, she always insisted two were enough. She didn't think the fact we had to stop and do this three or four times a day undermined her argument.

She jumped back in, slammed the door and smiled at me, then started slapping her thighs to the music again as we drove on. The hippie thing was just a piss-take. We'd met at a boogie just outside Sydney. She was in her late twenties and had been travelling for the last six or seven years, working the bars, fruit-picking, hitching rides. It had started as a gap year, then she'd forgotten to go home. 'The beaches are better here than in Berlin.' She'd laughed. 'I bet the same happens to you.'

She'd hitched a ride north with me. Why not? It was only a couple of extra thousand miles in the magical mystery tour that she called her life. I was hoping for a little bit of that myself now.

Silky stopped slapping her thighs and went and dug around on the back seat for some water. She clambered back beside me, sorted out her towel, and passed me the bottle. 'So, who exactly is Charlie?' With the Libertines and the wind rush in full swing, she had to shout.

'Tindall? Known him for years. We worked together.'

She held back her hair with her free hand as she took a swig. 'Doing what? I thought you worked in a garage, not on a farm.'

'That's just what he does now. We used to do loads of stuff – a little bit of freefall, that sort of thing.'

'Is he still jumping? Is that what we're going to do?' She jerked her thumb at the five-cell Raider rig on the back seat.

'No idea, I just wanted to catch up with him while I'm here. You know how it is. You're really close to someone for a while, then you don't see or hear from him for years. Doesn't make you any less of a mate.' I picked up the map that lay between us and threw it at her. 'Except we have to find him first.'

Four hours of long straight roads and one petrol stop later, and we were approaching a small town that sounded more like a tongue twister than a place on the map. The instructions Charlie had emailed me took us past a store with a tin roof and three saddled horses tied to a rail. We took the track left immediately after a blue letter box at the roadside, made out of a milk churn nailed sideways to a post.

We turned a corner or two and a haphazard collection of red tin roofs and a water tower started to take shape in the distance through the heat haze. We had arrived at Charlie's farm. Well, his son-in-law's, but all the family had chipped in. They'd sold their houses and moved to Australia lock, stock and barrel. Once Charlie had reached the magical age of fifty-five, God's own country had welcomed him with open arms – as long as he took out private health insurance and didn't expect an Australian pension. His own had kicked in when he'd left the army, though it was hardly enough to keep him in caviar and champagne. Charlie had been offered a commission and taken it. As an officer, he could stay in an extra fifteen years, instead of getting binned at forty.

We drove down half a mile of track, post-and-rail fencing either side of us. About a hundred metres from the house, a woman on a horse, waving like a lunatic, overtook us. I couldn't see much of her face under her baseball cap, just this huge smile. I slowed, but she waved us on. She stopped at a gate and we carried on along the track.

'Who was that?' Silky didn't sound jealous. A perpetual traveller couldn't be.

'Probably Julie, the daughter. The last time I saw her she was about seventeen with a face full of zits. That would have been a good fifteen years ago.'

We pulled up by the house, alongside a weather-beaten Land Cruiser and a pick-up truck that had seen better days.

Charlie stood on the veranda to welcome us, a big man in a green T-shirt. With his cropped, dark red hair, he was on his way to doing a pretty good impression of a traffic light. I could see Silky trying not to stare too obviously at the grey socks he insisted on wearing under his sandals. 'Don't worry about it,' I said. 'It's a Brit thing.'

Hazel came out and slipped an arm through her husband's. She was dressed more or less the same as him, except her feet

50

were bare. They both walked down the steps and out into the sun to greet us.

Charlie was heading for sixty but still looked as fit as a butcher's dog; there wasn't an ounce of lard on him, and that ginger hair somehow added to the healthy outdoor look. The sun hadn't been kind to him though; his skin was more burned than tanned. He thrust out a hand, small and out of proportion to the rest of him. He certainly hadn't shrunk with age; he was still a good two or three inches taller than me, but his grip wasn't as strong as it once had been. 'All right, lad? Glad you've come.' He kept eye contact to make sure I knew it.

We finished shaking and Hazel took over. I put an arm around Silky's shoulder and introduced her to them both.

'My name's really pronounced Silk-a,' she corrected me. 'But Nick calls me Silky. It's maybe easier if you do the same, otherwise you could confuse him.'

Hazel still had the same long, dark brown hair, and very clear, untanned skin. Her eyes had wrinkled with laughter when she was younger; I remembered her beaming behind the counter in Dixons in the precinct, always happy to use her employee discount for any Regiment guy who came in. They looked older and wiser now. Maybe sadder, too.

Hazel started to hustle us into the house. 'Sure you can't stay more than a night?'

'No, we've got to move on. There's a boogie in Melbourne on the ninth.'

Silky took Charlie's arm as we hit the steps up to the veranda. 'Do you still parachute? Nick said you used to.'

'No.' He gave me a questioning stare. 'Not any more.'

2

'While she's freshening up, lad – what does she know about work, besides the parachuting?'

It was a question Charlie had to ask. He didn't want to put his foot in it.

'Nothing. She thinks I'm a panel-beater.'

'With a boss who lets you take the year off? Or did you tell her you're retired? She's obviously got a bit of a soft spot for the elderly.'

I returned his grin just as Hazel came back into the living room with a tray of orange juice and glasses.

'I hope he's not trying to sell you a horse, Nick?'

A few notes of German drifted down the stairs as Silky relaxed under the shower.

'Nah, he's been giving me a hard time for not following his example.'

'But you're too young to retire . . .'

'I mean about not getting my hooks into a gorgeous girl like he did.'

Hazel smiled as she put the tray down. 'Has he told you about the lovely life we have now?'

'Not yet, but I'm sure it'll only be a matter of time!'

Hazel fussed around like a mother hen as she rearranged all the things neatly on the coffee table. Eventually she poured three glasses and we clinked them in an unspoken toast.

I pointed out of the window. 'Was that Julie I saw riding?'

Hazel's face lit up. 'She'll be over soon. She phoned to say she'd seen you.'

'The pair of them – like that, they are.' Charlie went to cross his fingers to show how entwined the two of them were, but couldn't quite manage it. His forefinger seemed to have a mind of its own. He brought his thumb and little finger into play instead, as if he was on the phone. 'And when they're not together, they're never off the blower. And Hazel emails the kids every day after school.'

'Maintenance, my darling.' Hazel looked me in the eye. 'If you don't keep checking the roof, then next time there's a storm . . . Don't you agree, Nick?'

I looked at the family gallery on the sideboard; the usual mishmash, some black and white, some colour, in a variety of silver and wooden frames. Wedding photos with '70s hair-styles; then their two kids, Julie and Steven, at all the different stages: big ears; no teeth; zits . . . Then the ones of Julie's wedding, and her own children; by the look of it they had about four of them. The air round here was obviously good for raising more than just horses.

My gaze fell on one of a young man in a Light Infantry beret and best Dress Number Twos staring proudly into the camera, the Union Jack behind him. Steven's passing-out parade must have been about 1990, because Charlie and I had still been in the Regiment; I'd thought he'd burst with pride when he told me. I didn't know much about him though, beyond the fact that he'd been seventeen and the spitting image of his dad.

'How's your boy doing? He still in?'

Hazel's eyes dropped to the floor.

I wondered what I'd said, then I noticed: there weren't any other pictures of him.

Charlie leaned across and took Hazel's hand in his. 'He was killed in Kosovo,' he said softly. 'Ninety-four. He'd just got promoted to corporal.'

He put his arm around his wife. I sat back in my chair, not sure what to say to avoid adding to the wreckage.

'Don't worry about it, lad, you weren't to know. We kept it to ourselves pretty much. Didn't want GMTV round, filming us going through the family album.'

Hazel looked up and gave a brave smile. She'd probably got over the worst of it during the last ten years, but it must have been a nightmare.

Silky drifted in, breaking the moment, smelling of soap and shampoo. She'd put on a pair of pale blue cotton trousers and a white vest, and her wet hair was combed back.

There was an awkward silence. Hazel busied herself pouring another glass of juice. 'I bet you feel a lot better for that.'

'The shower or the singing?' Silky smiled as she came and sat beside me. Whatever she was about to say next was drowned out by the blare of a car horn.

Hazel looked relieved. 'Julie.'

Seconds later, a flurry of feet and young voices bomb-burst into the house, shouts and shrieks echoing off the wooden floors. The door flew open and four boys with sticky-up crew cuts and untanned skin ran into the room. The older two, about eight and seven, came up to me and thrust out their hands. 'You're Nick, aren't you?' They had strong accents. Their two little brothers ran back outside.

I bent down and shook. 'And this is Silky.'

'That's a funny name.'

'You pronounce it Silk-a really. Nick calls me Silky because he's not very good with complicated words.'

Silky loved kids. Her older sister kept sending pictures of her twin seven-year-old boys to Silky's PO box in Sydney.

Every time we stopped in anywhere for more than a few days she got her mail forwarded and I would have to sit and listen to Karl and Rudolf's latest adventures.

'Where are you from, Silky? You talk funny!'

'Funnier than Nick? I come from Germany. It's a long way away.'

Julie and her husband Alan came in with Charlie, the two younger kids hanging off his leg. We made the right noises as we shook. Alan's hands were big and rough. He was a bushman to his marrow, and wasn't particularly fussed up about the visitors.

Charlie took charge. 'Right! I'd better get that barbecue lit, hadn't I? Who's coming to help me?'

It was obviously the standard call to arms. All the kids jumped up and down with delight and charged outside.

3

Two hours later, everybody was stuffed full of chicken, steak, prawns and Toohey's. Silky sat with Julie and Hazel on the settee; conversation flowed like they'd known each other all their lives. Alan sorted out a DVD for the kids, who were flaked out on cushions on the floor. He threw it in and, maybe sensing Charlie and I could do with some private time, sat down to watch it with them.

'Why don't you jump any more?'

Charlie was standing with me by the jug of coffee on the sideboard. We weren't ready for it yet; we were both still on cans. 'Wasn't fair to Hazel. Her nerves were bad enough as it was.'

Silky joined us with three empty cups. She nodded at the gallery as she poured. 'Charlie, you were in the army?'

'Yes.'

'You haven't changed, have you? Look at you!'

Charlie smiled at the picture of his son. 'I've put on a few wrinkles since then – and lost a bit of hair.'

I shot a glance at Hazel. She was smiling at Charlie for being so kind. Silky poured their coffees and went back to the other two, completely oblivious.

Charlie held up his can to me in a toast. 'The good old days.' We touched tins and he took a swig. 'What about Silky? Any plans?'

'Nah, I'm just letting her sleep with me till I find somebody better.'

He frowned at my bad joke. 'You're a knobber then. She seems a really good girl. Make the best of it while you can, lad.' He looked at the sofa then back at me. 'So, you want to come and watch the sun go down, or what?'

He couldn't have made it more obvious he had something he wanted to talk about if he'd tried. He lifted two new cans and I followed him out onto the veranda.

He leaned on the rail. A couple of hundred metres away, a group of horses kicked up dust in the paddock.

Charlie sat on a bench and motioned me to a swing seat opposite. Whatever was on his mind, he didn't seem ready to talk about it yet. My eyes followed his to the horse grazing on its own in a corner.

'You know what, Charlie? You were the one that I picked. I never told you that, did I?'

The training major always gave just one piece of advice to the newly badged troopers. 'When you get to your squadron, shut up, look and listen. Then pick one man you think is the ideal SAS soldier. Don't let him know you've picked him, but watch and learn. There will be times on operations when you don't know how to act or react. That's when you ask yourself what your man would do.'

Charlie had started out as the one I picked, but he very quickly became even more important to me than that. In my mind, I awarded him the highest accolade one soldier could ever give another. I could honestly say that I would have followed him anywhere.

He took another swig and rested his can on the rail. 'I

know, lad. I used to see you watching me. You learn much?'

'I think I did. In fact I thought about you on the last day of that Waco job. Do I deck the bloke or not. I know I made the right decision.'

'I'm not sure everybody at Waco did.' Charlie turned his head to look at me. 'Remember that young lad from DERA, the gas man? He killed himself a year later.'

I hadn't heard. I'd left the Regiment by then. 'His name was Anthony. He was all right.'

He sat back in his chair. 'Good men, fucked over by the system. It's nothing new.' He picked up his beer with a trembling hand, as if the emotion of the moment was getting the better of him. 'You know, I fell for it when I was a lad. I really did believe all that shite about Queen and country. We were the good guys, they were the bad guys. It took me thirty-seven years playing soldiers to realize what a load of old bollocks it was. Maybe you got there sooner? That why you got out?'

Charlie wouldn't know what I'd done after I left, and he would never ask. He knew that if I wanted him to know, I'd tell him.

'Sort of.'

He looked back at the solitary horse in the corner of the field. 'Did you know I was in the troop when my boy was on foot patrol in Derry?'

I nodded. A couple of guys had had sons in the green army, and all of them had been operating over the water at the same time.

He gave a little self-mocking laugh. 'I used to kid myself that every PIRA guy we dropped meant one less who could take a pop at my boy. Kind of felt I was looking out for him. But we weren't doing the job full throttle, were we? We were only dropping the ASUs [active service units] that Thatcher and Major thought would hold up the peace process.' His eyes narrowed. 'We were actually protecting Adams and

MacGuinness so they could have secret talks with our "We do not deal with terrorists" governments. Seemed there were good baddies and bad baddies, something I hadn't really thought of before.'

I shrugged. No one had ever officially admitted it, but we had all known what was going on. Eliminate the ones who were objecting to any sort of progress, then hope the rest were going to fall in behind our guys, Adams and MacGuinness. 'Maybe it worked. We've got a sort of peace.'

'Whatever. Only thing that mattered was, all the time I was running around working was time I didn't have to sit and worry about Steven.'

He gazed at the horse, lost for a moment in a world of his own. 'And afterwards . . . after he was killed . . . I didn't care how they did it, just so long as they kept me busy.'

I lifted the can. 'Must have been grim, mate.' I hesitated. 'I've kind of been there myself . . .' I tailed off again, because I wasn't sure what I was going to say next. In any case, Charlie was giving me that slightly challenging look you see in the eyes of the bereaved when people say, 'I know exactly how you must be feeling,' and they have no fucking idea. I shrugged. 'She wasn't my own, but fuck, it felt like she was. If it had hurt any more, I couldn't have taken it.'

Charlie shifted in his seat. 'Who was she? Stepdaughter?'

'Kev Brown's kid – he was in Eight Troop, remember?'

Charlie tried to, but couldn't.

'He and Marsha had made me guardian in their will.'

'Oh yeah, I heard about that. Shit, I had no idea it was you who'd stepped in.' His voice dropped. 'So what happened to her?'

'She got killed two years ago in London.' I stared down at the can. 'She was fifteen. I took her back home to the States and buried her, then, well, I buried myself, a bit like you.'

Charlie nodded slowly. 'Then you just wake up one day and wonder what the fuck it's all about . . .'

'Something like that. I always used to pretend I didn't give a fuck, but, well, you know, I loved her. Losing her fucked me up big-time. Next thing I knew, I was sitting at the wheel of a combi with long hair and a wrist full of these things.' I jiggled the friendship bracelets.

Charlie smiled. 'I guess everybody deals with it the best way they can. Know what Julie bought me for Christmas? Slippers. Fucking slippers! Ever since Steven died, that's how she and her mother want things to be. They want to live in a bubble. Everything nice and fluffy, and Steven's a happy face in a photograph. That's what this place is all about. It's Hazel's own self-contained eco-climate, like a fucking Eden Project for happier times.'

He took another swig of beer and looked me square in the eye. 'Coming here was the worst thing I could have done, lad. Far too much time on my hands. People look at me and think I have a slice of paradise, but it's driving me fucking mad. If you keep moving, keep doing, there's no time left to think. But now I spend half the day thinking about him. It's that same old feeling I had over the water, that I should have been there, should have been looking after him. I know there was nothing I could have done, but that doesn't stop you thinking it, does it?'

He gave me a rueful smile as he nodded over towards the paddock. 'You see that one in the corner, the bay? He was a stallion once. In his prime he covered three or four mares a day, and spent the rest of the time kicking down stable doors. He doesn't get to use his gear at all these days. Too knackered. Only difference between him and me is that instead of eating grass and shitting all day, I'm pruning the fucking gum trees and watching the sun set. You know the best thing I could do for him?' His jaw tightened. 'Put a fucking gun to his head and put him out of his misery.'

I chanced a smile. 'Or buy him slippers, mate.'

'Yeah, or buy him slippers. But some guys do it for themselves, don't they? Guys like Anthony. I used to think they were copping out, taking the coward's way, but I'm not so sure any more. Maybe they're the smart ones.'

I didn't know where he was going with this, and I didn't get the chance to find out. Julie pushed the door open and hurried from the house, a child's hand gripped in each of hers. She had a horrified look on her face, completely at odds with the bright tone in her voice. 'That was a silly film – come on, let's go. It's bedtime anyway.' Something not very good had happened inside, and she was trying to make light of it. She shepherded them down the steps just as her mother appeared in the doorway. Hazel looked distraught.

Charlie got up and took a couple of steps towards her, then jerked his head at me to go and check.

I pulled open the screen door and went in. Silky and Alan were standing in front of the television. This was no kids' DVD; the screen was filled with jerky, urgent images. I heard screams and the rattle of automatic gunfire.

Silky turned to me. 'It's near Russia somewhere. A siege. They're shooting children.'

The picture cut to soldiers trying to make entry into a big square concrete office block. The rolling captions announced that terrorists were holding an estimated three hundred people hostage. The town of Kazbegi was in the north of Georgia, on the border with Russia. Many of the hostages were thought to be women and children.

I watched as a small group of soldiers fired their AKs wildly into the windows and others tried to make entry with sledgehammers.

The camera shifted to an armoured vehicle ramming into a door. Screams filled the TV's speakers.

Women and children tumbled out of the building, only to be caught in vicious crossfire. Black smoke billowed through broken glass. Elsewhere, I could see panic-stricken faces pressed against the panes.

Soldiers gesticulated wildly to get them to stand aside,

but it wasn't happening. They were frozen to the spot.

The picture cut again to a reporter hiding behind an armoured vehicle, her pretty dark eyes wide as saucers as she extracted and processed information from the chaos. All around her, what looked like half the army was popping up and firing pistols and assault rifles. I was watching a gangfuck, Georgian style.

As two attack helicopters rattled overhead, she shouted into her microphone, in an Eastern European accent with an American twang, that the building was a regional government office; a census was being conducted and that was why there were so many people inside. The attack was thought to be an Islamist militant group protesting against the Caspian pipeline. Fuck knows how CNN had got someone there so quick, but they had. The breaking news caption now put the death toll at thirty.

Silky held her hands to her face. 'Oh my God, those poor kids!'

A soldier ran across the screen. Cradled in his arms was the limp body of a child, his clothing charred and smouldering.

There was an explosion inside the building. The camera shuddered as a rapid flash hit the windows on the first floor. Glass blew out, then smoke billowed from the holes.

I could hear a series of shouted orders, but the chaos continued. Usual story; more chiefs than Indians.

A couple of soldiers who had successfully made entry jumped back out of a ground-floor window, one of them with flames dancing on his uniform.

The camera zoomed in on a fleet of ambulances coming down a road, some civilian, some military. The two helicopters still rattled overhead.

Two blood-covered women dashed from the building, gathering up whatever dazed and bloodied children they could as they ran.

There was another prolonged and totally indiscriminate

exchange of gunfire as the camera zoomed in on two kids jumping from a first-floor window to escape the flames.

Hazel hit the remote and the TV died. 'Enough. Not in my house.'

4

I sat next to Silky on the veranda as the sun came up, listening to last night's events being endlessly dissected on the radio as I cut orange after orange for her to put through the juicer. Getting the Tindalls breakfast seemed the least we could do to repay their hospitality, and I hoped it might help put a spring in their step. The atmosphere had been pretty subdued after Hazel switched off the TV. We'd helped clear up in near silence, then gone to bed. Hazel hadn't been at all happy about the way the real world had come in uninvited, and Charlie had been tense, preoccupied.

'Hear that?' Silky whispered. 'They now estimate about sixty dead and a hundred and sixty injured.' She poured another few oranges' worth of juice into a jug. 'That's over half the people who were in the building. It's terrible.'

'It's not so bad, you know, as sieges go.' In the corner of the paddock, the old bay was treating himself to an early-morning dust bath. 'You have to work on the basis that they're all dead from the beginning anyway. Even a single survivor is a bonus in a situation like that.'

She stopped squeezing and straightened up. 'I keep thinking

about that poor child. The one who'd been burned. Did you see the soldier holding him?'

I cut another couple of oranges and passed them across. It seemed to be taking an awful lot of fruit to produce not very much juice. 'The place was probably rigged with explosives. We saw one lot go off. I'm surprised there aren't many more dead.'

'But all those soldiers looked out of control. They didn't know what they were doing.'

'You know, if twenty per cent or fewer get dropped it's a success. What those soldiers were doing was reacting to what was happening, whether it was the correct thing to do or not.'

'Dropped? What is dropped? Killed? For a panel-beater, you seem to know an awful lot about these things . . .'

'Don't you box-heads read *Time* magazine?'

Silky pulled a face before going back to her task. 'You certainly don't. The only magazines you read have parachutes on the cover.'

I was still laughing when Hazel appeared in the doorway in her dressing gown. Her hair was a mess and her eyes were red and shiny.

Silky jumped to her feet. 'Hazel, are you all right?'

A tear rolled down her cheek. 'He's gone.'

'Gone?' I said. 'What are you on about?'

'He's not here.'

A lot of thoughts raced through my mind in the next split second, and all at a thousand miles an hour. Charlie had withdrawn into his shell after the news broadcasts. 'That stuff really seemed to get to Hazel,' I'd said. 'She's been like that ever since Steven died,' he'd replied. 'She wants to shut out the real world, keep us all from being hurt like that again. That's what this place is all about.'

He'd been very morose all evening, come to think of it, but I'd put that down to the Toohey's; it had been looking more and more like he had a drink problem. And all that stuff about shooting horses ... fuck, he wouldn't have taken it into his head to drive off into the night and top himself, would he? He wouldn't have been the first.

Silky wiped her hands on her jeans and wrapped her arms around Hazel. 'Charlie has gone somewhere? Would you like some coffee, or maybe some tea?'

I glanced across at the parking area at the side of the house. The Land Cruiser was missing. 'Maybe he's gone to fetch some croissants.' I gave her my biggest smile. 'I noticed a little bakery about a thousand miles back.'

Silky glared at me as she comforted Hazel. 'It's not funny, Nick.' She was right; wrong time, wrong place.

'I'm sorry. You sure he hasn't left a note or something?'

She shook her head. 'He didn't say anything to you? You two were talking together a long time out here.'

Silky's head bounced between the pair of us as she tried to get Hazel to sit down. 'Anyone want to tell me what's going on?'

I touched her hand. 'Later.'

She got the hint. Hazel finally sat down and Silky disappeared inside the house to make that tea she'd promised.

'I'm scared that something's happened, Nick. He wasn't himself when he came to bed. You sure he didn't say anything?'

Silky was back in the doorway. 'Hazel, the telephone's ringing. Do you want me to—?'

Hazel was already moving. Silky stared at me quizzically but I wanted to listen, not speak.

I started through the door, but Hazel was already on her way back. 'That was Julie. The Land Cruiser's at the train station. What's happening, Nick? Everything's going to fall apart again, I just know it . . .' She buried her face in the front of my shirt, and clung to me like a woman drowning.

At last she raised her head. 'Please help me find him, Nick. Please . . .'

5

Even with the door closed, the racket Julie's kids were making carried into her father's office. Then the TV came on, and cartoon voices took over from their shrieks and the clatter of small feet across wooden floors.

I looked up from Charlie's desk. 'He won't have done anything stupid, Hazel. You know that's not his style.'

She nodded as if she wanted to believe me, but couldn't quite bring herself to. 'I pray you're right, Nick. I want him home.'

She'd already told me Charlie had been suffering from depression over the last few weeks, and the episodes had been getting worse and more frequent. She wanted so much to convince herself he wasn't off in the bush having a final dark night of the soul.

'Promise you'll try to find him for me?' She sounded lost, bewildered. She had changed out of her dressing gown but her hair was still a mess, and she'd given in to little bouts of weeping over the last hour. I'd never seen her look so vulnerable, and I wanted to do whatever I could to make her smile again.

She leaned down and switched on the worn, stained-plastic

PC for me. I listened to the modem shaking hands with the server on the line. I certainly wasn't going to admit to what Charlie and I had talked about. Maybe without realizing it I'd said the wrong thing and got him all sparked up. 'You go back to Julie, Hazel. I'll give you a shout if I find anything.'

As she left the room, the PC played the Windows music and went into msn. It was a very uncluttered office; the desk, the swivel chair I was sitting in, a filing cabinet, and that was about it. A Venetian blind over the window cast big wedges of light and shadow. There was a strong smell of wood.

The monitor sat in front of me, covered with kids' stickers. Shrek had a starring role on the mouse mat. A glass tankard full of sharpened pencils and pens, engraved with a winged dagger, doubled as a paperweight.

Family pictures were Blu-tacked to the walls. It didn't surprise me to see that there were none of Charlie's SAS days. There'd always been two types of guy in the Regiment: the ones who displayed nothing to do with their past, no certificates or commendations, no bayonets or decommissioned AK47s dangling off the wall. Work was work, and home was home. Then there were the others, who wanted it all to hang out for the whole world to see.

I picked up the tankard. Everyone got presented with one when they left. I couldn't remember where mine was. The squadron sergeant major had handed it to me almost as an afterthought when I gave him my clearance chit. 'Hold on,' he'd said. 'Here, I think this one's yours.' He'd fished around under his desk and given me a box, and that was that. 'See you around.'

Fair one. I was the one who'd chosen to leave. When you're out, you're out. There isn't a Good Lads Club or annual reunion or any of that malarkey.

I read the engraving and had to laugh. *To Charlie. Good luck. B Squadron.* By Hereford standards, that was emotion running amok.

I went through the paperwork it had been keeping in place; unpaid bills for fencing posts and animal feed, and two or three utility bills that had reached the red stage.

I started to mooch around on the PC. The only documents on the desktop were one about poultices for horses' feet, and something about the exchange rate between the Australian dollar and Turkish lira. I knew they'd honeymooned in Cyprus. Maybe Charlie was planning a surprise return trip. Maybe he'd just gone into the city to pick up the tickets.

The email folder didn't yield much either. The bulk of it was Hazel's daily exchanges with Julie and the kids, even though they lived within spitting distance. I wondered what it must be like to be part of such a strong family unit. Maybe it was a bit too claustrophobic at times. Maybe Charlie had just gone off to find himself some space. Enough of that; I was starting to sound like Silky.

I spent the next hour searching all his document folders, but found nothing. I went online. The browser's history had been cleared. What did that mean – that Charlie was hiding something, or just that he was a good housekeeper? Whatever, if he'd been planning something he didn't want Hazel to know about, he would hardly have left a sign saying THIS WAY on his PC.

The filing cabinet had four drawers. I opened the bottom one, P–Z, and pulled out the folder marked T. Charlie had done himself proud. The last couple of years' phone bills were not only in date order, they were itemized. I pulled out the last couple of quarters and ran my eye down the lists.

It didn't take long to spot a pattern.

Over the last month or so, and with increasing frequency, there had been several long calls to an 01432 number in the UK.

I looked at my watch. It was just after 9am, so still well before bedtime back home.

I picked up the phone and dialled.

PART THREE

1

'Hereford.' A finger prodded me in the shoulder. 'You wanted to know when we got to Hereford.'

I struggled to open my eyes. I hadn't realized the train had stopped. Lucky I'd asked the old lady opposite to give me a shout, or I'd have woken up in Worcester.

I thanked her and headed for the door, feeling like a zombie. After a two-and-a-bit-hour journey from Paddington, I'd changed at Newport for the local commuter to 'H', as it was known to guys in the Regiment. Before we'd even left London, my lids had been drooping and my chin was on my chest. Too many time zones and twelve thousand miles in cattle class were against me.

My conscience was weighing pretty heavily, too. I felt bad about lying to Silky. 'Going to the station to see if he's left any-thing in the wagon' was hardly the same as 'I've spoken to the broker and it sounds like he's accepted a job offer somewhere, so I'm flying halfway across the world to find out more. You know that bit about being back here tonight? I'll actually be thirty thousand feet over Singapore by then, but apart from that, everything I said was true and we can trust each other always, honest.' But what else was I supposed to do? The only way to find out where Charlie had gone was to put in a personal appearance. The broker wouldn't help me. His job was to match guys and work, not tell them to go home. The only way I was going to be able to fetch him back to his family was to physically grab hold of the silly old fucker and find out exactly what the problem was, and then see if I could help.

Maybe it was being separated from her for the first time in three months that did it, but I had a terrible feeling I was missing Silky already. She had a stupid accent and an irritating habit of understanding people much better than I did most of the time, but I'd got used to her being around, and it wasn't at all a bad feeling. The lying thing wouldn't go down well, of course, but Hazel would explain and I'd make it up to her somehow when I got back. Whenever that was. And if she was still there.

As I stepped onto the platform, carry-on in hand, I had a go at wiping off the dribble soaking into the front of my leather bomber jacket. The old lady must have thought I was pissed.

I wandered out to the taxi rank. Not much seemed to have changed. There was a new superstore opposite the station, but that was about it.

I climbed into a cab and asked for Bobblestock. The driver, a guy in his mid-fifties, eyed me knowingly in the rear-view of his old Peugeot 405. 'Been far, have you?' The locals loved the Regiment being based in their town, and not just because of the amount of money they spent. This guy was drawing all the wrong conclusions from a bloke with a tan who looked like he'd slept in a hedge.

'Yeah.' I tried to rub my face back to life. 'I can't remember the name of the road but I'll show you where it is when we get there.'

I spotted a new pub and a couple of shops that hadn't been there long, but otherwise Hereford was exactly as I remembered it. I'd left the Regiment in 1993, and I'd never been back since. The only thing I'd left behind was my account at the Halifax. I wondered how much interest I'd made on £1.52.

Bobblestock had been one of the first of the new breed of estates that sprang up on the outskirts of towns in the Thatcher era. The houses were all made from machined bricks and looked as if they were huddled together for warmth. With 2.4 children inside, a Mondeo on the drive, the minimum of back garden and front lawns small enough to cut with scissors, these places had about as much character as a room in a Holiday Inn. The developers had probably made a killing, then bought themselves nice period mansions in the outlying villages.

Crazy Dave lived on the high ground of Bobblestock, which he proudly told me had been Phase Three of the build. That was the only landmark I had in my head, but it was good enough.

'Just here, mate.'

We stopped outside a brick rectangle with a garage extension that looked as if it had been assembled from a flat-pack. The house to its right was called Byeways, the one to its left, The Nook. Crazy Dave's just had a number. Typical. Crazy Dave had been in Boat Troop, A Squadron. I knew him more from the café downtown than from work. We both used to spend our Sunday mornings there, drinking coffee, eating toast and reading the supplements. Him because he was trying to avoid his wife; me because I didn't have one.

Crazy Dave had earned his name because he wasn't; he was about as zany as a teacup. He was the kind of guy who analysed a joke before saying, 'Oh yeah, I get it. That's funny.' In all the time I knew him, he never understood why shitting in someone's Bergen was funny. But for all his faults, being as straight as a die made him perfect for his new job. Discretion was everything. When I'd asked him about Charlie over the phone, he'd admitted the old fucker was on the books, but wouldn't give me any wheres or whens. He did invite me round for a brew, though, any time I wanted to chat; so, well, here I was.

There was no car outside, but I could see movement through the living-room window. I paid the driver and walked up the concrete ramp that had replaced the front steps.

I rang the bell and the door was opened almost at once by two guys on their way out. They looked young and fit, obviously either having just left the Regiment, or being about to. They were both dressed, like me, in Timberland boots, leather jacket and jeans.

I closed the door behind me as the two guys walked away. The staircase was dead ahead, and fitted with one of those stairlifts that Thora Hird used to flog in the Sunday supplements.

Dave's voice came from down to the right somewhere. 'Straight through, mate. Out the back.'

I walked into a no-frills living room; laminate flooring, three-piece suite, a large TV and that was about it. The rest was open space. French windows opened onto the garden.

'I'm in the garage, mate.'

I crossed a small square of lawn to where another ramp led up to a pair of doors set into the garage wall – a recent addition, judging by the fresh mortar and brick edging.

The garage had been converted into an office. There was a stud wall where the up-and-over door would once have been, and no windows. Crazy Dave was sitting behind his desk. He didn't get up. He couldn't.

2

I went over and shook his hand. 'What the fuck did you do to yourself?'

Crazy Dave wheeled his way round in front of me, in a very high-tech aluminium go-faster chair. 'Not what you think. Got bounced off my Suzuki on the M4 by a truck driver from Estonia and took the scenic route. Did a tour of the central reservation, then checked out a fair amount of the opposite carriageway. Six months in Stoke Mandeville. My legs are fucked. I'm still in and out of hospital like a bleeding yo-yo. Plates in, plates out; they don't know what the fuck they're doing.' He looked me up and down. 'Fuck me, you don't look too good yourself. Fancy a brew?'

Not waiting for my answer, he spun the wheels past the sink and towards the kettle in the corner. 'So that was me out of the Regiment. Too handicapped even to be a Rupert. I get disability pension, but it hardly keeps me in haircuts. Then this landed on my plate. Madness not to.'

There had always been a broker knocking around Hereford. He had to be ex-Regiment because he had to know the people – who was in, who was getting out – and if he didn't, he had to know a man who did.

There was a clink of mugs. 'Had to turn the garage into a fortress, of course. The doors have drop-down steel shutters. Got to be firearm secure because of all that gear.' He nodded at the desk. All he had was a phone, a notebook, and two boxes of plain postcards, but to people wanting to know which companies were doing which jobs, they'd have been worth more than a whole truckload of AK47s.

'How's it all work, Dave? I've never been to a broker.'

'Guys come in, or phone me and say they're looking for work. I bang their details down on a card and put them into the box marked "Standby". See the other box? That's for "Bayonets". They're the boys who are actually working.'

I hoped the kettle was going to boil soon. Admin stuff might be fascinating to Dave, but I now knew all I needed to.

No such luck. A light started to burn in his eyes. Maybe he was crazy after all. He was like a trainspotter who'd just been asked to give a guided tour of the Orient Express. 'The system's simple. A company calls and asks for four medics, say, and a demolitions guy. I go into the Standby box and shuffle through the cards from the front, until I've got the requirement. They get a call. If they want the work they get moved from Standby to Bayonets. If they don't, their card goes to the back of the box. Once they've finished that job, if they still want to be on the books, they go into the back of the Standby box.'

What could I say? I gave him the sort of look that I hoped he'd mistake for total fascination.

The kettle finally rescued me. Crazy Dave busily squashed teabags as I settled in the chair the other side of his desk. He wheeled himself across to me with two mugs in one hand.

The choice was Smarties Easter Egg or Thunderbird 4. I settled for Smarties; it wasn't quite so chipped and stained.

'So, what do you want to know about Charlie?'

'He's a dinosaur, Dave; he's far too old to be fucking about. Hazel wants him home.'

He manoeuvred his way back to his side of the desk. 'She still putting up with the old fucker then?'

I nodded. 'Talking of which, your kids OK?'

He sat back in his wheelchair and had a sip of the brew. 'Married and gone, mate. The boy's in London, fucking about with some Polish model, and the daughter's married a pointy-head. Got a nice place in town.'

Dave had lived here for over thirty years now, but he still called everyone a pointy-head, as if he'd just turned up.

I took a sip of my own tea and nearly choked. It was three parts sugar.

He grinned from ear to ear. 'Even the ex-missus has married a pointy-head. One of the local coppers. What about you, Nick? Married? Divorced? Kids? The whole catastrophe, I shouldn't wonder . . .'

I shook my head and smiled. 'I think I may still have a German girlfriend back in Australia, but I had to leave her in a hurry because of you. She isn't going to be impressed.'

He grinned again. 'Them box-heads have always got the hump about something or other.'

We could have waffled on. I could have told him about Kelly – he'd known her Dad, Kev. But we'd done the social bit, and I was here to find Charlie.

'Can you give me some idea where the old fucker's gone? I promised Hazel I'd give him the lecture. You know how it is.'

Dave gave a smile that told me he did, and he'd heard it a hundred times. 'You know I can't tell you anything, mate. It's the deal with the companies: they don't want anybody knowing what jobs they've got going on. And if everybody went home as soon as their wives started honking, there'd be hardly any fucker working.'

He put down his mug and gripped the arms of his wheel-chair. He lifted himself a couple of inches out of the seat and held himself there; maybe something to do with circulation, or to stop pressure sores developing on his arse.

'What about yourself, Nick? I haven't heard your name mentioned on the circuit; what you doing?'

'Oh, you know ... Stuff.' I shrugged and smiled. 'Look, Dave, I don't need to know what Charlie's up to. I just want to be able to phone up Hazel and say I spoke to him.'

He put his tea down and wheeled himself back alongside me. 'Sorry, mate, but you're fucked. Apart from security, what if you convinced him to head back for the pipe and cocoa? I'd have to find a replacement. And anyway, he was gagging for a job. I didn't make him come to me, did I?'

He swivelled the chair and headed off towards the door. 'Tell you what, I'm going for a dump. I've been trying to put a toilet in here, but planning won't let me, the bastards.' He whistled through the French windows and down the ramp.

'Hey, Nick, watch this!'

I got up and went to the door just as he lifted his front wheels and did a 360. 'I've got to close up, mate. Want to wait in the front room and finish your brew? What about a pint, later?'

I followed him outside and watched as he locked the garage doors with one of a bunch of about half a dozen keys.

We went into the living room and he carried on to the bottom of the stairs. As I sat down he transferred himself onto the lift. Then he selected another key from the bunch, pushed it into a control box on the wall, and gave it a turn. The chair glided slowly upwards.

'You need a hand, Dave?'

'Nah, it's rigged up like a monkey's climbing frame up here.'

The moment I heard the bathroom door close, I was on my feet and heading for the kitchen. No sign of the fuse box. I tried the cupboard under the stairs. There were two rows of cutout switches encased in a neat rectangle of plastic, but not one of them was labelled. Fuck it; I turned the whole lot off at the master switch.

I went to the control box, grabbed the bunch of keys, and headed for the garage.

Charlie's card was right at the front of the Bayonets box. It didn't say who for, where, or what the job was, just that Dave had booked him a hotel room in Istanbul.

I locked up and went back to the living room.

'Nick! The fucking power's gone. Nick, you there?'

'Coming, what's up?'

I got the key back in the box just as Dave eased himself off another wheelchair at the top of the stairs and onto the lift. He hammered away at the down button like a lunatic.

'See? I can't even have a fucking dump in peace. Try a light for us, see if the power's gone.'

I hit the hall switch. 'Where's the fuse box?'

Dave told me and I headed for it. A few moments later the microwave in the kitchen buzzed a power-cut warning and he started to make his way back down.

'Dave – sorry, mate, but I can't stay for that pint. If Charlie's in touch, tell him to phone home – Hazel's lost something and he's the only one who knows where it is.'

3

Istanbul
Thursday, 28 April

One of the first things I always noticed about a new country was the smell. In the arrivals lounge at Ataturk International it had been of strong aftershave; in the back of this cab it was even stronger cigarettes. The driver was already sucking on his second since leaving the airport.

The traffic was chaos, and to add to the misery the driver sang along, between drags, to the loud Arab pop music that blared from the radio. He kept turning his head for approval, like he'd mistaken me for Simon Cowell and I was about to sign him to a billion-lira contract. His blue-eye talisman swung wildly from the rear-view mirror as we hurtled from one side of the road to the other. I hoped it worked as well with articulated lorries as it did against evil spirits; the driver's eyes were everywhere but on the road.

Every leg of this journey had been a nightmare, Australia to Hereford, Hereford to Stansted, Stansted to Turkey. Stansted on its own deserved some sort of prize. It felt like I'd spent longer there than I had in the air from Brisbane.

I'd made my way to it from Crazy Dave's without checking flights. I'd assumed one of the bucket carriers would be my best bet, and I just hoped I'd walk straight on. But of course I'd missed the last one by an hour, so had to spend the night stretched out on a row of anti-sleep seats in the terminal. And because I got there late, I'd missed the last of the baguettes at the only café still open. I settled for four packets of salt and vinegar instead, and two large coffees that proceeded to keep me awake all night.

Even though the weather was cold, grey and blustery, I kept the back windows of the taxi open, partly because I needed the ventilation, and partly because I thought it might help me in a crash. We finally got to the Barcelo Eresin Topkapi hotel without being flattened. The journey had been only three cigarettes long.

I hadn't had time to go online and check the place out, but it looked pretty impressive. A drive swept past the front of a large, four-storey building that wouldn't have been out of place among the grand hotels along the Croisette in Cannes.

A huge banner over the entrance welcomed the architects of Germany to their very important conference. That was what I assumed it said, anyway. All I'd learned during my two years in Sennelager as an infantry soldier was how to ask for a beer and half a chicken and chips, and I'd normally ended up with two; if they asked me whether I'd like anything on it, I'd just order it all over again.

I paid the driver and headed through a pair of towering glass automatic doors into the lobby. An ornate rope barrier guided me towards a metal detector, maybe a hangover from the bomb attacks in 2003. Whatever, the security guard, whose shirt collar was at least three sizes too big for his neck, just waved me past, then busied himself hassling a couple of locals coming in behind me.

Three or four blond girls were clustered on a portable exhibition stand to the right of reception. The display space behind their hospitality desk was lined with photos of glassy, high-tech buildings, and they could hardly move for the piles of goody bags on either side of them. The architects were clearly getting the warmest of welcomes.

The lobby was constructed entirely of dark wood and pale marble. I kept walking, looking for signs that would point me to the bar, a café, even a toilet – it didn't matter, so long as I looked as if I knew where I was going.

I headed for a big leather armchair at the bottom of a flight of marble steps where people sat drinking tea. I ordered myself a double espresso, and tried to resist the urge to put my head back; it wouldn't have taken me long to flake out.

The coffee took for ever to come, but it didn't matter. I waited and watched. A group disgorged from a plush Mercedes coach and were shepherded straight to the hospitality desk.

I picked up one of the 'This place is great' type brochures. The hotel, it told me, 'distances itself from and to the following point of interests: only 3 kilometres from the famous Covered Bazaar, Suleymaniye Mosque, Blue Mosque, and Topkapi Palace'. All the rooms had a 'luxurious bathroom' and, what was more, 'own private hairdyer with a parallel line are all individually yours'. Wasn't Charlie the lucky one?

I'd never been to Istanbul before. All I knew about it was that spies used to be exchanged at the railway station, and the Orient Express stopped here before it crossed the Bosphorus. When it came to the Turks themselves, I just had my step-father's words ringing in my ears. 'Don't stand still or they'll nick your shoelaces,' he used to say about anyone east of Calais. I guessed it might have been like that once, but when I looked outside I didn't see a steamy bazaar full of shifty conmen. I saw sleek women in Western dress and steel-and-glass trams gliding along a broad, boutique-lined boulevard. If I hadn't known better, I'd have said I was in Milan. The newer cars had a little blue strip on the side of their number plates, optimistically preparing for EU membership.

I looked around for any sign of my coffee. Maybe I'd try giving Charlie a call.

When it finally arrived, I took a sip from the thimble-sized cup and eyed up the house phones between the reception desk and the lifts. I'd call Charlie to tell him I was downstairs. If there was no answer, I'd wait out on the street and just keep a trigger on the place until he returned – which I hoped wouldn't be long, because I was going to fall asleep soon whether I wanted to or not.

Should I call Silky and Hazel back at the farm? I hadn't emailed or spoken to them since leaving Brisbane. Better to wait till I had some definite news, I told myself – though the truth was I wanted to avoid having to explain where I was to Hazel for as long as I could.

I slipped a couple of bills under the saucer and wandered over to the phones. As I picked up the receiver, the lift pinged. A crowd of Germans and Turks came past, swinging their conference goody bags.

The operator rattled off her hellos in Turkish, German and English.

'Listen, the architects' conference . . .' I smiled broadly; when you do that, it transmits to the listener. 'I'm the English-speaking organizer in reception, and a Mr Charles Tindall has gone up without his welcome pack . . . Could you possibly put me through to him?' I flicked through my imaginary notepad. 'He's in . . . let's see, Room 106 . . . or is that 206? I can't read this writing.'

'Mr Tindall is in 317. He is with the conference?'

'Well, I've got a welcome pack for him. Oh my word, here he is right now . . . Thank you very much for your help. Mr Tindall, here's your—'

I put the phone down, and seconds later was pressing the button for the lift.

4

I followed the signs to rooms 301–21, down a wide, carpeted corridor. Room 317 was near the end, on the left; its windows would look out onto the boulevard. A Do Not Disturb sign hung from the door handle.

I knocked and took a step back so he'd have a good view of me through the spyhole. 'It's Nick.' I gave him a big grin.

The door opened.

'I've come to pay back that three quid I owe you.'

Charlie was wearing jeans and a pullover he could only have bought from a shop catering for colour-blind customers. He wasn't smiling as much as the bloke who sold it to him must have; as he ushered me past, I wasn't too sure if his expression was one of surprise or anger.

I walked into a big, well-furnished room, dominated by a mahogany bed and a window that filled an entire wall. I could just about hear a tram rumbling below us. He still hadn't unpacked his carry-on, which lay open with his washing and shaving kit and a few pairs of socks on display, but there was a black laptop sitting on the desk next to the TV, lid up and screen working.

Charlie was close behind. 'Er, don't tell me, you were just passing.'

'Had to get my finger out and find you, didn't I? You spoken to Hazel yet?'

'You're joking! She'll rip my head off and drag it down the phone. I emailed, said I'm fine and I'll call later.'

I went and sat down on the bed. If he decided to chuck me out, he'd find it more difficult if I'd made myself at home. 'Do us a favour, will you? Get a plane home with me, and I can go back to my German without your wife killing me.'

He opened the minibar under the TV and brought out two cans of Carlsberg. He handed me one and we both pulled back the rings.

'Sorry about that.' He leaned against the desk by the TV and took a mouthful. 'She can be a nightmare when she's got the blood up. I'll call her tonight to explain, now I know how long I'll be away.' He smiled briefly before taking another swig. 'How'd you find me?'

I told him about the power cut at Crazy Dave's. He laughed so loud they probably heard him on the tram.

I was feeling too out of it to laugh, or even to touch the beer; I just rested the can on my chest as I stretched out on the bed. 'I don't want to know the job, mate. That's your business. But if you're serious about working, you could do much better than here. What about Baghdad, or even Kabul? The money's better. Four-fifty to five hundred a day for a team leader, even for a geriatric.'

'Oi, less of the team leader. Anyway, who said anything about Istanbul?' He took a long swig of Carlsberg and studied my face. 'Three days' work and all my problems are sorted.'

It was my turn to smile. 'Sorted? What the fuck you on about? You're already sorted. You're living the dream.'

'Hazel's dream . . .' He sighed. 'Look, I'm happy to go along with it. Since Steven died, the only thing that's kept her sane is having the whole family around her. But a farm don't run on horseshit. The pension only just about pays the mortgage, for fuck's sake. Cash flow, it doesn't exist. This job will pay off the debts in one swoop, and then some.'

The high sweat-to-bread ratio sounded worrying. It normally signalled a job no one else wanted to touch with a ten-foot pole.

'How much?'

He smiled again, and this time it was the really annoying smile of someone who knows a secret you don't. 'It's a one-off. Special senior citizen rates. Two hundred thousand US.'

'Fuck me. You dropping Putin or something?'

'Nah, I turned that one down.'

I raised my can to my mouth, then realized the taste of beer was the last thing I wanted. 'Whatever. You're too old for this shit. Go home; make Hazel happy. Let me get back to my German.'

Charlie kept looking at me and smiling, like the thing he was keeping to himself was the secret of the universe. 'It's not just about the money, lad.'

'I knew it. All that waffle about that horse of yours . . . then that stuff on the TV . . . you just want to get out there and do it again, don't you?'

'I wish.' He turned his back on me to gaze out of the window, and when he turned back, the smile had evaporated. He just stood there and stared at me for a long time, like a cop on the doorstep with bad news, searching for the right words to tell me. He looked down at his trembling hand, then back at me.

I finally twigged. 'You're sick, aren't you?'

He looked away. 'You mustn't tell anyone this, especially Hazel. You up for it?'

I nodded. As if I was going to say no.

He stared at me again for what seemed like for ever, and in the end he just shrugged. 'I'm dying.'

I was so tired I wondered if I'd heard right. '*What?* What the fuck's wrong with you?'

He looked out of the window again. 'MND, mate. Motor neurone disease. Well, one of the forms of it. A few Yanks who were in the Gulf have got it as well. They're trying to find a connection, but it's pretty academic. By the time they do, it will be too fucking late.'

'You're kidding me?'

He shook his head. 'I wish.'

It was my turn to stare. I didn't know what to say. The only person I could think of with motor neurone disease was Stephen Hawking. Did this mean Charlie was going to end up buzzing around in a wheelchair and sounding like a Dalek?

'What's the prognosis?' I put the can down on the side and swivelled round to get my feet on the carpet. 'I mean, is the bad stuff inevitable?'

'It's already happening.' He took another swig of beer before holding the can out towards me. 'Sometimes I have to really concentrate just to pull the ring on one of these things. Sometimes it's a bit difficult turning door handles. It's been going on for six months. I went to see a doctor on the quiet – ' he pointed his finger at me, the can still in his hand – 'and it needs to stay that way. At least until all the money's in the bank. I want something to cushion the blow for Hazel when I tell her.'

He siphoned up the last of his beer and this time I decided to join him.

'Does it have to get worse? I mean, maybe a few trembles is as bad as it'll get?'

He shook his head slowly. 'Sure as night follows day.' He sounded almost matter-of-fact. 'The next step is memory loss, then my speech gets slurred. Then I won't be able to walk or swallow . . . Five years on average, and that's me gone.'

'Stephen Hawking's been going for donkey's years.'

'One in a million. It's five years, some much quicker. I

wouldn't mind that. Once it gets to the stage where Hazel's spoon-feeding me mashed banana, I'll get her to kill me anyway.' He started to laugh, maybe a bit too much. 'Or maybe I'll see just how much of a mate you are.'

5

We nursed our second can of Carlsberg in silence. I was still on the side of the bed; Charlie was by the TV, staring out of the netted window. I didn't feel like drinking, but at least it was cold and purged my mouth of three days' worth of airline shit on a tray. I wished it could have washed away Charlie's bad news as well, but it didn't. I felt sorry for him and his family, and that was a strange feeling for me to have. Normally it would just be a case of, tough shit and I'll kill you when it's spoon-feed time.

'It makes sense now.' I couldn't stand the silence any more. 'But what if your hands start disco dancing while you're working?'

'Chance I've got to take.'

'Crazy Dave know?'

'Crazy Dave's a good man, but he's not in the charity game.' He shrugged and gave me a smile. 'I just told him how much cash I needed and if there was a job that paid it, I'd be there. It's my last payday. Hazel will need the money. And you were right about the horse . . .' Charlie took the final swig from his can and put it down on the desk. He bent and stuck his head half inside the fridge as he rummaged among the drinks and chocolate bars. His voice was muffled. 'I don't want to spend my last few breaths stuck in the corner of a fucking field.'

Charlie hadn't seen the state Hazel was in after he'd done the runner. 'Why not go home and explain everything to her, then come back? What if you fuck up and don't get home? That'll be two Hazel's lost, and all she'll remember is you fucking off.'

He stood up with two cans, water this time, and handed me one. He placed his on the desk and had a go at opening it. This time his middle finger made a meal of getting under the ring pull.

'Well, lad.' The can finally fizzed. 'She's going to lose me whatever I do. This way at least she gets some compensation. I'm staying here.' His eyes gleamed and there was certainty in his voice. He was suddenly the Charlie I knew of old. 'Better to burn than fizzle out. I'll do the job I'm contracted to do. Then I'll go home and face the music. She'll calm down after a while. She loves me really.'

He fixed his eyes on mine. 'You want to come along as shot-gun?' He brought the can of water up to his mouth and tilted his head to drink. His eyes swivelled so they kept contact with mine. 'No pay, mind – that's all for Hazel. But I'll pick up the costs and get you back to your German, Club Class.'

I couldn't help but smile; it almost turned into a laugh because the situation was so ridiculous. I'd never worked for nothing in my entire life. I'd even charged my mum twenty pence to go to the corner shop for a pack of Embassy Gold. 'But you haven't even told me the job.'

Charlie detected the flicker of interest. He fished a USB memory stick out of his jeans and plugged it into his laptop. A dialogue box asked if he wanted to carry on with the movie clip from where he'd left off, or go back to the beginning. He tapped the keyboard and we got a jerky picture of a ten-foot brick wall with broken glass cemented into its top. A succession of Ladas trundled down the potholed road alongside it. I could see only the top two floors of the worn-out and pitted brick cube the other side of the wall, but every window was protected by a heavy grille that sat proud of the building so it could be opened outwards. The camera passed the graffiti-sprayed gates. Two wall-high metal plates closed the house off to the public. They looked as if they had been there as long as the house, rusting and battered, held together in the centre by a lever lock.

The picture curled as Charlie poked the screen. 'Fucking amateur bag fit.' The camera had been concealed in a bag of some kind, with just a small hole cut into it. If the lens had been pressed right up against it they might have got a full picture, but they'd done it so badly it was blurred round the edges.

'What are we looking at?'

'This, my lad, is the home of a government minister, in that most upright and enlightened of landscapes, the former Soviet republic of Georgia. He goes by the name of Zurab Bazgadze – though I like to think of him as plain old Baz.'

'Great. And?'

'I'm going to pop in there and do a little job.'

'No job's that little, for that sort of cash. You covering your back?'

He grinned. 'That's why I'm thinking you should come along and help me.' He pulled at his jumper. 'This wasn't the only thing I bought duty free.' He stood up, walked over to his carry-on, and extracted a small digital camcorder. Its red light glowed. 'I thought it was him at the door again...' He powered down the device. 'I'm building up as much of a security blanket as I can lay my hands on. If I get stitched up, he'll go down with me.'

'Who the fuck are you on about?'

'The world's fattest American, with one of those fuck-off whitewall haircuts.'

Charlie came back to join me at the laptop. He pulled out the memory stick and waved it at me before it disappeared into his pocket. 'He dropped this off, and the laptop – and before you ask, don't.'

He was right. I didn't need to know who this man was. If I did go with Charlie and Whitewall found out I was also on the ground, Charlie could say that I knew nothing about anything. He wouldn't have shown me the tape now anyway. I had nothing to do with the job.

'I don't want to know. I'm more worried about you getting caught. Those shaky old hands of yours will see out their days with thumbscrews attached to them. They don't fuck about in Georgia, mate.'

'Piece of piss getting into that target, lad. Who d'you think did all those banks in Bosnia?'

'I thought about you when I read the story.'

Towards the end of the Bosnian war, the Firm needed to get their hands on the financial records of certain government officials and high-ranking army officers who were taking bribes from the drug and prostitution barons. MOE guys from the Regiment hit a whole lot of banks. The idea was that when the new country was formed, we could make sure we kept the dodgy ones out of the picture, and got the good guys in. Not that it had worked, of course. It never does.

'Yeah – should've skimmed off a few bob for myself while I was at it, shouldn't I? Wouldn't be here now . . .'

'What is this little job you're doing, then?'

The screen went blank and Charlie looked up at me. 'Can't tell you just yet. But come along as shotgun, and I'll tell you in-country. I've got to hit the place this Saturday, leaving here at dark o'clock tonight.'

'Why Saturday?'

'Baz is away, but he'll be back Sunday. So I can't hang around chatting; it's make-your-mind-up time, lad.'

He raised an eyebrow, waiting for a reply.

'Read my lips, Nick. It's decision time.' He locked his eyes on mine. 'Which means you've got to dig deep, and ask your-self a big question.'

'How big?'

'None bigger, lad.' He took a deep breath, and adopted the kind of intense expression you use when grappling with the mysteries of the universe. 'I mean, it's the twenty-first century. So answer me this: just what kind of sad fuck goes round with a whitewall any more?'

He laughed like a drain.

He laughed so hard he had to hold his sides.

'Tell you what, Charlie,' I said wearily, 'you call Hazel and tell her you're OK and I'm here, and I'll think about it.'

PART FOUR

1

Tbilisi, Georgia
Saturday, 30 April

My sleep was broken by an announcement from the flight deck
I didn't understand a word of, and the plane began its descent.
I looked out of the window, hoping to catch a glimpse of the
city, but the cloud cover was too low and it was still pitch dark.
Baby-G told me it was nearly 5.30am. I just loved red-eye
flights, they really set you up for a good day out.

I dug around in the seat pocket for the printouts I'd done at
the internet café in Istanbul. I'd had a day to kill after Charlie
had left the city, and I always tried to find out as much as I
could about any alien environment I was about to go into.
Apart from anything else, if I had to get out quick time, I'd
need all the help I could get.

I tended to hit the CIA's world report website for facts and
figures, and backpacker chatrooms for real-time information; it
paid to get the view from both ends of the food chain. If I
needed more, I'd log on to Google.

The Russian Federation, referred to in the local press as 'the
aggressive neighbour', loomed over Georgia to the north, and
the two weren't exactly cosying up at the moment. Since the

fall of communism, Georgia, always a predominantly Christian country, had become an independent state, very pro-West, very pro-Bush. Pro-Bush meant anti-Putin, whichever way you looked at it, and that definitely put the main man at the Kremlin's nose out of joint.

What pissed him off even more was the fact that America and the UK had already given millions of dollars in arms and equipment to the Georgian military. It was the last thing he wanted happening in his backyard – which was why he hadn't pulled out his troops, armour and artillery, which were officially still there as 'peacekeepers'.

To the east lay Azerbaijan, one of the countries lucky enough to have a shoreline bordering the oil-rich Caspian Sea. Despite being Muslim, it too was backed big-time by the US, for reasons that weren't hard to see. The BTC pipeline, built by a consortium headed by BP and on the brink of coming on-line, stretched a thousand miles from Baku and passed just south of Tbilisi as it made its way through Georgia towards the Mediterranean coast.

To the south-west was Armenia, a country I'd always reckoned must be completely devoid of any men between the ages of twenty and forty. They were all busy elsewhere, running drugs, prostitution and extortion in every city in the West, as well as every other racket that used to be Mafia copyright until these guys muscled in.

Also to the south-west lay the all-important Turkey, feeling pretty pleased with itself these days for owning the business end of the pipeline at Cheyhan, where fleets of supertankers would soon be waiting to ferry enough of the black stuff to keep the 4x4s of the UK and the east coast of America on the road for the foreseeable future. It probably felt very secure, too; the huge US air base at Incirlik was right on its doorstep.

A million barrels of oil a day were going to start pouring through the three-foot-six-inch-wide pipe some time in 2005. It would take six months to travel the thousand miles – not that

Turkey would care. They knew they were now such a pivotal part of the process as far as the US and UK were concerned, that fully fledged membership of the EU was all but guaranteed, however reluctant the French and Dutch might be. Those EU-style number plates were much more than just optimism.

The Caspian Basin had often been at the centre of international attention. Back in the nineteenth century, when Tsarist Russia was having a bit of handbags with the British Empire, Kipling called the fight for oil the Great Game. Two hundred years later, the game was still very much on, but with a whole lot more players.

Everyone wanted a piece of the action. Russia had built a pipeline to the Black Sea coast. China was getting stuck in too. Some of the largest untapped energy reserves on the planet – an estimated 200 billion barrels – lay beneath the Caspian, and since the collapse of the Soviet empire it was very much up for grabs.

The US had military advisers in Georgia to train the army. The Brits were doing their bit by supplying equipment, transport and logistics and the whole effort was called the Partnership for Peace programme – in theory rebuilding Georgia's post-communist army, but in practice training them to protect the 'energy corridor'. The threat of sabotage by Islamic militants and ethnic separatists was constant. Whenever the boys were taking time off from harvesting their poppy crop, it would make an irresistible target.

The funniest thing I read was that the Russians had gone and built a base alongside each of the US ones, so the two sides just sat there eyeballing each other. So peace and harmony was not exactly the name of the game, particularly when you bore in mind that the Georgian government was rated one of the top ten most corrupt institutions on the planet. It all added up to a possible big-time fuck-up for Disco Charlie, which was very much why I was here.

The plane touched down and I rescued my carry-on from the overhead locker. Most of the other passengers seemed to be men, either large Turks in raincoats, liberating their packs of Marlboro, ready to light up as soon as they were inside, or locals dressed from head to toe in black. The only pair of jeans in sight was mine, bought cheap in the market, along with a jumper with a nice nylon sheen to it that was even scarier than Charlie's.

I pulled up the collar of my bomber jacket and followed the other punters across the rain-lashed tarmac to the Soviet regime's idea of a state-of-the-art terminal building, a mausoleum of concrete and glass. In the bad old days it would have been adorned with more than a few stirring portraits of the local-boy-done-good, Iosif Vissarionovich Dzhugashvili. Or, as he preferred to be known, Uncle Joe Stalin.

2

The inside of the terminal had been given a bit of a tart-up within the last decade or so, but it looked to me as though it had been done by the same crew who did the railways back home after privatization – the ones who'd given a lick of new paint to the old rolling stock and fixed for us to pick up a free magazine as we got on, in the hope that we wouldn't notice that all the carriages were still in a shit state, the toilets didn't work, and nothing arrived on time.

The immigration hall consisted of four passport control booths, each with a smiling young woman sitting behind a glass screen. I couldn't make up my mind whether they were a girl band in their spare time, or Maria Sharapova's training partners. I joined the visa line. So far, this country smelt of wet greasy hair.

Ahead of me was a column of raincoated Turks, staring daggers at the No Smoking signs. They obviously hadn't been expecting them. Behind me, maybe six or seven people back, I heard a couple of Merseyside voices. I turned as casually as possible to check them out.

There were three or four of them, two with beards, all

dressed in Gore-Tex jackets and practical walking trousers, and big practical boots. If it hadn't been for the green flowery BP logos on the tags hanging from their laptop bags, I'd have assumed they might be here to open an adventure centre or run a management bonding seminar.

I turned back. At the head of the line, two immigration officers were too busy smoking and chatting to bother helping anyone get the paperwork necessary to pass through immigration and possibly be reunited with their bags.

The Turks were really getting pissed off. I wasn't sure if it was because of the wait, or the fact that the immigration guys were hammering through the Marlboros while they couldn't. At last, fag break over but still waffling to each other, the uniforms starting picking up passports and glowering at their owners. Charlie wouldn't have had to go through this yesterday; he'd been waiting in Istanbul to arrange his visa in advance. He'd wanted to leave nothing to chance; unlike me, he hadn't fancied the idea of leaving himself to the mercy of the Chuckle Brothers and the Spice Girls up ahead.

I finally reached the front of the line. The immigration guys sat behind a glass screen, at a Formica-covered desk about level with my waist. The younger of the two grabbed my blue US passport and arrivals form without even giving me a glance. He thumbed through the passport and finally raised his head. His face was completely expressionless. 'No visa?'

Why the fuck else would I bother standing in the visa line? I smiled. 'I was told to get one from you.'

If I'd had the time to go and queue up all day and get one from the consulate in Istanbul, it would have cost me forty US dollars. Now that I was here, the price had gone up to eighty. That was the theory, anyway. I couldn't wait to hear how far these boys thought they could push their luck.

He didn't smile back. 'Hundred twenty dollar.'

'One twenty?' I toyed with the idea of aiming him at the website, but immediately thought better of it.

'Hundred twenty dollar.'

I pulled the cash from my wallet and handed it over. It wasn't the extra dollars I begrudged, so much as the principle of the thing. He looked at me for a couple of seconds, his gaze level. 'Hey . . . Why you come?'

'To find my friend.' The best cover stories are always based on the truth. 'He has left his wife and is travelling here. I've come to take him home.'

He leaned across to his mate, who was still gobbing off to him about something or other. The old guy nodded and smiled; he'd probably clocked the fact that he could now afford to stop by a hooker on the way home.

My guy counted out the hard currency, stuck the visa into my passport, and even fixed me a receipt. It was only for eighty dollars, but at least the visa was full-page. I gave him a grin to show him I thought I was getting my money's worth.

I picked up my carry-on and headed for passport control. The Spice Girls all wore shiny brown uniforms. Their new national flag was emblazoned on each arm: the cross of St George, with a smaller cross in each of the white quadrants. It looked like something Richard the Lionheart would have daubed on his shield before storming Jerusalem.

3

I wandered outside. A huge concrete awning spanned the area, probably built in the '50s to celebrate a bumper Soviet wheat harvest. Beneath it, people were jockeying for position, trying to coax their pre-Stalin-era trolleys in the direction of the taxi rank. Across the road, taxi drivers stood drinking coffee outside a row of brightly lit wooden sheds while they waited for their fares.

As I stood there trying to get my bearings, the management bonding crew climbed aboard a gleaming white Land Cruiser that I imagined was all set to whisk them away to a hot mug of tea and a full English.

I wandered over to join the ever-lengthening taxi queue. A haphazard procession of square, boxy Ladas swung towards us, their signs fastened precariously to their roofs with a couple of bungees, the same trick Silky pulled with surfboards.

The Georgian women in front of me all seemed to be either skinny as rakes, or built like bowling balls. Thirty seemed to be the point when the one turned into the other, though it was quite difficult to tell; all of them, even the ones who should have been grey, had hair that was dyed jet-black, or as dark red as a plum.

My turn came for a Lada, and a very nice mustard-and-rust one it was too. I got into the back. The windows were steamed up and the radio was going full blast in an attempt to drown out the noise of the wipers scraping across the smashed windscreen.

'The Marriott, mate. Marriott Hotel.'

The cigarette stuck to the driver's bottom lip bobbed up and down as he nodded. But the taxi didn't move.

'The Marriott. MA-RRI-OTT?'

'Marriott! Marriott!'

The penny dropped and the Lada lurched off at a rate of not that many knots, possibly because the windscreen looked like it had been on the receiving end of a burst of semi-automatic and he was trying to see through the web of cracked glass.

The meter was covered in grease and fag ash, and had probably never been turned on. I leaned forward. The driver was in his sixties, with a bushy grey moustache and grey, slicked-back hair that curled around the collar of a black polo-neck jumper.

I rubbed my thumb and forefinger together. 'How much?'

He gobbed off at me and of course I didn't understand a word. Most of it sounded like Swahili, with the odd click and guttural embellishment here and there.

He remembered to turn on his headlights while he was talking, and we picked out a 110 hardtop Land Rover parked at the roadside. It was unmistakably Brit military; dull green, with MoD plates.

The driver had left his wagon and was leaning against the wing. Bulked out with a blue waterproof jacket, shaved head, stonewashed jeans and very smart, still sparklingly clean Nikes, he had to be American. Maybe he was dropping off or collecting 'advisers' for the Partnership for Peace programme.

I was still none the wiser about the fare as we followed a wide dual carriageway towards the city centre, just over ten miles away. I only knew that because of what I picked up off the web. There were no road signs at all, just billboard scaffold over the road that had probably once carried posters celebrating the wonders of communism. Now they seemed to be saying the same sort of thing about Coke and Sony.

As we reached the outskirts of the city, drab concrete apartment blocks sprang up on each side of the road. They'd been given a recent lick of paint, but not in any colour you'd have chosen sober. Some of the giant cubes were green, some purple. One was yellow.

This wasn't what I'd been expecting, good roads and fresh paint. To cap it all, even at this time of the morning, in the dark, there were women out sweeping the road with the sort of brooms that Harry Potter played Quidditch on.

A convoy of olive-green military trucks towing artillery pieces passed us, going the other way, as we came into the city proper. I knew Tbilisi lay at the foot of three massive, steeply inclined hills. The river Mtkvari ran through it, north to south. We were entering from the flatter ground to the east.

As it became more built up, so did the number of dogs. They were everywhere, if not loose and pissing against every car within reach, then on a leash and being treated to their early morning walkies.

A blue-and-white was blocking the way. The two guys inside the shiny new VW Passat had their heads down for a nap; by the look of things, they'd got a bit tired running stripy police tape from each wing mirror to the wall on either side. My grey-haired friend peered through his screen, cursed and hung a right.

The smoothly surfaced road immediately gave way to a minefield of water-filled potholes big enough to hide a bus in. My driver joined all the others slaloming from side to side to avoid them. I wasn't sure how some of them managed it, without any headlights.

This was more like the Georgia I'd been expecting. Maybe the tourist board didn't want to deprive the punters of the authentic gulag experience, and the police were there to make sure there was no chance of us missing it. At least there were a few road signs now, in Russian Cyrillic and a language I supposed was Georgian, though the words looked more like rows of twisted paperclips.

The taxi driver crossed himself every time we passed a church. I couldn't tell if it was out of respect, or alongside a prayer of thanks for surviving the manic driving of his fellow countrymen and the Jurassic-scale potholes.

We crossed the Mtkvari, the fastest – and brownest – river I'd ever seen, to the west bank and the city centre. The Marriott was on the main drag, another stretch of flat, freshly laid tarmac that paralleled the river. It looked every bit as big and impersonal as any I'd stayed in, though I could see it was one of the newest and smartest in the chain before I'd even got out of the cab.

Chandeliers the size of hot-air balloons hung from the ceiling of an atrium eighty feet high. Everyone inside looked as though they'd just stepped out of an Armani ad before heading for their early morning breakfast meetings; all of them, both reception staff and guests, were dressed in varying shades of black.

According to the bulletin board in reception, it was the Marriott's honour to welcome the BP Georgia conference, and they looked forward to welcoming all delegates at 2pm in the St David Room. Capitalism wasn't just being embraced in this neck of the woods; it was being bear-hugged, then having its contact details Bluetoothed into every Blackberry in sight.

4

'Room 258, sir.' The concierge handed me my room card.

I thanked him and turned away, but he hadn't finished.

'One moment.' He searched under the counter top. 'This is for you.'

I took the bulky envelope. On the back was written: 'From C.T.'

I bent to pick up my carry-on, but a young bellboy beat me to it. He guided me the four paces to the lift. I hardly needed the help, but I didn't want to upset hotel protocol and get myself noticed. Besides, there was no way he was going to let go of the bag, or the tip.

He pressed the call button. 'You have travelled to Tbilisi before, sir?' The accent probably came from watching American TV shows. So did the grooming; he had hair so clean and sculpted he could have auditioned for *The OC*, and there wasn't a zit or hint of stubble on his cheek.

I smiled and made all the right noises as we let a briefcase-toting American major in BDUs get out of the lift before taking it to the third floor. 'No, but it looks very nice to me.'

He nodded and agreed, but treated me to the sort of look

that said he doubted I was in any position to judge, if my choice of outfit was anything to go by.

When we got to the room, he showed me how to work the air conditioning and TV, and even took the trouble to explain that the two-litre bottles of Georgian mineral water beside it were complimentary. I knew, but I didn't interrupt his patter. I wanted to be the grey man; or as much of one as I could be in an orange-, green-, brown- and blue-patterned jumper.

After he had completed his routine, he took a bow and gave me a very big smile. I pushed a five-dollar bill into his hand before he had a chance to go for an encore. I didn't have a clue how much that was in local hertigrats or whatever they were called, but he left a very happy bunny. Like almost anywhere, in Georgia the US dollar was king.

I took in the thick plush curtains, furniture and fittings. It made a welcome change from the shitholes I'd normally had to put up with when I was on a job. Then I peeled open Charlie's envelope.

The Motorola pay-as-you-go cell phone was fresh from its packaging. It would have been the first thing he bought after arriving. I sparked it up; there was only one phone number in the display for me to ring, so I pressed it at the same time as I hit the TV remote. I always liked seeing if other countries had to suffer their way through the same shit programmes that I watched.

Charlie answered immediately, tearing the arse out of his Yorkshire vowels like one of the Tetley tea folk. ''Eh oop, how art thou, lad?' He sounded as though he'd swallowed a fistful of happy pills.

'Shut up, you nugget. I'm in 258. You?'

'One-oh-six.'

'I'm going to sort my shit out – see you in about thirty?'

'Okey-dokey.' He killed his phone.

RTV1 was the default channel. It was good to see that today's Russian housewife wore the same gently exasperated

111

expression as her Midlands cousin when she watched her boys covering themselves with mud on the footie pitch, and that Tide washed away all her problems too.

I shoved the two-pin charger plug into a socket and checked the bars. Charlie would already have done it but there was no harm in a top-up, especially in the power-cut capital of the world.

I flicked channels again. Russia's Weakest Link looked exactly the same as the American show (which looked exactly the same as the Brit version) except that the woman asking the questions had brown hair and no facial tics.

I checked out the room safe, though I had nothing to put in it. All the US dollars I'd drawn from an ATM in Istanbul, about fifteen hundred of them in fives and tens, would stay with me. My passport would stay with me too. I only did it out of habit, in case the last guest had left me some valuables. I had probably been doing it since I was a kid checking out the coin return in phone boxes and cigarette machines. I'd never found anything then either, but you never know.

I scanned the minibar too. All the normal miniatures, but not as much vodka as I'd have thought. Coke. Fanta. A local beer covered in paperclip writing and a bit of Russian. A couple of small mineral waters with the same label, Borjomi, as the litre bottles by the TV, but without the nice little card telling me it was the pride of Georgia, and an arrow on a map pointing to a town somewhere to the west of the city. The rest were berry and fruit drinks.

I settled for a can of apple juice.

Sitting on the bed and feeling totally exhausted, I flicked through the remaining twenty-two channels. Most were Russian; a couple seemed to carry local news, and of course there were CNN and BBC. I left it on a Paperclip channel and glanced outside as I headed for the shower.

The weather was still miserable. It had stopped raining, but it was a gloomy, cloud-ridden dawn. The street directly below me was already clogged with a mixture of Western cars and trucks, and old square Ladas straining under the weight of too many sacks of spuds lashed onto their roof racks.

Beyond it were a lot of grand buildings a couple of hundred years old, which I knew from my map housed the government. A few museums, domes and church spires from even further back rubbed shoulders with the tightly packed brick cubes that lined the narrow, steeply climbing streets.

At least the communist planners had had a stab at preserving the grandeur of the centre, and built most of the crap far enough away from city hall that they didn't have to see it. By the look of things, when their work was done here, they'd probably gone and had a crack at Hereford.

The green hills that surrounded the city soared above the rooftops, and seemed close enough to reach out and touch.

I put my fluorescent nylon socks over my hands, jumped into the shower, and used them as flannels to give both them and me a wash.

My first glimpse of the foyer had told me I should have hit some local fashion websites before I came; market gear just didn't cut it here. But fuck it, Charlie's job was tonight, so I'd be out of here by tomorrow . . .

Well, that was if I did it.

I wanted to know exactly what it was first.

And coming here was the only way I'd find out.

5

Who was I trying to kid?

I knew I had to save old Disco Hands from himself, otherwise why would I be here?

But I wasn't going to tell the old fucker yet. He'd have to work for it.

I had a few concerns. It felt like too much of a rush. I would have preferred time to tune in to this place, but that wasn't going to happen. And besides, it was why Charlie was getting paid big bucks.

He'd have to think on his feet. And if they started to wobble, I'd be there to hold him up.

Five minutes later I dried myself, watching what had to be the best recruiting ad for any army in the known universe. It took me a moment to realize it wasn't a Colgate commercial. Every trooper in sight had the sort of clean-cut, sharply chiselled smile your average Georgian mum would die for; quite a few of them were busy swooning in the audience as the parade moved past them. I was expecting to see the bellboy any minute.

The music oozed serenity as the camera lingered on envious

younger brothers who couldn't wait to join up, and older sisters who only had eyes for their older brothers' new mates. And all the while, Richard the Lionheart's flag fluttered alongside the Stars and Stripes, the two occasionally entwining in the breeze.

It was all very moving. I had half a mind to sign up myself. And as Charlie often used to say, that was all you needed . . .

Leaving the defenders of the motherland saluting the flags, I headed downstairs with money, passport, phone and wet hair.

I needed a brief. After that, our plan was to be seen together in public as little as we could. We'd do our own recces, only get together for the job, whatever that was, then leave separately for the airport the next day.

Our return flight to Istanbul was at 10am, but it didn't matter if we missed it. There were flights within the following couple of hours to Vienna or Moscow. That at least guaranteed an exit from Georgia, and once we were clear, we could sort ourselves out for a plane back to Australia.

I could see if Silky was still talking to me, and he could go and die.

Room 106 had a Do Not Disturb sign on the door handle, in Russian, English and Paperclip. I gave a knock and stepped back so the silly old fucker could see me through the spyhole.

The door opened and a very smiley Charlie let me in. He'd gone for the oilman look, complete with a scuffed-up pair of US desert combat boots. The only thing missing was the green flowery logo.

He looked me up and down. 'Making an effort to blend in, I see? You look like those blocks of flats on the way in.'

The curtains were drawn; all the lights were on. The laptop was rigged up on the small desk by the window. A town map was spread out on the bed, unmarked. Alongside was a collection of improvised picks and tension wrenches. I sat on the edge of the mattress and picked up one of the lengths of coat-hanger wire. It had a two-inch shaft, then a right-angle bend; the other end had been twisted into a circle.

'You already done the locks recce for this little job of yours?'

'I could see everything from the video.' He went and sat in front of the laptop and pushed the memory stick into the USB port. 'Have a look.' He freeze-framed on a shot of the large double steel gates. 'See? Piece of piss. It'll take me about ten seconds.'

He was right. It was just lever lock. It would be easy to defeat, even without a recce. At least that would get us into the yard and out of view.

'What happens when you're inside? You still haven't told me.'

He flipped down the screen and looked at me. 'It's a covert CTR [close target recce]. I – hopefully we – have to open a safe and nick whatever documents are there, lock everything up again, and drop the stuff in a dead letter box. Old Baz will never know; we'll be in and out without leaving a fart print.'

He paused.

'It'll be like being over the water again, eh?'

True; we'd done enough covert CTRs of PIRA houses, looking for weapons or explosives, or putting in listening devices, to fill the housebreaker's handbook. But this was different. 'It sounds like a lot of cash for just a bit of nicking. You know where – and what sort – the safe is?'

Charlie couldn't help smiling. 'Nope, and it doesn't matter. Even a dickhead like you knows that locks are designed to be opened. Besides, why do you think I'm being paid so much?'

I stood up. 'Do you know what you're lifting?'

'Nope. Just anything inside the safe, handwritten or printed.'

'You know why it has to be lifted covertly? Why not just get a local lad to blow the thing up?'

'Don't know, don't care. Could be one of a thousand reasons.'

'He live alone?'

'Yep, all on his lonesome, in that big old house. What a waste.'

'You know what this Baz guy has done, or what he's about to do?'

Charlie knew I'd be hitting him with questions like this for hours if he didn't shut me up. 'Take a breath, lad. Everything's in hand. I'll be finding out all I need to when old Whitewall turns up at nine. He'll have to tell me; it's too near the witching hour for him to fuck me about, and I won't do the job if he doesn't tell me the reason why.'

'What's he coming here for?'

'I gave him a kit list in Istanbul.'

Charlie went through it all: fibre-optic equipment; big holdall of pick gear to cover all the safe options; all the other tiny details that never leave the expert's mind.

Charlie was grinning like an idiot. He loved talking work stuff; it was like he'd been let out of the paddock. 'Why the long face, lad? I know it's about two donkeys' worth of kit, but we need it to cover all eventualities, not to mention our arse.'

I was listening, but just now the kit was unimportant. 'It's your arse I'm worried about. And mine. Charlie, you know fuck all. You could land up in a world of shit, mate. You could get thrown away with the rubbish once this job's done.'

6

'I know it's risky. That's why I want you to come. I'm thinking if the wheels start to fall off you'll be there to help put them back on. But I'll know more about the job after nine . . .'

I didn't answer; I wanted him to work and I wanted to know more about Whitewall and Baz, and why he needed to steal documents from a safe.

'Look, I've already started to protect myself, and FedEx'd the first tape of the fat one to Hazel. I told her not to open it, just keep it safe. There's fuck all on it, but at least it's a start.' He got up and headed for the brew kit above the minibar. 'It's all right, Nick, really.' He pointed at the bed. 'Park your arse and I'll make us a nice cup of tea.' He sounded like somebody's granddad. Which of course he was.

I moved the map out of the way and sat down again. My face felt hot. What was I so worried about – the job, or his safety? I couldn't work it out.

The little plastic kettle started to bubble. Charlie had his back to me. 'So, lad. You with me?'

He ripped open a couple of sachets and dropped the teabags into two tiny coffee cups. We weren't going to get much of a brew out of them. 'Just like old times, eh?'

'No, Charlie, it's not like old times. We're using our own passports. We don't know what the fuck we're heading into. We are not in control of the job.' I stared at his back. 'I'm not doing it unless we know more . . .'

I tailed off, exasperated. 'What the fuck am I saying we for?'

Charlie liked that one. His shoulders shook so much it looked like he was chuckling with his whole body.

He calmed down after a minute or two and had another go at digging into the milk tubs with the back of a spoon. 'You think I don't know all that stuff? It's why I need you here, lad, like I said. To ride shotgun.'

He turned and handed me the brew.

'What do you say?' His eyes had turned a bit liquid, and I wasn't sure it was just because of the laughter. 'Piece of piss if we're two up . . .'

I took a sip of the weakest tea I'd ever tasted. 'What's his name again?'

'Zurab Baz-your-father. Something like that.'

'For fuck's sake, you don't even know his name. You on drugs or something?'

'Hang on, I remember. It's Bazgadze. But his name doesn't matter, does it? I know where he lives and it's not as if we're going to see him. We do the recces today and get on with it tonight. Then we're gone. I'll even pick up a nice bottle of duty-free, to take home for Hazel. Do you know this country invented wine?'

I moved the map so I could stretch out, and dumped the tea on the bedside table. 'How was she?'

'A bit scratchy, but she knows you're with me.' He was all smiles again. 'Silky was out riding with Julie.'

I realized I was smiling too. It had only been a few days, but I was missing her. I'd got used to being around her. It was certainly a lot more fun hanging out with her than with this old fucker.

119

Charlie had touched a nerve and he knew it. 'If you like, you can even get back into Hazel's good books by saying you're dragging me back, we're not even doing the job. What do you reckon?' He thumbed the number into his cell. 'Go on, give her a ring.' He threw it on the bed. 'I told her you'd try and talk me out of it anyway.'

I left the cell where it landed. 'What if we can't get in tonight? There a Plan B?'

'Nope. Now or never. Go on, give her a call.'

He gave up his own attempts to drink the undrinkable. 'I'm staying, lad. I've got no choice. She thinks we're still in Turkey, by the way. Tell her you're bringing me back tomorrow.' The smile had gone. This was serious. 'Please.'

I picked it up and hit the call button. It took an age before the ring tone started, but it got lifted after just one ring.

'No,' I said. 'It's Nick.'

'When's your flight? Do you want us to meet you at the airport?'

'Tomorrow. He's seen sense at last.'

'Thank you so much, Nick.' I didn't think I'd ever heard anyone sound so relieved. 'Thank you, thank you. When are you getting in?'

'It's going to depend if there's direct flights out of Istanbul. It's a nightmare. Is Silky there?'

I heard Hazel's muffled reply, then Silky's voice. 'I'm missing you, Nick Stein. You're coming back tomorrow?'

'Um, listen, we're on a cell, it's costing a bomb. I'll call you when we get a flight, OK?'

'OK.'

'And Silky?'

'What?'

'I miss you too, box-head.'

I cut the phone and threw it back on the bed. 'Thank fuck this isn't a video phone.'

'You don't want her to see you looking miserable?'

'No, I don't want her to see this jumper.'

I picked up the map. 'Right,' I said. 'How the fuck are we going to crack this, then?'

7

The sky was heavy and grey and busy slicing off the tops of the hills. Cars splashed their way through puddles the size of tennis courts. The pavement glistened round the bus stop where I sat waiting for Whitewall to show up. It was going to be a horribly muggy day.

I was across the road from the hotel, keeping trigger on the entrance. The plan was that I'd give Charlie early warning of any 'possible' going in. The camcorder was rigged up in his room to record the handover of kit, and his replies to Charlie's questions. The tape would become a major part of our security blanket if the wheels did come off. We'd cache it – along with anything else we'd been able to get our hands on – and make sure that Crazy Dave knew we had a few shots in the locker to keep Whitewall or whoever from fucking us about.

I was right next to the front window of a gun shop. Punters waiting for their buses could check out an almost endless display of shotguns, rifles and chrome-plated pistols to meet their every need. I had already seen a couple of guys walk past with shoulder holsters over their sweatshirts, and they weren't using them to carry their deodorant. The sweatshirts were black, of course. In Georgia, black was the new black. The men mostly wore black leather over black. Every one of them over the age of thirty looked like he'd just spent the night standing outside Tbilisi's answer to Spearmint Rhino, fucking people off.

The streets leading uphill from the main drag all looked like they hadn't seen a lick of tarmac since the time of that bumper harvest. There were more potholes than there were Ladas to fall into them, and the pavements had crumbled so badly there was no longer any kerb.

Hordes of scabby-looking dogs were all set to spend the day chasing bits of swirling garbage in the wind. There was enough rubbish on the ground and enough fading plastic bags caught in the trees to form a fourth hill which would enclose the city completely.

Another ten minutes went by. Except for the gun shop and the odd mobile phone store and café, the main drag seemed to be lined with bookstores. As I watched the old, bunker-shaped Russian trucks jockeying for space along the boulevard with streams of brand new Volvos and Mercs, I realized there were no traffic lights. Come to think of it, we hadn't driven through a single one all the way from the airport. Either the drivers were very polite here, or no one would have taken a blind bit of notice.

Just before nine o'clock, a two-tone Mitsubishi Pajero 4x4, silver bottom, dark blue top, pulled up outside the hotel. It was three up. Even from this distance I could see that the passenger in the rear was the size of a small tank. He waddled out onto the pavement, opened the back door and took out a large, light-coloured bag, then disappeared through the glass doors. The driver kept the Pajero static. There had been quite a few limos and 4x4s picking people up and dropping them off, but this felt like Whitewall.

I hit my cell phone. The SOP for this job was to leave nothing but Charlie's number as the last call, and I was only doing that

123

in case I forgot it. 'Got a possible carrying two donkeys' worth.'

I decided to dice with death while I waited for the possible Whitewall to re-emerge, and crossed the road to get a better view of the two up front. They were side on and directly in front of me as I slalomed across the final stretch. The two boys were straight from Thick Bouncers central casting. Mid-thirties, lots of black leather. Both were clean-shaven and bald-headed, and the driver had perfectly manicured hands draped over the wheel and a pair of black-framed gigs.

The plate was pressed steel, white background, black letters before the numbers 960: a local registration, not military or diplomatic. The engine was still running, so the rear passenger obviously wasn't intending to be inside for long.

I felt the phone vibrate in my jeans pocket. I took the first option right to get me out of line of sight and hit the green.

'He's on his way down, lad. See you in ten.'

8

Charlie took the tape out of the camcorder. He was already gloved up.

The CTR kit was laid out on the bed, alongside a navy-blue canvas satchel the size of Imelda Marcos's shoe bag for us to carry it all in. He needn't have bothered improvising his own lever-lock wrenches; it looked like Whitewall had delivered one of every type ever manufactured.

'Whitewall had two local slapheads in tow. Mafia or oil? Makes you think, doesn't it?'

'Might do, if I did bother to think about it. But I'm not going to, lad. It gives me a headache.'

'Fair one.'

I took a pair of rubber gloves from the bed and started to put them on. If Whitewall or his slapheads had left DNA or prints on the kit, that was up to them, but I wanted it to remain sterile of Charlie and me.

'Come on then, old man. How did it go?'

'I told him I wouldn't do the job unless I knew what was happening. So he talked me through it while I gloved up and pulled out the bits of kit one by one in front of him.'

There was everything a budding burglar could wish for, from lock picks, rakes and tension wrenches to mini-Maglites, a keyring torch, and rubber door wedges, but one particular bit of kit was missing. 'Where's the weapon, mate? Every man and his dog here has got one.'

'Not needed. Like I said – in and out without leaving a fart print.'

He picked up the fibre-optic gear and worked the cable so that the end of it wriggled like a worm. 'Seems our man Baz has got his grubby little fingers in just about every pie within reach. He's in with the militants up north, and he's taking backhanders from the Russians. Both groups want to sabotage the pipeline, which not only fucks up the supply but also puts the lives of Yank and Brit construction workers at risk.

'Whitewall wants to knock all that firmly on the head, but first he needs to know what Baz has got tucked away in that safe of his – you know the sort of thing: who's on the take; who's got the Semtex hidden under their bed, and so on. Once he's got all that int in his hot little hand, he – and I guess that means the US government, meaning the oil companies, now you got me thinking – can go to the Georgians' top bollocks and bubble him. The appropriate authorities can swing into action and bingo, everyone can have a love fest.'

He turned and looked me in the eye. This time he wasn't smiling. 'Now, you happy with that? You can see the tape if you want.'

I shook my head. No need. 'Not if you believe him.'

'Makes sense to me. Not that it matters, either way. As I said, lad, I'm still going to do it. If those hairy-arsed militants start hitting the pipeline, people will get killed. The contractors know the risks; they're well paid for it. But the other poor bastards don't – the ones who'll be guarding the fucking thing . . .'

I remembered the fresh-faced kids from the recruiting commercial. And then I understood. 'I guess they'd be about Steven's age . . .'

126

'You're not wrong, mate. Good lads getting fucked over; it's the same in any language. Who knows? Maybe I can save some other parents from the nightmare Hazel and I have been through. It's not why I'm doing this, but it would be a fuck of a bonus.'

His face lost all expression as he thought for a moment about his boy, but he managed to cut away from the feeling almost as quickly as it had come. I knew that process all too well. I always hoped it would get better with practice.

The creases in his face returned. 'Actually, fuck the money, I should be getting a Georgian MBE for this! You want one?'

'Whatever's going,' I said. 'What's the plan?'

'Two options. Whitewall says Baz'll be out the house until Sunday morning. He's off to some national park to kiss babies, or whatever the fuck you do to win votes in this neck of the woods. So we have to go in as soon as we can tonight, and find and attack the safe. We lift whatever's inside, close up again behind us, and go and catch the morning flight.'

'What about the DLB? Where are we dropping the stuff?'

He'd forgotten about the DLB, I could see it. 'Didn't I tell you? A cemetery, about ten minutes from the house. Whatever we find goes into a plastic bag and inside a stone bench, next to someone called Tengiz. It's no problem, he's buried just past the main gate.' His look changed from silly grin to friendly smile. 'Lighten up! Just because I'm not frowning as hard as you are, doesn't mean I'm not working.'

He opened up the map.

'Anything else you might have forgotten to tell me, you silly old fucker? What about Plan B? You said you had two options.'

He looked slightly sheepish. 'Plan B doesn't exist, lad. I thought it'd sound better if we seemed to have a few options to play with.' He liked that one. His smile was as wide as the Mtkvari, but it was clear he was still trying to recover from his fuck-up.

'Tell you what, Charlie. Why don't I go and do my walk-past

now? You can spend some time sorting yourself out with this shit.' It was a gentle reminder that he needed to check everything on the bed was working before his walk-past. 'We'll RV in the cemetery and find this DLB. Then we'll split, and come back here for the brief.'

I nodded at the tape next to the TV. 'What's the plan with that? Tell you what –' I picked up the tape and shoved it inside my jacket – 'I'll take it. You've got enough shit to carry.'

I did up my jacket. 'You positive you want to go through with this?'

The smile vanished. He was going to give me a bollocking. I put my hands up. 'I know, I know. This will be the last time, promise. I just want to make sure your senile fucking brain has taken all the risks on board.'

He toyed with the pick set. 'It's got to be done.' He tried to extract one of the picks from its retainer but seemed to find it difficult. He dumped it quickly on the bed before he thought I'd had a chance to notice.

I turned to go, but got called back. 'Oi, shit for brains – let's see if anything's rubbed off during my years of painstaking tuition. One: Whitewall couldn't find out Baz's date of birth – can you? And two: we need five or six towels and a couple of extinguisher inners for tonight . . .'

I nodded and turned back towards the door.

'And make sure you nick them from the penthouse floor. If there's a fire, the posh fuckers can burn . . .'

PART FIVE

1

I came out of the hotel and turned right along the main drag, checking the town map I'd got from the front desk. Everyone else on the street was either a local draped in black or a Westerner in regulation Gore-Tex jacket, polo shirt and Rohan trousers. It had certainly been dress of the day in the Marriott. The reception was full of them emerging for breakfast; the café was a sea of Outward Bound.

I followed the main drag, paralleling the river somewhere to my right. It was 11.26 and a lot busier now as I passed the spruced-up opera house, theatres, museums and parliament. They were beautiful buildings, hailing from an era before Joe Stalin turned up with a few million truckloads of ready-mix. I couldn't understand it: from what I'd read there were still a few statues to him left standing, and plenty of old Soviets who rated him their greatest ever leader – pretty scary considering he'd massacred a million or so of his devoted comrades.

Above me, just before the cloud cut off the sky, was a telecoms mast the size of the Eiffel Tower, beaming out pictures of US flags and smiling Russian housewives 24/7.

There were quite a few locals out and about at this time of

the day, and I definitely wasn't the grey man. I didn't have the sort of skin that tanned in five seconds like theirs did, my hair wasn't black and my eyes were blue. I was blending in like Santa in the Congo. People were looking at me as if they all had come to the conclusion that I must be a spy, or there to do any number of bad things to them.

A police blue and white Passat cruised past. The two guys inside had AKs on the back seat. They both looked me up and down before the driver gobbed off to his mate about the weirdo. Fuck 'em, I'd be out of here soon enough. Besides, they were probably just jealous of my jumper.

All the same, I was beginning to feel more worried about this job – or, more truthfully, about Charlie. Which probably meant I was a little worried about me, for being stupid enough to go along with him. I couldn't quite work out how he could rattle off the kit list, yet forget about the DLB . . .

Then I thought, fuck it, so what? I'd see this through. Charlie needed me. He was all that mattered. He might have disco hands and have difficulty remembering what the fuck he was up to, but at least he was still here. Every other friend I'd ever had, whether we'd still been at the embryonic stage or reached the point where we were wearing each other's clothes, was dead.

I was doing this for Charlie; he was doing it for Hazel. I couldn't let him down. He was in the hotel at the moment, probably flapping a bit about whether or not I'd noticed that there were times when he couldn't even pick his own nose. Maybe he was flapping big time, not knowing if he was going to be able to keep his shit together long enough to see the job through. The thing he most needed right now was to know that he could depend on me, and that made me feel good.

Maybe I'd also be doing my bit to save a young squaddie or two on the pipeline. I'd seen what happened to a family when their much-loved son was zapped, and I realized I didn't like it one bit.

I had a shrewd suspicion that I was really trying to concentrate hard enough on Steven and Hazel to allow me to avoid thinking about Kelly and me, but I just didn't have the bollocks to admit it to myself. So I thought of Silky instead and that felt much better. I knew I'd rather be on a beach with her than fucking about in a Georgian politician's backyard.

I crossed the road and passed an English bookshop/café/internet joint. A high-pitched American female voice screeched through the open door: 'Oh-my-*God* . . . that-is-*sooo*-cool.' I made a note to give the place a miss.

I felt myself smiling. The fact was: I missed Silky. Months of sitting on a psychiatrist's couch hadn't cleared my head anywhere near as effectively as bumming around for a few months with a freewheeling, freethinking box-head.

Maybe I'd just get back to her and crisscross the continent in that van for years to come. Maybe this job would be my swansong as well.

I passed the city's newest landmark. No doubt about it, the new McDonald's was the glossiest, brightest building on the main drag. Its brown marble walls were extra shiny this morning after their coating of rain. New converts lined up with their kids for a Georgian McBrunch.

There weren't too many Ladas parked up outside. Being the new thing in town, it was the domain of dark-windowed Mercs, and even a Porsche 4x4. You didn't get cars like that by working for a living in this part of the world. Their drivers-cum-bodyguards were gathered under a nearby tree, dragging on Marlboros and pausing occasionally to flick ash off their obligatory black leather sleeves.

An old man in an even older black suit jacket pointed at parking spaces with a small wooden truncheon, as more shiny cars full of rich kids came to stuff their faces with American imperialistic calories. I was even thinking about getting super-sized myself.

It wouldn't be long now before I turned off the main; it was easy to tell because McD's was featured big-time on the map. Just as well, because I couldn't read the street names in Russian and Paperclip.

My plan was simple. If possible, I would do a full 360 of the target house, until I'd seen as much of it as I possibly could. My priorities were defences and escape routes. That was if I didn't get picked up by one of the VW blue-and-whites. They buzzed around the city like flies, or just sat there, lurking in lines of parked cars while their passengers watched and smoked.

I turned left on the second junction and walked uphill into a swathe of narrow roads and cramped houses that hadn't had their wash and brush-up. Suddenly I was in the real Tbilisi, the part that was poor and decaying, and I realized that I felt at home in it, away from the land of fresh paint and shiny new tarmac.

Small bakers sold bread and cakes from a hole in the wall. Cars swerved round potholes and pedestrians who'd stepped into the road to avoid craters in the pavement. Abandoned vehicles and bulging bin bags littered the kerbs. Maybe it was garbage day. Or maybe it was just a hangover from the communist era: the belief that anything inside your four walls was your responsibility while anything outside was the state's had come hand in hand with the hammer and sickle.

It was easy enough finding the house numbers; they were stuck to the wall on two-foot-square plastic panels that also carried the street name in Paperclip and Russian. It felt like another depressingly uniform throwback to the old days, but I guessed at least it meant the postman wasn't going to make a mistake with the Christmas cards – unless you lived in one of the fancier places. They seemed not to have to advertise themselves.

Electric cables ran in every conceivable direction above my head, emerging from what looked like homemade junction boxes stuck on trees. Maybe they were; when the electricity supply is as erratic as it was here, people will always come up with ways of making sure they get their share. Rainwater dripped from gutter pipes that disgorged their contents straight into the street. I was starting to get an uncomfortable film of sweat down my back as I climbed.

I carried on uphill, the sweat now flowing freely. After navigating three crossroad junctions I got to what I hoped was Barnov Street. The target house was along here, on the left somewhere.

Old, once-elegant buildings stood shoulder-to-shoulder with the odd modern lump of glass and steel. Without exception, they were protected by high walls, some plastered and painted, some just rough concrete blocks.

I passed the French and Chinese embassies. A small hut stood outside each of them, complete with bored-looking security guard reading the morning paper. Despite appearances, and the holes in the road, this was obviously the upscale end of town.

Ladas weren't the limo of choice up here, either. The only badges I'd seen blocking the narrow pavement in the last few minutes were VW and Mercedes. But strangely, not many of the drivers were wearing black. A lurid Hawaiian number went past in a Saab, smoking a cigar and shouting into his mobile, but still finding the time to check his slicked-back hair in the rear-view. He didn't look like he was en route to an ambassadorial reception.

This had to be mafia land. Good for them, but not good for Charlie and me. There was going to be an unhealthy amount of protection around this neighbourhood.

2

I didn't know its number, but I could tell I was at the target house from what I remembered of the bag-fit video footage.

The top of the ten-foot-high wall glistened with broken glass. Not a problem to climb over if we had to, just a little bit time-consuming. And I was right, no number boards for the posh houses up here.

I passed the rusty sheet-steel gates on my left. So far I hadn't seen any more on this recce than the film had shown me, except some fresh Paperclip and Russian graffiti had been daubed on the gates. The keyhole was a simple three-lever device that Charlie's bits and pieces would defeat in seconds.

I caught a glimpse of a blue vehicle in the gap between the gates. There were two inches of clearance at the bottom, and a bolt at the base of each was rammed into the ground on the inside. Unless there was another exit, chances were Baz was at home.

The high wall continued for about three or four metres before it turned left at the junction. I followed it, and immediately saw that I still wasn't going to learn any more about the target than I already knew.

On the other side of the road was a nightclub/restaurant/bar called the Primorski. The neon was dead, but pictures outside its big black doors showed dancing girls straight out of Las Vegas, feathers in their hair and hardly any other kit on.

The rendered wall gave way after a few metres to bare concrete blocks, before turning once more onto a new road. I didn't follow it left. A blue-and-white was parked up. I headed right instead, towards the cemetery. In any case, Charlie would be coming up that parallel road and would see exactly what I could from where I stood: that the crumbling buildings were crammed together so tightly, the target might as well be a terraced house with another row behind it.

If we fucked up and needed to do a runner, the easiest escape route was going to be up onto the high ground, towards the telecoms mast. There was no habitation up there. We might even be able to move along the higher ground under cover of darkness until we got level with the Marriott, and then down to get a taxi for the airport.

I now had to check the cemetery DLB, which was up on the higher ground ahead. We might even be able to see inside the target's yard from there. I walked past a parade of shops that seemed to sell nothing but shoes. I texted Charlie: *Bring binos.*

I got back an *OK*, deleted it, and headed up the road.

The very last shop sold food. I stopped and bought a bottle of water. It was the same stuff as they had in the Marriott minibar and on top of the TV, the pride of Georgia.

At least Charlie had remembered one thing correctly. The cemetery really was no more than ten minutes away, and it was simple to find. All I had to do was follow the old folks hobbling there on their sticks, against the flow of a funeral procession heading home.

Cars that looked more abandoned than parked filled a large open area of hard-packed mud on the opposite side of the road. Maybe they were waiting to fill up at the brand new, jazzily lit petrol station to the right, so freshly opened the concrete forecourt was still white. I entered the cemetery through a knackered iron gate attached to the remains of a broken-down wall and ran the gauntlet of the dozen old women selling flowers and long skinny candles.

The cemetery itself was as busy as a mall, and unlike anything I was used to in the West. Instead of neat lines of headstones, this place was a labyrinth of large family burial areas, each fenced off with wrought iron or low brick walls.

Men and women sat chatting away to each other, cradling flasks of tea or coffee, at tables fixed to the ground close by the graves. One old guy was drunk, even this early in the day, and ranted at one of the stones. I had the feeling he was getting his own back for a lifetime of nagging.

Water taps were sited every twenty metres or so along the central path, and people were either washing out their cups or refilling vases at most of them.

A woman sitting at a table full of candles tried to sell me a few when she saw me empty-handed, but I kept on walking, keeping to the central path. The most luxurious areas, I noticed, were immediately adjacent to the pathway. You obviously paid a premium in this country to keep your shoes clean. Off the pathway, people had to squeeze between other family plots to get to their own. One had a glass-covered oil painting of a dancing clown set into it. A fine, black granular substance was spread on the ground between the plots, and it obviously worked. There wasn't a weed in sight.

I tried to look like I was doing the same as everyone else, browsing at other people's tombstones as I made my way slowly to my family plot. I was looking for Tengiz's final resting place. All Charlie had been told was that it was along the main path. I had no idea if I was looking for a man or a woman, not that it was going to matter. We'd be fucked either way if the inscription was in Paperclip.

Our luck was holding. I came to a large black marble headstone in a square plot covered with white stone chippings, cordoned off by a newly painted white wrought-iron fence about two feet high. I saw now why Whitewall had chosen it. Engraved portraits of four defiant-looking men stared out at me, with the single English word Tengiz chiselled beneath a whole load of Russian and Paperclip.

There was a black marble two-seater bench with a solid-looking base, and a rusting, galvanized rubbish bin, full of dead flowers, set off the pathway to one side. If it was left there permanently, I'd use it as a marker.

A line of women were sitting by the next plot, knitting and chewing sunflower seeds. They were gobbing off at warp speed, and there was a fair amount of tutting and eyes raised to the clouds as I passed. I wondered if it had anything to do with the jumper.

I checked the rest of the main path just in case there were another five Tengiz plots to choose from, but there weren't. It was time to see if there was a vantage point up here from where I could look down into the target yard. If there wasn't, we'd be going in blind.

I spotted a place, right on the edge of the cemetery, where a lone wooden bench faced out over the ghetto. There was a sheer drop of about twenty feet down to the road below; the main gate would be along the road to the left somewhere. To get there, I had to pass rows and rows of quite recently installed headstones, each engraved with a picture of a young man or woman who seemed to have died in 1956. It looked as though, after the fall of communism, the bereaved had at last had a chance to commemorate some of Stalin's million or so victims.

I reached the bench and sat down. All I had to do now was try and work out which house belonged to Baz.

I called Charlie, who was still shopping for binoculars. 'I've found a possible on the path. We just need to check that the block supporting the slab isn't solid, otherwise I've got the wrong one. If you follow the perimeter left from the main, mate, I'm up on the high ground.'

3

Charlie joined me on the bench about twenty minutes later. By then, I had worked out where the target was, and could just about make out the blue vehicle in the yard and most of the front of the house that faced the yard, and us. There was a front door with a window each side and another two directly above them on the first floor. But from this distance, we'd need binos to see any detail.

He had a carrier bag in his hand. 'Fucking hell, I thought graveyards were supposed to be havens of tranquillity. It's like a fairground here.'

'What do you reckon on the DLB, old one?'

'The four guys eyeballing God by the flower bin? It's got to be the one. The bench support is a square of four sections. It's got to be hollow inside. Anyway, I'll find out tonight, won't I?'

'I picked up a comic for you at the hotel. Something to keep you occupied while I do all the work.' He fished a newspaper out of the bag, followed by a pair of green miniature binos, still in their packaging.

It was the *Georgian Times*, an English-language weekly that

141

came out on Mondays. I studied the front page as he unpeeled the binos.

George Bush was to visit Tbilisi on 10 May, on his way back from the VE Day celebrations in Moscow. *TBILISI IN ANTICIPATION OF GREAT VISIT*, yelled the headline. Then: *TBILISI LOOKS LIKE A PARROT*.

It seemed the locals were honking about the yellows and pinks being splashed all over buildings to cover the grime.

'It all makes sense now. Dubya on his way, new tarmac roads. I bet he's like the Queen, thinks the whole world smells of fresh paint and floor polish.'

Charlie snorted with laughter. 'Thought you'd like it. Maybe the rush on this job has something to do with his visit. You know, sort out any local difficulties before the main man shows up.' He shifted the binos up to his face and got busy focusing them.

I flicked through the rest of the paper. It didn't seem to go a bundle on world news. Most of the spreads were devoted to groups of smiling people shaking hands outside some local company's HQ, with a caption saying wonderful things about partnership in enterprise, and the importance of spreading the message of Georgian business worldwide. One small article announced that the government had demanded yet again that the Russians pull back their forces. But yet again the Russian answer was yeah, yeah, like we said, wait until 2008 – or words to that effect.

I scanned the rest of the page. 'Hot pipeline news,' I said. 'Says here it's coming in on time. It'll start pumping by the end of May.'

'Not my cup of tea, lad.' The binos were lined up on the target. 'I went straight to page three. Check it out – lovely pair of peaks.'

I turned back. 'Oh yeah, good one.' I was looking at a picture of the hills of Borjomi National Park. 'That's where the water comes from.' I read the piece more closely. 'Oh dear, seems somebody's fucked up. The pipeline goes straight through here, and a fuck sight too close to the natural springs. Georgia's biggest export will be history if there's a landslide and the pipeline fractures. There's shit on in the government. "Pressure groups demanding an enquiry," it says here. The World Wildlife Fund are leaping up and down. There's all sorts going on. Did you find the horoscopes?'

Charlie was still studying the target. 'Fuck, Nick.' The binoculars trembled in his hands. 'Looks like there's proximity lighting – and a couple of cameras covering the inside of the courtyard. Here, what do you think?'

I swapped him the paper for the binos. A group of old women passed behind us, each with a burning candle in one hand and a bunch of flowers in the other. They were all dressed in black and bundled up in headscarves.

I looked down at the house.

'That his Audi?'

'Yep, blue and in shit state. I even have the plate for later on. If he's on the take like Whitewall says, you'd think he could afford a decent motor.'

He was right about the lighting; the corner nearest us had CCTV and arc lights mounted on both front corners of the house. Under each arc light was a black plastic cylinder that we'd have to assume was a proximity detector. We hadn't seen any of it during the walk-pasts because they were at first-floor level, hidden by the wall.

One camera on the right-hand corner was angled in the direction of the gate and another covered the side of the house, aiming towards the rear, just like the camera on the left-hand corner. There'd be another one at the back, no doubt. I studied the gates.

'I still think the bolts are manual.' I lowered the binos. 'Did you see them on your walk past?'

'No. What do you reckon about the two outhouses?'

The binos went back up. The only windows that would get

143

any light into the ground floor would be the ones by the front door. There was a gap of no more than two metres between the wall and the house at the sides and rear. Maybe the building had originally had a fence and no neighbours.

Two small brick outbuildings faced the house, about ten metres across the cracked concrete courtyard. If we came in through the gate, they'd be down to our right, the Audi dead ahead and the front door to our left. 'Good place to hide while we sort our shit out? If he's in, at least we'd have somewhere to sit and think.'

The front of the house was flat. Three steps led up to a recessed porch. The door was solid natural-coloured wood, with two lever locks on the right, one a third of the way up, the second a third of the way down, and a handle in the middle. From this distance I couldn't tell if the handle also had a lock. The floor was lined with cracked, blood-red quarry tiles and a coir mat.

I felt a few specks of rain on my face. Mist was rolling in from the other side of the city. Three young guys walked past. They had their hoods up on their multicoloured nylon shell suits, and they were trying hard not to look furtive, but failing.

Charlie grinned. 'Looking for somewhere to try out a bit of home-grown poppy from the north, I fancy.' He wiped the moisture from his cheek. 'So the house – piece of piss, or what?'

'Don't know yet. I need to give it some thought once we get back to the hotel. You?'

'Easy. Chances are, any motion detectors down there are just for the lights, maybe they even kick off the CCTV as well. Why rig them up to the alarms? They'd go off every time a bat flew past. Poor Baz'd be up all night, wouldn't he?' He took the binos from me. 'Know what, lad? I think we should just go for it. Street lighting is shite. Through the gates, do the old anti-detector crawl, up to the main door. I'll get that open, do the business, and then we'll get our arses up here and DLB the lot. Then it's back to the hotel in time for breakfast. A nice early one, mind, because I've got a very important appointment with Air Georgia.' He brought down the binos and grinned at me. 'That sound like a plan?'

'Sounds like a fucking nightmare.'

He pulled open his jacket and shoved the binos inside. 'Give me a few. I can walk past that nightclub for any escape routes round the side.'

I picked up the paper again. 'OK, I'll follow in fifteen.'

Charlie stood up and rested his hand on my shoulder. 'Listen, lad, I want to say thank you . . .' He paused, and seemed to have difficulty swallowing. 'For a while there I thought you weren't coming. That worried me. I really do need your help, so thanks.'

I didn't know what to do. My head sort of froze. Fucking hell, what was he going to do next? Kiss me? 'I hope you remember the way back, you silly old fucker . . .'

Charlie smiled; he knew it was just a bit too much for me. Man to man, my comfort zone with emotions didn't extend much further than the message on his glass tankard.

'Maybe, maybe not. If I get lost, I'll ask a nice policeman. Fucking enough of them about, aren't there?'

He walked away and I instantly regretted not telling him how I felt. He was my friend, and of course I would never have left him. But that was another of my many problems. I only ever knew what to say after the event.

I looked at the paper for another ten minutes, my mind full of what-ifs. What if Baz was in the house? What if he met us as we were trying to go up the hallway? What if there wasn't even a safe?

To me, three hours of planning for three minutes' work was always time well spent. But maybe Charlie was right. What was I worried about? We would go through the plan, and all the what-ifs, at the hotel.

I found myself thinking of Silky again, and concentrated hard on all the positive stuff. It took about another five minutes to realize it wasn't working. Try as I might, I couldn't overcome my biggest concern: that Charlie might forget what the plan was once we were on target.

I got up from the bench and started walking down the slope, past row upon row of the young smiling faces of the 1956 dead. They all looked about the same age as Steven was, when he, too, became a good lad fucked over.

4

The rain had stopped, and there were even a few stars pushing their way through the breaks in the cloud.

I made my way past the opera house, taking the same route as earlier. It was my job to clear the area from the direction of the hotel; Charlie was doing the same from the other side of the Primorski.

The streets and pavements were still busy, even half an hour before midnight. Most of the shop lights were on, and McD's was heaving. I'd hoped Tbilisi wasn't a city for late-night people so our life would be easier, but no such luck.

I'd left the hotel at about 8.30, after asking the concierge for a couple of suggestions for places to eat. It sounded perfectly normal, as the hotel was jammed with the Gore-Tex version of the UN. The BP Georgia conference had ended and the restaurant and bar boasted even more European languages than polo shirts.

Not that I was in any position to take the piss. Charlie had been in charge of buying us both some oilman kit to change into for the flight. We'd be getting wet and shitty later on, trying to make entry, so would need to smarten up a bit before we

147

exited the country. I had a rather fetching blue sweatshirt with matching Rohan trousers and a slightly padded khaki jacket to come home to. With that on tomorrow, I should be close to invisible.

I had checked that the screechy American had left Prospero Books, the English bookshop, café and internet place, and went and logged on with a hot chocolate and sticky bun. It seemed to be a general meeting place for Brit and US expats working on the pipeline, and at their respective embassies. Or it might just have been the only joint around that had its own generator, so when the power failed they could stay online.

My first big question for Google was Baz's date of birth. With luck there'd be a list of Georgian politicians somewhere, with personal information; whatever, I'd just get in among the web and find it.

One approach to cracking the combination of a safe is to crack the psychology of the owner. Surprisingly often, combination locks are left on their factory settings – usually 100, 50, 100. I wasn't too up on eastern bloc defaults, but Charlie would be.

If you bin the default and choose a new combination, chances are you'll spend the whole time flapping in case you don't remember it; it's the same as it is with PIN numbers. So people tend to use numbers they know, like their birthday, car registration or phone. If they choose random numbers, they are almost certain to write them down somewhere. An address book is usually a good place to start looking.

It was easier than I could have hoped. The Georgian government had a website, and they published personal details. Baz was only forty-five; he was born on 22 October 1959. He must have had a hard life, though; his picture showed a balding man with a few wisps of grey hair, skinny as a rake. He could have done with a few of the sticky buns I was getting down my neck.

The small sign above every PC kindly reminded users that

148

they must not erase their history. Maybe the shop had to hand a printout to the police every twenty-four hours, or perhaps they checked it after every user. Trying to cover up my history as comprehensively as possible, I wiped it clean then had a quick look at today's helping of doom and gloom on CNN's website.

Two junctions past McD's, I took the left and headed uphill towards Barnov. The river was behind me, the big telecoms mast up to my half-left, its warning lights blinking red. The ambient glow from the main drag faded as I moved further into the residential area, and nothing much took its place apart from what spilled from behind curtains and the occasional car headlamp. Up here the street lighting wasn't just poor, as it was around the target; it was non-existent.

My cell vibrated in my jeans pocket as a blue-and-white cruised downhill. I pulled it out and hit green.

'All clear my side, and the obvious is pretty busy.' He had cleared the road that paralleled the target street, leading to the obvious, the Primorski club, checking there hadn't been a murder or anything that might persuade the blue-and-whites to pile in and block off the street. He'd said he wanted to be there fifteen minutes before me; team leader and all that. It wasn't my place to argue; he was the mechanic; I was the oily rag.

Charlie was carrying all the MOE kit in the satchel, over his shoulders. All he needed to complete the mature student look was a roll-up and a woolly hat. To help me blend in, I'd bought myself a black Tbilisi Dynamo basketball cap. It also covered the black ski mask that was folded on top of my head, just in case we fucked up and kicked off any of the CCTV cameras we could see, or any that we couldn't. So confident was he that I was going to stay, Charlie had bought it for me before I'd even got there.

I started to feel the trickle of sweat down my back once more as I made my final checks. I ran through my jeans pockets, just in case I'd inadvertently kept some loose change since leaving the bookshop, and made sure my clear rubber gloves were still there. It wasn't as if they were going to jump ship on their own, but it made me feel better to check again that they hadn't. Check and test, check and test; that was what this game was all about.

I had the gloves but no change; the charity box in the bookshop had done well out of my tradecraft skills. Everything else was in the room safe, and my entry card was shoved behind the toilet next to the hotel's restaurant. Going on a job sterile was something that always felt uncomfortable to me. Not having my passport meant not having a means of escape. But if we got caught, we lost our passports and they knew who we were. This way, if we got caught and escaped, we still had a chance of making it out of the country. I also had $400 dollars in cash rolled up in my jeans pocket. Not for any particular reason, it just made me feel a little better.

I made sure the mini-Maglite was in my bomber jacket's left pocket. If I tested it any more, I'd run the battery flat. The heavy steel CO_2 canister from one of the fire extinguishers was secure in my right. It was about nine inches long and as effective a truncheon as I could wish for.

Charlie had the other one I'd extracted from the pair of fire extinguishers I'd borrowed from the top floor of the Marriott. They were our make-like-burglars kit. If we did get compromised, the 'actions on' would be the same as we employed over the water: fight our way out and nick something, maybe even mug the person who compromised us.

I had a final look at my boot soles for stones, and after a quick jump up and down to check for noise and to make sure the canister wasn't going to fall out, I was ready. I just wanted to get this over and done with and start listening to flight attendants with Australian accents as soon as possible.

5

The French and Chinese embassies were lit up like Christmas trees, and their guard huts leaked wailing, almost Arabic music. The odd set of headlights cruised up or down the street, but Barnov was mostly shrouded in darkness.

The target house was coming up on my left. No lights from the top windows. No neighbour's windows lit that over-looked the gates or yard. So far so good.

I called Charlie. 'Clear.'

'Still clear this side. See you in two.'

The phone went dead and this time I'd memorized his number so I deleted it before powering down. Everything was now clear on the phone, not that it would mean much if we got lifted. They could still trace numbers in and out.

I watched the mature student coming downhill from the Primorski end. The street looked clear behind him. I had no idea what was going on behind me, but that didn't matter. If Charlie saw a problem, he would just carry on walking when he got to the gate. Same for me. We would then do a complete circuit and come back and try again.

He got to the gates before me, unshouldered the satchel and

placed it gently on the ground. A new layer of Paperclip graffiti had been sprayed on them since we'd been there earlier. At least it covered up the rust. He did one last check round, then dropped to his knees. I got my back against the left-hand gate and kept checking the area as I put on my rubber gloves.

Charlie was peering through the two-inch gap at the bottom. It must have been OK the other side. The Audi obviously wasn't there, because he pulled his homemade tension wrenches from the satchel and got to work on the lock. Maybe it made him feel better to use his own kit rather than the one-stop-shop option that Whitewall had delivered. Who cared, as long as he got us into the yard in quick time?

There was the faintest scraping of metal against metal as he began to attack the lock. It really did feel like old times. I even had a moment of déjà vu, back to a time when we were operating over the water, doing a CTR together on a house in the Shantello estate in Derry. We were looking for a PIRA timing device that they planned to add to four pounds of Semtex and plant in a community centre on the other side of the river. A team in the Bogside, a couple of miles down the road, were watching a player and his wife who were out on the piss. Before closing time, in an hour, we had to try and get into their house, find the device and make sure it would never finish its job.

We got in through a back window, and the first objective was to clear all the rooms to make sure they hadn't left kids asleep upstairs, or someone in the front room with headphones on listening to music.

We finally got to the attic landing. I climbed onto Charlie's shoulders, lifted the trapdoor, and heaved myself into the loft space. His job was to pass up a Maglite so I could have a good look around before I committed myself to the search.

I dangled my hand ready to receive, but nothing happened. I leaned down further, in case he couldn't reach, and then a little more, to the point where I was nearly falling out of the hatch. I looked down to see what the problem was, and realized he was moving the Maglite lower and lower, just for the hell of it.

Charlie had to block his mouth with both hands to stop himself snorting with laughter. At least he thought it was funny. In the end, like with most CTRs, we found fuck all. The pubs closed and we had ten minutes to get out and leave everything exactly as we'd found it.

Charlie was taking for ever. A lever lock is very basic; even with improvised gear, it should have taken no more than thirty seconds to open. I took my eyes off the road and gave him a gentle kick. 'For fuck's sake, get on with it, you senile fucker.'

His shoulders rocked with silent laughter just as headlights came downhill from our left. I broke away and started walking up the road towards the Primorski. I knew that Charlie would be getting to his feet and following suit, hands in his pockets, as I had, to hide the gloves. We'd both do a circuit.

The vehicle, a big Merc, hung a right, down towards the Primorski, just as I made the same turn. It pulled up at the kerb, and three girls in their early twenties got out, followed by a man of fifty something. The girls were dressed in spangly gear that sparkled and dazzled in the pink and blue neon. Maybe that was why Grandpa still had his sunglasses on. Wafts of high-octane perfume and cigar smoke filled the air as I walked past. The club's black doors were held open for them by security and I heard a low rumble of talk, music and laughter.

I turned left to carry on with the circuit. I was worried about Charlie. It had been taking him far too long to open the gate. I sparked up the phone. If he'd remembered, he would have done the same. 'Listen, are we going to get in there, or what? Get your finger out and get on with it.'

A car passed him as he replied, but I swore I heard him laugh. 'Let's give wisdom and experience one more go, then bull-headed youth can have its chance.'

The phone went dead but I kept it in my hand. A couple more cars bounced and splashed their way across the potholes. I eventually got back onto Barnov.

I called Charlie. 'That's me back on the main.'

He'd have been making his circuit on the other side of the street so we didn't pass each other too closely. Sure enough, I could soon see him in front of me, crossing the road so that he was on the target side. A Lada rumbled past from behind me, missing the club junction and heading uphill.

Charlie wasted no time as we reached the gate again. Down on his knees, he kept the satchel over his shoulder this time. I looked down and saw he was fighting two battles, one with the locks and the other with his hands. I gave him a nudge in the leg. 'For fuck's sake, get on stag. I'll have a go.'

He looked up and shrugged. We swapped places. 'Fucking hell,' I muttered as I got to work. 'This lock's nearly as old as you are.'

The tension wrench was still in place. I felt the pressure of the lever against it at the top of the lock before it turned, then the gate was open. I pulled out the pick and handed it to Charlie.

I slipped off my baseball cap, rolled the ski mask over my face and put the cap back on. Charlie did the same. I didn't worry about anything else; that was his job. If he saw anything untoward, he'd deal with it.

I pushed the left gate inwards very gently, just enough to squeeze myself through the gap. There was no telling how sensitively the motion detectors had been calibrated, or what their range was. I inched my way along the right-hand gate, heading for the wall. As long as you're far enough away from the sensor and against a solid background, nine out of ten times you can get away with it.

Once I hit the wall, I stayed flat and waited for Charlie. He moved his head and shoulders back against the gate and pushed it gently to, without locking or bolting it. This was our only known escape route, and we wanted to keep it that way.

A loud, male Paperclip monologue fired up close by in the street. I couldn't hear a reply; he was probably mad, drunk, or on the phone.

I looked to our right. We were about three or four metres from the outbuildings that were going to cover us while we tuned in to the target and carried out final checks before making entry.

Hugging the wall, I started moving. Slowly, really slowly.

The band in the Primorski struck up with Boney M's 'Brown Girl In The Ring'. The audience's polite applause was followed a few seconds later by a volley of raucous cheers. The Vegas girls must have made it onstage.

A minute or two later we were safely behind the out-buildings and Charlie's mouth was against my ear. 'I like this one. It's Hazel's and my song.' His shoulders did a little jig. 'Brings back a few memories.'

I stifled a laugh. 'I'm very happy for you both. But let's not have those hands of yours doing all the moves.'

He was probably grinning like an idiot under his ski mask, but I knew he must be as worried as I was about his condition.

He turned his head and spoke gently through the fabric. 'We'll give it just a bit longer, then go and have a decent look at that door lock, eh?' Charlie had always tried to make ops like this sound like nothing more than a bit of DIY, but he was overdoing the nonchalance now.

He retrieved the binos from the satchel and peered round the corner of the brick sheds. He passed them to me. They weren't NVGs [night-viewing goggles], but they certainly helped my night vision. I checked out the CCTV first, then the door. Nothing had changed.

The band segued from Boney M to Sinatra. A group of three or four highly excited male voices moved past the gates. Maybe they were looking forward to dislodging a feather or two, or maybe they just thought New York was their kind of town.

We checked yet again that our phones were off and nothing was going to fall out of the satchel, and Charlie put his mouth back up to my ear. "Eh oop, lad, we might as well get on with it, mightn't we?'

PART SIX

1

So far, we seemed to have been right about the light-and-camera motion detectors, if that was what they were; they covered the front of the house and the courtyard area between it and the gate. The two on each corner of the building swept the narrow alleyways between the house and the perimeter wall. We hoped we wouldn't need to check out the set-up at the rear.

Only one aspect of the security arrangements didn't make sense. The wall the far side of the courtyard, facing us as we came through the gate, didn't seem to be covered at all. It didn't take us long to decide it was our best route to the front door.

We edged along, Charlie ahead of me, our backs against the decaying brick wall. It was still very muggy, and the inside of my ski mask was soon clammy with sweat and condensed breath.

The only sounds up until now had come from the club and the occasional passing nutcase, but there was a sudden flurry of footsteps on the pavement by the front wall. There were at least two people out there; one of them was coughing and sniffing his way towards us.

He stopped just the other side of the gates for a good old spit; I could see the silhouette of his shoes at the centre of the two-inch gap beneath them. I hoped he didn't decide to pop inside for a piss. I edged further back into the shadows. There was a burst of raucous French mockery from his companion. I didn't speak much French, but enough to know that our throat-clearing friend had left a trail of snot down the front of his shirt.

They moved on, and so did we, working our way round to the corner of the house. The camera focused on the gate was mounted on the wall above us, with the motion detector immediately beneath it. We had to assume that it was angled towards the porch, so the light would go on when Baz went into or came out of the house. We'd have to make it think we were part of the floor this time, rather than the wall.

As we eased ourselves downwards, the Primorski band switched into Johnny Cash tribute mode, which must have put a big smile on the faces of the men in black. While they walked the line, we started to kitten-crawl the last four or five metres. Hugging the ground, we pushed ourselves up, as slowly as possible, on our elbows and toes, just enough to move forward, an inch or two at a time, along the cracked wet concrete path. We moved our eyes, not our heads, to see what lay in front of us; mine were already aching from the strain of keeping them right at the top of their sockets.

Charlie had to nudge the satchel ahead of him before he got to move himself. He finally got his head level with the three tiled steps leading up to the front door, and stopped dead, checking for any sign of a motion detector inside the porch. We hadn't seen one through the binos, but we'd had to plan on the assumption that there was one.

He lay there for another fifteen seconds or so, then started to slide the bag forwards again. Slowly, and with infinite care, he and the satchel moved up the steps and out of my line of sight. All I could hear was his laboured breathing, punctuated from time to time by the click of high heels and the occasional peal of laughter heading in the direction of the club. Didn't anyone sleep in this place?

I sucked in a lungful of air, lifted myself on my toes and elbows, and moved forward another four inches. I breathed out as my wet jeans and thighs made contact with the concrete once more.

There was a burst of applause at the Primorski as the band performed the closing bars of the Georgian version of 'Jumping Jack Flash', and in the momentary silence that followed I sensed rather than heard another sound, like something being dragged, from much closer by.

It felt as if it had come from the window above me, but I didn't dare move my head to check. I held my breath, mouth open to cut down any internal body noise, and listened.

I raised my eyes as far as I could towards the porch. There was no sign of Charlie. He would have been doing the same: stopping, listening, tuning in.

Whatever it had been, it didn't happen again. The only sounds now were distant laughter and the music of the night.

I breathed out, breathed in, kept my mouth open, and strained to pick up even the slightest vibration. Still nothing. Had it come from the window? Impossible to tell.

I waited another thirty seconds or so. If someone upstairs had spotted us, surely they would have done something by now.

I started to edge forward. We had no option but to treat this like an advance to contact. If you stopped every time you heard a gunshot, you'd never close in on the enemy. If there was someone in the house, or we'd been seen, we'd know about it soon enough.

161

2

My head eventually drew level with the bottom step. I resisted the temptation to take a shortcut and rush the last few feet. That's always the time you get caught.

Charlie was on my right, the side the door opened. He'd pulled up enough of his mask to be able to press his ear against the wood.

I finally made it inside the porch, and sat against the rotting brickwork. I didn't know which felt worse: the sweat on my back or the residue of rain-soaked concrete on my front. Charlie's left knee was on the doormat. He would have checked underneath it for a key – well, you never knew your luck – and that it didn't conceal a pressure pad. He moved his knee off the mat, pointed down at it as he kept listening.

I pulled the rubber up and saw that one of the four-inch-square tiles had no cement around it. I lifted it, and it appeared Baz had scraped out enough concrete to hide a set of keys very nicely. But of course they weren't there. Maybe Baz had switched on a bit since coming up with that one. Why do people think no one else would ever think of looking just by the door?

I slid the CO_2 canister from my bomber-jacket pocket and slipped it up my left sleeve. The elastic cuff would hold it in place. Having it up the right sleeve, ready to drop into your hand when required, was just film stuff. You rarely got a good grip on the thing, even if it did fall conveniently through your fingers.

The two keyholes were a third of the way down the door, and a third of the way up it. The handle in the middle wasn't attached to either of them.

There was no need for any discussion about what came next; we'd both done this enough times, from Northern Ireland to Waco. Charlie shone his key-ring torch inside the lower of the two locks and had a good look at what he was up against. I hoped his hands had calmed down. I didn't want to have to take over again.

I pulled his mask back down over his ear, then leaned over above him and pushed slowly but firmly against the top of the door to test for give. If it didn't budge, chances were it was bolted, and that would be a nightmare because we wouldn't be able to make entry covertly. Worse still, it would mean that Baz was inside, or that he'd left by another exit, and we would have to run the gauntlet of the motion detectors to find it.

It gave. No problem.

Charlie turned his attention to the top lock, and I gave the bottom of the door the same treatment. It, too, yielded. That wasn't to say there wasn't a bolt midway, but we'd find out soon enough.

A helicopter rattled across the sky on the far side of the river and the band sparked up with a jazz number to send it happily on its way. Charlie pointed to the top lock and gave me the non disco-dancing version of the thumbs-up. That was a bonus. Then he pointed at the lower one and did the thumbs-down, and got busy with the wrench.

I left him to it and sat back, knees against my chest, wet denim stinging my thighs and sweat going cold on my back. It

163

was always better for the one working on a lock to do everything himself. If I held the torch, I'd be throwing shadows in all the wrong places, and we'd just get in each other's way.

The only problem was, it gave me a little bit too much time to think. Why did Baz use just one of the locks? Had he decided to have a quiet night in? Had he just nipped out for a swift half at the Primorski? Or was he just a lazy fucker, and in a rush? It wouldn't be the first time. I'd carried out CTRs on houses and factories protected by some of the most sophisticated alarm systems in existence – or they would have been if anyone had bothered to switch them on. Whatever, the quarry tiles were starting to numb my arse. Charlie was taking far too long.

I leaned forward. Even in the gloom, I could see his fingers were going nineteen to the dozen. Fuck that. I slipped across and put my hands over his, to stop him going any further.

Charlie held the tools out like chopsticks to try and convince me everything was fine. I took the torch and shone it on his right hand. It was trembling like an alcoholic with the DTs.

He sat wearily back against the wall and put five fingers in the torch beam, opening and closing them twice.

I nodded. I'd give him ten minutes, maybe fifteen. He wanted to do this, he had to; not just because it was what he was being paid to do, but because we both knew it was his very last time out of the paddock.

I understood that, but we didn't have that much time to fuck about. It would be first light just after 6.30, and we needed to have filled the DLB by then.

I decided to make the most of it. At least it gave us a chance to listen out for anything that might be happening the other side of the door.

Time well spent tuning in, I kept telling myself. It didn't sound any more convincing this time than it had the first.

3

I waited for the full fifteen, but by the end of it Charlie had defeated the bottom lock. Still on all fours, he packed the picks and wrenches away before easing the door open a few inches, so it didn't creak or bang tight against a security chain. He waited a moment to see if any alarms kicked off, then poked his head through the gap to have a quick look and a listen.

It was time for me to get my boots off, ready to do my bit. The ski mask was clammy round my mouth, the back of my neck was soaked with sweat, and the rest of me didn't feel much tastier, but fuck it, we'd be done with this by first light, and knocking back a couple of beers on the plane by midday.

I shoved my boots down the front of my bomber jacket and zipped them in, then liberated my Maglite and the CO_2 canister.

Charlie crawled back to where I'd been sitting. He'd get his own boots off, prepare the camcorder and wipe the porch dry with one of the towels I'd nicked from the hotel. When Baz got home, there mustn't be the slightest trace of our visit. The subconscious takes in everything; when the mat isn't at exactly the same angle, when the dust on the table has been inexplicably disturbed, little alarm bells start to ring. Most of us don't hear them because we're not smart enough to listen to all the things our brains are trying to tell us. But some people do, and Baz might just be one of them.

I peered round the door. The place reeked like every auntie's house I'd ever gone into as a kid, of over-stewed tea, old newspapers and stale margarine.

I held my breath, opened my mouth, and cocked my ear. The only sound was the gentle ticking of a clock, off to my right. The opening of a door at night changes the atmospheric pressure in a house ever so slightly, but sometimes just enough for even a sleeping person's senses to pick up.

I let go of the door and, keeping control of it with my left shoulder, stepped inside. I hooded the lens of the Maglite with my fingers, leaving just enough light to see there was a staircase rising steeply along the external wall to my left and a longish hallway dead ahead with two doors on either side of it.

A strip of flowery carpet ran down the centre of what looked like a parquet floor. The parquet was the first piece of good news I'd had since we made it through the front gate; it wouldn't creak. The walls were bare, apart from a couple of framed pictures above a wooden chair with some coats thrown over it.

Baz didn't seem like much of a homemaker, at first glance, but he was certainly keen on security. As I flicked the Maglite to my right, a floor-to-ceiling, steel-barred gate glinted in the beam, hinged to swing across the main entrance but opened flush against the wall. There were two receptors each side of the door and flat bars lying on the floor with a pair of padlocks.

I checked Baby-G. It was 2.28. We still had to find the safe, let alone defeat it. At this rate, we might be here for hours – and we only had about four and a bit left until first light.

Charlie made only the faintest of sounds as he shouldered the satchel and came in behind me. I was going to be in charge of the next phase, the room clearing; he would keep control of the noisemaker, the bag.

166

I covered the torch lens with a finger so that just enough light came out for us to move, leaned back and spoke softly into his ear. 'Let's just check for another exit. We need to concentrate on finding the safe.'

Charlie thought for a second, glanced at his watch, then nodded. I moved off, keeping to the nine-inch-wide strip of parquet at the right-hand edge of the carpet, so as not to disturb the pile, and trying to avoid rubbing against the walls.

I took two paces and stopped to give Charlie room to come in. He was already taking IR film with the camcorder, but handed me two rubber doorstops as he went past. Thank fuck his brain hadn't been in 'Oh I forgot' mode when he wrote down his kit list.

I closed the door softly behind me, and shoved one immediately below each of the two lever locks. If Baz came back unexpectedly, they would buy us a bit of time to play burglar. If he was already upstairs asleep and tried to do a runner, they would help make sure he didn't get outside in a hurry, and start shouting for help.

Charlie switched the camcorder to standby. The plan was to record the layout of the place wherever we went, then check it on the way out to make sure we'd left everything exactly as we'd found it.

The doors off the corridor were all open, and I headed for the first one on my right. It was a living room, and by the look of it, Baz's answer to Mrs Mop hadn't been too energetic with her feather duster recently, though she had remembered to wind the grandfather clock. The dark wooden furniture and faded wallpaper somehow matched the smell.

Black-and-white pictures of a couple on the mantelpiece. His parents, maybe. Pictures of him as a little lad. Magazines littered across the floor, some quite recent ones in Russian, some in Paperclip.

The first phase of a house search is always a quick once-over. It would be pointless doing a detailed inspection of every room in sequence, only to find what you're looking for smack in the middle of the very last room, three hours later. It's on phase two that you start moving sofas, lifting carpets, looking up the chimney.

The two picture frames in the hallway held large, sepia photographs of the house during happier times. There were no bars on the windows, no other buildings in sight, and no wall, just a three-foot-high fence to keep the horses from munching the grass that had pre-dated the courtyard.

We reached the door at the far end. It was hinged inwards on the left and open about an inch. I shone the torch round the frame to check for telltales. I couldn't see anything. I signalled to Charlie and he filmed the gap.

I nudged it open with the end of the canister. It didn't take long to realize this was the kitchen. The smell of margarine and old papers was so strong here it nearly made me gag, even through the ski mask. More old furniture; a wooden table and a couple of chairs. The cooker looked like Stalin might have done his baked beans on it. Had Whitewall pointed us at the wrong place?

I opened the door fully and found myself facing the external wall. Set into it, directly ahead of me, was what would have been the back door – if it hadn't been covered completely by a large steel plate, bolted firmly into place.

I turned to Charlie and nodded. We were in the right house.

4

I shone the torch around the kitchen from the doorway, picking out dented old aluminium pots and pans hanging from hooks over the cooker, and a half-drunk bottle of red wine on the table next to an open newspaper. A fly-screen in the corner seemed to lead to some kind of larder. Jars and cans glinted behind the mesh.

I stood and listened for another three or four seconds, but the only noise was the ponderous ticking of the clock. I turned back up the hallway, tapped Charlie on the shoulder, and aimed the torch at the door to our right, about three paces ahead. The small red LED on the camcorder began blinking again.

It was only just ajar. I checked for telltales round the frame, then gave it a gentle push. There was a window opposite, protected by an external grille, but completely filled by the perimeter wall.

It looked like I was in somebody's sewing room. A Singer treadle sat in the far corner, next to a wooden bench top, but there were no half-made clothes or swatches of material. There were no cupboards. Swirly carpet covered most of the wooden floor, apart from a couple of feet around the edges. The fireplace looked like it hadn't been used for years, not since the last time the pictures hanging either side of it had got within reach of a duster.

I walked round the edge of the carpet and checked the pictures for telltales, intentional or otherwise. The one on the left was of a bunch of flowers in a vase. There was nothing behind it except a paler square of wallpaper. There was no safe under the one of a mountain, either.

I made my way back into the hallway and signalled to the door opposite; Charlie was right behind me, recording.

This was much more promising. It was obviously Baz's office; what looked like Bill Gates's very first prototype was sitting on a desk in front of the window. Files and newspaper cuttings were strewn all round it, and on the floor as well. The shelf along the wall to my right had bowed under the weight of too many books. There was a cupboard in the far corner – a light oak veneer, flat-pack job, rather than somewhere Uncle Joe might have hung his uniforms.

I moved out of the way to let Charlie past. He panned the camera left to right before we started moving stuff around. Using the torch to make sure I didn't step on any of the paper on the floor, I headed first for the desk, in case there was a number on the phone. There wasn't.

We had better luck with the cupboard.

Having checked for telltales, I pulled open the door and bingo, we'd found what we'd come for.

I stepped back to let Charlie see the prize. He filmed the whole thing inch by inch, every bit of chipped grey paint, every word of Russian Cyrillic, no doubt proudly announcing its manufacture by royal appointment to the Tsar. It was about two foot square, and solid. The door was hinged on the right, with a well-worn chrome handle on the left, then a large keyway, and a combination cylinder dead centre. Once Charlie had the position of each on film, he handed me the camcorder, tested the handle, shrugged, and fished inside his bag.

I shoved the canister back up my sleeve and let him get on with it.

He brought out a towel and laid it in front of the safe. The bag was wet and he didn't want to leave sign.

5

Charlie knelt on the towel in front of the safe, the bag to his right, and carefully unrolled the fibre-optic viewing device from a strip of hotel towel. Every item in the bag had been wrapped to prevent noise or damage.

I fired up the camcorder and went over to Baz's desk, filming everything on the top first, then the positions of individual drawers. There were about ten of them each side, designed to hold a thin file or a selection of pens. Some were slightly open, some closed; some pushed further in than they should have been.

I lifted the telephone, but there was nothing taped underneath. There was a small wooden box beside it, loaded with pens, pencils, elastic bands and paper clips. No joy there, either.

I checked for telltales on each drawer, and went through them one by one. I found sheet after sheet of paper in Paperclip and Russian, but no key to the safe, or anything scribbled down that resembled a combination.

I looked over at Charlie. Torch clenched between his ski-mask-clad teeth, fibre optic inside the keyway, he was manipulating the controls like a surgeon performing arthroscopy – except that he was doing it on his hands and knees, with his arse in the air. He was attacking the day lock first, in case it was the only one being used.

It was decision time. Nothing had turned up on this sweep, and I could spend all night searching this place for the key or any hint of a combination, and the more I looked, the more I would disrupt the area. I called it a day and went and knelt down on the towel, waiting until Charlie was ready to speak to me.

It was as quiet as Tengiz's grave now – quieter, probably, if the knitting circle were still gobbing off right next door to it. The only sounds were the old disco-dancer's manic breathing and the distant ticking of the clock, and once or twice a vehicle in the distance.

He finally removed the fibre optic and leaned towards me. I got my mouth into his ear. 'How long do you reckon?'

He rolled the fibre optic into its piece of towel, and replaced it in the satchel.

That was a good sign; you never leave anything out that you're not using; it gets packed up straight away in case you have to do a runner.

'Piece of piss, lad. The day lock is warded, and the combination, well, it's a combination. Anything up to four hours. Don't worry, there were loads like this in Bosnia.' He paused and I knew there was a funny coming. 'Any longer than that and I'll let you blow it.' This time I could see the grin, even behind the nylon. He shoved the key-ring torch back in his mouth, taking the mask with it.

He was right; the ward lock, at least, was going to be easy. It was basically a spring-loaded bolt into which a notch had been cut. These things had been around since Ancient Roman times. The key fitted into the notch and slid the bolt backwards and forwards. It takes its name from the fixed projections, or wards, inside the mechanism and around the keyhole, which prevent the wrong key from doing the business.

Charlie tucked the fibre optic away and unwrapped a set of what looked like buttonhooks, fashioned from strong, thin steel. All being well, one of them would bypass the wards and shift the bolt into the unlock position.

In next to no time I heard the deadlock clunk open, and Charlie's head swayed from side to side in triumph as he packed the hooks away.

The combination cylinder was next. This time, the lock would be released once an arrow on the left-hand side of the dial had triggered the correct sequence of numbers. Our problem was that there was no way of telling when the tumblers had reached their correct position; the only noise we'd hear was when the lever finally descended into the slot, once the right combination had been dialled.

Charlie started rotating the cylinder left and right. He may have been trying Baz's number plate first, or running through the Russian factory default settings.

Once he'd exhausted the obvious ones, he would have to go through every possible permutation. In theory there'd be about a million of the little bastards, but the good thing about old and low-quality cylinders like this one was that the numbers didn't have to be located precisely; up to two digits either side of true and the lock would still open, which cut the possible combinations down to a mere 8,000 or so. It wasn't what Charlie might call a piece of piss, but even with his hands wasting away he should be able to rattle through them in a few hours. He told me once that he really never thought about what he was doing; he just switched onto autopilot.

He leaned over to me. 'DOB?'

He hadn't asked me for it since my trip to the bookshop because there was no need. If I hadn't found Baz's date of birth, I'd have told him.

'Twenty-two ten fifty-nine.'

His hands started to turn the cylinder: 22 anti-clockwise . . . 10 clockwise . . . 59 anticlockwise . . .

For some reason, that was the most commonly used sequence of movements.

I realized I was holding my breath.

Nothing. No sound. No falling lever; no question of simply turning the handle and hearing the bolts slide back into the door.

Charlie played with the three number sets in sequence, but varying the direction of rotation.

After a dozen or so other attempts, he tried 22 anti-clockwise, 59 clockwise, 22 anti-clockwise.

There was a gentle clunk from inside the door.

Charlie picked up his torch and shone it round the floor to make triply sure that he'd left nothing lying around.

I could have opened the safe while he did so, but there was a protocol to be observed at times like this. That honour belonged to Charlie.

He turned back when he was satisfied everything had been packed away. He pulled down the handle. The bolts retracted from both the hinged and the opening side, and it swung open with a small metallic creak.

Charlie still had the key-ring torch in his mouth, and his head was inside the safe. I leaned over him. There was a shelf in the middle, and it held just two items: an open box of antique jewellery, maybe his mother's, and a blue plastic folder.

Charlie didn't need the camcorder to remind him how the folder lay; he lifted it straight out and handed it over. A quick sweep of the Maglite revealed about twenty pages of hand-written Paperclip.

It didn't look much, but it was obviously worth two hundred thousand US to someone.

He hardly had time to shrug before the door burst open and the lights came on.

6

There were two of them, hollering at us in Russian or Paperclip. They were both carrying suppressed pistols with big, bulky barrels; we raised our hands very slowly, so they couldn't fail to notice that, unfortunately, we weren't. I kept my left elbow slightly bent, to try and hold the CO_2 canister in place.

They were in their early thirties; short black hair, jeans and leather jackets, lots of gold rings and bracelets, and both looking confused about the situation.

Their faces weren't masked, and that was bad news. They didn't care about being identified. One was dark with stubble; the other had bloodshot eyes. I wondered if he'd stopped by the Primorski on the way over.

Their yells increased in volume, and reverberated around the room. Just having our hands up obviously wasn't enough.

It looked like the one with the bloodshot eyes was in charge. He glared at me and opened his leather jacket repeatedly with his spare hand. I got the message. Keeping my right hand up, I unzipped my bomber very slowly with my left. My boots dropped onto the carpet. Charlie followed suit.

They now knew that neither of us was carrying, but that didn't stop the shouting. I didn't know what else they wanted, and I wasn't going to ask. I didn't want them to know we were Brits. I shrugged my shoulders and twisted my hands.

They gobbed off at each other, very quickly and aggressively, then Red Eyes moved towards Charlie, pistol steady, while Stubbly covered him. He waved his free hand again, shouted, gesticulated at the floor.

Charlie got it: the boy was after the folder.

He reached down and picked it up with his left hand, keeping his right in the air. Red Eyes took a step forward, grabbed it, and jammed his weapon into Charlie's neck. I could see Chinese characters engraved along the barrel. It was old and really well worn, but that didn't matter. It would still fuck Charlie up if he pulled that trigger.

Keeping the muzzle right where it was, Red Eyes bent down and reached into the safe. The jewellery found its way into his jacket pocket with the speed and precision of a conjuring trick. For a finale, he yanked off Charlie's mask, then gave me the same treatment.

He took a couple of steps back to survey his handiwork. They both stood there for several seconds, one each side of the doorway. Red Eyes muttered something to his unshaven friend, placed the folder on the desk and started to flick through its contents. Stubbly kept moving the muzzle of his weapon from my head to Charlie's and back, just in case we hadn't got the message.

They barked stuff at each other as Red Eyes turned the pages. I didn't know what to do next. I had been in the situation enough times myself to recognize the look and sound of uncertainty. Finally he looked up, glowered at the two of us, and pulled out a cell phone.

I glanced over at Charlie, who was studying the floor so closely he appeared to be trying to memorize every fibre of the carpet. I knew that look. He was wondering how the fuck to get us out of here. I hoped the silly old fucker would come up with something before these boys got permission to top us.

There was a series of rapid beeps as Red Eyes punched in the number. Whoever was at the other end answered immediately. Red Eyes studied each of us in turn, giving what sounded like a description, then picked up the document and quoted a couple of chunks from it. Then he looked at us again. I didn't understand what he was saying, but I got the drift. Whatever problems they'd expected to have to deal with in the house, they now had two extra ones, and they were less than happy workers. As if I was.

There was nothing we could do to help ourselves immediately, so I studied Stubbly's weapon instead so I'd know what to do with it when I got my hands around the pistol grip. The power of positive thinking.

His finger was on the trigger and the safety was off; the lever on the left-hand side of the grip was down. These kinds of suppressed weapons normally had both a single-shot and semi-automatic capability. With the one, you loaded manually, pulling back the top slide and letting it go forward to pick up a new round from the magazine each time you fired. With the other, the top slide wasn't locked in position, so you just kept firing until the magazine was empty.

I didn't know what setting Stubbly had gone for, but something told me it wasn't single shot.

Red Eyes was still waffling into the phone and riffling through the papers when we heard a metallic rattle from the direction of the street. He stopped in mid-sentence. There was a loud creak as the front gates swung open.

Red Eyes closed down the conversation by running out into the hall.

He was back in less than ten seconds, and not at all happy. He rolled up the folder, thrust it into his jacket, yelled a couple of instructions at Stubbly and disappeared again.

Stubbly stood his ground and raised his weapon a few inches.

There was no time to think.

I lunged at him, aiming my shoulder at his gut. He tottered backwards under the impact, hit the wall, and before he could recover I dragged him down with me, my hands flailing. I didn't really care if they made contact, as long as they got in the way of him controlling the weapon. With any luck I'd bang against it myself.

I felt Charlie's legs pushing against me, then heard a sound like a watermelon hitting a pavement. He'd given Stubbly's skull the good news with his CO_2 cosh.

I let go and kicked myself away. It was Charlie's call; he could climb aboard him if he needed to.

I scanned the floor for the weapon, but couldn't see it immediately, and didn't have time to search.

I ran out of the room, shoving my right hand into the left sleeve of my bomber jacket as I went. Red Eyes was ahead of me, throwing out the stops. The door swung back and the hall was flooded with light.

The gates into the street were open.

Baz's Audi swept into the courtyard.

I sprinted along the carpet as Red Eyes half ran, half tumbled down the porch steps.

There was a shower of glass as he emptied his magazine into the driver's window and he pirouetted like a matador as the vehicle coasted past him, into the wall.

I took the steps in one, canister in hand. Leaping up before he had a chance to collect himself, I swung the heavy metal tube down onto the top of his head. The weight of my body coming back down to the ground gave the hit enough force for me to hear his skull crunch.

He dropped like a cow under a stun gun and I followed suit, brought down by my own momentum. His weapon skidded across the wet concrete. I grabbed it, turned and fired into his skull. The third time I squeezed the trigger, nothing happened. The top slide stayed back, waiting for a fresh mag to reload.

Fuck closing the gate. I dropped the empty weapon and ran back into the house in case my disco-dancing mate needed a hand.

There were gunshot wounds in Stubbly's chest and just below his right cheekbone, and a pool of dark, deoxygenated blood spreading across the carpet. Charlie was as cool as a cucumber. He'd slipped his mask back on, and was hoisting the satchel over his shoulder. 'Give me five,' he said. 'I'll try and find the CCTV monitors. There might be tapes.'

I grabbed my own mask off the floor and pulled it over my head as I legged it back to the front door.

7

I went straight to the gates. Fuck checking outside, I just slammed them shut and got the bolts down, then carried on struggling to put on the mask. I only had one eye uncovered. I must have looked like the phantom of the fucking opera.

There was a big drum roll and a clash of cymbals from the Primorski, followed by a round of applause. If I hadn't been so knackered, I'd have taken a bow.

Broken glass, spent brass cases, wet concrete and two pools of blood glinted in the courtyard lights. Fighting to get my breath back, I ran over to the car.

It looked like someone had thrown a bucket of red paint across the car's interior. The driver's body was slumped, face sideways, over the central console. It was Baz all right, and he didn't look good. He'd taken rounds in the head, neck and shoulder, and his once-grey hair was crimson.

I checked the front end. The bumper had absorbed most of the punishment, and one of the headlamps was cracked, but I reckoned the Technik was still Vorsprung. I pulled the door open, grabbed hold of Baz's arm and dragged him clear.

By the time I returned to the house, my throat was as dry as sandpaper.

'Charlie!'

'Up here.' His voice came from the landing.

'Dead body. Bring some bedcovers down, anything. Got to cover the car seats.'

I ran into the office and grabbed my boots. No time to do them up properly; I shoved the laces under the tongue so I didn't trip up. Speed was everything; we had to get out of here.

Back in the yard, I rolled Red Eyes over and pulled the folder from his jacket. Charlie jumped down the steps with two multicoloured bedspreads dragging behind him.

'Any luck with the CCTV?'

He shook his head. 'Could be anywhere – on that PC, for all we know. Let's just fuck off and get on the flight. You OK with that? Or stay and look some more? I'm up for it if you are.'

I stood by the car. He was right. Why waste time on a blood-filled target, with three dead bodies for company? 'Let's go.'

We threw the bedspreads over the front seats.

Charlie dumped the satchel in the back and I jumped into the driver's side. I knocked the remaining shards of glass out of the window frame while Charlie checked the road.

The moment the gates were open, I hit reverse. Charlie secured the gates as well as he could, and jumped in beside me, lodging his pistol under his thigh. We started uphill, towards the blinking red lights of the telecoms mast.

As we passed the left to the Primorski, two stretch Mercs were picking up a crowd of very young women and very old men.

At last we were able to pull off our masks, and Charlie started to giggle. 'Well, you fucked up there, didn't you, lad?'

'Heads up, we got police.'

A blue-and-white had turned into our road, heading down-hill towards us. It was slow, taking its time. I checked Charlie – did he have blood on his face? He checked me – if I had, it was too late. We passed them; they looked over and two red spots of heat between their lips got brighter as they sucked.

Charlie nodded at them. 'Evening.'

They passed Baz's house without stopping.

'Evening? If they'd heard you they'd've stopped us just to investigate that accent.' I couldn't stop myself from laughing. It wasn't the joke, it was pure relief.

Wind gusted through the driver's window. I took a hand off the wheel and slid the folder out of my jacket. It was looking a bit the worse for wear but at least there were no bullet holes in it.

Charlie scanned the streets for blue-and-whites. 'They must already have been in the house, waiting for Baz to come home, make him open the safe, get whatever it was we've got here, then drop him.'

'I thought Whitewall said he was away at some national park or something, till the morning? And since that was bollocks, where does it leave us with everything else?'

I swung the wheel right and left, weaving between the potholes. 'Maybe they were waiting for him to turn up in the morning. They'd have seen us coming into the yard. That must have been what we heard – those fuckers in the front room. When we opened the safe for them, they must have thought it was Christmas.'

I took a left, up towards the cemetery. 'I knew I should have looked in the larder . . .'

'If you had, they might have just dropped us.' He started to laugh again. 'But hey, we're still here, aren't we? A quick trip to the DLB and then it's bye-bye Georgia.'

We bounced over the open ground opposite the cemetery. There were still quite a few cars parked around the place, and Charlie pointed under a tree, where the ambient light from the petrol station finally gave up trying to penetrate the darkness.

I switched the engine off and killed the lights. I sat there, just looking and listening. 'You OK?'

'I'm fine. But the old hands are wobbling a bit. Maybe you should do the drop-off at the DLB. I'm not sure I'm in the slab-moving business any more.'

'Done.' I smiled. 'Then it's back to the hotel for a shit, shave and shower. Thank fuck it's Sunday. With luck, Baz won't be missed till tomorrow.'

8

Charlie wrapped the batch of paper in a plastic bag. 'Every page is numbered, mate, there's a signature block on the last one, and anything that's been crossed out has been initialled. I reckon it's a statement.'

'So who were Red Eyes and Stubbly?'

'Fuck it, who cares? Let's just dump the gear and get out of here.'

'You got any rounds left?'

He pulled the pistol from under his thigh and pressed the magazine release on the left of the grip. 'Two in here.' He pulled back the top slide. 'One in the chamber.' He let the slide go again, replaced the mag, set the safety catch and passed it to me. 'That's made ready, safety on.'

I double-checked the safety catch before shoving the pistol down the front of my jeans and the plastic bag into my bomber pocket. As I got out of the Audi I gave myself the once-over. We still had to make it back to the hotel tonight, and pass muster with the night staff. Even in Tbilisi, they didn't like their guests covered in other people's blood.

I pulled out my phone and switched it on. 'I'll call when I'm done. If you see any dramas coming in, just give us a call, OK?'

Charlie nodded as he slid into the driver's seat. His job was to keep the trigger on the entrance.

'I'll need your torch as well.'

He handed it over.

'See you in a bit.' I headed straight for the open gate. There was no time to lurk about in the shadows. It was just a case of straight in, get it done, and back to the hotel before first light.

I checked the phone for a signal as I hit the main path between the burial plots. The glow from the petrol station was doing its best to bathe everything – headstones, benches, tree trunks – in BP green. I had no complaints; it meant I could see where I was going.

A car drove past the entrance, sounding like its exhaust was bouncing along the road behind it. Apart from that it was quiet. Even the knitting circle had called it a day.

My marker bin loomed out of the shadows. The four guys on Tengiz's headstone were still gazing at the heavens. I couldn't make up my mind whether they were doing it out of sheer admiration, or just waiting for an answer that never came. I shone the beam along the wrought-iron fence to get my bearings, and then picked out the bench. I moved across the plot and tried to slide the top slab away from the base. I only needed a one-inch gap, but this was one chunk of marble that looked as though it wasn't going anywhere tonight.

I bent down and gave it a second shove, this time with my shoulder. There was a low, grinding noise as it moved, and a quick flash of the torch confirmed I had the gap I needed. In went the bag of papers, the torch went back in my pocket, and I started to pull back the slab.

There was a crunch of feet on gravel behind me.

I spun round. A figure closed in on me, arms raised, blocking out every shred of ambient light. This boy was huge.

I stepped to my left as the arm came down, trying to check it in mid-stride. I was lucky. Steel clattered against stone as something very unfriendly fell from his hands.

I grabbed the bottom of my bomber jacket with my left hand and pulled it up, trying to grab the pistol grip with my right. But he was ahead of me. He yelled and lunged, hands the size of grappling irons gripping my arms and trying to wrench them from their sockets. I stumbled backwards over the low fence and we crashed onto the pathway.

My shoulder hit the kerb and my attacker fell on top of me, crushing the air from my lungs. I arched my back, kicking, bucking, struggling to get my hands down, trying to get him away from me so I could draw down.

The top of his head pushed hard against my chin. My teeth weren't clenched and I bit my tongue.

Eighteen, maybe nineteen stone of him pressed down on me, keeping my arms pinioned above my head.

'Charlie!'

I could feel the blood spurting from my mouth as I shouted. I bucked and kicked, but his body was still moulded to mine, pressing against the weapon.

'CHARLIE!'

He let go of my arms and decided to throttle me instead. Massive fingers closed around my throat and I felt his saliva spray across my face as he strained to push my Adam's apple out through the back of my neck. My head felt like it was going to explode.

There was nothing I could do but kick and writhe like a madman. I managed to get my hands round his neck as well, but his muscles simply tensed like steel hawsers under my fingers. I shifted them down to grip the lapels of his jacket, using them as leverage to dig my thumbs into the soft, fleshy area between the collar bones, at the base of his throat.

He was going to have to use his hands to deal with mine. If he didn't, he'd choke to death. Unless I did first.

My face swelled to bursting point under the pressure of his grip.

He pushed down his chin, tensing his neck even more. Fuck, he was big. His stubble took two layers of skin off my hands.

My head pumped, my eyes blurred.

I dug harder and he lifted his head.

His hair flicked against my face. I felt his bristles rasp across my cheek and smelt his sourly alcoholic breath. I knew he was going to try and finish this with his teeth.

9

I shook my head, trying to keep it moving, hoping I'd have a chance to get in there first.

When his nose was only inches away from mine, I got my chance. I lunged, and my teeth caught him just on the bridge. I bit down on the hard bone above the cartilage and kept on going. He flung his head from side to side in an attempt to shake me off, but I was like a terrier hanging onto a stick.

At last his grip slackened on my neck and his hands moved up my face. I managed to screw up my eyes before he got there with his thumbs. He pressed them into my sockets, but I just bit harder. Blood spurted over my face.

He went berserk with pain, thrashing about like a game fish under a harpoon.

I let go of his throat and threw my hands round the back of his head, pulling it towards me so I could get a better purchase with my teeth. Then I bit as hard as I could, working my head from side to side as I did so.

My jaws closed and the bone collapsed like a peanut shell. His sinuses exploded.

Blood and snot spurted from the hole in his face and he let out a scream of rage and pain.

I pulled away from him, kicking and punching, trying to get him off me. But he still held on.

I managed to turn us onto our sides, and force my hand down between us until it could close around the cold metal of the pistol grip. I brought the muzzle up beneath his armpit, released safety, and squeezed.

He took the round full in the chest.

I squeezed again.

Nothing.

There hadn't been room between us to allow the top slide to move backwards and forwards fully enough to reload.

I pushed myself away from him, scrabbling at the top slide with my fingers until I got enough grip to rack it and release it.

I lay on my back for a moment as he writhed beside me. Then I rammed the muzzle into his chest and squeezed the trigger twice.

I crawled away and sat against Tengiz's stone. The only sound louder than my choking attempts to regain my breath was another car passing along the road. This one seemed to have parted company with its exhaust entirely.

My tongue had swollen to the roof of my mouth. My Adam's apple felt like it had been kicked right against the back of my throat. I sat there, gobbing out blood between my jumper and my sweatshirt, trying to leave as little DNA as possible on the ground.

I fished out the mobile, gulping oxygen to slow down for Charlie to understand me. It rang just once before he answered.

'Back the car up to the gate. Get the boot open. We've got a drama.'

He didn't answer; he just closed down. He knew what was going into the back.

I rolled over and scrabbled about, trying to locate whatever the Hulk had been aiming to cut me into little pieces with. My fingers touched the cold steel of a gollock. No half-measures for this boy; he might have called it a machete, tree-beater, it didn't matter. What did was that the thing wasn't buried in my head.

Fuck that. I'd been lucky this time.

I crawled over to the bench, still trying to gulp in air, my mouth still filling with blood. I spat it into my jumper, and managed to heave the slab far enough to get my hand through the gap. I fished about until my fingers brushed against the plastic bag. The papers went back in my jacket pocket. Until the Hulk had turned up, I'd given Whitewall and whoever pulled his strings the benefit of the doubt, but I wouldn't any longer. Charlie and I were being well and truly fucked over. No one was getting this now. It was ours.

I groped around with the torch and found the pistol. I pushed it back into my jeans, and shoved the machete down the front of its previous owner's trousers.

I grabbed his hands, and started to drag him down the pathway. We couldn't just leave him here. The elderly are early risers, and for all we knew there could be a steady stream of widows from first light.

I could see Charlie bumping the Audi across the road, then turning and backing it up.

I reached the tap and started to wash myself down.

Charlie walked through the gate and saw the body on the pathway. 'Fucking hell, lad.'

'You've been stitched up, mate. Fucking Whitewall had this knucklehead waiting for you with a gollock.' I pointed down at the handle sticking out of his waistband. 'I've got to clean up, then I'll give you a hand.'

I washed as best I could and pushed back my wet hair, trying to look a bit respectable for the hotel. I filled a couple of plastic drinks bottles that someone had left by the taps, and went back to the plot to rinse away the most obvious splashes of blood. I didn't want the Sunday morning knitting circle to miss a stitch and call in the blue-and-whites.

Charlie and I somehow managed to heave the Hulk into the boot, torso first. For a moment the rest of him was hanging down across the Audi's rear bumper, as if he was bent over, being sick.

There was rustling, and the crunch of gravel behind us. Bodies on the pathway.

No time for talk: I grabbed the gollock and ran back into the gloom. My eyes out on their stalks, I checked each side of the path as I ran to where I thought the noise had come from.

I stopped just past Tengiz, took cover behind a tomb, and listened.

More rustling, left of the path.

I ran for it between two plots. They heard me and took off. I headed for the shouts of scared Paperclip.

Jumping a low wall, I crunched over the gravel of a plot. I could make out two shapes, maybe two plots ahead, stumbling over fences and walls, trying to get away. I jumped again and fell onto plastic sheeting. A body was under it, moaning, not moving.

Gollock up, I kicked myself free and pulled the plastic away.

One of the shell-suit crew stared up at me, tourniquet still in place around his arm, not moving a muscle. The plastic was pulled between two plots to make a shelter. I shone the torch beam in his eyes, and his pupils remained fully dilated. If he was looking into the future, he didn't have to look far.

The others were well gone now. There was nothing I could do but head back for Charlie and hope they'd been too fucked up to see anything. But I knew, deep down, that if they were, they wouldn't have been jumping around as they had.

We each grabbed a leg and swung him in. I closed the lid and Charlie took off his jacket and jumper and started to wipe blood off the back of the car.

'He was waiting for me,' I said. 'He knew you'd be here. Which means I wouldn't mind betting those two at the house weren't there by accident either.'

Charlie carried on with his cleaning while I checked the area for stray shell suits and any other machete-waving psychopaths.

'I hope you got the full wad up front, mate. It's a total fuck-up, but we'll protect ourselves with the document. Whatever's in it must be pretty important; every fucker seems to want to get their hands on it.'

The cleaning was taking too long. 'Let's just fuck off and sort everything out when we get back under cover.'

We got in the car, me behind the wheel.

'I've got a problem, lad.' Charlie looked like he'd just seen a ghost.

'What?'

'I've only got half.'

'You what? What the fuck were you thinking of?'

Charlie raised a hand. 'Hold on, everyone's in the driving seat except for me. I had two choices. Take the job as it was, or leave it.'

I headed for the nearest area of darkness, the high ground towards the TV tower. I couldn't believe he'd been so stupid. You always demand all the money up front. You never know who's fucking about with you. I started shouting at him as we bounced back into the shadow of the trees. 'Didn't you think you could be stitched up? What the fuck was going through that wobbly old head of yours?'

He said nothing as we twisted and turned our way towards the darkness.

As I parked up, in what I supposed was a fire break in the pine trees that blanketed the mountain, he finally turned and faced me. It was his turn to shout, and I could feel the force of his soundwaves against my face as well as in my ear. 'I'm fucking dying, remember? I need the cash. What would you have done? Assume Crazy Dave would come begging, and just walk away? Think about it.'

I'd known I was wrong as soon as I'd opened my mouth. 'I'm sorry, Charlie. Fuck it, it doesn't matter. Let's get the kit in the boot, and then get the fuck out of here. As long as we've got that document, we're going to be OK, I'm sure of it.'

'Yeah,' Charlie quipped. 'If all else fails we can put it on eBay.'

PART SEVEN

1

Sunday, 1 May

The terminal was heaving with passengers waiting for international flights, and every single one of them had been delayed.

It was 10.09 on a Sunday; only a matter of time before the Audi would be discovered. Even in Georgia, bloodstained seats and a shot-out window must be a curiosity.

Our flight to Vienna should have taken off at 10.30, but we weren't even being allowed to check in. There was only one departure gate, and only enough room airside for one planeload of passengers.

We'd covered our tracks as effectively as we could, but that didn't stop me feeling uncomfortable. Red Eyes and his mate hadn't done us any favours when they'd ripped our masks off, and it wouldn't take Inspector Morse to link us to Baz's Audi and the bodies in his driveway. I just wanted to get the fuck out of here. Freedom felt so close I could spit at it, but we were still the wrong side of the glass partition.

I sat by the garden sheds across the road from the terminal. At least the benches were dry; the sun had done its stuff, and now peeped intermittently through the banks of slow-moving cloud.

A lot of us had moved out here to escape the crush, and the taxi drivers were really pissed off about it. They didn't want to share their world with a load of foreigners. The shed owners weren't too happy about it, either. Each of them sat behind their identical chocolate- and gum-laden counters, making it very clear that the portable black-and-white TV on the shelf behind them was a great deal more appealing than the potential customers in front.

A bored-looking anchorwoman with big black hair was presenting a news programme on all three screens. It was obviously another slow day at the network. We were treated to endless vistas of grand buildings, or lingering shots of Georgian soldiers in US BDUs, with Richard the Lionheart insignia stuck all over them, sitting purposefully in the back of trucks, or running courageously up and down hills.

We'd made it to the hotel just before four. The kit had stayed with the body in the boot. We had to walk back into the city clean, just in case a curious blue-and-white wanted to know what we were lugging about this time of the morning. Charlie's jumper and the weapon went down an open manhole that no man or beast in their right mind would consider even going near, then we'd played a couple of drunken arseholes back from a night on the piss, jackets inside out and tied round our waists to cover the worst of the blood and mud. As it turned out, nobody raised an eyebrow. It was just another Saturday night in downtown Tbilisi.

I'd retrieved my card from behind the cistern, had a shit, shave and shower, then headed for Charlie's room with my old clothes under my arm to spend a little quality time covering our tracks. I pulled the CTR tape from its casing and burned it, with the help of the hotel's complimentary matches, and flushed the ashes down the toilet. Even our cell phones got the good news from my boot heel after a wipe-down to dispose of prints. We'd come into this country sterile, and we had to leave the same way.

The Marriott tape stayed with us; it was just too valuable to lose control of. There was a world of potential shit between us and Brisbane, and we needed to keep as much bargaining power to hand as we could.

After enough room-service breakfast to feed a couple of Charlie's horses, we binned our clothes in the kitchen skips behind the hotel, along with the remains of the camcorder. The tape was in my new, oil-worker chic, dark blue Rohan trousers, and I had slipped the first ten pages of the document in Baz's safe inside a magazine, in the pocket of my new khaki jacket. Charlie, waiting in the terminal, had the other half. He was going to come out and buy something from the shop when it was time to leave. That would be my signal to follow him back in.

I felt sorry for the old fucker. Once such a strong, solid, dependable performer, and now so screwed around by disease that he was finding it hard to grip anything firmly for more than five minutes. I could only begin to imagine his frustration. Just like Ali – king of the world one minute, a wreck the next. But unlike Ali, Charlie had a half-empty wallet into the bargain.

I had been thinking about that wallet a lot since this morning. Instead of keeping the papers as insurance, maybe we should cut a deal.

I felt a call to Crazy Dave from Vienna coming on. I'd persuade him to put us in touch with whoever the fuck had dreamed up this job, and give them the chance to buy the papers for the rest of Charlie's two hundred grand.

As a bonus, I'd try and resist the temptation to rip their heads off for forgetting to mention that we'd be sharing house-room with a couple of maniac jewel thieves, and a graveyard with a machete-wielding cousin of the Incredible Hulk. We'd keep the two tapes of Whitewall and a copy of the papers as a little memento of our Georgian adventure, in case they changed their minds later, or suddenly found themselves in the mood to give us 200K's worth of pain.

I didn't have too many illusions about Whitewall. He was probably just as expendable as we were, and they'd bin him as easily as they'd planned to bin Charlie. But at least we had something up our sleeves that he wouldn't want to become regular Sunday afternoon family viewing.

I suddenly realized that, for the first time in my life, I didn't give a fuck about the actual money. I wanted it for Charlie and Hazel's sake, of course, and because I never liked the idea of being turned over, but that was it. The thing I was really looking forward to was calling Silky. I needed to hear her voice again.

But I didn't fancy explaining to either of the girls that we'd be coming back via Hereford – that we had to see an old mate, and would therefore be a day or two later than we'd promised – so I decided to leave that bit of the conversation to Charlie.

2

Next time I looked at my watch it was 11.05. I was slouched over an espresso thick enough to tar a road, watching a Georgian celebrity chef do something interesting with an onion and a couple of oxen.

The delay was beginning to worry me. Once Baz's Audi was found with a present in the boot, the police would be swarming all over the house, trying to work out how Father Christmas had dropped by there as well. Or it could be the other way round. Whatever, it didn't matter which way this nightmare unfolded. If there was any CCTV footage in the can, it wouldn't be long before they were huddled round a monitor, watching the fuck-about in the yard.

Had I left any DNA at the cemetery? It was too late to worry about it now. But I did, just a bit.

Adrenalin and caffeine were taking their toll. I could almost feel the tension pumping round my body. At least the pain in my Adam's apple was starting to ease.

I took another sip of my now-tepid brew and concentrated on looking as bored as everyone else, but the bites in my swollen tongue made that easier said than done. Shit, it hurt. I wouldn't be putting away any packets of salt and vinegar for a while.

Five flights had been delayed so far. I heard the occasional Brit and American voice, and now and then a snatch of French and German, but most of the chat seemed to be in Russian or Paperclip.

A hardtop 110 Land Rover was still parked outside the terminal, either waiting for a pick-up, or until the driver was sure his passenger's flight had actually taken off. For his sake, I hoped he'd brought his thermos and a paper.

Two men came out of the terminal, dragging their carry-ons behind them, and headed towards the sheds. They wore the international uniform of the travelling fifty-something American executive: blue blazer, button-down shirt, chinos, very shiny loafers and a laptop bag for good measure. They were clearly in a good mood, and anxious to share it. Some guys who'd been chatting in French, and switched instantly to English as they approached, were today's lucky winners. 'Hey, good news, fellas. The Vienna flight's at 12.25. We gotta check in now.'

There were sighs of relief and jokes about Georgian in-efficiency as the crowd gathered their bags and headed for the terminal.

I stood up just as Charlie emerged from the main entrance, laptop bag on his shoulder. He saw me, up and ready, and turned back.

I was about to follow when I caught a glimpse of the latest TV news bulletin. And what I saw made my body feel so heavy, all of a sudden, I had to sit down again.

Baz's Audi filled the screen.

Then the camera cut to a glistening pool of blood in the mud, directly under the boot. Some of the rubber stops must have been missing from the drainage holes.

The reporter gobbed off, then a policeman answered a series of questions. A string of Paperclip flashed along the bottom of the screen, with what I assumed was a summary of the morning's breaking story.

The camera homed in on the open boot, where the Hulk lay curled up like a baby, the satchel still shoved behind his back. He was big, and a lot darker-skinned than most locals.

It zoomed in even closer on the entry wounds. An ambulance crew stood by as forensics guys took swabs and checked for prints.

I took a casual sip of stone-cold coffee. Third-party awareness: I couldn't look as if I was flapping. There were still people around waiting for their flights, chatting, smoking, ignoring the TV.

I tried to calm myself. I mean, so what? We'd be checking in any minute. In just over an hour, we'd be airborne.

Then my heart switched to rapid fire again, and it wasn't because of the coffee.

With a still of the Audi filling half the screen behind him, a reporter was poking a microphone under the noses of three teenagers in multicoloured shell suits outside the graveyard. Two of them seemed to be explaining what they had seen. The third looked so out of it he wouldn't have known if anyone had fallen on top of him anyway. The first twos' hands charted a course across their zit-filled, heroin-racked faces; I tried not to admit it to myself, but fuck it, what was the use – they were describing what I looked like.

Then it was back to the studio, where the anchorwoman spoke for a few moments. They flashed up a shot of the target house, with blue-and-whites all over the street, and cut to a close-up of the cameras mounted on the wall.

A few seconds later they broadcast the pictures that killed any hope I had of boarding the 12.25 to Vienna.

3

A few seconds of fuzzy, black-and-white CCTV footage flashed up, at the point where I'd turned back to the house after dropping Red Eyes.

They reran it, then freeze-framed on my face. The image was blurred, but they made up for that by cutting to an artist's impression. It was the first drawing anyone had ever done of me, and I wished they hadn't.

The next CCTV clip showed us both masked up as I got into the Audi and Charlie opened the gate. So it was official. I was in the shit. It didn't matter if they were calling *me* Baz's killer, or Red Eyes, or even all three of us. They had a face and were looking for it.

Head down, I made my way across the road to the terminal and the endless check-in queue. I found Charlie and got eye to eye. As I walked away, he followed.

I headed for the toilets. I stood at a urinal and Charlie took the one next to me. All the cubicle doors were open; we were alone.

'It's hit the news. You're OK, but they got my face.'

Charlie wasn't fazed. 'What we going to do?'

'*We*'re doing nothing, mate. *You*'re going to catch the flight. I can't risk it – even if I make it airside, what if I get pinged? There's TVs in there, mate. I'm better off staying landside. Maybe I'll try for Turkey by road.'

There was no hesitation from him. 'I'll hire a car. We'll get to the border by tonight, dump the car, and walk across. Piece of piss. Let's go.'

He started to move but I grabbed his arm. 'I don't need your fucking hands disco-dancing all over the country. Besides, they even check what you look at online. For sure they'll be checking car hire, and will be asking questions before you get the key in the door. Too risky. Take the papers, get the flight, get to Crazy Dave, and stand by. As soon as I get into Turkey I'll give you a call and see you in H. I think we can still get you the rest of the money.'

Charlie wasn't listening. 'Wait here.' He shoved his laptop bag at me. 'Bung the tape and papers in here. Just in case you get lifted, at least I might have something here that'll get you out the shit. Follow me, lad.'

He turned and walked out of the toilet, striding towards the terminal exit as I shoved everything in the bag, like a fumbling PA following in the wake of his boss.

Why couldn't he just do what he was told for once? I got up level with him.

'Fuck it, Charlie, just get the flight. I got an idea how to get your cash, it might even get me out of the shit as well.'

He still wasn't listening. His eyes were fixed on the glass exit doors. 'We're wasting time, lad. Once we're out of here we can worry about money. But for now, just shut the fuck up and follow.'

We walked out of the terminal. 'Wait here.' Charlie carried on straight towards a young guy in a blue sweatshirt, sitting at the wheel of the 110.

Charlie had his serious, purposeful warrant officer face on as he marched up to the vehicle. The driver, a young white guy with a crew cut, watched him all the way to his window. A green, heavy-plastic sleeve lay on the dash. It was the 110's work ticket folder, a log of the hours and mileage done, and had DUTY VEHICLE stencilled across it.

Charlie tapped on the glass and motioned him to wind it down.

'Duty driver? You dropping off or picking up?' Charlie spoke like he was giving the guy a bollocking for having done something wrong. Soldiers tend to react better to that tone of voice, because nine times out of ten they have.

'Dropping off.'

Charlie exploded. 'Dropping off, SIR! What camp you from, son?' He turned and pointed at me. 'Stay where you are! I haven't told you to go anywhere. Bring my bag here.'

I jerked my head. 'Yes, sir.'

'Well, bring it here, man. At least be of some use. I don't know who I'm even handing it over to. What the fuck is wrong with this man's army?'

I joined him and handed over the bag. Charlie made a show of looking for papers in the side pocket, eventually back to the driver. 'What camp are you from?'

'Camp Vasiani, sir.'

'That the only camp in this area?'

'Yessir.'

'That's where we're going then.'

Charlie bounced back to me, still in bollocking mode. 'Why weren't any joining instructions sent to me?'

'I don't know, sir,' I said. 'I sent an e-mail requesting—'

'Not good enough.' Charlie was in full flow now. 'Why isn't there anyone here to pick us up?'

'I . . . I don't know, sir.'

'You don't know, sir? Oh, is that so?' Charlie opened the rear door, slotted in the laptop and pointed at me. 'In!'

I saw it now. Charlie wanted me in the front because we were going to do a bit of hijacking.

He glowered at the driver as I got into the front passenger seat. 'How far to camp?'

'Just under an hour, sir. But I have to get permission to—'

Charlie's hand told him to shut up. 'Just drive. The flights are all leaving now; you're leaving nobody behind. We'll sort it out on the way. Can't your fucking officers even organize a pick-up?'

He jumped into the back as the duty driver leaned across and flicked a switch on his radio, a small green thing tucked into the dash.

Charlie was quick off the mark. 'Just get going, I don't need to talk to anyone. No one seems to know what day of the week it is anyway.'

The driver was flapping as he leaned back towards Charlie. 'But, sir, I gotta call in when I leave, and I gotta tell them if I dropped off OK. It's a standing order.'

There was no way we could stop him; it all had to appear routine. After all, Charlie was the one moaning about inefficiency. He was hardly the sort of man who would break a standing order.

'Well, get on with it then. Let's go.'

The driver started up the 110 and we left the airport perimeter. Charlie gave me a wink as he waited for the boy to finish speaking into the boom-mike headset.

'That's right. Two pax for our locale. But no work sheet?'

He shrugged at whatever was being said in response.

Charlie's hand loomed over the driver's shoulder. 'Give me that.'

He barked into the headset. 'Who is this?' There was a pause. 'Well, Sergeant Jay DiRita, I did not receive any joining instructions, not even the name of the person I have come all the way from Istanbul to see!'

Charlie listened to DiRita. 'Oh, is that so? You don't have any visitors scheduled for today? Well, Sergeant DiRita, now you do. We will be there soon to try to make sense of this total cock-up.'

207

He passed the headset forward to the driver and sat fuming out of the window.

I looked out at the parrot-coloured apartment blocks lining the dual carriageway, and hoped we got out in the cuds soon, so we could bin the driver and head for that border.

I scanned the dashboard. 'Got a map?'

4

We continued along the dual carriageway towards the city. I glanced from time to time at the parrot-coloured apartment blocks while the duty driver over-concentrated on the road to avoid having to catch the eye of the monster in the back.

The map he'd handed me wasn't much more than a commercial traveller's guide to the main drags and towns, but at least I could see the Vasiani region, about thirty Ks north-east of the city. It looked like our current route would take us to the right, around the bottom of Tbilisi, then up towards the camp.

'You haven't got a better one, have you? I like to know where I'm going.'

He kept his eyes on the road. ''Fraid not, sir. The duty wagon only ever gets to go to and from the airport, and once we're on this road, there's not a helluva lot of choice.'

He took a right onto a single-carriage road. We were no longer in parrot country. A mile or two later we reached the mountains, and wove our way towards a sky filled with doom-laden clouds, massing for another downpour.

As we made our way down the other side, I saw the glare of

brake lights. There were a couple of vehicles ahead of us, both slowing. Our driver changed down through the gears until we were creeping along at walking pace.

A hundred or so metres ahead, grey nylon sandbags had been piled into sangars each side of the road, and large concrete blocks had been positioned between them to channel the traffic.

I heard Charlie shifting in his seat behind me, and knew he'd seen it too. The same thoughts must have been racing through his head: were they going to ask for passports or ID? And even if they weren't, had they read their papers or watched the news?

He leaned forward to give the driver another bollocking. 'What's the VCP for? Do we have to stop?'

'Yessir. There's checkpoints on all the approach roads to the city.'

On the far side of the VCP, a rusty old coach leaned precariously under the uneven load of crap strapped to its roof, and a line of cars waited impatiently behind it while soldiers with body armour and AKs checked out its passengers.

Charlie passed me the laptop bag. 'Sort this thing out. I can't get it to work.'

'Yes, sir.' I took it and got my head down. I made a bit of a meal of opening it up and fucking about with the power button until the screen started to flicker.

We were now the third vehicle in line. A Georgian soldier was heading towards us on the driver's side, his weapon slung over his shoulder. A group of his mates were gathered on my side of the road, in the shadow of the sangar.

'Can I have your IDs, sirs? They'll want them alongside my work ticket.'

'Unbelievable,' Charlie fumed. 'We're here to help these people, and all they do is mess us around. Do we look like bloody militants?'

The squaddie got to the vehicle in front of us. He leaned

down to speak to the driver, who was ready with some kind of ID. They had a bit of a chat and the squaddie pointed to the sky and shrugged, probably moaning about the weather. He took a step back, waved the driver through, and sauntered towards us.

I leaned even further forward, completely absorbed by the problem with the laptop.

'Sir, I need—'

'Fuck this.' Charlie was out of the wagon, his back straight as a ramrod, his shoulders squared.

'You!' He jutted his jaw at the Georgian. 'Stand up straight, man!'

Some orders are understood by every soldier in any language. The squaddie snapped to attention.

'Why are you holding us up? You think we have all day?' Charlie was gripping him big-time now. Looking him up and down, inspecting him. This boy was back on the parade ground.

'Please, sir, he can't understand you.' The driver was half out of his cab. 'Please, let me . . .' He tried to placate the angry officer, at the same time as exchanging a knowing look with his fellow squaddie.

Charlie flicked the open map-pocket flap on the Georgian's combat trousers. 'What's this, man? Get your act together! Buttons are there for a purpose; they're not just decoration! Sort yourself out, soldier!'

I held my breath as Charlie got back into the vehicle. I thought he might have overdone it with his Starship Trooper impression.

The squaddie hesitated for a moment, dark thoughts furrowing his Slavic brow. Then he reached down and fumbled with his trousers. The other guys on stag kept well out of it.

'Right, let's get this wagon moving.'

The driver reached for the folder on the dash. I gave the laptop screen my total attention.

He wound down his window and passed the paperwork through as Charlie prodded my shoulder and treated me to the same kind of bollocking.

I nodded obediently and tapped the keys some more, then looked up to the skies for salvation. The Georgian hurriedly flicked open the folder and checked its contents.

Charlie was incandescent. 'Come on! Get a move on!'

No way did this boy want to be treated to another helping of what Mr Angry had to offer. He scribbled a signature on the work ticket, then handed the driver his millboard for him to do the same. Almost in the same motion, he waved us through.

We negotiated the concrete chicane and came alongside the bus. The driver looked a little concerned about my performance with the laptop, and I could hardly blame him, especially now that I packed it up and passed it back to Charlie.

'I think everything is fine, sir.' I glanced at the driver and rolled my eyes. *Officers, eh?*

The driver hit the net. 'Hello. Duty Vehicle through checkpoint Alpha. Over.'

'Roger, duty vehicle. Checkpoint Alpha. Out.'

Charlie sat there glowering. I could almost feel the heat of his anger on the back of my neck, and I knew the boy on my left could too.

I tried a little gentle fishing. 'What a drag for you . . . How many of these things do you have to get through?'

'Just the one, sir.' I could hear the relief in his voice. The last thing he wanted was for Charlie to get revved up for an encore.

We emerged into a huge valley, with a network of rivers and streams, and at least ten Ks of undulating ground separating the mountains on either side. It was big, tree-covered country out here, Switzerland without the cows.

Even though we had escaped the confines of Tbilisi it was still going to be difficult lifting this thing. The traffic wasn't anything like as busy as it had been in the city, but there was a constant stream of military trucks, full of bored Georgian squaddies rolling their heads from side to side, and packed-out buses with sacks of spuds and bags and all sorts strapped on top, bouncing between towns and slowing down only to squeeze past each other on the narrow stretch of crumbling tarmac.

We passed yet another of them, heading towards the city, and drove into a depression a couple of hundred metres long. We were in dead ground. It was as good a place as any.

I held up a hand. 'I need a piss.'

The driver slowed immediately, and pulled up on the grass verge.

I got out and walked round the front of the wagon, so I could position myself on the driver's side, before moving towards the rear and going through the motions. Charlie also got out and stretched his legs. He wandered past the radiator grille and seemed to spot something. He pointed underneath the bonnet, then looked up at the driver. 'What is this? Driver, get out!'

The squaddie jumped dutifully out and joined Charlie at the front of the vehicle. I turned and followed, two steps behind.

Charlie was still bumping his gums. 'Who's responsible for this wagon? Look at the state of it.'

The driver looked, but he couldn't see anything wrong. 'But, sir, I can't—'

I closed my hands around his mouth and jaw and jumped on his back. I pulled his head into my chest, wrapped my legs around his waist and toppled backwards.

5

I landed in the grass, with him on top of me, and hooked my legs through the inside of his. The boy didn't resist for a second or two, then he started to kick and flail his arms.

'It's OK, mate, it's OK,' Charlie said.

I pulled back even harder and kept my body and legs rigid.

'We're not going to hurt you, mate. Just calm down. Come on, composure . . .' Charlie leaned over him and raised his finger, as if scolding a child. 'Cool it, son, we're not here to hurt you. There'll be no pain.'

He jerked and writhed even more in response, so I reined him in more tightly still.

Charlie went through his pockets and tossed the contents onto the grass. I knew he'd be checking for a cell. If he had one, it would have to be dumped as soon as we were down the road. There'd be no point in calling Crazy Dave with a warning order that he had a lot of shit to sort out, and no point in taking it with us, in case it was tracked.

He stepped back. 'Nope, he's not got one.'

The boy was breathing a little easier now.

Charlie pointed at him again, and this time his tone was

almost apologetic. 'Listen, son, we're going to take the wagon, and we're going to leave you here. I know it won't be your idea of a perfect day out, but just accept it. If you start playing silly buggers, we're going to have to slap you about a bit, and take you with us. If you behave, we'll let you go. Now that's not rocket science, is it?'

He nodded as best he could with his head still compressed against my shoulder.

'I'm going to let go of you now,' I said. 'I want you to just roll off and start walking away. That's it, mate, that's all you have to do. OK?'

His breathing slowed a little and he gave something approaching a nod.

'OK, here we go.'

I released my grip, untangled my legs, and he did exactly as he'd been told.

Charlie kept an eye on him as I got to my feet and moved round to the driver's door. 'That's it, son, just walk away. Well done.'

Charlie jumped into the back seat and I switched on the radio. If anyone was going to start gobbing off about us, I wanted to hear it.

We were good for fuel. The tank was three-quarters full. No surprises there – duty wagons were always topped up after every job, ready for the next.

I glanced over my shoulder. Charlie had the laptop bag on his knees. 'On the metal or cross country?' I threw him the map.

'Shows fuck all.' He studied it for a few more seconds and shook his head. 'So I guess we're committed to this, unless we see a minor they haven't bothered to include.'

'It takes us straight through Vasiani . . .'

Charlie pored over the map again. 'Maybe, maybe. But if we get past it, we can box around the city and then head south.'

He looked up at the ground to our left, then behind him. 'Or

215

we head back cross-country, get around the VCP, then back on the road and south. We can't go back through the city. It'll be too easy for them to ping us in this thing once the driver manages to get an SOS out. He'll be flagging down a vehicle the first chance he gets.'

He paused. 'What you reckon, worth a go?'

We drove on for another five minutes to make sure we were well clear of the driver, then I chucked the 110 into four-wheel drive and headed left, off road. Once we were out of sight of it, I'd parallel back past the VCP.

The wagon lurched and skidded in the soft ground. The days of intense rainfall had saturated and loosened the soil. It wasn't ideal, and we didn't have much time to spare – it'd be a couple of hours, max, until the driver ran back to the VCP and raised the alarm and everyone would be looking for the 110 – but we didn't have a whole lot of choice.

If we got stuck, we'd just have to dig the fucker out. At least we weren't on the steeper ground. A combination of heavy rainfall, steep slopes and a surface loose enough to overcome the gravitational pull that kept it in place was the recipe for landslides.

We dropped into dead ground and turned left, but it was no cause for celebration. If anything, the conditions were worse. Glutinous mud sucked at the wheels and we sank down almost to our axles. I checked out Baby-G, then glanced at the dash. We had been going just over thirty minutes, and only covered a couple of Ks.

I turned back to Charlie. 'This ain't going to work, mate. At this rate we won't even be past the VCP by the time he's raised the alarm. He might even be there now if he's hitched a lift.'

'Nothing's changed, lad. If we head back onto the road, we're committed.'

I grabbed the map and traced the route round the north of the city, in case we could head west and chuck a left towards Turkey. I also looked out for filling stations, but I didn't see any marked.

'That's got to be better than being stuck right here. At least we get to make distance. That's what we need, mate. What do you say, cut our losses?'

6

I stopped just short of the crest of the hill and Charlie got out.

He scrambled up to check the dead ground in front of us, dropped onto his hands and knees as he neared the skyline, and crawled the last few metres. We didn't want to run the risk of piling straight over the top and discovering that our old mates at the sangar were right there in front of us.

He waved me up and jumped back in as I drew level with him. He leaned through the gap between the front seats. 'The road's two hundred the other side of the rise. No way have we passed that VCP.'

I edged the wagon uphill. 'We'll soon find out, one way or the other. Fuck 'em.'

The time comes when you just have to accept your options are running out and go for it.

We hit the road, hung a left, and I flicked the 110 back into two-wheel to conserve fuel.

No more than a minute later, we saw the duty driver ahead of us. He spotted the wagon and started waving us down.

Charlie laughed. 'Bet he changes his mind when he sees who it is.'

He was right. As we got closer, the guy did a double take and legged it into the trees.

Another quarter of an hour and we had to slow for an oncoming truck, overloaded with turnips. A few fell off and bounced across the top of our wagon as we manoeuvred round each other.

We came to the top of another rise and the dead ground opened up before us. The camp was in the distance, maybe a K off the road, along what looked like a newly laid gravel track.

It was the size of a small city. Dozens of green twenty-man tents stood in smart, regimented lines along the side of a chain-link-fenced compound. To their right lay a maze of Portakabin-type structures with satellite dishes on their roofs, either linked in terraces or connected by concrete roadways.

Five or six Hueys were parked in a neat line beside a helicopter pan.

The main drag continued for maybe three Ks past the junction towards another camp on higher ground.

Charlie leaned forward again. 'Fucking hell, they've got the whole army here!'

He wasn't wrong. 'Any bright ideas?'

He shook his head. 'We've got to keep on going for it. Nowhere else to go. And we're in a company wagon, aren't we? Let's hope the driver hasn't got to the VCP yet and they just give us a nod.'

I put my foot down and we accelerated past the turn-off to the first camp. The track was actually hardcore, and stretched a K or so to the main gate, where massive US and Georgian flags fluttered shoulder to shoulder in the breeze.

The fields either side of us were a hive of activity. The Partnership for Peace programme was in full swing. American unarmed-combat instructors in green T-shirts and US Marine Corps spotty-camouflage BDU bottoms were putting Georgian troops through their paces. They looked as though they were having a great time, kicking the shit out of the happy boys

219

from the recruitment commercial while their mates force-fed infantry fieldcraft to patrols in arrowhead formation.

No one gave us a second glance.

So far so good.

The 110 started to shake and rattle as the road surface quickly deteriorated the other side of the junction. I kept my foot to the floor as we moved uphill towards the second camp.

I dropped to third on the steeper gradient and the 110 ate it up. I was starting to feel good about this.

'Hello, duty vehicle, duty vehicle. Is that you on the hill? Report. Over.'

I looked down at the radio and then at Charlie. He shrugged his shoulders. Somebody with nothing better to do was watching us through their binos. So what?

I changed down to second to get a spurt on past the camp at the top of the hill, in case they'd been instructed to stop us.

'Duty vehicle, do not go any further. Repeat, do not go any further. Return to our locale. Over.' Maybe they needed the wagon back to pick up the CO's sandwiches.

We ignored it again. The throttle was flat to the boards. The engine screamed as we headed on up the hill.

'Do not cross the demarcation line. Crossing the demarcation line is contrary to standing orders. Repeat, return to this locale. Over.'

'Demarcation line?' Charlie's head was level with mine as he too peered up the hill. 'These two places in the middle of a union dispute?'

'Something like that.' I nodded in the direction of the flags flying over the gates of the camp, now about 150 ahead on our left. They weren't the Stars and Stripes or anything to do with Richard the Lionheart, but the white, blue and red horizontals of the Russian Federation.

Charlie's head was level with my right shoulder. 'Fuck it, let's just keep going; take our chances. There's fuck all else we can do.'

220

We began to parallel the camp's front fence. Men in uniform swarmed around in confusion alongside never-ending lines of tents and vehicles. By the look of it, they were getting stood to.

There was now a major flap on at the main gate. I slowed as armed men spilled out on the road. Were they throwing up a roadblock?

The radio blared at us again. 'Duty vehicle, status report. Over.'

I kept my eyes on the uniforms up ahead. They'd obviously dressed in a bit of a hurry; some had combat jackets that weren't done up, some didn't have helmets. But they all had AKs. Run one of them over and they'd open up big-time.

'I'm not going to stop. I'm just going to keep going, but real slow. You up for it?'

I looked back at Charlie in the rear-view.

He winked. 'So which one are you, Butch or Sundance?'

7

We were level with the main gate and the speedo flickered near twenty. Nobody on the road seemed to know what to do. They were all mouthing the Russian for 'What the fuck's a British 110 doing up here?' Thankfully they all still had their AKs slung rather than in the shoulder.

Charlie started to wave. 'How's it going, lads?'

They stared back, then some of the younger ones smiled and returned the wave. NCOs started shouting angrily, trying to get something organized.

We trundled past, Prince Charlie in the back still doing his greet-the-people bit. Still nobody challenged us.

The radio barked. 'Duty vehicle, turn around, turn around. Do not stop; do not take any action that is deemed aggressive. If apprehended, comply with their orders.'

'Shut up, you twat,' Charlie said, smiling broadly at his new subjects.

I flicked the radio off.

Moments later, we were clear of the confusion. I was braced for shots, but none came. We were going gently downhill, no longer in view from the American camp.

The fence line stopped. Charlie turned and looked back. 'Still no follow-up. Let's keep going. Get that foot down, lad.'

Absolutely no argument with him on that one.

For maybe thirty minutes we saw no junctions, no options, no VCPs, just lots of undulating green to our front, a forest to our left, and a valley to our right. The engine was gunning and we were up to ninety Ks an hour in some places where the road surface allowed it.

The duty driver must have reached the VCP by now. But so what? We were well out of the area. There'd be a Welcome to Tbilisi VCP waiting over the horizon somewhere on the road, just itching for the chance to stop us any way it could, but we'd cross that bridge when we came to it. For now, I was feeling pretty pleased with myself.

Then I heard something all too familiar, and my heart sank.

I looked at Charlie and could tell from his expression that I was right.

He wound down his window.

The noise was louder and unmistakable.

The steady throb of heavy rotor blades cutting the air.

They had a pipeline to protect: of course they would have a QRF [Quick Reaction Force] on standby. I just wished they hadn't taken the quick bit so much to heart.

Charlie bounced around in the back to try to pinpoint where it was coming from. I leaned forward over the wheel, straining my eyes up into a still-empty sky.

The steady beat seemed to come up level with us, and then the Huey broke out of the dead ground to our right, no more than a couple of metres away.

For the two seconds it was overhead, the 110 almost stood still under the pressure from its downwash. I could see the pilot quite easily. Both the side doors were pulled back, and the space between them was heaving with dark green BDUs and the odd two or three in US Marine spotty-camouflage.

They waved urgently, pointed weapons, gestured at us to stop.

223

Bollocks. They'd have to land on top of me before that happened.

I kept my foot down.

The Huey flared away and disappeared into dead ground ahead. Moments later, another set of rotors started beating the air behind us.

Charlie leaned over the back seat. 'Here it comes. Shit, it's low!'

Huey Two passed directly over us, just feet away, following the road. I could see the soles of combat boots resting on the skids and AK barrels sticking out of the open doors.

The 110 shook violently. Maybe they really were going to try to land on top of us.

Charlie scanned the sky. 'Where's the first one gone?'

'Fuck knows, but I think this one fancies us. Look.'

It had scooted about 200 metres ahead, and flared up as it turned back round to face us. The heli's skids bounced onto the road and troops started jumping into the haze of its exhaust fumes.

From our right, and closing in, I heard the slap of another set of rotors. Huey One passed more or less level with the 110 as it moved to take up station behind us. It was going to drop its troops to cut us off.

Fuck this. I yanked the wagon hard left, over the rough ground towards the treeline. There weren't enough of them to find us in there.

Huey One immediately turned back towards us and swooped like a kestrel onto a field mouse, settling at a hover just feet above us. A spotty uniform leaned out, feet on the skid, one hand gripping the door frame. He fixed me with a stare and shook his head slowly, then moved the index finger of the other slowly across his throat.

'Fuck him, don't stop, lad. Nearly there.'

We had maybe 300 to go. My head bounced off the roof as the wagon took on the terrain. It shook, rattled and tipped from side to side, but still kept going.

The heli moved ahead and landed. More troops fanned out and took up fire positions between us and the treeline.

I swung the wheel half right. Safety was just 200 away now.

Huey Two had picked up its men from the road and was back in the game, coming at us from the right.

'He's coming real low, lad . . .'

Charlie kept up a running commentary while I concentrated on the driving. It was still in two-wheel; I wasn't going to stop the momentum to get it in four.

'They got caltrops!'

I kept my foot hard to the floor, leaning over the wheel, urging the 110 closer to the cover of the trees. The rear of the wagon went momentarily airborne and the back wheels spun with a high-pitched whine, like a propeller out of water. We had to beat the caltrops.

Huey Two had come in above us. Its downwash pummelled the wagon from side to side. It moved just ahead. A spotty uniform was perched on the skid; a ten-metre strip, peppered with three-pronged spikes, swayed from his hand towards the ground.

I swerved right again, paralleling the treeline. Just over a hundred to go.

Charlie pulled the tape and papers from the computer bag, ready to run. 'The other heli's up! Here any second. Get that fucking foot down.'

The caltrops were only metres ahead, coming in left to right.

'Stand by . . . stand by . . . they got us!'

The caltrops fell and the tyres hit almost immediately.

8

The steering wheel vibrated violently in my hands for several seconds then the wagon simply came to a halt. Tyres deflated, the wheel rims had just ploughed into the mud.

Both helis were on us. BDUs jumped out metres away, weapons up. The guys would be pumped. Some looked nervous, some like they just wanted to chalk up a kill.

I raised my hands very slowly and obviously and placed them on the dash, where they could be seen.

A black guy in spotty-camouflage, two bars on his lapel, shouted from the front of the wagon, over the roar of the helis. 'Get out of the vehicle! Get out of the vehicle!'

We didn't fuck around.

Baby Georgians swarmed round and kicked us to the ground. Hands searched us. Pockets were pulled out, jackets ripped open.

One of the Hueys took off again and hovered above the 110 as I got turned over onto my back and searched some more. A winch cable descended from its belly, at the end of which hung a set of wide nylon straps.

The downwash was heavy with the stench of aviation fuel.

My face was splattered by earth, grit, and rainwater from the grass.

Thanks to the caltrops, the wagon wasn't going anywhere without help, even if the BDUs had wanted to risk another international incident with the Russians. The Georgian boys were all over it like a rash, rigging the webbing straps. This beat the shit out of another day in the classroom.

AKs bore down on us and the black guy loomed back into my line of sight. He carried out yet another search, oblivious to the buffeting of the downwash.

'The driver's OK! We dropped him a few Ks from camp. He's fine.' I took a deep breath so I could make myself heard over the two sets of rotors. 'We didn't touch him, he's OK!'

People can get very dangerous if they think one of their own has been hurt.

My hands were grabbed. The cuffs had solid steel spacers instead of chains. You can't flex your wrists in them. They were closed far too tight, but I wasn't complaining. I just looked down, clenched my teeth, kept my muscles taut, ready for another kicking.

The captain grabbed hold of the spacer and gave it a tug. I was totally under his control. He jumped the caltrops, and started running towards the second Huey. It was just too painful to do anything but follow as best I could.

I looked behind me and saw Charlie quick-timing to keep up with his escort.

The captain jumped aboard first. He hauled me up and shoved me into one of the red nylon webbing seats that ran down the centre of the cabin, facing the doors. Charlie's man did exactly the same from the other side.

The Georgians leaped on board behind us, and the heli lifted. I got a great view of the other Huey, hovering above the 110. It was just about rigged up and ready to go.

The troops it had ferried in would have to stay behind; I guessed they'd come back for them after dropping us off.

As we crossed the main drag, a line of overexcited locals peered up at us from the windows of a rusty old coach loaded with suitcases, shopping bags, chickens in cages, all sorts, on the roof rack. I guessed theirs would be the last happy faces I'd be seeing for a while.

We flew over the bus, giving the Russian camp a wide berth to the left. The captain had pulled on a set of headphones and talked fast into the boom mike. The noise of the engine and the rush of the wind made it impossible to hear what he was saying, but I knew it had to be about us.

The inside of the Huey hadn't had anything done to it since it left Mr Bell's factory in the 1980s. The walls were still lined with faded silver padded material, and the floor's non-slip, gritty paint had worn away before some of these squaddies were even getting the hang of their first water pistols.

We hugged the side of the valley, using it as cover from the Russians who'd be up there, somewhere, radioing a progress report to Moscow.

We flew low and fast, trees, animals and buildings zooming past in a blur.

We tilted left and right, following the contours. Wind blasted the interior as we took a particularly sharp right-hander. I gripped my seat between my legs to stop myself being tipped into the trees.

We levelled out then surged over the ridge and Camp Vasiani spread out ahead of us.

The fieldcraft training was still in full swing, but I now knew it was just for show. The real Partnership for Peace programme was being played out here in the Huey. Guys like the US Marine in the seat beside me would stay in charge, while the Georgian boys would do the housework and smile for the cameras.

We hovered over the concrete pan and came in to land. Exhaust fumes and downwash gusted into my face.

No sooner were the skids on the ground than we were manhandled in the direction of a waiting 110.

228

In the distance, the other Huey appeared over the ridgeline, the Land Rover dangling from its belly.

Down here, confusion reigned. The Georgians bundled us into the back of the 110. One of their mates was driving, and the others formed an armed escort. Four outriders sat astride dull-green quad bikes. The marine in charge wore body armour, helmet and wraparounds, and had an M16 slung across his back. The bar on his lapels and the top of his helmet marked him out as a lieutenant.

We were bounced around the camp perimeter and eventually arrived at the Portakabin complex. I didn't bother coming up with any scenarios. I'd have no influence on events, so I was going to take things as they came. I just had to accept I was deeply in the shit: if they didn't know it already, they wouldn't take long to realize that they had a local TV and newspaper star on their hands. And once they did, well, every minute I wasn't banged up in a Georgian police cell with a crew cut and thumbscrews was a bonus.

We turned into an open square lined by groups of the cream-coloured, aluminium Portakabin modules. The 110 stopped, and the quad bikes pulled up around us.

The lieutenant dismounted and shouted a series of orders.

Three US Marines stood to on our right, in body armour and Kevlar helmets, weapons in the shoulder. Their message was clear. 'Hands up! Show me your hands! Hands in the air!'

I spotted the air-conditioning units on the roofs of the modules. I had a feeling we'd be needing them.

PART EIGHT

1

The one-bar ran around barking orders into the open door of one of the Portakabins and the marines moved forward. We did exactly as we were told; we each had a muzzle in our face.

We waited for instructions; the trick is to show no sign of fear, or any other emotion that might spark people off. Be neutral; do what you're told, when you're told.

'*You!* You with the dark hair,' the marine closest to me shouted. 'Get out of the vehicle, and get out real slow. The old one, stay where you are.'

I stifled a grin. Charlie wasn't going to like that one bit.

More marines tumbled out of the Portakabins into the square, clad in body armour and Kevlar helmets but not carrying weapons. I had the feeling we were about to meet the reception committee.

I got out slowly, making sure they saw my hands at all times, and that I made no jerky movements.

The guy covering me came round to my side of the vehicle and stopped a couple of metres away, his barrel pointing into the centre of my chest. He leaned into the weapon, butt firmly in the shoulder, aiming down rather than up so that if he had to shoot, there'd be less chance of the round hitting someone else on the way out.

It was now Charlie's turn to be hollered at. I heard rather than saw him step down from the wagon. I wasn't going to turn round until the man with the semi-automatic said he wanted me to.

Two or three rubberneckers stuck their heads out of the windows on the far side of the square. A whole lot of others came right outside and gathered in a circle around us.

'What's happening, man? They steal the 110? Must be Russians.'

'Nah, drug dealers.'

'No way. They're terrorists, man. Fucking militants.'

These guys obviously spent more time watching reruns of *Fantasy Island* than checking the local news, but I knew it was only a matter of time before they made the connection with Baz.

My escort gripped the spacer bar on my cuffs and yanked my hands in front of me, and a couple of his mates gave me a brisk search. They didn't seem at all pleased about us nicking their wagon.

A set of hands grabbed each of my arms and half carried, half dragged me along the hard standing and up two wooden steps. We turned down a wide, windowless corridor. Grey lino covered the floor and extended six inches up each wall instead of skirting board. Fluorescent light bounced off glossy white walls.

The marine ahead of us was clearing a path through the onlookers. 'OK, guys, the show's over. Back in your offices, please. We got this situation under control. Come on, people, let's move here.'

We arrived at a pair of windowless double doors, heavily scuffed at the bottom where they'd been repeatedly opened with the help of a boot.

We barged through three or four sets in all before we finally stopped outside a bare room, furnished only with a single aluminium chair and a table.

Charlie was no longer behind me. I didn't like that at all.

One of the guys pushed me inside.

The lino-and-white-wall combo was clearly all the rage in this neck of the woods.

They turned me round and sat me down. Then, without saying a word, one of them grabbed the spacer bar and yanked my cuffed hands behind my head. The weight of my arms pulled it into the back of my neck, so I tried to hunch up, to take some of the pressure off my wrists.

I was pulled back up by the hair. 'Sit straight, you fuck.'

Four guys and a woman stayed in the room with me, all in uniform, with radio earpieces and pistols in black nylon leg holsters. One of them kept hold of my spacer bar, his knuckles digging into the back of my neck.

Their eyes drilled into me.

The woman stood in front of me. 'Undress.'

If she was here to embarrass me, she was a lifetime too late. I'd had to eat my own shit before now, and I'd do it again if it stopped them climbing aboard me. Anything was better than getting a kicking.

The cuffs were released and blood rushed back into my hands as I started to pull off my kit.

Except for the gentle hum from the air-conditioner vents high on the wall, the room was silent.

She dug into her box of tricks and snapped her hands into a pair of surgical gloves. I noticed a badge with two snakes coiled around some kind of stick on her lapel. Medical corps.

I stood with my clothes in a heap at my feet, awaiting instructions, though I had a good idea where this was leading.

She pointed to the chair. 'Sit down.'

I did as I was ordered and the four guys formed a semicircle in front of me. One of them had a can of mace at the ready;

235

another held a Taser. It was almost as if they were willing me to start something.

The metal was cold on my bare back and arse but I didn't have time to think about it. The woman pushed my head back and dug around in my mouth with a spatula.

I could smell smoke on her shirt. I hoped she wasn't too pissed off about being called away from her cigarette break, because I had the feeling this was about to get very intimate.

I wondered what they were looking for. Drugs? A miniature bomb under my tongue? Or were they just putting me through the wringer?

More important, where was Charlie?

She put the spatula aside, and probed around my gums with a finger.

What next? A free orange suit and daily trips to the interrogation room on a handcart? Who the fuck did they think I was?

She checked my ears, then dipped back into the box for a party-size tube of KY jelly. I was obviously going to get the full Saddam.

She squeezed some onto the first and middle fingers of her right hand. 'Stand up, bend over and touch your toes.'

I had only one consolation: it was going to be worse for her than me. I'd been saving up all day for a dump.

I felt her finger slide in, have a good dig around, then withdraw.

'Stand up.'

I avoided looking her in the eye. I didn't want to give her even the hint of a smile.

The heel of a boot slammed into my back and sent me flying towards the wall. I knew that was just for starters. They'd warm themselves up with a few more of the same before mob rule took over. They really did have hatred in their eyes.

I took the fall, curled up tight, and waited. Boots advanced on me across the floor. I kept my face covered, but one eye open.

One of the radios crackled and the wearer quickly pushed in his earpiece to keep it private. He conveyed whatever had been said to him to the others in hushed tones. They looked at me, clearly disappointed. That was it, then; they must know I was the TV star. It was now Georgian police time. I tried to kid myself it was a better option.

The medic pulled off her glove and deposited it into a plastic bag and bundled all her toys back into the box. She pointed at the chair. 'Sit.'

I got to my feet, but not quite quickly enough. One of the guys helped me on my way with his toecap.

The aluminium hadn't got any warmer. I heard the slurp of KY as I shifted position, then the sound of gaffer tape being ripped off a roll.

2

They grabbed my wrists and forced them up against my temples, then got busy with the tape. They wrapped it around my hands and head like a bandage, then down under my chin for good measure.

I clenched my fists as tightly as I could, trying to create some slack in the tape when they'd finished. Even a little bit of play might mean my circulation wasn't cut off. I knew I wasn't going anywhere in a hurry, but knowing that I was resisting in some small way made me feel better.

Next they turned their attention to my arms, binding them together just above the elbows, locking them firmly under my chin.

No order was given, but they suddenly stepped back as one and left the room.

I glanced around me. My clothes were gone, and there was no way out.

My hands more or less covered my ears, but I'd heard the door being locked from the outside, and the four ventilation grilles were no larger than letter boxes. Besides, they probably had me under CCTV.

I leaned forward and rested my elbows on my knees. Sweat stung the skin beneath my chin. I must have stayed like that for an hour, maybe more.

I tried to keep optimistic.

I'd fallen in more than my fair share of dung heaps over the years, and while I might not always have come up smelling of roses, I'd been able to keep a certain percentage of me shit-free and easy on the nose.

I'd taken a bit of punishment along the way, but somehow always managed to get away with it. I guessed that was one of the reasons I'd carried on doing these stupid dickhead things.

Try as hard as I might, I couldn't avoid the thought that maybe this time would be different.

3

I could hear muffled speech in the corridor. I lifted the gaffer tape as far as I could away from my ears. Heated or just frustrated, I couldn't tell which, but there were certainly a few 'Goddams' and 'No way, their asses are ours' being bandied around out there. It sounded like something bad was happening for them, but of course that didn't necessarily mean something good was happening for us.

That cell in Tbilisi suddenly seemed very close again.

Boots and tyres crunched across the gravel.

I hated times like this, not knowing what the fuck was happening. Maybe the police were already here, working on Charlie first? He might not be in great shape these days, but they wouldn't get much out of him.

They'd probably tell me the old fucker had confessed everything, but I knew the last thing Charlie would do was give them any ammunition. His hands might swing into disco mode and his memory might let him down, but some things are so deeply ingrained they're second nature.

I spent a moment or two wondering where the silly old fool

was. If I got out, did I run around and try and find him? Without a doubt. Even bollock-naked and with my hands taped to my head, I'd still try and break down every door along the corridor until I found him. Then all we'd need were two sets of clothes, our passports and some kind of transport out of here, and Bob's your uncle.

Back in the real world, I did my best to uncurl myself and stretch my back and legs, trying to relieve the pain in my muscles and the pressure points against the lino.

It started to get cold, so I reversed the process. They'd probably adjusted the air conditioning, to soften me up before they came and read me my horoscope.

Half an hour or so later, I had to stretch out on the floor again, every bone in my body aching. Which god had I pissed off so mightily this time? What wrong turning had led me here, my arse leaking KY jelly, my head mummified with gaffer tape, just when things had started looking up?

Deep down, I'd always known that I'd fuck up big-time one day, but it had never bothered me much.

Until Kelly came along.

Funny how a snot-nosed kid with a moth-eaten teddy bear can make you pay attention.

I was never the knight in shining armour she deserved, and nothing I did would stop me blaming myself for failing to save her life, but even now I was back in my old familiar world I realized normal service hadn't quite resumed.

I knew I was always destined to be smack at the bottom of the food chain, and I'd almost got to like it. But Kelly made me dare to think for a moment that there might be something better around the corner.

And now Silky was doing it all over again. She'd become my gatekeeper, my interpreter in a world that spoke a language I barely understood.

What was she doing right now? What was she wearing? What kind of stuff would we do together when I got back? I would take her tandem jumping again for sure, maybe train her to freefall.

I couldn't believe how much I missed her. For the first time in as long as I could remember, the sum total of my feelings wasn't 'bollocks to that'. I was actually looking forward to being with someone, and really wanting it.

If I ever managed to get out of here, I wouldn't moan at her for the way she strapped her board on top of the VW. I'd even let her play the Libertines all the way from Cairns to Sydney and back again if she wanted to.

In the meantime, I curled myself up again, like the body in the boot of the Audi, closed my eyes and tried to think good things.

It was all I could do for now.

4

I lay on the cold hard floor, my hands locked like a vice to my head, my body numbed by pins and needles, no matter which way I turned, no matter how often I stretched.

At least the room was warming up now; someone had thrown the switch on the air conditioning a few minutes ago and hot air was streaming out of the duct alongside me. I sat up and shuffled across the lino on my arse until I was directly in line with it.

The odd Huey cruised overhead, and I could catch snatches of conversation along the corridor.

They still didn't seem to know who we were. Drug dealers was a popular choice, and since we were white, we pretty much had to be Russian. Mafia, maybe.

One guy reckoned we were Brits because the driver had said so, but that got short shrift. Everyone knew that Brits were fucking stupid, but not this stupid, surely.

I didn't allow myself to get too carried away, though, and I was right.

There was the sound of hurried footsteps outside my door, and the good news came through loud and clear. 'Hey, just heard about these two fucks. They killed that politician, you know, the guy on the news? Yeah, shot the guy in the head twenty times and left him in the trunk of his car. Our guys caught 'em trying to get away.'

I lay there for what seemed like hours, bored now that I knew what was in store.

I moved closer to the door, to try to hear more. Mostly I wanted to know where Charlie was, but I would have settled for the time. All I heard was the squeak of boots and the odd bollocking about the noise.

I was gagging for a drink; it was a lifetime since those espressos at the airport.

I started to feel sleepy and guessed it must be getting late. I tried to nod off, but I couldn't; every position I tried was just too uncomfortable.

More time passed; then I heard shoes, not boots, approaching down the corridor.

The door was flung open and the room was plunged into darkness.

There were two of them gripping me, one either side. They were in civilian clothes; my left foot pressed against a metal buckle on a pair of muddy loafers, and I was treated to a cocktail of stale nicotine and leather on my right as I got hauled off the lino.

I was prepared to bet all of Charlie's three quid that the jacket was black.

Then all I could smell was turnips as a scratchy nylon sack was pulled over my head. It came down to my elbows.

My two new best mates exchanged a word or two in Paperclip; I was starting to get the hang of it now. Then they dragged me out into the corridor. Pinpricks of fluorescent light glinted through the weave, and I could see more grey lino through the gap at my waist.

We turned left, through a set of swing doors, then on again, through another.

A gust of cold air played across my bare skin, shrinking everything except the goose bumps. I started to shiver as we moved out onto a short flight of wooden steps.

Chips of gravel punctured the soles of my feet as I was bundled through the open tailgate of a waiting estate car. The back seats were down and I landed on a haphazard combination of scratchy woollen and furry nylon blankets.

I wriggled as far forward as I could, hoping to bump up against Charlie, but my only reward was banging my head against a spare car battery and having my nose attacked by the overpowering stench of urine and damp dog. Another blanket was thrown over me and the tailgate slammed shut.

This wasn't good.

I had a feeling I knew what kind of policemen these guys were, and you wouldn't want to stop and ask them the way.

The front doors opened and closed and I felt myself bounce around a bit as the two of them sorted themselves out. The engine fired up and we crunched our way past the Portakabins. I closed my eyes, to try and maintain some sense of direction.

I heard some chat, then the strike of a match, and nicotine-laden smoke began to do battle with the smell of dog.

I wasn't scared about what might lie ahead. I just felt depressed.

And hungry.

And, much to my surprise, pretty fucking lonely.

5

We came to a halt and the driver wound down his window. He rattled off a series of short, sharp instructions to someone in Paperclip, then I heard the creak of a barrier being raised and the car rolled forward once more.

We rumbled over the kilometre or so of hardcore towards the main and took the left. No surprises there. The Georgians weren't any fonder of their old mates from the Russian Federation than the Americans were.

We moved smoothly along the metalled road, with only the occasional shake and rattle as we encountered a good old-fashioned pothole.

I tried to time this stretch by counting off the seconds, and got to twenty minutes without a pause.

The two in the front were still enjoying themselves. They switched the radio on and listened to some Georgian songs that seemed to involve a lot of wailing. Maybe it was the same station that played in embassy security huts?

At no stage did they acknowledge I was there. Maybe they'd forgotten me. That would have been nice.

There'd been no steep climbs up or down, so we were still

following the valley. Why weren't we going over the high ground, stopping at the VCP then heading back to the city? And if we weren't, was that a good or a bad thing? I had a nasty feeling I knew the answer.

Ten minutes more and this definitely wasn't normal police stuff. We still hadn't got anywhere near the high ground; if we'd been going back to the city we would have done so by now.

I shuffled around, trying to get more blanket over me. My goosebumps were on the retreat and I wanted to make the most of it while I could.

Something about being warm and cocooned set me thinking about Silky again. I was confused. I knew I'd done the right thing coming here with Charlie, but at the same time, all I wanted now was to be back with her in Australia. Not just as an alternative to lying in the back of a car on my way to what was probably going to be the beasting of a lifetime, but simply because I wanted to be with her. She smelled a whole lot better than these blankets, for starters.

I thought about her lying next to me on the beach, and sitting beside me in the passenger seat of the VW. My mind rambled. I couldn't think of a single moment with her that hadn't been good. I thought about the time she said, 'We're a good fit, no?' She was right, we were. I missed her.

So what were we going to do when I got back? There was still the trip to the red centre; to what I called Ayers Rock and Silky and everybody else seemed to think was now Uluru.

Before meeting Silky, I'd have cut away from any fearful thoughts in a situation like this – even cut away from good stuff at the same time. I probably would just have lain here. But fuck it, I liked it this way. There was still sailing in the Whitsundays, and Kakadu National Park, and New Zealand. All the places we'd spoken about when we were travelling together. I wanted to go to them all, and I wanted to go to them with her.

The gearbox made a muffled complaint and the car slowed. We turned onto much rougher ground. I curled up tight.

The engine cut out.

Both front doors opened and there was the crunch of shoes on stones.

The tailgate was lifted and the blanket pulled away. The cold air hit me like a slap in the bollocks.

6

I was dragged past another vehicle, across a stretch of wet grass strewn with rocks and scree.

The night wind chilled me to the bone; my skin was like a freshly plucked chicken's.

We stopped and I heard the sound of a heavy kick on wood. A door swung open and I was pulled through it into what felt like a sauna. The air was heavy with the odour of damp and bottled gas.

I stumbled forward a few paces then felt pressure on my shoulders. My arse connected with a plastic chair. Above me, I could hear the gentle hiss of burning gas. I leaned forward, clenching my teeth, waiting for them to give me the good news. I expected to get yanked upright any second, but they let me stay as I was.

Then, even more surprisingly, they pulled off the sack.

I kept my head down but my eyes went into overdrive. I was in a small room with rough stone walls and a compacted earth floor. In front of me was a blue plastic collapsible picnic table with metal legs, which looked as though it had come straight out of an Argos catalogue. Two hurricane lamps sat at either end of it, their shadows dancing across the walls. My passport and Charlie's lay in between them.

The driver and his mate were behind me, breathing heavily after the exertion of frogmarching me from the car.

A pair of US desert boots appeared on the other side of the table. The chinos above them looked as though they'd been inflated by a high-pressure hose. A thin-barrelled .22 semi-automatic was pointing straight at my forehead, held rock-steady in a latex-gloved hand.

When I saw who it belonged to, the Georgian secret police suddenly seemed like the soft option.

My luck had finally run out.

Towering over me was at least 250 pounds of fat, topped off by an all-too-familiar whitewall haircut.

I didn't like the way he was holding the weapon, but it didn't look nearly as scary as he did.

Jim D. 'Call Me Buster' Bastendorf, the man we'd rechristened Bastard at Waco, had hardly changed a bit in the twelve years since I'd last seen him.

7

I looked down again, but kept my eyes on the weapon.

All of a sudden, my hands felt strangely comfortable round my head. All the same, I clenched my teeth and closed my eyes. I had fucked up and had to accept whatever followed.

If he wanted me to beg, though, he had another thought coming. Fuck him. He was going to do what he was going to do, whatever I did, so what was the point?

I heard him move around the table. His nostrils whistled as he bent closer. Then I felt him jam the muzzle hard into my right hand.

I flinched as the working parts clicked. I couldn't help it.

I opened my eyes. Bastard was still above me. He liked how I'd reacted; it made him smile.

'Now, son, who the fuck are you?'

'You've got my passport. Give it a read.'

He looked down at me. I knew from his expression that he still hadn't made the connection between me, Anthony the Brit fag scientist, and a compound full of dead Davidians, and I wasn't going to help him out. I was in enough trouble already.

'You're no American. Where you from?' His brow furrowed

as he studied my face and let his brain flick back a few pages. 'I know you from somewhere, don't I?'

'Listen, we have you on film, handing over equipment at the Marriott in Istanbul and—'

The first punch was to my right temple and caught me square on. I managed to stay on the chair, but it was a while before my head stopped ringing and splinters of light stopped dancing in front of my eyes.

'Shut the fuck up! You're in deep shit, boy! The police want your ass, big-time. You're responsible for the murder of their answer to that Bob fucking Geldof guy, and they don't see the funny side of that. And you know what? I'll give those fucks just exactly what they want if you don't offer me a little cooperation.'

He hit me twice more. My hands took some of the pain but the second blow took me down onto the hard earth floor and came fucking close to dislocating my shoulder.

'That's what I want, cooperation!'

I tensed, eyes closed, knees up to my chest, ready for more.

I didn't look up.

Bastard was a difficult man to ignore, but in my opinion it was well worth the effort. The heat on my back was good and I made the most of it while I waited for the starbursts in my head to burn out.

The two boys leaned down either side of me and heaved me back up onto the chair. I felt the cold steel of a blade against the right side of my chin. I flinched again, but was patted gently on top of my head.

'Relax, Nick. The guys are just having a little fun.' He'd put his Mr Nice Guy hat on, and although it was never going to fit, at least it made a change. 'They're just gonna cut the tape off you. Relax, son. We don't wanna risk slicing out those baby blues now, do we?'

They dug a pair of scissors into the gaffer tape and started to cut and pull. As the tape was yanked away, it took clumps of my hair and eyebrows with it. There was a positive side to it, though; I felt the blood rushing back into my arms.

'Sit up, Nick. Enjoy the party.'

I tipped my head a little and looked behind me. A patio heater fuelled by a king-size propane gas bottle was doing its bit for global warming, and the two boys were the shiny-headed bouncers I'd seen in the Pajero outside the Marriott. Both were still in black, and the one on the right was giving his gigs a polish.

'How you doing, Nick, you OK?' Bastard drew up another plastic chair on his side of the table, all sweetness and light. The weapon had gone but the gloves remained.

An aluminium thermos now sat between the lamps. The passports had gone.

'Go on, son. Smell the coffee. It's good and strong.'

I flexed my fingers, leaned forward, took the flask, and started to unscrew the lid. At times like this you've got to take whatever's on offer. You've no idea when it's going to come your way again. Besides, I'd been gagging for a brew for hours.

The two boys behind me shuffled from one foot to the other. I couldn't decide whether they were just enjoying the heat, or readying themselves for the next bout in the programme. Whatever, it was clear they were still in the red corner, and I was still in the blue.

The venue for tonight's entertainment was, as far as I could tell, an old farmhouse with exposed roof beams and tiles. The holes in the wall, where I guessed there had once been windows, were blocked with grey nylon turnip sacks like the one I'd been wearing.

I poured hot black coffee into two plastic cups and pushed one across the table with a smile. It smelled really good. 'Where's Charlie?'

He took a sip. He knew what I was doing. If I got drugged, he did too.

The coffee stung the cuts on my tongue, but so what? It

tasted as good as it smelled, and warmed me all the way down to my stomach.

'Any chance of my clothes?'

He shrugged. 'Sure.' He leaned back in his chair, lifted another grey sack from the floor and tipped my kit out in front of me.

I dressed quickly, checking my pockets as I went. No cash; definitely no passport. Nothing, apart from Baby-G. But then what was I expecting?

'Has Charlie got his?' Part of your job under interrogation is to look after your mates. Charlie was in bad enough shape already, without going hypothermic.

Bastard gave me a nod, and sampled a little more of his coffee. 'You guys look out for each other, don't you? I like that.' He put his cup back down on the table. 'Hey, I'm sorry about what happened just now. But you know –' he made a pistol with his fingers and pulled the trigger at me – 'finding out that Chuck had brought someone on the job with him, well, it made me a little crazy.'

He still had a supersize smile glued to his face, but I wasn't too happy about that. He'd been a little crazy the last time we'd met, and that hadn't taken us anywhere good.

8

His smile broadened. 'I like to know what's going on; I like to get things done my way. I just needed to let off some steam. Guys like us, we need to do that from time to time, don't we, Nick? You understand.'

I understood all too well. It wasn't about letting off steam; it was about showing everyone within a 500K radius who was boss.

I took my time tucking in my sweatshirt. This wasn't about the 110, Baz and the police. This was about something much more important to him, the job.

I sat back down. 'So help me out here ... Having Charlie dropped, once he'd done the safe. That's getting things done your way, is it?' I risked a smile too. 'Looks like it was just as well I came along.'

'I didn't have anything to do with that. Whichever fucks on the top floor – ' he pointed skywards – 'made that decision, they didn't ask me along. All I know is that Chuck was going to do the job, and I supplied the support, the kit, the information, that kinda thing. What do you think I am? A fucking animal? Hell, Chuck's one of us, one of the good guys.'

'Who's on the top floor? Military? The oil guys?'

He shook his head slowly and gave me a pitying look. 'You know what, Nick? I like you, but do you think I'm fucking stupid? Come on, man. All you need to know is: I saved your asses today. You're a wanted man. Any longer in that camp and you'd have been picked up and shovelled like shit into custody.' His eyes sparkled unpleasantly. 'Hey, I know what they do to guys like you in those cesspits. Not good, Nick, not good at all. They're fucking psychos in there.'

I was sure he was right, but my mind was elsewhere, trying to work out what to say next, how to keep well away from those particular cesspits. The one I was in was bad enough.

'Hey, enough of that shit. I'm sorry, really sorry, for monstering on you just now. But when I got the news about you two at the camp . . .' He laughed a little too loudly and took another mouthful of brew. 'I guess it's kinda worrying having a pistol to your head. But you should be thanking me for not letting you get handed over. Those guys in the camp? They got really pissed when they found out you weren't no fucking terrorist.' His jowls quivered. He was enjoying every minute of this. 'Hey, can you believe that?'

I could, actually. If they had been able to stick me with the terrorist label, I'd have been halfway to Guantanamo Bay by now.

I wondered why he hadn't said anything about the laptop bag. Or the papers and tape. He must be saving it up for later.

'But, you know what, Nick? You did a helluva job saving your asses out there, considering the problems you had.'

This wasn't the Bastard I knew. But then, this wasn't Bastard – this was just a good old boy fronting a set of interrogation techniques, and me shutting up until I needed to speak.

He was deploying what the manual called 'Pride and Ego Up'. He thought I'd be feeling devastated by the capture, and would respond to praise for a job well done. Any minute now he'd be telling me he understood my feelings, and we'd bond big-time over a few more cups of coffee.

But what he didn't know was that my pride and ego had been well and truly hung out to dry more years ago than I cared to remember. He'd have to dig a whole lot deeper, if he wanted to find any traces of either.

I nodded to show how glad I was that he understood me. 'We did all right.' I got more brew down my neck. 'Who was that at the house and cemetery?'

'No idea.' Bastard shook his head slowly, as if Red Eyes, Stubbly and the man mountain with the machete had all dropped out of a clear blue sky. 'Whatever, those fucks sure messed up a good operation.'

He leaned across the table, nodding in agreement with himself as he pulled two cigars from his Gore-Tex jacket. 'People think it's a science, but they forget about the bit you can't control, and that's the target, right?' He offered me one and I gave a polite shake of my head. But I poured myself some more coffee and got it down my neck, just in case he decided he'd gone far enough with this and it was time to wheel in Bad Cop again.

He lit up and inhaled appreciatively. He seemed to have kicked his old tobacco-chewing habit. Maybe this was his idea of a healthier option.

Was he waiting for me to start gobbing off, trying to fill the dead space? If so, I was going to disappoint him.

No way would I respond to any of this by opening up and saying stuff that could dig me and Charlie a deeper hole. In a strange way, knowing there was somebody else in the shit with me for a change made me feel more confident, and I knew Charlie would be thinking the same. He wasn't going to let me down; I wasn't going to let him down either.

'You know what?' Smoke poured from his mouth. 'You turning up with Chuck like that? That was one big surprise. Yessir, he kept that set of cards pretty close to his chest. How's it working with you guys – you planning on splitting the money?'

I nodded. 'Down the middle.'

'That's one heap of change . . .' He sucked on the end of his cigar, as if he suddenly couldn't make up his mind whether to chew it or smoke it. 'But I think you should've got more, Nick. Seems to me you did the lion's share, getting you both out of the shit. Only fair, don't you Brits say?' He flicked away half an inch of ash. 'I suppose it was Chuck's idea to make this a two-hander?'

'Had to be, didn't it? Otherwise I wouldn't have known about it.'

It didn't sound like he knew anything about Charlie's disco hands. This time a thread of spit hung between cigar and lip as he drew the Havana away from his mouth.

If you're anywhere long enough, you tune into the environment. Every house feels strange the first time you go into it, but give it half an hour and you begin to feel at home.

That still wasn't happening to me here, though; the only familiar elements in this room were the hiss of the gas heater and the smell of cigar smoke.

9

He studied my face, waiting for me to say more.

But I wasn't going to fill any gaps, not while he was still trying to be my new best friend. Later, perhaps, when we got to the page in the manual that had pictures of crowbars and broken bones; that would be the time to gob off enough bullshit to try and keep him and his two Georgian mates off my back.

'Did Chuck tell you what the job was about?'

I pushed the mug away from me and nodded. 'Too many people messing about with pipeline security?'

'Yessir, they sure are. These Georgians are one corrupt bunch of motherfuckers.' He beamed over my shoulder. 'But hey, so what? What's new, fuckheads?' He continued smiling and nodding at the boys in leather behind me. 'Don't worry about those fucks, Nick. Hari and Kunzru there, they don't understand a word. They're so shit stupid they can't even tie their own shoelaces. Ain't that right, motherfuckers?'

I heard murmurs behind me. This was clearly Bastard's version of Partnership for Peace, and it was working just the way he liked it.

He leaned forward and took another puff. 'Yeah, damn right.' More smoke poured from his mouth. 'You're a pretty smart guy, Nick. I'm sure you wanna get this sorry business over with, and get home to your loved ones.' He clenched the cigar between his teeth and treated me to his widest grin yet. 'And I'm with you on that one, pal. This is my last job. I got sun and sand to retire to, rolling cigars on dusky senoritas' thighs – you understand where I'm coming from?'

He waved the cigar expansively at me. 'You know what, Nick? I should have been more careful when I went to meet with Chuck, then we might not have found ourselves in this . . . predicament.' He paused, and gave me a conspiratorial look. 'I bet the tapes were your idea, eh? Trust Chuck to bring along another guy just as smart. You guys are killing me.' He stood and shook his head in frank admiration.

Behind me, Hari and Kunzru shifted impatiently. I heard the rasp of a match and caught a blast of sulphur at the back of my throat.

Bastard delved around in his Gore-Tex and pulled out my dark blue passport. It was so new, the embossed gold US eagle on the cover glinted in the light of the hurricane lamp. 'Not been a citizen long, have you?'

'No.'

'What're you involved in, stateside?'

'I used to work for a marketing company. They got me citizenship. But I was made redundant a while back, so here I am with Charlie. Can I see him?'

'All in good time, son. How did you get caught up in this line of work? You ex-military? You tapped into that broker guy, back in the UK?'

It was pointless lying. Of course I was, or Charlie wouldn't have hired me. 'I knew Charlie and the broker in the army. Charlie asked me if I wanted work. I did. A dollar doesn't go far these days, especially when you haven't been earning for a while.'

He nodded, not believing a word of it; on that score, at least, we were even. 'I got a problem you can help me with, Nick.' He picked a speck of tobacco leaf from his lip and studied the wet end of the cigar a little too carefully for more stray bits. 'You can understand I'm kinda nervous; Chuck tells me he has two tapes of the hotel meets. You were about to say the same, no?'

He didn't give me time to answer – not that I had any intention of doing so.

'He also says you've got the very thing we –' he gestured with his hand as if we were all in this together – 'are in this fucked-up country for . . .'

I did my best to look completely blank.

'Those papers . . .'

What was he saying? That he didn't have them?

'You see, those papers . . . well, the people I work for really need to get their heads around whatever they contain. And those tapes? I could find myself in a very embarrassing situation if they go public . . . it'd kinda fuck up my retirement plan.'

I could imagine that a video showing someone handing over the kit found in Baz's boot, and then talking about the job, would fuck up any kind of plan, let alone a retirement one.

He ramped up the smile to full megawatt capacity. If he wasn't careful, his face was going to explode. 'I need you guys to help me out, right? You're just too smart for me, what can I say?'

He leaned across the table and steepled his fingers, cigar and all. That smile must have been killing him. 'Why don't we clear this business up tonight, and we can all be on a flight out of this goddamned shithole of a country first thing?'

Hari and Kunzru shuffled their feet again and I prepared for the worst. It must have shown.

Bastard relaxed. 'Don't worry about those fucks just yet, son.

I'm suggesting an easier way out. What about it, Nick? What do you say?'

What I said was nothing. He was doing a good job of hiding it, but he was hurting. Fuck him, he wasn't getting any help from me.

'Nick, we all need to get out of this place. But if you're gonna fuck me up the ass, there'll be nothing I can do to stop these two doing what they do best. I can't let that stuff be out there – you understand that, don't you?'

I did understand. I understood he was flapping. What had Charlie done with the papers and tape? The only place I could think of would have been checked by a finger and a tube of KY. 'Let me talk it over with Charlie, see what he thinks.'

'He's already told me he'll do whatever you say. I'm trying to be reasonable with you. Fuck him, man – you gotta start thinking of yourself. You're the one on the TV; you're the one ID'd at the cemetery. He's laughing.' His throat was tightening with frustration. 'You're a wanted man, Nick. Every man and his dog is out there looking for you. Him? He's got no face. He can walk . . .'

His gaze became still more intense, but the cracks were beginning to show. It was a bit like watching a volcano starting to erupt. 'I'm your way out. Where can you go, what can you do, unless I help you? You got no passport, you got no goddam cash. And I'm the only one standing between you and those Georgian fucks out there looking to nail your ass. I can make it happen, Nick – either way.'

He was scraping the barrel. He'd tried the pride and ego thing; tried to be really nice with it, but now he was jumping straight into Pointing Out the Futility, to make me see all hope was lost. But the only thing I could see was Bastard moving into territory he felt more comfortable with, the land of the out-and-out arsehole.

I still didn't answer.

'You're fresh out of options, guy. I can get these two to drive you to Tbilisi right now and hand you over to the fucking animals who call themselves the police in this sorry town . . . I can make things happen, good or bad.'

He patted the passports in his jacket. 'You're in a deep hole, my friend, but I'm throwing you a rope. I can get you out and back stateside. I'm running out of ways here to explain I'm the only one who can do that for you.'

Now he was trying the incentive approach, and after that there was really only one place he could go. We were running out of road.

I leaned forward and down, and tied my bootlaces. I didn't want to lose them in the course of what I was pretty sure was about to happen. Then I looked up and nodded. 'I'll need to talk to Charlie.'

He jumped up and slammed his fist on the table. The flask and cups went flying. Even the guys behind me took a step back. 'You fuck! I want those papers and tapes! Give me! Your face is on every TV screen in Georgia . . . You're in deep shit . . . The Georgian police are screaming for your blood . . . Unless you do exactly what I say, I'll hand you right over to them . . . You tell me where they are now, or I'll rip your fucking heart out – you hear me, boy?'

Eyes down, I kept my jaw tight, clenched my teeth, waited for the punches. This time it was Fear Up, and it was working well, because this was what he was born for.

'Sit up, before I make you.' He perched his knuckles on the table like an ape, nostrils flared and whistling as his over-weight body sucked in oxygen to fuel the outburst.

His gut heaved as he leaned towards me. 'Things will get very painful, very soon, man. You're leaving me no choice.'

'Let me talk to Charlie, square things away.'

His reply was half-shout, half-scream. '*You got absolutely nothing to talk about.*' His words echoed round the walls and his fists came off the table. He pointed at me with a finger the size of a sausage. 'You're getting me fired up, man.'

He stormed round the table and I tensed every muscle, ready to take it. He swung an open-handed slap across the side of my head. The force of it took me straight to the ground.

My head spun. Stars burst in front of my eyes. Instinctively, I curled into a ball.

I sensed him bending towards me. The gust of cigar breath told me I wasn't wrong. 'Give up the tapes, give up the papers. I got contacts – high-up, government contacts – that can make good things happen for you. Think about it, asshole. Think about it while I go back to Vasiani and smooth out the mess you made with the army. And you know what? It's those contacts who are saving your ass now so you got a chance to do the right thing.'

He passed behind me on his way to the door. I relaxed, and a second later his cigar breath exploded just inches from my face. 'Me? I'm going back to the real world tomorrow, so I gotta clean things up here one way or another.'

He took a slow breath, calming himself down. 'Tapes and papers, by the time I get back. Or these two fucks will rip them out of you before you spend the rest of your fucking miserable life in a Georgian shithole jail.'

He disappeared behind me. 'Taking a fucking military vehicle?' He gave a hollow laugh. 'You call that smart?'

The door opened and closed and he was gone.

He must have signalled to Hari and Kunzru on his way out. They grabbed an arm each and lifted me to my feet. One picked up a hurricane lamp and I got shoved out through a second door into an overgrown walled area at the back of the building.

We moved along a muddy path. I caught a glimpse of stars through a break in the cloud, and another building, about fifty feet away.

Hari – or Kunzru – got busy with the rusty bolt on the door. As it creaked open, I heard a wagon spark up in the distance and drive away.

I was pushed into pitch darkness. The door slammed shut behind me, and the bolt scraped back into place.

I couldn't even see my hand in front of my face. I sat down on the hard earth, and tried to get my bearings. There wasn't as much as a pinprick of light. I listened as Hari and Kunzru made their way back to the propane-heated room we'd just come from, finally slamming the door shut to keep out the cold that was already eating into my bones.

There was a movement beside me and I almost jumped out of my skin.

Then a voice boomed, 'You took your time, dickhead. I hope you've got that three quid you owe me.'

PART NINE

1

I was so relieved to hear his voice I burst out laughing. I felt my way over on all fours, heading in the direction his voice had come from.

'He tried everything, the fat fucker.' He chuckled. 'We had Ego Up, Fear Down, the whole A to Z.'

I knew Charlie felt the same way I did, really happy to be reunited, no matter how much shit we were still in. Neither of us was going to say so, of course. If he hadn't made a joke, I would have.

'I gave him an eight point five for his Fear Up. Suited him better, in my view.' I parked my arse next to Charlie, and lowered my voice. 'Where the fuck are they?'

'HF 51 KN.'

'What? You lost the plot?'

'The duty wagon. I shoved the magazine under the back seat. Better to hide it and take the chance it's still out there than hand it to Whitewall on a silver plate, eh? All we got to do now is get out of here, go and find the wagon, and use all that shit to get us home. You up for it, lad?'

'Big-time. Especially the get out of here bit.'

He was joking, but he was right. Fuck knows what the papers said, but as Bastard had confirmed, they were important enough for every man and his dog to want control of them. I was a wanted man – and that stuff sounded as though it was just what I needed to get unwanted. The tape wouldn't hurt our chances either, and if Bastard really did have friends in high Georgian places, and a casting vote or two at Camp Vasiani, that stuff might be our ticket out.

'His name's Bastendorf. Remember him from Waco? We called him Bastard. He commanded Alpha Pod.'

'I like the name, but I had fuck all to do with the Pods. He's hardly one to forget, though, is he? He recognize you?'

'No, and I want to be well out of here before he does. He's going back to the camp. If they've searched the wagon and found the gear, we're good as dead. Which is the way Bastard and his mates wanted you in the first place.'

'You notice if the twins are carrying?'

'Not a clue. We've got to assume so, haven't we?'

He rubbed his bristles. 'What do you say we just call them to the door and take our chances? With that wagon gone, at least the head count's down.'

I rested my head against the rough stone wall. He was right; the longer we stayed here, the more the odds were stacked against us. 'That just leaves Hari and Kunzru watching *Coronation Street* . . . How are your hands? They strictly ballroom tonight, or up for a bit of action?'

'Sound as a pound.' He clapped them together, as if that proved anything.

'So, we checking out of here, or what?'

'Yeah, but not your way. Fucking hell, that's *Mission Impossible*. Let's check the obvious first.'

We started groping along the walls for another door, or a hastily blocked-up window. We worked our way back round to the main door without success. I gave it a shove, top and bottom. The only resistance was in the middle, but it was solid. It was going to take a few big shoulders' worth to open it.

I put my ear against the wood, but heard nothing the other side. I ran my hand along the wall on either side of the frame, and it closed around a loose protruding stone. I suddenly had a thought.

I gripped Charlie's coat. 'Remember the Stoner in Colombia? That could be our way out.'

'Well fucking hell, you're not just a nice pair of buttocks, are you, lad?'

We got down on our hands and knees and felt around on the ground for more loose rocks. For this to work, we were going to need a couple each, big enough to fit in the palm of our hands.

Something the size of a brick would be the business.

2

Back in the late '80s, Charlie and I had been part of Thatcher and Reagan's 'first strike' policy in Colombia. The SAS were sent as advisers to help identify and destroy the cartels' drug-manufacturing plants in the rainforest.

We patrolled suspected areas, putting in OPs, planning attacks. We weren't supposed to carry out the attacks ourselves; that would have been one very hot political *patata*. We were there to aid and guide, usually one of us to every ten local anti-narcotics police.

Every time we gave the bad guys a slap on the wrist, they'd bring in the media and the politicians to celebrate, and we'd melt into the background and go and have a brew. The snappers were never told about an attack in advance. There was so much corruption that if you reported a sighting of a DMP, everyone on site would have evaporated in less than the time it took to snort a couple of lines of marching powder.

Even as it was, the attack helicopters would fly over the target compound, more often than not, on their way to pick us up. They didn't stop far short of trailing a banner advising the Cali and Medellin boys to leg it.

The day Charlie and I encountered the guy we came to call the Stoner, there'd been an operation that had gone as chaotically as normal. Most of the police had been chewing on coca leaves wrapped around a sugar cube, flapping big-time because they didn't want to get shot at. Half of them were only good for barking at the moon by the time the attack went in.

We didn't normally end up with too many prisoners during these attacks. The players stood and fought, and eventually got dropped, which suited us just fine. But this particular time one literally fell into our hands, because he'd been helping himself a bit too liberally to the merchandise. He was so out of it he didn't know if he was in the jungle or on the first manned flight to Mars.

While we waited for the circus to arrive, we put him into one of the 'factories', long sheds made of wood and sheets of wriggly tin, with long, low-troughed channels where the coca was laid out and made into paste. It wasn't exactly watertight as a detention centre. The one Charlie and I were in now was better.

Stoned out of his brain, he was still sharp enough to grab a rock in each hand. Arms windmilling frantically, he made a run from the hut to the treeline, taking down anyone who came within range.

The four of us from the Regiment had been sitting around, making a brew; watching the police do a bit of foraging in the generator-run fridges and dead men's wallets.

The cokehead had three guys down with severe lacerations to the skull before they gave up trying to arrest him and stopped him permanently with 7.62mm. The mixture of surprise and aggression worked well for him, and if his brain hadn't been so fried he might have got away.

We scrabbled around for a moment or two, but didn't have to look far. The walls were in bad shape, and the mortar was loose in places. It wasn't long before we had a couple of big flinty stones each. I felt my way to the door and tested the side opposite the hinges, trying to visualize myself ramming it. Just thinking about it made my shoulder hurt.

Charlie stationed himself to my left.

'I'll try first, old man.' I reached out in the dark, to move him back a little further. 'I'll give it three or four goes, then it's your turn. Once we're out into that courtyard and we're not stopped, it's got to be over the wall and take it from there. If we get split, let's be outside the Marriott every evening, somewhere within reach of that bus stop. Wait an hour between nine and ten. If we don't meet up after three days, we're on our own. OK?'

'Done,' he said. 'Now stop waffling and get on with it.'

'Listen . . .' I knew I was in danger of going soft in the head, but I wanted the stupid old fool to be sure of something. 'Before it all goes ballistic I just have to say . . . thanks for coming with me. You were a fucking idiot not to catch that flight, but thanks anyway.'

'You trying to get me back for what I said at the cemetery? I know, I'm a good guy, now shut the fuck up and get on with it, before you ask Hari and Kunzru to join us for a group hug.'

I reached out and touched the right side of the door with an outstretched fist. That was one pace. I moved back another two, making sure I kept perpendicular to it. The last thing I wanted to do was to charge into the wall, or hit the door at an angle. Either way, it would give Charlie a good laugh, but probably destroy my shoulder.

Two or three deep breaths, then I dropped my right shoulder and charged. The crash as I connected was so loud they must have heard it in Tbilisi. I reeled. I felt like I'd been hit by a car.

Charlie yelled, 'Get on with it! Come on! Come on! It's noisy now, stop mincing about.'

I took another three paces back, closed my eyes and ran again. It hurt like fuck, but the door definitely moved.

Charlie was straight in my face. He sprayed me with spit. 'And again! Again! Come on! Get on with it!'

Three paces back and *bang*. The door shifted a bit more and I sank to the floor in pain. I rolled to the right, out of his way. 'You go! You go!'

He crashed into it and the door immediately folded in on itself. The hinges had given way before the bolt.

I got up behind him, the pain in my shoulder and back masked for the time being by the adrenalin that was pumping around my body. We more or less fell into the undergrowth which lined the yard.

Two hurricane lamps jerked to and fro in the darkness as Hari and Kunzru bomb-burst out of the interrogation room.

I started running at them, windmilling like a man possessed.

The Georgians closed and I lost sight of Charlie as he went for the first one. The second got the contents of my left hand across his neck, or maybe his collarbone, I didn't know, didn't care. He screamed out as the rock in my right crushed his gigs against his face. The lamp slipped out of his grasp and I scored another hit on the back of his shoulder as he followed it down to the mud.

I kept swinging. I had to keep moving, keep hurting. My arms cartwheeled like a boxer on amphetamines.

I felt a hand grab my leg and I kicked it away. I brought both rocks down onto the back of his neck. The hurricane lamp rolled away, throwing wild shadows against the walls.

'Shit, Nick . . .'

Charlie was in pain.

He was lying next to a limp body, trying to get up off the ground, but his left leg wasn't helping. I couldn't see any blood, but it was fucked. The body below me writhed in agony, too preoccupied with his injuries to care about us any more.

I shouted out to Charlie. 'See if your one's got the keys! Keys! Keys! Keys! Money, anything.'

I fumbled in the pockets of my one's leather jacket and found a wallet, picture ID, empty holster on his belt, loose change and house keys. Charlie had more luck. 'I've got them! I've got them!'

I picked up the lamp and cash and scrabbled around to find my boy's weapon. It was a revolver, well past its best-before date, but it should still do some damage to whoever it was pointed at. I jammed it into my jacket and ran over to Charlie. He was trying to drag himself up the wall.

'Keys, where are the keys?'

I took them from him, hoisted his left arm around my shoulder and dragged him into the interrogation room.

We'd obviously interrupted a rather cosy evening. The radio was blasting out the Georgian Hot Hundred, and there were steaming mugs on the table, along with a car battery and a set of jump leads. It didn't take much imagination to work out how the boys planned to entertain themselves later on.

Charlie took in the brews. 'Stop, stop.' He poured them both into the empty thermos and we carried straight on out to a Lada estate. It wasn't locked.

I helped Charlie into the front right and eased myself behind the wheel. We were soon doing a twenty-five-point turn as I tried to head it back down the track.

Panting for breath, Charlie ripped open the glove compartment and checked it for anything useful.

I looked over at him. 'What happened?'

Charlie gave a not-so-convincing laugh. 'Slipped on the stones. I can't believe it. My ankle, I've twisted the fucking thing.'

'We'll sort it. You get any money? Weapon?'

'Got both.' His nose wrinkled. 'Oh fuck, I hate the smell of wet dogs.'

3

My foot hit the floor as soon as we reached the tarmac, and the Lada's engine made an awful lot of noise while it thought about responding. Eventually the speedo edged around the dial. I didn't think we were going any faster, but at least it made us feel better.

Charlie put the light on to check his badly cut left hand. It looked as if some of the flint had splintered and gone into his palm, but there wasn't much he could do about it, except apply pressure by ramming it against his leg. He opened the wallet I'd thrown at him with his right, and pulled out cash and a laminated ID card.

'Look at old fucking bone-dome here.'

The card belonged to Hari Tugushi. A declaration in Paperclip, Russian and English confirmed his official accreditation by the Georgian government.

Charlie wound down his window and lobbed Hari's wallet out into the night. Kunzru's soon followed before we got stuck into the brew, trying not to spill any as the Lada rattled down the road.

'You see that battery, lad?'

'Yep.' I didn't want to think about it too much.

'Wouldn't want those wires attached to your bollocks, would you?'

'No.'

'They wouldn't have managed mine, of course. Those clips were way too small.'

I smiled at him. 'Makes you think though, doesn't it? These guys weren't fucking around. If they had their way, you'd never see Hazel and the grandkids again.'

'It's not ideal, lad.' He shrugged. 'But I'm dead anyway, remember? It's different for you.' He paused. 'Don't waste any time fantasizing about that little box-head of yours, though – you should be working out how to get us across the border. It's your big chance to show the world what you picked up from the master.'

'That's the thing . . .' I hesitated. 'I have been worrying. I have been thinking about her. It's the first time something like that has ever worried me. You've had it your whole life, haven't you?'

He shifted about in his seat. 'Fucking hell, don't tell me you're finally thinking of joining the human race?'

'How did you mix it? You know, "What the fuck am I doing here? I'd rather be at home doing I don't know what, mowing the grass or finding the cat, or something"?'

'It was all about trying to hang on to the balance. And that meant finding somebody like Hazel, somebody who understood what was going on in this thick head of mine, and was prepared to live with it. But it's a partnership, lad, which is one of the reasons she's going to be pissed off with me at the moment. After all those years, she thought she'd served her time, just like me.'

He had another look at his bleeding hand. 'But it's that fucking stallion in the paddock, Nick; that's what got to me. And with these fucking things starting to behave as if they've got a mind of their own – well, I just had to do it without her this time. If you know they understand what's going on, even if they disagree, you don't have to worry about the Hazels of this world when you're in the shit. You know they'll be counting on you to use what brain you have to get out of the shit and get back home . . .' He tailed off. 'Make any sense?'

I nodded. 'Suppose so.'

'Good. Remember to write it down, lad. Something else you've learned from the expert.'

We must have been travelling for about twenty minutes along the valley floor when the Lada's engine started to groan and we headed uphill. As we approached the crest, I killed the headlamps and edged forward, hoping not to see a VCP looming out of the darkness below us.

It was worse than that. Less than a K away was a large cluster of American lights illuminating the rows of twenty-man tents and Portakabins. A few Ks beyond that, on the higher ground, was another light cluster. But these belonged to the Russians.

'Vasiani,' I muttered. 'I suppose at least we know where we are.'

Charlie looked up from his first aid. 'We'll have to bin Turkey for a while, lad. We need that gear back.' He nodded down at the lights. 'Listen, it'll be suicide trying to get in there and find the duty wagon. I say we go for it in the morning. At least we know where it'll be. Let the fucking thing come to us.'

'You think that wagon's going to be back on the road?'

'Course – that thing's gonna last longer than me, lad. Whoever's running the transport pool down there would already have slapped on new tyres and done a jet spray under the arches. Come on, it's a fucking army, isn't it? What they holding it back for, forensics?'

He was right. It was the duty wagon and that was that. Every vehicle was allocated to something or other, and if this one had done a bit of cross-country, so what? That was what they did.

Charlie kept his eyes down. 'He tell you he was leaving tomorrow?'

'Yeah – more of the futility stuff, I thought.'

'Maybe, maybe not. But I know I'd want to get the fuck out of town if I didn't have control of whatever we got in the back of that 110 – wouldn't you?'

He turned to me and I could make out just a little of his face in the ambient light from the valley. 'It'll be a fucker, but all the more reason to go to the airport, no?'

Two or three sets of headlights fired up and moved around inside the camp. Then one of them broke away and headed towards the main gate.

'We'd better assume the twins had phones, Charlie boy. We got the Russians or that VCP to get past. Or – you want to get out and leg it? Even you'd be better cross-country than this thing.'

Charlie reached for the dash, smearing blood onto the plastic as he started rocking backwards and forwards in a not terribly serious attempt to make the Lada go faster.

He caught my expression. 'Russians. Got to be done. I'm not hopping over these hills all fucking night or risking bumping into that squaddie I ripped apart.'

I put my foot down. The acceleration was so feeble that his rocking actually seemed to help.

'That's it, lad – to boldly go where no Lada has gone before.'

I changed down into third, trying to get a burst on. The engine whined, but that was about all it did. I rammed the gearstick back into fourth.

My eyes strained to pick out the holes in the road. I didn't get much joy from the Lada's headlights – even on full beam they only lit up about two feet in front of us. The junction right was coming up. The other set of headlights was coming fast down the track towards it.

If we didn't get past first, the other wagon would block us off.

'Come on! Keep it going!' Charlie rocked as if he was having a fit.

There was nothing I could do but keep the car pointed in the right direction and ram my foot down.

By the time we reached the junction the engine was not too far short of cardiac arrest. The other wagon's headlights were immediately to our right, about four hundred metres away.

Flecks of saliva sprayed me as Charlie urged us on. 'Keep going, lad, come on.'

The engine groaned again as we started to head uphill. It wasn't steep, but it was clearly steep enough.

The whole vehicle shook as we rumbled over the rough tarmac and I threw the wheel left and right to swerve around the potholes.

'That's it, lad. Keep going . . .'

The other headlights came to the junction and turned to follow. It didn't take long for them to start closing in.

The lights of the Federation camp were less than a K away. I changed down to try to get a few more revs out of this fucking thing, my face almost against the windscreen as I tried to read the road.

Charlie checked behind. 'It'll soon be in spitting distance, lad. Keep that foot down.'

As if I needed telling.

Into fourth. The engine squealed.

The Russians' floodlights were getting closer, but the hill was getting steeper.

Our speed dropped. Into third. A burst, then slowing.

Into second. We both jerked as the gear kicked in and the engine screamed.

'It's a Pajero, Nick! Got to be Bastard!'

Even as he said it, the 4x4's lights flooded the inside of the Lada and we got the first nudge. It actually speeded us on our way.

'Is it Bastard? You sure?'

Charlie was still twisted in his seat. 'Who gives a shit? Just keep your foot down!'

Another slam into the back. Another jolt forwards. If it was Bastard, maybe they'd do without the helis. That had been all about the duty wagon, not his shit.

Not far to the Russians now, maybe four hundred.

The next collision was to the rear nearside. The back of the Lada slewed to the right. All I could do was keep the front wheels facing forwards and my foot on the floor.

The back fishtailed and I spun the wheel like a lunatic.

'He's backing off, Nick, he's backing off. Well done, lad, just keep those fucking wheels straight.'

We were coming up to the Russian camp's fence line.

I checked the rear-view. Charlie was right, the headlights were receding. Whoever it was, he was bottling out. Charlie checked behind us one final time, then relaxed back into his seat.

The Federation flag fluttered high over the floodlit main gate. Four fresh-faced guards stirred in their sentry posts, and started to prepare a traditional Russian welcome. They were in camouflage uniforms and helmets, AK assault rifles slung across their chests. They stared at us in a certain amount of confusion as we gave them a cheery wave.

'Maybe we should stop,' Charlie said, laughing. 'One of the lads might fancy making us an offer for the car.'

'You can leave it to him in your will, you stupid old fucker.' The lights from both the camps disappeared and we dropped into lower ground. 'Sooner I get you back, the better.'

4

Monday, 2 May

The line of taxis outside the terminal hadn't moved much in the hour since first light. When the odd cab did leave the front of the rank, the drivers behind didn't start their engines to shuffle forward, they just got out, leaned back in through the window, and pushed.

I had the trigger on the terminal entrance from the other side of the road. I was past the three garden sheds, sitting on the concrete between overflowing rubbish skips and four old abandoned buses in the small, potholed car park. I blended in well; I was wearing a black woollen hat I'd found in the boot of the Lada, that smelled like it had been worn by a wet bloodhound. The big ear flaps made me look like one too, but it helped hide some of my face.

Blue-and-whites had been cruising past every few minutes, and one was static right now by the sheds. The two cops inside drank coffee and smoked.

Charlie and I had come right into the lion's den, but there was no other way. Our only chance of retrieving the papers and tape was to get into the duty wagon. There were two fixed points where we knew it would be during flying hours – at the camp and at the airport.

We could have tried to wave it down on the road, but SOPs for military vehicles usually precluded them from stopping – and after the stunt we'd pulled yesterday, every driver would be on red alert. A hijack was out of the question; instead of dead ground, you need an open stretch of road, so you can identify the vehicle before you hit it in the dark. Our current plan wasn't perfect, but it was the only one we had.

I checked Baby-G. It was just after eight. Charlie had hobbled into the terminal ten minutes ago to get into position. He had to take the lead; I couldn't run the risk of being recognized.

The idea was simple: the wagon turns up to drop off or pick up; Charlie sees it through the glass; walks out, lifts it, heads into the car park behind me; I'd jump in and we'd head for the border. This time he wouldn't just bark a whole lot of orders, but rely instead on his weapon. He had a little 9mm Makharov, the sort of thing James Bond used to tuck into his dinner jacket.

Assuming there weren't any delays, all the international flights were gone by midday. If Bastard showed up for one of them it would be one fuck of a big bonus for us, even if the 110 didn't show.

We had gone through dozens of what-ifs. What if he turned up before the 110? We had to hold him until it came, and use him to get the gear out. What if he turned up after the 110? Well, we would never know because we'd be gone – unless Charlie managed to find out what flight he was on.

What it boiled down to was that we would have to take the situation as it came – otherwise we'd still be out in the cuds a week on Wednesday, going through thousands of options. Fuck it, let's just get on with it and get out of here.

My revolver was also Russian, and looked like it had seen action in the Crimea. It still had seven big 7.62 rounds in the cylinder, and that cheered me up a lot. Given that our plan stank worse than the dog blankets, it was the only thing that did.

I slumped down against a skip, sliding my legs under the one in front of me. The guys in the blue-and-white finished their brew and drove off. I craned my neck to look along the building. Two more policemen had taken up position outside the terminal. After yesterday's nightmare, word had obviously got round.

After dumping the Lada in the city at about five this morning, we'd hidden up and waited for the place to come alive a little before approaching a taxi. Between them, Hari and Kunzru had had exactly 127 Lari in their wallets – about $70, as it turned out. The taxi driver had pocketed about ten, and Charlie had custody of the rest. He was going to need it to grease a palm or two at the check-in desks to see if his best mate Jimmy Bastendorf was leaving today. Charlie wanted to arrange a birthday surprise for him when he got home and wasn't sure when he was flying. Was it today, or maybe tomorrow? In a dirt-poor country, even loose change can get you anything.

A rust- and grime-covered yellow bus pulled up at the stop outside the terminal, its exhaust pumping out diesel fumes you could cut with a knife. Most of those disembarking looked as though they were airport workers, but there were one or two others with suitcases. The airport was coming to life.

Charlie appeared through the fumes, lurching across the road like Long John Silver. His hand had been OK when he left me, just cut and sore, but his ankle had swollen like a balloon, even though I'd tried to strap it up with a couple of strips of blanket.

He had a newspaper in his hand. 'Bastard's off to Vienna, we've got him.' He lobbed it in my direction and it fell between the skips as he carried on past. 'Here's the bad news.'

He had to do a circuit now, maybe check something out in the car park. Nobody just exits a terminal and crosses the road, only to cross straight back ten seconds later.

I crawled over to the paper, then back to where I could still keep trigger in case there was a drama. If ten blue-and-white Passats screamed up to the terminal and dragged Charlie away, I needed to know.

He'd chucked me a copy of the *Georgian Times*, the English-language paper. Folded inside was a large bar of chocolate. I ripped the foil off and popped a chunk into my mouth, but when I scanned the front page my throat went dry.

Most of it was covered by a grainy photograph of the yard in front of Baz's house. The banner headline screamed: *'SAINT' SLAIN!*

It went on in a similar vein, to bemoan the savage killing of the most honest and incorruptible public servant the country had ever seen. This wasn't the picture Bastard had painted, but that wasn't much of a surprise.

A force for all that was good and just has been callously cut down, it cried. *Who has perpetrated this evil deed? The finger of suspicion can point in many directions, all of which this country needs to cut out like a cancer.*

For weeks, the walls of St Zurab Bazgadze's house had been daubed with warnings not to pursue his crusade against corruption at all levels of government, the journalist wrote. *In our wretched country, many words spell wrongdoing – words like 'minister' and 'militant', 'business' and 'privatization', 'pipeline' and 'oil'.* It seemed Baz had been a thorn in the side of them all.

Charlie still hadn't come back from his hobble-past. Blood pulsed in my neck as I read on.

The two other dead bodies found at Baz's house had been identified as members of the militant gang behind the recent siege in Kazbegi. But who were the other two men caught on CCTV, one masked, one unmasked? Were they now in possession of the affidavit which the Saint had been due to swear in front of the cameras for *60 Minutes*, exposing the rampant corruption in Georgian society?

According to a police insider, the safe in Bazgadze's house

had been found open, and the CCTV also showed one of the masked men taking a folder from the body of one of the militants. If this was indeed the affidavit that *60 Minutes* claimed to have been waiting to receive, then exposure of its contents would be very embarrassing for the government, as the programme was due to be aired on the eve of President George W. Bush's forthcoming visit.

I sat and chewed chocolate, my mind spinning. Good guy gets fucked over – nothing new there – but what had the militants been doing at Baz's house?

It got worse. The inside pages were teeming with maps and photographs.

TRAIL OF MURDER: SAINT'S CAR FOUND IN TBILISI ALLEYWAY – GRISLY CARGO

If there hadn't been a perfect artist's impression of me under the headline I might have laughed.

It was followed by a shot of the Audi up the track, with the boot open. Witnesses had seen two men drive it to the cemetery and load a body into the boot. Beyond that, apparently, was only 'murky speculation'.

I'd read enough. I refolded the paper and swallowed the last four chunks of chocolate.

That 110 couldn't arrive a minute too soon.

5

As Charlie got back to the terminal, a two-tone Pajero, silver bottom, dark blue top, sped past the main doors, one up. It was too far away for me to be able to ID the driver, but the sheer bulk of the silhouette at the wheel made me stay with it as it continued past the garden sheds.

I scrabbled along the skips and watched it turn into the car park. The Pajero bounced over puddles and potholes, heading towards the derelict buses closer to the terminal. The nearside wing was damaged. I had a feeling I knew why.

I lost sight of it behind the buses, and I turned back to scan the front of the terminal. Still no sign of the 110.

I heard a door slam behind the buses.

He'd have to cross a hundred metres or so of open ground before he got to the terminal. A straight line would take him very close to the skips. We were going to be in the shit if the 110 turned up right now and Charlie carried on implementing Plan A. The driver would have to come with us; we couldn't have any more of them running around the country.

No time to think. Bastard was waddling towards the terminal, dressed in the US business uniform for the over-fifties. He pulled an aluminium wheelie carry-on behind him. Whatever we had in those papers, it had got him all fired up. It would have been bad enough for him losing control of the papers Saturday night. But now? With the Istanbul and Marriott tapes out of his control as well, he definitely needed to do the same as us – just get the fuck out. I guessed he wasn't too anxious to land a starring role on *60 Minutes*.

I let him pass the back of the sheds, then crawled out from between the skips to get behind him.

A roll of fat quivered above his shirt collar. Pulling my hat down low, I followed in step.

'Oi, Bastendorf!'

I gave him a big happy face as I closed in, but stayed just beyond grabbing distance.

His face clouded. 'How the fuck do you know my—?'

'I've got Kunzru's weapon. I want our passports.'

He rolled his head back and laughed. Maybe he was amused by the hat.

'Passports, I want them.'

'Get the fuck! I shout out right now and you're history, ass-hole. I'm walking. What you gonna do, pull steel and gun me down in front of the fucking terminal?'

'Yes.'

You never make a threat that you can't carry out, and Bastard knew it. He could see my hand over the front of my jacket.

His nostrils flared. He breathed very slowly and deeply. 'I burned them.' He enjoyed telling me that.

Over Bastard's shoulder, I could see a 110 pull up in front of the terminal, its rear doors already opening. Charlie would be out any minute. He didn't know we had the Pajero now; that there was now no need for desperate measures. All he had to do was bluff his way into the back and retrieve the gear.

Maybe Bastard had the passports on him, maybe not. We'd soon find out. I nodded over his shoulder. 'You're going to turn round and head for the one-ten.'

'The what?'

'The Land Rover. Move.'

I came up on his left, eyes peeled for Charlie. Cars and buses moved between us and the 110, temporarily blocking the view.

Bastard gobbed off far too confidently for someone this deep in the shit. 'We going back to town? You thinking of turning yourself in, or do you just like stealing military vehicles?'

The wheels of his carry-on rumbled along behind us as we made our way to the road. Two guys stepped out of the 110, luggage in hand. Charlie would come out as soon as he saw them check in.

'Get your arse moving. Go and tell the driver you were in the duty wagon a few days ago. Pull up the back seats, tell him you've lost something. I don't give a shit what you say, just pick up what's under there.'

He stopped in his tracks. 'You fuck!'

I pushed him forward and carried on walking, eyes peeled for Charlie steaming through the terminal doors. 'If you say anything to the driver or start fucking about, I'll drop you. Understand? I've got nothing to lose.'

'Fuck you.'

'I'll take that as a yes.'

Charlie emerged from the terminal. His gaze was fixed intently on the 110 a few metres ahead of him.

We started to cross the road and I could now see the front plate. HF 51 KN. Different driver but the same vehicle, apart from a brand new set of tyres.

Charlie was closing in on the driver's door when he finally pinged us. I shook my head and he carried on hobbling.

Two police walked out of the terminal, one of them tapping a couple of cigarettes from a pack.

I could see Bastard weighing up his options as they came towards us, sharing a lighter. His eyes bounced between them and me.

I couldn't turn away or try and hide my face. It would only attract their attention.

Fuck it; if they pinged me, there was nothing I could do about it.

I was on autopilot. It was the only way.

They passed us. Then we passed Charlie, who was waiting for a bus to pull out so he could cross over to the sheds.

Bastard looked at me. 'What I'm reaching for now is my wallet, OK?'

I held back a metre or so as he approached the driver's window. He started talking even before the guy had finished winding it down.

The two policemen had stopped by the terminal entrance and were leaning against the wall, enjoying their smoke break.

Bastard thrust his ID in the driver's face. I could tell he was talking from the way the roll of fat wobbled against his collar.

I concentrated on the driver's face. Young, Latino. Most importantly, betraying no sign that Bastard was telling him the truth.

Bastard moved around to the rear doors of the 110. The Latino turned and leaned across to help him lift the seats.

Bastard emerged with the magazine in his hand and tapped a goodbye on the window. We turned and headed back the way we had come. The policemen hadn't moved, but they had stopped chatting and seemed to be watching Bastard closely.

I held out my hand for the magazine.

Bastard hesitated. 'Do I get my flight now? Hey, I was going to let you go if you came up with the goods.'

'Keep walking. We've got plans for you.'

I heard laughter and out of the corner of my eye I saw one of the policemen pinch a fold of skin on his neck and give it a good wobble.

A second or two later, it started to rain.

6

Nobody talked as I drove the Pajero away from the airport perimeter. You could cut the atmosphere with a gollock. I drove; Bastard was next to me in the passenger seat. He knew I had a pistol tucked between my legs out of his reach but within mine, and that Charlie had another behind him, but there was no knowing what he might do if he saw an opportunity to escape. If I was him, I'd be gone the first chance I got.

I pushed the heater to full blast, to get rid of the condensation. It had only been a short walk back to the 4x4, but we'd all got drenched.

I'd given Bastard a physical search when we got in, but he didn't have the passports on him. Charlie was emptying his carry-on across the back seat.

I flicked the wipers from steady to rapid and threw Charlie a map from the side pocket. 'Which way?'

He opened it out. 'This is a fucking sight better than the one in the one-ten. Looks like just over two hundred Ks to the Turkish border.'

'Four or five hours, maybe, as long as we don't have to go off-road?'

He shook his head. 'As the crow flies. But I reckon the best route's south until we hit the pipeline, then follow it south-west.'

It was good thinking. What could be more normal than three Westerners mooching along that route – especially with official government accreditation in Mr Bastendorf's wallet? It looked like someone had gone mad with a rubber stamp, then added, in Paperclip and English, that he was a welcome guest in their country, and should be given every assistance in carrying out his important work for the government. The added bonus was the $450 he had tucked away to go supersize when he hit Vienna airport.

I felt safer now I was in a vehicle, but I knew it was an illusion. If we hit a checkpoint we'd still have to bluff it big-time and bank on Bastard getting us through. Our two pistols should help persuade him to do that. Besides, he might be the world's biggest arsehole, but he wasn't a fool. He was a survivor.

Bastard coughed up a mouthful of phlegm, and started unwinding his window. He gobbed it out through the two-inch gap.

'I don't remember saying you could do that.' My hand reached for the pistol. 'Don't make another move unless I say so, you understand?'

Bastard scoffed. 'You think that's scaring me? My mama done better.'

I concentrated on the road, barely visible through a near-solid curtain of rain.

My guess was, Bastard wasn't in the FBI any more – or at least, he certainly didn't carry any ID to say he was.

Charlie finished checking the carry-on. 'No mobile here either.'

Bastard stared straight ahead. 'I said I didn't have one. Why the fuck would I need one now? The local things don't work stateside, do they?'

'Heading home, were you? What happened to the dream of the dusky señoritas?'

'Go fuck.'

Even dog-legging it, we'd probably still get to the border well before last light, which would give us time to find a decent crossing point. I wasn't going to tell him yet, but Bastard was coming with us. Georgia was in the good lads' club with the USA these days, and probably had all sorts of pooling arrangements between police forces. Following Bush's 'If you're not with us, you're against us' doctrine, any enemy of Georgia's would be an enemy of America's, and right now I seemed to be top of Tbilisi's Most Wanted.

We skirted the city to the west and soon swapped the shiny new dual carriageway for a more familiar, knackered metalled road. Old guys sat behind tables at the verge, sheltering from the rain under trees and bits of plastic, trying to sell jugs and bottles of ancient engine oil.

Bastard scoffed. 'Fucking stuff's been through every truck in sight about sixteen times.'

Charlie and I didn't respond. Bastard was trying to draw us in. He'd tried aggression, and now he was trying to lighten the mood and get all chummy.

The road ahead was flanked by giant cubes of grey concrete. Rusting steel skeletons jutted through their flaking skin. There had been no pink or orange facelift around here. Washing hung from the windows, getting a second rinse.

Bastard tried again. 'I guess this particular boulevard didn't make it onto the presidential route.'

We continued to ignore him. If he thought we were going to be sharing toothbrushes by the end of this trip, he was receiving on the wrong frequency.

I zigzagged round puddles for a kilometre or two, then we hit a sign for Borjomi, 151 kms.

That cheered me up; the pipeline ran through Borjomi.

Dark cloud blanketed the high ground and I flicked on the

lights. We weren't the only vehicle on the road, and we were all competing in the giant pothole slalom. It could only be a matter of time before there was a pile-up in the gloom.

Puddles the size of bomb craters had claimed a couple of dilapidated Ladas. They still had exposed spark plugs, Charlie Clever Bollocks had explained to me, and flaked out nineteen to the dozen once they encountered a bit of moisture.

I glanced back at Charlie again. He seemed all right, no shakes, just sitting there, staring out of the window. Four or five hours from now, I could get him and his disco hands on a plane home.

7

The air con was still doing its stuff to keep the windscreen clear on the inside. We were well out of the suburbs, up in the high ground and shrouded in mist, when the tarmac stopped abruptly and we hit a wide gravel track.

Charlie sparked up from the back. 'How are Hari and Kunzru?'

Bastard shrugged. 'How the fuck should I know? I got the call; at least one of them was still breathing. I was heading back there when I saw you guys on the road. Anyway, fuck 'em. Welfare ain't my responsibility.'

The mist cleared as we wound down the side of the mountain. A wide, fast-flowing river sparkled in the sunlight below us. Apart from the vivid brown scar that cut across the lush green of the valley floor, we were back in *Sound of Music* country.

Bastard jerked his thumb towards the point at which the line of freshly turned earth cut back towards us and started to run level with the road. 'There's your pipeline.'

'Where's the metalwork?' I'd been expecting to see something above ground, as I had in the Middle East.

'They've buried it. Makes it a whole lot tougher to blow up.'

Charlie leaned between us. 'Our old mates the militants?'

'Militants, Kurdish separatists, Muslim extremists, Russian assholes, you name it. They all either want a piece of the action, or to use the thing as a bargaining counter.

'The Kurds wanna split from the Turks: you give us our country, we don't fuck with your pipeline.

'The Russians, well, they just want to fuck the pipeline up, period. Perestroika, my ass; the Cold War never ended for those guys.

'And closer to home, there's the Georgian politicos, doing side deals with whoever comes within reach – and charging the oil companies a fucking fortune to give the pipeline house room in the first place.'

Charlie nodded. 'And we have a few bits of paper tucked away explaining where our late lamented friend Mr Bazgadze fitted into all this.'

Bastard glowered at him. 'Don't count on it, asshole.'

The rain started again. I flicked the wipers back into overdrive, but still had to press my face against the windscreen to see where we were going.

Bastard squinted through the curtain of water ahead of us. 'But who gives a shit? My job was just making sure things ran real smooth.'

'Fucked up there then, didn't you?' Charlie tapped the package in his jacket pocket. He'd wrapped the camcorder tape and the documents from Baz's safe in a plastic bag he'd found in Bastard's carry-on. 'And I'm no expert here, but the local media seem to be painting a rather different picture than the one you gave us . . .'

Bastard couldn't help himself. 'Hey, I only told you what I'd been told myself.' He gave a deep, frustrated sigh. 'I'm not the decision-maker here. I'm like you guys; I'm a worker bee – a worker bee who just wants to get the fuck out of here.'

I'd promised myself to stay out of this, but my blood was

starting to boil. 'Worker bee, my arse. You're a fucking maggot. You feed off situations like this, and leave the real worker bees to pay the price.' I changed down to take a bend. 'Remember Anthony, the Brit you slapped around at Waco?'

He went quiet for a moment. The rain was now hammering so hard on the Pajero's roof it sounded like we were trapped inside a snare drum, but I could almost hear his mind whirring. 'Anthony? Anthony who? I don't remember slapping any Brit at Waco.'

'Yes, you do.' My eyes were fixed on the mud-covered gravel ahead. The Pajero was starting to slip and slide, and I had to fight the wheel to correct it. 'He designed the gas you used, but shouldn't have, remember? He committed suicide about a year afterwards. He couldn't live with the guilt.'

'Oh, *that* Anthony . . .' Bastard ran an index finger over his moustache. 'Sure I remember him . . . fucking Limey fag. He shouldn't have been there. Never send a boy to do a man's job . . .'

I swung the Pajero up a track that suddenly opened up to the left. We bucked over the pipeline towards a stretch of trees.

I shouted back at Charlie. 'Let's see if this arsehole's bollocks are as big as his mouth.'

I braked hard at the treeline, killed the ignition and shoved Bastard towards the passenger door. 'Get the fuck out! Now!'

I swivelled in my seat, leaned back against my door and kicked at him with both feet as he scrabbled for the handle. 'I was there, I was with Anthony. I saw the whole fucking thing . . .' I kicked him again as his door swung open and he slithered out into the mud.

He picked himself off the ground, his face a mask of fear and indignation. 'It wasn't me who gave the order. That was way above my pay scale.'

I followed him out while Charlie rummaged in the back of the wagon.

'I thought you'd got the message about that worker bee shit,'

I yelled through the rain. 'None of those kids stood a chance, and you enjoyed every fucking minute!'

'Bingo!' Charlie gave me the thumbs-up, slammed the rear door and headed for the Pajero's bonnet.

'Wait until I've climbed aboard him.' I brought my pistol up. 'I'm going to have this fucker.'

Bastard backed away until he was pressing against the front wing. 'Hey, I knew it wasn't right. I knew it was wrong to kill those people.' He raised his hands, half pleading, half trying to make me keep my distance. 'Those were American citizens . . . my own people . . .' He pointed at me. 'Our people.'

'Down! In the mud! Now!'

He slid down the side of the vehicle and slumped against the wheel. The rain kicked up the puddles all around him. We were both soaked to the skin. My sleeve weighed heavily on my arm as I raised my pistol to his head.

'Who are you working for?' My first kick caught him square in the ribs. 'Who gave the order to drop Charlie?' My second disappeared into the mountain of flesh that spilled over his waistband. 'What's in those documents? What the fuck happened at the house?'

Charlie had released the bonnet and was now standing on the other side of him.

Bastard heaved air into his lungs and his face tilted up towards me, eyes screwed up against the rain. 'What you gonna do, son? Pull that trigger? Fuck you, then. Just get on with it. '

Charlie shook his head, then leaned down and clipped one of the Pajero's jump leads onto the roll of fat above Bastard's collar and held the second against his ear.

Bastard screamed and his whole body shuddered. He collapsed like a rag doll, legs splayed out in the mud.

The jump lead was still clamped to his neck. Charlie handed me the other and slid into the driver's seat.

I gave Bastard another kick, just because I wanted to.

Charlie fired up the ignition, and gave the pedal a squeeze.

Bastard said nothing, just lay there whimpering, listening to the steady throb of the Pajero's engine, staring down at the mud. He was starting to get the message.

8

'Look at me.'

He kept his eyes down.

I jammed my clip against the top of his ear.

He squealed, arched his back and collapsed again.

I leaned over him. '*Look at me . . .*'

He stayed where he was, but this time his eyes came up to meet mine. Rain streamed off my chin and onto his face.

'This is very simple.' I waved the jump lead in his face. 'You talk, and I keep this away from you.'

He jerked his head to dislodge the crocodile clip from his neck, but it stayed right where it was.

I kicked his hand away as he tried to reach up and grab it.

When he started to talk, I could hardly hear him above the sound of the rain. 'It was a simple operation that got fucked up. We just needed those papers, no hassle, everything clean.' He scrabbled in the mud and hauled himself back up against the wheel. 'It's out of my hands now. That's why I was getting out of this shithole.' He stared into the trees.

I moved the clip back into his line of sight, and held it no more than a centimetre away from his nose. 'You're not answering the questions. Who the fuck are you working for? Who are these powerful friends of yours you said can make things happen?'

'The politicos, man. Same old story. The guys Bazgadze was gunning for. That's why they wanted what was in his safe. That's all I know.' He glanced up at me. 'And all I wanna know.'

'You still with the Bureau? Is this some covert FBI fuckabout we've been sucked into here?'

He shook his head slowly and his gaze dropped back towards the mud. 'Those fuckers spat me out four years ago. Chewed me up and spat me out, with just enough of an annuity to buy myself a cigar every Fourth of July. Why do you think I ended up in this goddam shithole?'

I wasn't buying the sympathy card, and brought the clip a fraction closer to let him know.

'I was in the job thirty years, and for what? Jack shit, man. So when these guys step in and offer me a retirement plan—'

'What happened at the house?'

'The guys I work for, there are six of them, OK? Partnership for Peace isn't high on their list of priorities; well, partnership gets their vote, but peace can go take a dump. They want to keep things exactly the way they are. US dollars are flying in by the planeload, and a lot of them get diverted their way. They pay the militants to threaten the pipeline, just to keep things on the boil. Nothing bad, nothing physical – just the occasional fire-work display. Nobody gets hurt. It's just good, old-fashioned commerce. I'm just there to—'

'Yeah, we know,' Charlie said. 'You're just there to smooth the way . . .'

Bastard looked up at him and risked a smile.

I kicked him. 'Get on with it.'

He slid his legs up as close to his chest as his gut would allow. 'This Bazgadze guy, he'd been getting more and more of a problem. The whole sainthood thing wasn't good for business. And neither was getting found out just before Bush arrives to rally the troops for the war on terror. So the plan was, steal the papers, find out what he knows. Lean on the guy. Warn him off . . .'

He raised a hand to the jump lead still clamped onto his neck. 'Can I take this thing off? I'm fucking helping you here.'

I shook my head. 'You're helping yourself. That still doesn't explain what happened at the house, or at the cemetery. Who the fuck were those guys?'

'Bazgadze wasn't any more popular with the militants than he was with my politicos. There's this fuck, Akaki, he runs them. He just couldn't wait. If Bazgadze had proof he was on the take, he wanted him dead. He's a fucking psycho, he's out of control. It's not the way to deal with guys like Bazgadze – he's a fucking god around here. It's gotta be subtle.'

'What, like you?'

The rain was so hard it felt like a madman with a staple gun was attacking the back of my neck.

Charlie wasn't happy – and not just with Bastard's explanation. 'We better start getting a move on.' He pointed beyond the trees, where mud and loose debris were breaking away from the side of the hill and gravity was doing the rest. 'The road's taking a pounding.'

I kicked Bastard to his feet.

'So what happens now?' he said.

'What happens now is you shut the fuck up, or we connect those jump leads to your bollocks. You're coming with us, and later on, when we're in Turkey and out of this shit, you're going to call a few of your high-powered mates. We're going to make a little deal, and this time you're going to be the broker.'

9

The curtain of water in front of us was now so solid I had to slow the Pajero to a crawl.

The noise was horrendous. We'd had to open all the windows, to try to deal with the condensation from our soaking clothes. The heater was going full blast, but it didn't stand a chance.

Bastard was trying without success to shift some of the mud off his clothes and skin. He looked like he'd just crawled out of the black lagoon. He paused mid-scrape and had a crack at getting back into the good lads' club. 'Hey, Nick, believe me, I'm sorry about that Anthony guy. I'm sorry about the whole goddam thing. It was a really heavy time.'

'But it didn't have to be, did it?'

Bastard fidgeted some more. 'It wasn't like that. Just think what would have happened if Koresh and his buddies had gotten away with giving the finger to the ATF. Law and order would've lost all credibility. A thing like that couldn't go unpunished. Anarchy, lawlessness – gotta be nipped in the bud, or you end up like this shithole.'

Rain crashed onto the car like breaking waves. The wipers were on full power, and still I couldn't see a thing.

Charlie had arranged himself across the back seat, weapon tucked under his arse, legs draped over the carry-on. It was one of those airtight, fireproof, everything-proof aluminium things that come with a lifetime guarantee and a thousand-dollar price tag.

I got to thinking about what Bastard had said when he was plugged into the mains, and it didn't stack up. When it came to being fucked over, I was the world's leading expert, and the smart money didn't say anything like Bastard wanted us to think it did. There was something a whole lot more serious going on here than a little light spring-cleaning before the US President arrived.

I kept an eye on the pipeline scar to our left; more often than not, now, it was the only way of telling we were still on the road. The river had burst its banks an hour or two ago, and raged along the bottom of the gradient to our right.

Bastard glanced over his shoulder and leaned towards me, as if he had a secret to share with his best mate. 'Nick, listen. What about you and me making a deal? Let me go with the papers and tapes when we get to Borjomi; I'll call my guys, see to it you're off the wanted list, and make everything cool once you two get into Turkey. We've had enough of this shit, don't you think?'

He nodded at Charlie, whose head was wobbling from side to side as I bounced the wagon along the track.

'Just tell him I got out for a dump and made a run for it. Hey, how's he to know . . .'

Things weren't looking good out there. Brown slurry cascaded off the high ground to our left, carrying rocks and broken branches across our path.

Bastard wasn't giving up. 'You and me, Nick, we're both really in deep shit. We're singing off the same hymn sheet here.'

'Why don't we start with *Swan Lake*, lad?' Charlie sparked up from the back. 'We'll hum it, you go jump in it.'

I glanced in the rear-view. He'd turned onto his side, knees bunched up, and was chuckling quietly to himself. 'You've got two problems with your plan, Fat Boy. One –' he tapped the top pocket of his jacket – 'it's all in here. Two, running isn't exactly your strong suit. You couldn't even bend over to run a bath, for fuck's sake.'

There wasn't time to laugh.

A river of mud ten metres wide sluiced off the hill and hit the wagon broadside, pushing us to where the road fell away to the river below.

I swung the wheel to steer us into the skid, but nothing happened.

'Charlie, out the wagon!'

The mudslide gathered weight and momentum, and started to spill in through the open windows.

I grabbed the edge of the roof and hauled myself out of the gap.

Bastard was sliding his fat arse towards the passenger door. He could look after himself.

The Pajero was beginning to tip. I wrestled the rear door open and dragged Charlie clear by the shoulders.

He tumbled out on top of me as the vehicle slewed another couple of metres, then finally succumbed to the sheer weight of mud and cartwheeled down towards the river.

A dozen or so metres away, Bastard struggled to get himself upright.

Charlie blinked as the rain lashed his mud-caked face.

'Papers and tape?'

Charlie tapped his pocket and nodded.

We both heard a sound like an approaching train.

I looked up, but before I could shout a warning the knee-high surge of mud and debris had gathered Bastard up and swept him over the edge.

PART TEN

1

The Pajero had landed upside down at the river's edge, five or six metres below us, doors open, windscreen smashed. It bucked and wallowed as water the colour of chocolate pounded against the wreckage. Any second now it would be snatched away and hurled downstream.

Bastard hadn't been any luckier. The river at this point was around thirty metres wide, and I watched as he floundered, went under, and bobbed up again about halfway across, almost indistinguishable from all the other lumps of debris swirling downstream.

I started ripping off my jacket.

Charlie rolled his eyes. 'Nothing we can do, lad. Fuck him. Anyway, we got Crazy Dave.'

I shook my head. Later, Bastard could die a slow and painful death, as far as I was concerned, but right now he was here, and Crazy Dave was a million miles away. 'He's our route out of this shit! He's got the contacts; he can get us over the border.'

There was nothing Charlie could do to help. His ankle was fucked, and the rest of him was falling apart. This one was down to me. I pulled my shirt out of my trousers and half jumped, half tumbled down the slope towards the maelstrom.

The water surged past at a fearsome pace, carrying all before it. Huge branches crashed over the rocks ahead of me.

There was a screech of tearing metal as the Pajero finally lost its grip and thundered downstream. I watched it for about a hundred metres, until the river bent sharply to the left and it disappeared.

And that was where I spotted him. The force of the current had carved out the subsoil for a ten-metre stretch along the far bank, exposing a latticework of tree-roots that gleamed white against the mud, like the ribs of a putrefying corpse. Bastard had his arm hooked through one of them.

He didn't stand the slightest chance of hauling himself up and out of the mud, let alone over the edge of the bank. There was no way I'd be able to either, and I hadn't spent a lifetime on the Big Mac diet.

I could see he was yelling at me big-time, but I couldn't hear a thing above the roar of the water.

I scanned the stretch of river between us. He must have fetched up where he was after being catapulted into it mid-stream. I'd need to enter the water much further up if I was going to have a chance of hitting the bank before I was swept in the wake of the Pajero, and on around the bend.

I scrambled over the mud thirty or forty metres upstream, past the jagged skeleton of a small wooden footbridge that had been unable to withstand the force of the flood.

I plunged in up to my calves and pushed on, fighting the freezing current until I was up to my waist and the sheer weight of the deluge whipped my legs from under me. I kicked and thrashed, but might as well not have bothered. Nothing I could do would stop me going under.

I went with the flow until my lungs threatened to burst and I started taking on water through my nose and mouth, then somehow managed to kick myself back to the surface.

My head spun and my eyes were streaming, but I caught sight

of him again as I fought for breath. Like me, he was struggling to keep his head up, clinging to the tree root for dear life.

The water took me under again and I was suddenly more concerned about sucking in air than getting to the other side.

I wrestled my way to the surface once more, and saw that I was now almost at the far side. I could let the current do the rest.

Seconds later, my fingers closed around Bastard's tree root.

He was cold, disoriented, frightened. He grabbed me, desperate to stay afloat, but only succeeded in pulling me under.

I kicked and jerked my way back up, fighting to keep my grip on the root as the current tore at my legs.

'*No!*' I kicked out at him. 'Compose yourself, for fuck's sake! *Stop!*' Down at this level, the roar of water was deafening.

I jack-knifed away from him, trying to keep him at arm's length. I knew he was panicking big-time, and there was no way I wanted us to head to the bottom of this vortex together.

The bank was steeper than I'd thought. There was a chance I could heave myself out, but it would take a crane to lift him clear.

'We've got to swim back across! I'll help you, but no grabbing . . . We won't make it if you fucking lose it, OK?'

He stared at me with glazed eyes, his teeth chattering with cold. 'I can't swim.'

For fuck's sake.

I scanned the boiling surface of the water on either side of us. The trunk of a pine tree had lodged itself against a rockslide just short of the bend in the river. Its roots faced slightly upstream, creating a V-shaped breakwater. The aluminium rectangle of Bastard's carry-on glinted among the debris bobbing in the slower-moving water at its centre.

Bastard was staring at me wild-eyed. He tried to speak but couldn't.

I let go of the tree root and crashed hard against the fallen pine.

I grabbed the carry-on and flung my free arm over the trunk. I hooked a leg over a branch, but the rest of me still trailed in the river. I let myself be buffeted by the force of the water until I managed to draw breath and heave myself up. I lay there for a moment, my knuckles whitening as I fought to hang on to the handle of the carry-on. Then I started to crawl slowly towards the bank.

I hauled myself upright and made my way back upstream.

Bastard saw me coming. 'Get me out of here, now!'

It was like being accosted by 250 pounds of stranded bull walrus.

'Hey! I'm here . . . *Here!* What the fuck's keeping you?'

For a split second I toyed with the idea of cracking him on the side of the head with the carry-on and watching him float away. Then I gave myself a reality check. If we lost Bastard, we lost our broker. I began to lower myself down the bank and back into the water.

'This is our raft,' I yelled. 'Grip the fucking thing as tight as you can and don't let go. I'll hang on to you. Now kick . . . *Come on, kick!*'

He nodded obediently but didn't move. The carry-on bounced up and down in the swell between us.

Bastard was experiencing Fear Up big-time at first hand. He couldn't bring himself to let go of his anchor. I punched down hard on his hand to get him to release, and we were away.

I locked my hand on the collar of Bastard's blazer, kicking to propel us out into the current to clear the fallen tree.

Bastard was putting all his energy into keeping his head above water.

'Get kicking! Fucking help me here!'

The signal finally made it from his ear to his brain and he kicked. The current grabbed us and we thundered past the pine tree. The further we travelled, the closer we were being thrown towards the far shore. It was only a matter of time before my boots hit the riverbed.

I struggled to my feet and half pulled, half dragged Bastard into the shallows. A few moments later, he was lying beside me on solid ground.

I took off my shirt and T-shirt, and twisted as much water out of them as I could. To make the most of what was left of my body heat, I had to get some air into the fibres. That was what I told myself anyway. The rain soaked them as fast as I could wring them, but somehow the whole process made me feel better.

I put the shirt and T-shirt back on, then knelt to take off my boots. I fumbled to undo the laces with numb, trembling fingers. Finally I wrung out my jeans.

Once I was dressed again, I tucked everything in, trying to minimize the number of ways in which the wind could get to me.

A familiar voice boomed down at us from what was left of the road. 'That was really big of you, lad, but you needn't have bothered.'

I looked up at Charlie and shrugged.

His eyes twinkled. 'I could easily have made do with a carrier bag.'

Bastard lay beside me like a beached whale.

I kicked him. 'Time to move. Check you've still got your ID.'

Bastard dug around and pulled out his wallet.

He gave it a squeeze and fished out the laminated card. 'You really do need me, don't you?' He had the faintest of knowing smiles on his face. 'Well, fuck you.'

2

The mudslide had demolished the road, leaving little more than a trail of boulders and uprooted trees in its wake. Even if we'd managed to hang on to the Pajero, we couldn't have gone any further.

I slumped down next to Charlie and fought my way back into my jacket. After my *Baywatch* experience, the effort of pushing Bastard back up the slope had almost finished me off. He sat a little way away from us. I hoped he might be suffering from a touch of wounded pride, at the very least, but if he was, he wasn't going to let us see it.

In a completely futile display of defiance against the still-torrential rain, he had fastened all three buttons on his blazer and pulled up the collar. Amazingly, he'd hung on to both his shoes, and apart from a few bruises, seemed little the worse for wear.

'I've no weapon,' Charlie muttered. 'You?'

I shook my head. 'It was a simple choice: the seven six two or you. Fuck knows why, but you won out.'

Charlie grinned, but only briefly. 'Better not hang about, lad. We need to get a move on. Doubt we'll make the border before tomorrow, in this shit. The road the other side of town won't be a pretty sight either. So, first stop Borjomi, sort our shit out, hit the local Hertz kiosk, and crack on, eh?'

'I reckon we've done about a hundred and thirty odd K, so it can't be much more than twenty to tab. Four or five hours maybe, even with you in Hopalong Cassidy mode.' I got to my feet and grabbed Bastard by the scruff of his neck. 'I'll grip him; you just keep that ankle moving.'

Charlie set off and I manhandled Bastard to his feet. Normal service had been resumed; he was complaining about everything in the universe. I didn't envy him the next few hours though. Charlie and I were soaked, but at least we had a layer of outdoor wear and, more importantly, we had boots. Bastard was going to have to tab in wet loafers, and they weren't built for it any more than he was. His feet would be blistered to fuck before we'd gone a thousand metres.

'Time to get going. We've got a little brokering to do, remember?'

Bastard didn't reply, so I gave him a shove. It was like trying to fast-forward a hippo; he didn't budge an inch.

'Time to go, Big Boy.'

'Fuck you!' He obviously liked that phrase. It was his default reply.

'I'm doing you a favour, mate. You're not going to last five minutes out here on your own in that gear, are you?'

We kept on the road, or what we could see of it. Large cracks had opened across it, and water sluiced through them like they were storm drains. We had to move as fast as we could: not only to get to Borjomi as quickly as possible, but also to keep our drenched bodies warm.

I looked ahead of us. Charlie might have been the cripple, but he was doing a whole lot better than Bastard. His body swung from side to side as he tried to compensate for his swollen ankle, but he'd been in this kind of situation more times than he could count. On a tab, you've got to get from

315

A to B, so you just crack on with it. It's pointless worrying about the weather, your physical condition, or how pissed off you feel. It doesn't help you make the distance any quicker.

Bastard didn't get it. I guessed I couldn't blame him for feeling sorry for himself, but now wasn't the time or the place. I laid a hand on each of his shoulder blades and pushed.

He was grumbling big-time, but it wasn't helping him much. Bumping your gums doesn't get you to where you need to be. The only way you're going to do that is by putting one foot in front of the other as quickly as you can, and if it's not fast enough, then someone needs to come behind you with a cattle prod.

It was like being back in the infantry; I had been pushing or pulling flaking bodies since I was a sixteen-year-old boy soldier, trying to keep the slower guys up with the squad. It was all part of the deal. You moved as fast as the slowest man, but you had to make him as fast as you could. You carried his weapon, carried his kit, encouraged him, took the piss out of him – fucking well slung him over your shoulder and carried him if need be, not that I was in any hurry to try that with Bastard.

We'd been going for about an hour, and covered maybe four or five Ks, when Charlie limped off the road and heaved himself under a low fir tree. He lay back on the grass and stretched out his leg.

Bastard and I closed up on him.

'Thought I'd better hang around for you two lardasses.' He took a series of short, painful breaths.

Bastard couldn't even marshal the strength to move off the road; he just fell to his knees instead, and slid towards Charlie in the mud. It was probably the furthest he'd ever walked in his life, certainly in monsoon conditions and dressed in a blazer and loafers. His head slumped forward, displaying a very nice crocodile-clip-shaped bruise.

I left him where he was and went over to the tree.

Charlie was resting the sole of his boot against the trunk, in order to ease his damaged ankle.

I collapsed alongside him. I wasn't going to ask him if he was OK. If the time approached when he couldn't take any more, he'd give me plenty of warning.

Charlie grunted. 'We'd better step up the pace or we'll be stuck out here all night. If he could tab as energetically as he gobs off, we'd be there by now.' His face was lit briefly by one of his stupid grins. 'He's a bit like you, lad; he can talk the talk, but he certainly can't walk the walk.' He liked it so much he shouted a repeat for Bastard's benefit.

Bastard looked up, but either couldn't or didn't want to hear.

I wasn't looking forward to trying to keep Bastard on the move all night. If he couldn't shift his arse in daylight, he'd be ten times worse after dark. People like him become un-coordinated; they stumble, they injure themselves.

Bastard looked the part inside a Pod with a coffee machine at his elbow and a wad of tobacco in his hip pocket, but that was about it. He'd boast a good night out, but I didn't want to have to nurse him through one.

I doubted he'd ever gone more than a couple of hours between doughnuts.

I checked Baby-G, which was still chugging along after its dip in the river. It was 3.27, which meant only about another four hours before dark. At this rate, it wouldn't be enough.

Charlie moved his foot off the trunk of the tree and onto my shoulder. Bastard watched, and maybe it made him feel even more like Nobby Nomates. He sounded pretty sorry for him-self. 'How much fucking longer in this goddam shit country, man? How far we gotta go?'

'What's the matter, Big Boy?' Charlie watched him fiddle with his soaking wet loafers. 'Never been cold, wet and hungry before?'

I broke into a smile. 'Cold and wet, maybe. Hungry? I don't think so!'

Charlie almost choked with laughter.

'You fucks think we'll get there before dark?' Bastard scowled at us as he wiped the rain from his face. 'I don't want to be out in this shit all night long, that's for sure. And don't even think about leaving me out here. Nothing's changed. You fucks can't get out of here without me. Don't forget it.'

Charlie grimaced as his foot made contact with the ground again. 'Don't fret, Big Boy. We'll push your fat arse all the way to Turkey if we have to.'

He hobbled off up the road. I couldn't see his face, but I knew it would be contorting with pain with every step.

I'd have offered myself as a crutch, but he would only have fucked me off. He knew as well as I did that he wasn't the priority right now, whatever Hazel might think.

3

I pushed and shoved Bastard for another hour. He was slowing down, without a doubt. It couldn't have been easy shifting that bulk of his; I could almost hear those big wobbly thighs chafing together with every step he took.

We were still following the pipeline scar to the left of the road. The rain was a solid grey curtain.

As we rounded a sweeping bend into high ground, I saw a splash of white about 150 metres ahead of us. I wiped the rain from my eyes and looked again. It was the arse end of a van, static beside the road.

Bastard and I drew level with Charlie.

Charlie rested his arm on my shoulder to take the weight off his injury. 'Looks like our luck's in, lad.'

Bastard began sounding off as if he'd spotted an empty cab at theatre time and we were about to let it go. 'Hey, what're you fucks waiting for?' He shambled off up the road, trying desperately to make his legs move as fast as his instinct for self-preservation.

As we got closer, the white blur became a Mercedes van, up to its axles in the mud. Both sets of rear wheels were spinning, but the driver was only burying them deeper.

I dodged the spray coming off the tyres and made my way round the passenger side. I saw two shapes in the front seats, but they were too intent on working the steering wheel and gearstick to notice me.

I tapped on the glass.

The figure in the passenger seat spun around, clearly startled. I could see her dark eyes, as wide as saucers, through the rain-blurred window. She stared at me for several seconds then switched her gaze to Charlie and Bastard as they closed up behind me. I could understand her concern. We were in the middle of nowhere, in a torrential storm; we must have looked as though we'd just crawled out of a primeval swamp.

I unzipped my jacket, lifted it up, and turned from side to side. 'No weapons,' I mouthed. 'We . . . are . . . unarmed.'

I let my jacket fall as the others followed suit, but kept my hands up.

She wound the window down about six inches, but her expression made it clear that she still wasn't exactly delighted to see us.

'It's OK, it's OK . . .' I smiled. 'Speak English?'

She turned to the driver and said something in rapid-fire Paperclip. He took his foot off the gas and bent forward to see round her. He had a very short, just grown-out crew cut, and hadn't shaved for a day or two.

I kept my smile so wide my face was starting to hurt. 'English? Speak . . . English?'

The girl faced me again, her brow still furrowed. 'Who are you?' The accent was Eastern European, but with an American TV twang.

I spoke very slowly. 'Our car . . . It got hit . . .' I mimed a collision. 'The mud . . .'

The driver leaned forward again. 'We understand.'

Bastard appeared at my shoulder and pushed me aside. He pulled his accreditation from his soaked leather wallet and

320

thrust it through the gap. 'Borjomi,' he barked. 'Take us to Borjomi.'

If that was his idea of a charm offensive, our tab was far from over.

The woman took the ID.

Bastard didn't waste any time. 'We wanna get to Borjomi. See that ID? That says you take us.'

The two inside the Mercedes had another exchange in Paperclip, glancing at each of us in turn. I never liked not knowing what was being said in situations like this, particularly when I appeared to be the subject of the conversation, and the outlook didn't sound good.

Eventually she shrugged. 'Sure . . . It's not so far. No more than thirty minutes. We're going there ourselves, if we can get out of this mess.'

She passed the ID back and Bastard tucked it into his wallet. In the state he was in, I doubted she'd been able to match him with the photograph. I hoped she wouldn't recognize me.

Bastard reached for the handle to the sliding door halfway down the wagon, as if he already owned it, but she waved him away. 'You will have to dig us out first.'

She slid across into the driver's seat, and he climbed out. He was tall and lanky, maybe mid-twenties, and wore a black Gore-Tex jacket. He came round the front of the vehicle and thrust out a hand. 'I'm Paata.' He nodded towards his companion. 'And she's Nana.'

Charlie and I both introduced ourselves. I hoped that our expressions would help distance us from the tub of lard still wrestling with the sliding door.

Bastard glanced in our direction. 'Hey, this goddam thing's stuck.'

Paata shook his head. 'It's locked on the inside. Security. We'll undo it in a minute.'

Bastard pulled up his collar and went to lean against one of the few trees to have been left unscathed by the side of the road. He leaned forward, hands on his knees, resting his huge buttocks against the trunk. I tried not to laugh; he looked like a bear trying to scratch its arse.

Charlie and I grabbed the rear bumper and started to push and lift, trying to free the wheels from the ruts they'd created. Paata shouted out to Nana to keep them turning, then came to join us. He unzipped his jacket, to stop himself overheating. Me, I was looking forward to it. Mud flew like muck from a spreader as Nana floored the accelerator.

Paata yelled more instructions and Nana hit the pedal again. This time the wheels spun more gently.

Charlie and I leaned against the back door and tried to lift, then let go so it rocked back into the rut. I wasn't sure how much good we were doing. His hands were starting to shake like a demented percussionist.

'Paata,' Charlie called out. 'Have you had to get out of this stuff before?'

'Sure. I am an expert!' Paata gave us a beaming smile. 'Every time, I call a tow truck.'

'Good thinking.' I laughed. 'But not this time?'

'Cells don't work this far out. Not until Borjomi.'

Charlie tapped him on the arm. 'Thing is, lad, I've dug a few vehicles out of snowdrifts in my time. It's not as bad as mud, but the principle's the same.'

Charlie bent to inspect the axle. 'The mud clings to the undercarriage until there's no way to get any traction, and spinning the wheels only drives them deeper. Us three strong lads need to stay here, at the back, but Nana must help us rock the wagon back and forth. She needs to keep the wheels as straight as she can, shift quickly from first gear to reverse, and we'll get a nice rhythm going. When we manage to jump this thing free, she should keep it moving until it's on firm ground. And she should try not to spin the wheels if she can help it.'

Paata headed up front to pass on Charlie's instructions.

'Hey, driver,' Bastard shouted from under his tree. 'What

about getting me a hot drink?' He was well and truly back to his old gobshite self.

Paata sensibly ignored him.

The engine revved and the three of us started to push and shove. I wondered how much more of this Charlie could take.

Nana threw the Merc into reverse and Paata wiped a fistful of mud off his face.

'Open up the back,' Bastard yelled. 'I'll make the coffee myself.'

Paata muttered something under his breath. I thought I'd probably just learned the Paperclip for 'fuck off'.

Charlie took a step back. His ankle looked as though it was about to give way beneath him. 'Listen, Paata, this isn't going to work. You got a shovel?'

'I wish,' Paata said. His expression told me that if he had, he'd use it across the back of Bastard's head.

Charlie opened the front passenger door and burrowed inside. He emerged with the rubber mat from the foot well and handed it to me. 'You might be able to scrape enough mud away from the wheels with this to get some traction, lad.' He turned back to Paata. 'What about snow chains?'

Paata rattled off another sentence or two of Paperclip to Nana, and I heard the side door slide open and close. He re-appeared with two sets. Charlie dropped one into each of the furrows I'd scooped behind the tyres and threw in the rubber mat for good measure.

At Charlie's signal, Nana revved the engine once more and dropped the clutch. The wheels spun for a second and the Merc rolled straight out of the ruts and back onto firmer ground.

Bastard didn't waste any time getting his arse off the tree.

Nana climbed out. She was dressed in walking boots, water-proof trousers and an expensive black Gore-Tex jacket like Paata's. She couldn't have been more than about five foot six, and her features were almost elfin, but there was nothing fluffy about her demeanour. As she headed round the side of the vehicle, she looked as purposeful as a heat-seeking missile.

She gave the side door a quick double tap. There was a click and it slid open to reveal a bank of TV monitors set in an alloy frame which acted as a bulkhead to the cab, a stack of aluminium boxes, and an even more purposeful man with a huge beard and biceps the size of Bastard's thighs.

'This is Koba,' Nana said. 'I regret we live in dangerous times. Koba makes sure we come to no harm.'

She wasn't kidding. Koba wouldn't have looked out of place wielding a gollock in a Tbilisi graveyard. He studied us silently with dark, hooded eyes, as if trying to decide which of us to head-butt first.

'There's only room for another three of us here in the back.' Nana pointed at Charlie. 'Why don't you get in the front with Paata and stretch out your leg? It looks painful.'

Bastard didn't need a second invitation. He heaved himself inside and I followed. It was obviously an outside broadcast set-up. I put two and two together, and suddenly wished I'd hung on to my stupid hat.

I'd thought Nana seemed familiar. She'd fronted the camera in the broadcast from the Kazbegi siege.

4

I shifted a couple of cables out of the way to make room for my feet. I could see Paata and Charlie through the hatch, framed by the TV monitors, as we set off. Beside them, someone had taped a montage of images from Nana's recent past.

One of them showed her in Fiona Bruce mode, posing at a news desk, wearing make-up and an earnest smile. Captions in Paperclip, Russian and English promoted her for some kind of award. She had certainly kept herself busy. She had exposed corruption in all sections of government, 'unearthing entanglements of network and patronage at all levels'.

Another shot showed her alongside the Georgian army, covering the siege by Islamic militants in Kazbegi, on the Russian border, not even two weeks ago. According to the cutting, she'd been the first journalist at the scene, and reported live for CNN.

Nobody talked. Nana was very tense and edgy, and it set the tone. The soundproofing in the cab did a perfect job of muting the rain, and it accentuated the awkward silence.

Bastard, true to form, remained oblivious. 'Now where the fuck's that coffee?'

Nana reached into one of the large nylon zip bags on the floor and handed him a stainless steel thermos.

As Bastard unscrewed the top, Koba watched his every move.

'Do you guys work on the pipeline?' Nana asked. 'What are you, surveyors? Engineers?'

Bastard poured himself a generous mug, and the smell of coffee filled the van. 'Security.'

She turned to me. 'You security too? Do you have any ID? Koba likes to be sure about people.'

'It was in my bag, in our Pajero.' I did my best to look apologetic. 'We lost everything.'

She switched her attention back to Bastard. 'We're planning a documentary about the pipeline. Maybe we could do business one day.'

Bastard was getting the brew down him. It hadn't occurred to him to offer some to anyone else. 'Anti, I guess?'

'Excuse me? Oh, I see.' She flexed her fingers. 'Well, don't you think it's crazy for an oil pipeline to cut straight through a national park?'

Bastard took a deep breath. We were about to be treated to his state-of-the-nation speech. 'Listen, lady, you ain't getting the big picture. It had to come this way, to avoid the Russians down south. That place of theirs ain't called Military City Number One for nothing. Hey, it's you people who call them the aggressive neighbour, not us.'

It was clear Koba didn't like Bastard's tone and Bastard knew it. 'What the fuck you looking at, Lurch?'

Koba's deep-set eyes didn't even blink.

Bastard sank the last of the brew and I jumped in to try and stop things escalating.

'And you, Nana? Why are you going to Borjomi?'

Her eyes narrowed. I knew she didn't like me; I just hoped I didn't know the reason why. 'You probably won't have heard because it's just a little local matter, not part of the big

326

picture . . .' She glanced at Bastard, but her irony was clearly lost on him. 'Just over a week ago, militant rebels massacred more than sixty women and children in a village called Kazbegi . . '

I'd seen that look on her face before. Hazel and Julie had used it too. She tried to compose herself.

'A farming family in Borjomi lost their only child in the massacre. A little girl. She was seven years old . . .'

She paused again.

'We were with them on Saturday. We're going back because they are willing to go live and tell us what it is like to live under the tyranny of Akaki, the militant leader. He is no freedom fighter; he's a self-seeking, dictatorial thug. These poor people live in fear. But this couple, well – they have had enough.'

Bastard just started laughing. 'What the fuck are momma and papa gonna do? They think that's gonna change the world? They think that's gonna make Akaki drop his pants and run away? Shit, they'll just get themselves dead. Fucking dumb-asses.' He nodded at Koba. 'Ain't that a fact, Lurch?'

Koba shifted in his seat. He clearly recognized Akaki's name, and he didn't like it one bit.

Bastard couldn't contain himself now. He was on a roll. 'That Akaki . . . boy, he's caused us all a few headaches, over the years.'

'Headaches? *Headaches?*' Nana shook her head in disbelief. 'Yes, I suppose you could call them that . . . Did you hear of the murder of Zurab Bazgadze?'

She was talking to him, but I had a nasty feeling she was addressing me.

'The saint guy, right? The one who tried to get in the way of the pipeline?'

'With very good reason.' She glanced at Koba too. Her expression seemed to tell him that he needn't worry about ripping Bastard's head off. Any minute now, she'd do the job herself. 'As you may have spotted, the soil structure around here is extremely unstable. It's an area of considerable geological complexity, particularly vulnerable to landslides and earthquakes. In the event of pipeline rupture, there's a risk of catastrophic environmental damage.

'Zurab knew it would devastate the natural springs. Bottled water is Georgia's number-one export. The people round here, their livelihoods depend on it. No one championed their cause more vigorously than he did.'

'Zurab, eh? He a friend of yours, missy?'

'He became so. I interviewed him many times over the years; most recently, just before he died. He was here on Saturday, visiting the bereaved family. He was very good like that. A man of the people. We were to film him at length on Sunday morning, but he had to return to Tbilisi at short notice, so we were only able to grab a few minutes with him . . .'

Her look was defiant, but I thought I could see tears in her eyes.

'Now, of course, I wish we'd tried harder to persuade him to stay.'

I leaned forward, elbows on my knees. 'You're *60 Minutes*, right?'

She nodded.

That figured. The *Georgian Times* had said that *60 Minutes* and Baz had been due to have a love fest when he presented his affidavit.

'We got sensors in the pipes to show up any fractures,' Bastard said. It was as if he hadn't listened to a single word. 'It'd be sealed in days.'

Somehow, she managed to keep her cool. 'By which time the whole area would be contaminated. That's precisely why Zurab got an injunction to stop the pipeline coming this way. But your . . . friends . . . got it revoked. Zurab said that the decision came all the way from Washington; that your freedom-loving president intervened.'

328

Bastard wasn't really listening. His face was boiling up nicely, as if he'd just caught this woman setting fire to the Stars and Stripes. 'Hey, lady, that saint of yours knew you people were getting a good deal out of this. If it weren't for us, you'd still be living in the dark ages. We're bankrolling you. We're giving you independence, freedom and stability – and in exchange for what? A few miles of metal tube. My president is even taking time out to come here and show you guys he means business. What more did your fucking saint Zurab want from us?'

Koba was looking more and more pissed off. Nana soothed him with a few mumbled words and shook her head sadly. 'Zurab just couldn't understand why, if you're so devoted to democracy and stability, you support a government whose corruption knows no limits. The people see very little benefit from your so-called altruism, so the people think you are just here for the oil.'

Bastard's face had turned purple. 'You know what, lady? I don't give a fuck. Bazgadze and his kind make me sick right up to my back teeth – complaining about this, complaining about that. Jesus, you were spending all day lining up for bread before we came along, yet all he did was complain about your government, my government, the Russians, the energy corridor. But you know what, lady.' He put his finger to his temple, compressing the veins until they bulged. 'I don't give a shit if the Georgian government are driving round in Cadillacs. That was his problem, not mine.'

'I agree, it was his problem. But it is also mine, and Georgia's – and make no mistake about this, it's yours as well. Zurab was right. He knew your country was more interested in oil than democracy. Democracy is just an excuse, a convenient flag to wave. You are behaving no differently here than you do in South America, Africa, the Mid-East. You invest in the military, keep corrupt governments happy, and build bases for your own troops to protect your oil interests. Meanwhile, our

329

people, their people, the people who really matter, get nothing.'

I leaned back against the aluminium boxes. Charlie's 'little guy getting fucked over' theory was receiving its most articulate airing yet.

'Zurab knew very well that you, America, use the war against terrorism and paranoia about national security to underpin your foreign deployments, while your military becomes the protection force for every oil field, pipeline, refinery and tanker route on the planet. And the price we will all pay is higher than you can possibly imagine. You think it is measured in dollars, but it's not. It's measured in blood.'

There wasn't a whole lot even Bastard could say to that, but he didn't have to. Paata turned and leaned back through the bulkhead. 'We are here.'

5

Seconds later, Charlie poked his head through the hatch. 'Doesn't look much like the centre of the country's number-one export business to me, but there you go.'

I glanced through the windscreen. A few houses were dotted each side of the valley, increasing in number as the road climbed towards a cluster of roofs about 500 away.

The whole area was lush, green, and very wet. The muddy tracks and rough wooden fences and shacks had an almost medieval flavour. Apart from a handful of chickens scuttling about and a few cows mooching around in the fields to our left, the place seemed to be deserted. The torrential rain was keeping the villagers indoors, and I couldn't blame them.

The track ahead of us had been shored up with broken bricks and lumps of wood. Ominously, I didn't see any sign of a 4x4. I wondered how long it would take us to get to Turkey by horse and cart.

Charlie turned to Paata. 'What now?'

'Back to where Nana did the Kazbegi interview. We need to keep the Mercedes out of sight. Nana isn't everybody's favourite girl around here. She should be, but she isn't. She likes to poke her nose into places people don't want her to.' His jaw tightened. 'The farmer let us sleep here, with the truck. He's a good man. He and his wife are the ones we've come back to see.'

We passed a dilapidated farmhouse, and turned right along a track. We pulled up in front of a huge barn, built of unmilled wood with gaps between the planks, and a roof of heavily patched and rusty corrugated-iron sheets. Paata jumped out to open the doors.

Bastard took it as his cue to started bumping his gums again. 'That ID says you gotta help me. I want a truck.'

'I'll ask Eduard,' Nana said sweetly. 'He's waiting inside.'

Paata slid back in and we drove a dozen or so metres into the centre of the barn. It was about three times the height of the wagon, and could easily have taken another six vans each side of us.

The whole place stank of decay and old manure, but at least it was dry. There were no tools or machinery in sight, not even a bale of hay. All I could see was a roughly hewn wooden bench in the far corner, by the remains of a small fire. It looked like it was where this lot had got their heads down.

Nana said something in Paperclip to Koba. He nodded, and took up station a few paces to one side of us. He unzipped his jacket as Bastard fell out of the wagon.

'Where's this Eduard guy? I've got some business to take care of.'

She was trying to keep it light, but I could see she was worried. 'He'll be here. He's not the sort to break a promise.' She glanced uneasily at Paata, then at me and Charlie.

Fuck this; there was too much eye contact going on here. It didn't feel right.

'We've got to get going too,' I said cheerfully. 'Thanks for the lift.'

'Eduard will know if there's transport. I'll call him.'

I followed her line of sight to Paata and Koba, and sensed the tension between them. They were on starting blocks, waiting for something.

I looked back at Nana as she punched the buttons on her cell.

For just a second, I had a vision of a peasant farmer trundling along a bumpy track, fighting the wheel of his battered Lada as he scrabbled in his pocket to retrieve his Nokia.

A peasant Georgian farmer, with a cell phone. Who the fuck did he have to call?

My eyes shot back to Nana. Hers were glued to Koba, and the look between them told me everything.

She knew. She'd known all along. All that heartfelt, rabble-rousing shit had just been to keep us busy.

I walked over to Charlie. My eyes were fixed on Koba's feet, between us and the door. I wasn't going to join the eye-contact fest and make things worse. 'C'mon, mate,' I murmured. 'We're off.'

6

Charlie backed me as I took a pace towards the doors, ready to take on Koba if he decided to get in our way. It wasn't something I relished, but we were running out of choices again.

He took a pace towards us. It had gone noisy.

I charged at him, head down. Nana screamed, but Koba's hand moved faster. A split second later, I was staring down a shiny chrome barrel, three or four metres from my face. He covered all three of us, the twitch of the .357 Magnum Desert Eagle's muzzle making it clear that our next sensible move was to get down in the dirt.

I looked up at Nana. The cell was at her ear.

'Nana, what's the matter? What's wrong?'

Koba swung his boot into my side. I shut up and took the pain, which was a lot more comfortable than a round from a Desert Eagle. It was no accident that the massive, Israeli-built semi-automatic pistol was weapon of choice for every self-respecting US gang member.

Nana's eyes flashed beams of hatred down at me as she waffled away in Paperclip, and that didn't feel much better.

Paata pulled a couple of aluminium boxes from the van and

started dragging them towards us. I heard Baz's name mentioned a few times before she closed the cell down.

'You know very well what's wrong. The police are coming.'

Fuck Koba and that boot of his, it was gob-off-and-play-stupid time.

'But I don't understand ... why pull a gun on us? We haven't done anything.' I tightened up for another kick.

She came and knelt down by my head instead.

'Do you think I didn't recognize you? You killed Zurab. I don't just make the news. I watch it too.'

Stupid wasn't going to work.

'Wait, Nana ... Yes, I was there. Charlie and I were both there. But we didn't kill him. Akaki did, they were his people.'

She stared at me coldly, her hand up, blocking me off. 'So what? The only difference between you is that Akaki got there a little earlier. Was Zurab making too much noise for you? What does it matter? You all wanted him dead. Why else were you there? And this one –' she aimed a toe at Bastard's head – 'he carries government ID. What am I to make of that?'

Paata was busy setting up his camera stand and lights just a few metres from us.

Bastard had been uncharacteristically quiet so far, but being face down in the dirt wasn't going to keep him from his default setting for long. 'You don't lump me in with these two fucks, you hear? I'm pipeline security, period. Nothing to do with whatever these fucks got up to. That ID says you gotta help me, so do it.'

'I despise you.' Nana glared across at him. 'You are as guilty as if you'd pulled the trigger yourself.'

Paata had rigged up the lights, forward and either side of us, and started running the cables back to the van.

That was it then. Our big moment. Captured on camera by Nana Onani. I wondered what Silky and Hazel would make of it.

Charlie was obviously thinking much the same. 'Don't look

335

now, lad,' he muttered. 'We're about to have a starring role in Nana's answer to *I'm a Celebrity, Get Me Out of Here . . .'*

'That's got to be worth an Emmy, don't you think?' she said, then barked something to Koba in Paperclip. He nodded obediently. The muzzle of the Desert Eagle didn't waver a millimetre as Nana stood up and hit the cell keys again.

'We didn't kill him, Nana. You must have seen the CCTV. You didn't see me kill him, did you?'

'Save it for the camera. You'll all have your chance.'

She waffled into the cell, was put on hold for a moment, then started talking again.

Paata fired up the Merc's onboard generator and the arc lights burst into life. I could feel their heat on my face and back. My clothes started to steam.

Nana went into rapid-fire Paperclip mode; she checked her watch and waved her spare arm at Paata and his kit, as if whoever was on the other end could see. I could make out every mention of Baz's name now; I'd heard it far too often these last couple of days not to.

Paata knelt by the van to unpack a sat dish from something resembling a black golf caddie. Nana's exclusive was going to go out live, with us pleading our innocence straight to camera just before the police arrived.

Decision time.

Should we give up the papers now? Maybe we could still get out of this some other way, and hang on to them.

Bastard was going to say fuck all to her. Why incriminate himself?

But Charlie might . . .

I decided to hold off just a little longer, until we got ready for filming. Maybe we'd get to sit up; any chance we had to move was a chance to take action.

Nana finished her conversation and her gaze rested for a moment on something just beyond where we were lying. 'That bench?' There was sadness in her voice. 'That is where Zurab

336

sat on Saturday, when he took the call that made him go back to Tbilisi. If only . . . If only he hadn't gone . . . If only I'd asked him even two or three more questions, who knows how things might have turned out?' Her head jerked back towards me, her eyes full of loathing once more.

Charlie broke the silence that followed.

'Nana, we didn't do it. We can prove it. We have papers. That affidavit everyone's after? I've got it here – and a tape of this fat fuck setting the whole thing up.' He turned to Bastard. Their heads were just a couple of feet from each other. 'Pipeline security, my arse.'

7

The tape started to spin in the console.

Koba now had the three of us lying down beside the Merc's open door, but we could see everything we needed to. We had a pretty good view of one of the monitors; Koba and his Desert Eagle had a very good view of us.

To start with, Paata and Nana seemed more interested in what the fuck had happened to Eduard. I was getting the hang of this Paperclip now. Where was he? But then they went quiet as he concentrated on the screen and she flicked through Baz's papers.

The picture quality was nothing to be ashamed of, given what it had been through. It was a bit gritty and fucked up by the mud, but it was clearly and unmistakably Jim Bastendorf coming into Charlie's hotel room at the Marriott.

The little 10x8 screen didn't do full justice to Charlie's disguise, but it still brought a smile to my face. He'd remembered to keep his back to the lens, which was a smart move, given his outfit. He'd draped a towel over his head and shoulders, like a boxer, but no one was going to confuse him with Muhammad Ali. He'd topped off the whole ensemble with a shower cap.

Somebody said something, but the sound quality was poor. Paata rewound the tape a few frames and turned up the volume.

We all listened to Bastard telling Charlie the reason he needed him to get into the house on Saturday night. '*The fuck's away until Sunday.*' He pointed a finger at the bathrobe in front of him. '*So it's got to be Saturday night, you got it?*'

I flicked my eyes from the screen to the open barn doors. The rain-drenched track was beginning to look more like a duck pond. How long would it take for the police to arrive? And where would they come from? If there was a station in Borjomi itself, we could be seeing blue-and-whites any minute.

Koba was still standing, rock solid, a very professional three metres from our backs. What were the odds of gripping him and that .357 before we heard sirens? We had to be in with a chance. There were three of us, counting Bastard, and I guessed he'd pitch in. He'd gone far too quiet for my liking, but I knew he wouldn't want to be lifted any more than we did.

Nana looked across at me. 'Do you know what this says?'

I shook my head.

I had another go at explaining why we'd been in Baz's house, but she just carried on reading. I wished now that I had taken action when Koba had kicked us to our feet and walked us the dozen or so paces to the van. No matter what, she was going to wait for the police.

But what the fuck, I told her everything I knew; how Bastard came into the story, why we were at the house – and how the tape proved not only that Bastard was part of the operation, but that we didn't even know Baz was going to be there . . .

'Hey, lady,' Bastard chipped in. 'I just do what I'm told. I knew nothing about that killing shit. I didn't know he was gonna come home . . .'

He was wasting his breath. We both were. Nana's head was down, and less than halfway through the second page she lifted a hand to silence us.

The folder was on her lap. I watched a tear fall from her cheek and land on the page.

'Oh my God.' She stifled a sob. *'Oh my God . . .'* Her hand reached out and gently touched Paata's back. 'We must go live with this – right now.'

8

Nana's eyes devoured the remaining pages, and she had to keep wiping her face with the back of her hand to stop more tears from falling and smudging the ink.

Colour bars flickered to life on all three screens as Paata rigged up the dish just outside the barn doors. Koba sparked up behind us. I guessed he wanted to know the same things as the rest of us – what was wrong, what did it say?

The screens flickered. A woman in a blue jacket materialized in front of us, sitting at a desk in an empty studio. She pulled on her set of headphones and the speakers crackled. Sure enough, we were going live. 'Nana? Nana?'

Nana cut the sound and pulled on her own set of earphones and boom mike. She took a moment to compose herself, then started talking in low, urgent tones. Baz's name came up again and again as she looked down and quoted long chunks from the document. The woman in the studio looked horrified. Behind us, Koba was building himself into a rage. This wasn't good; Baz's text was supposed to help us.

When she reached the bottom of the last page, she closed the folder with a snap and shoved it into the side pocket of her Gore-Tex.

She exchanged a closing word or two with her colleague in the studio, who got up from the desk and disappeared off-screen.

Nana's eyes were still full as she removed her headphones. 'We planned to address parliament with Zurab tomorrow.' She was trying hard not to break down. 'We were going to film him presenting the contents of this document to us in front of his government colleagues, in front of the very men he was going to expose.' Her head shook slowly from side to side. 'But none of us had any idea . . . no idea that these revelations would be so . . . so . . .' She really had to search for the word. 'Abominable' was what she came up with, but I could see from her expression it still didn't fit the bill.

The word seemed to hang in the air, then her hand came up to her mouth again. I didn't know what to say – how could I? I hadn't a clue what it was she'd just been reading. All I knew was that Nana was a tough one, but Baz's stuff had turned her into a mess. And that it didn't look as though the document was going to help us get off the dirt and away from here.

'Nana, you believe us now? You need to let us go before the police come. *Nana*?'

She still wasn't listening. 'He wouldn't tell me . . . He thought it would put me in too much danger . . .' She turned to face us again, with red, hate-filled eyes. 'Believe you? Why? Why should I believe you? Explain it to the police. See if you can persuade them.'

'Listen, lady. I wasn't there. I just got told to deliver the bag. Don't you lump me in with these murdering fucks.' Bastard was nothing if not persistent. I almost found myself starting to admire him.

'*You! Shut the fuck up.*' Charlie clearly didn't feel the same.

We had to try to convince her before the uniforms arrived. It was unlikely they'd be speaking our language. 'Nana. Why would we give you this stuff? We've told you what happened. Did you see me kill him? No. All we were there for was the papers. If we were part of it, why would we tape this fat bastard?'

It wasn't working. She turned back to the monitors. They were rerunning the bulletin. The girl in the studio was talking, but there was no sound. At least, not from the screen. But we'd all heard the noise outside.

'Police.' Nana sounded relieved.

Paata came running back into the barn, screaming in Paperclip. I only managed to pick up one word, and it didn't sound good news to me.

I turned my head. Koba was still behind us. He looked like he hadn't enjoyed hearing Akaki mentioned any more than I had.

The scream of engines got louder. Koba got more and more agitated. Three or four wagonloads of militants, by the sound of it, and only one of him. I could see his dilemma.

Nana tried to calm him down, but it wasn't happening. The Desert Eagle was still pointed at us, safety off, and the muzzle waved alarmingly from side to side. His eyes brimmed with tears of rage.

Bastard just lay there. He seemed to be almost enjoying it. What the fuck was the matter with him?

Charlie turned onto his back.

'Calm down, Koba lad. Or point that fucking thing some-where else . . .'

I double-checked under the van, along the rear wall. No sign of a back door.

The vehicles were on top of us now. Charlie was the first to see them. 'Taliban wagons!'

I glanced back towards the doors.

Guys in black masks and green combat jackets, some with ponchos, swarmed out of Toyota pick-ups, laden with AKs, light machine guns and belts of 7.62 short.

343

Koba ran straight for them, screaming, sobbing, going ballistic.

I leaped up and grabbed Charlie. 'Let's go, go, *go!*'

The heavy-calibre .357 kicked in Koba's hands. I heard screams from both sides of the barn doors.

Charlie and I ducked down behind the van. Fuck knows where the other three had got to; I didn't care.

Bastard materialized behind us as two bursts of AK put an end to the Desert Eagle. Angry shouts echoed round the barn.

I looked under the van. Koba was writhing in the mud beside one of the wagons. Blood pumped from the holes drilled into his torso.

A big guy with wild hair and an Osama-style beard walked across to him, the butt of an AK in his poncho-draped shoulder. He leaned in and squeezed the trigger. The weapon kicked, and Koba's head exploded like a melon.

PART ELEVEN

1

Nana had balls, that was for sure.

She was straight over to confront Akaki and the first of his men who piled through the doors. She seemed to applaud his courageous victory over the cowardly capitalist lapdog, Koba, then she treated them to a blur of hands and Paperclip as she pointed to the satellite dish, the van, the arc lights, the camera.

But I didn't get to see her whole performance. Another wagonload had swarmed round our side of the Merc and were using their boots and rifle butts to corral us in the corner of the barn, near Baz's memorial bench. I'd already seen enough, though, to know that whatever she was on about, Akaki's men were very poor listeners.

I tried to look on the bright side. At least we got to sit down. I also tried to look relaxed and avoid eye-to-eye with the guys herding us. One of them had tucked Koba's mud-splattered Desert Eagle into his belt.

Bastard's eyes were everywhere, scanning the crowd.

Some of Akaki's boys were beginning to pull off their masks, exposing rough bearded faces and blackened teeth. There were a couple of teenagers still struggling to get past the bum-fluff stage, but most of them were in their late twenties or older. Whatever, they all affected the same swagger; they knew they were the big swinging dicks around here. They looked like battle-hardened Afghani mujahideen, right down to their choice of wheels. For a long time now, nobody I knew had called a Toyota pick-up anything but a Taliwagon.

Some had made a bee-line for the Merc, and were poking about inside. Others, worryingly, just stared at us with glazed, fucked-up eyes, like the junkies in the graveyard.

Nana was still trying to engage the group near the doors, but they were losing interest fast. Most of them were just giving her lecherous looks and sharing the sort of boys' talk that didn't leave much to the imagination.

Paata's eyes never left her. I hoped he wasn't contemplating playing super hero. One of us dead in the mud was enough.

Charlie still seemed to be looking out for the non-existent back door, and the treeline on the high ground beyond it.

Akaki's men took a deferential step or two back as he swept Nana to one side and strode into the barn. He stopped and surveyed the scene with wild, crazy eyes. Droplets of rain spilled from his curly black hair. He grabbed a handful of beard and squeezed out a pint or so more.

Nana was steeling herself to confront him when two blood-drenched corpses were dragged into the centre of the barn like dead dogs. They'd both taken several rounds to the torso, but the carefully positioned shots through their hands and feet told the most significant story.

Eduard and his wife had already had their interview.

Nana stormed across the barn, but Bastard was quicker. He jumped to his feet and brushed aside a couple of militants who weren't quick enough to step out of his way. 'Akaki, you miserable fuck!'

Akaki pulled his rain-soaked poncho over his head, to reveal a pair of Levi 501s, a US BDU jacket and the kind of woollen jumper that could only have come from the shop where Charlie and I had bought ours. He'd shoved some sort of semi-automatic into his shoulder holster and four extra AK mags in his chest harness.

He didn't even blink as Bastard approached; just raised a hand to calm anyone shaping up to blow holes in him. The expression on his face was that of a man who'd spotted a relative he'd never much liked, but had to put up with. They knew each other all right.

'*You!*' Bastard's finger jabbed in Nana's direction. 'Fucking Barbara Walters! Give him those papers; tell him I want out of here.'

The Merc's suspension groaned as he disappeared through the side door.

Akaki ripped Baz's papers from Nana's outstretched hand. She kept talking, fuck knows what about, but he was no more in the mood to listen than she had been ten minutes ago. He lashed out with his fist; she took the punch square on the cheek and crumpled to the floor.

Paata sprang to his feet but took the butt of an AK in the chest for his trouble. Nana screamed at him to stay put. Akaki bellowed at her and raised his hand to deliver another slap.

Bastard was firing on all cylinders. 'Happy now, you demented fuck? Got what you want?' He jabbed at Akaki with a sausage finger to emphasize every word. 'I nearly got killed because of you. Now get me out of here!' He kicked Nana in the ribs. 'Translate! Fucking tell him! Tell him the police are coming.'

Nana did as she was told; at least I thought she did. The word 'police' is pretty much universal.

Akaki just laughed, and one by one his men joined in. Yep, they were really shitting themselves that a couple of blue-and-whites were on the way.

Bastard wasn't fazed. I saw the outline of the Marriott cassette in his wet jacket pocket.

He turned his attention towards me and Charlie, as if the joke was on us. 'You two fucks really think I was coming all the way with you?'

He came and stood inches from my face. 'You know what? I should have gone to the cemetery and done the job myself, instead of hiring a moron with a machete to make a king-size fuck-up.'

He spotted Koba's weapon and hooked it out of its proud new owner's belt.

Fuck him; I wasn't going to flinch this time when he squeezed the trigger.

I looked him straight in the eye as he closed one hand on the grip and brought the other one up for good measure.

Nana screamed Paata's name but she needn't have bothered. Akaki roared an order and Bastard got an AK butt on the side of the head before he even saw it coming.

Charlie kicked the Desert Eagle away as it fell to the ground at our feet.

The militant leader stormed across and started yelling at Bastard, punctuating every sentence with a good kick to the American's prostrate bulk. The fat man only managed to crawl away as his attacker began to tire.

Nana translated. 'He says you can take Eduard and Nato's car. If you don't go now, he will kill you. He says that he imagines he's not the only person here who would like to see that.' She paused. 'And on that score, at least, he is telling the truth.'

Bastard reached Eduard's corpse on his hands and knees, and delved into the bloodstained pockets like a starving man fighting for food. A set of keys glinted in Paata's arc lights, and he staggered to his feet. His gut heaved. He stared at me, his nostrils flaring and whistling as his overweight body sucked in oxygen. He had things he still wanted to say, but he'd left them too late.

Akaki grabbed him by the roll of fat above his collar and frogmarched him all the way to the door.

Bastard disappeared from view, but he was still determined to have the final word. When Akaki's boys had finished applauding their beloved leader's most recent show of strength, his voice echoed along the rain-soaked track.

'I want those fucks dead! Kill them!'

2

I was starting to get the hang of Akaki; he wasn't a big fan of the long game.

He towered over Nana, pummelling her shoulder as he let her know what was on his mind.

Paata kept a watchful eye on the AKs just inches away from them as he translated for us. 'He wants an interview, right here and now. He has an important message for his fellow Georgians, and wants his words to be recorded for posterity.' He somehow managed to talk as calmly as if he was discussing overtime rates.

The three of us watched Nana's hands emphasize every word of her response. She wasn't backing down.

It was turning into quite a show. Even the guys guarding us were crowding round and tuning in.

'He's rambling,' Paata said, as Akaki turned up the volume another couple of notches. 'He says he wants to tell the world of his fight for freedom and against corruption. He says he will work to continue this battle, until victory – or until he meets God.' An edge of concern crept into his voice.

Charlie nodded. 'He knows he can come out with any old

bollocks he wants to now. He's got the papers, and Baz isn't here to disagree.'

I was worried about Nana. 'Why don't you guys just let him have what he wants? What's she giving him a hard time about?'

'She's telling him it's a great idea, but we should go and film him in the village. He needs to be seen out in the open, among his people, not cowering in a cattle shed . . . She says his film needs to have an epic scale; anything less would not do his message justice. She'll do the edit when she's back in Tbilisi.'

'Yeah, right. I bet he's really buying into that.'

'She has to try.' He sighed. 'He only tolerates people like us as long as we're of use to him. And when we no longer are, or if we do something that offends him . . .'

'We're history?'

Paata nodded. 'He slaughtered a French crew not so long ago . . .' He cocked his head. He'd heard something he didn't like. 'Oh shit . . . He's talking about the dish. He knows we can go out live.'

His eyes flicked anxiously between us and Nana. 'She's insisting they tape it, and in the village, not here . . . She's trying to give us a chance to escape, I'm sure of it.'

I glanced back at Akaki. His arm was raised, ready to give her the good news again. 'What's his take?'

'It's not good. I'm sorry.' The blood had drained from his face. 'She was calling him murdering barbarian scum on camera last week . . .' Paata's voice tailed off.

'Didn't go a bundle on it?'

Paata nodded gloomily.

Nana was turning away. She knew when to concede. Akaki gave her a parting kick in the small of the back to help her on her way. It must have been agony, but she was determined not to show it.

She limped the remaining five or six paces to the bench. 'Here's the deal . . .' The left side of her face was livid red and swelling. 'No pre-record. We go live or he kills us all now. He wants to sit right here on the bench and address not just his fellow Georgians but the USA too – and he wants to do it live.' Her eyes bored into Paata. 'Go and fix up the link.'

Paata hesitated. He knew there was one thing missing from her instructions. I grabbed him as he stood up. 'Take your time, mate.'

'No.' Nana was adamant. 'Get it rigged, and set up the link. Tell them who we have.' She looked him in the eye. 'We – need – the – cavalry . . . Understand?'

We all did now.

Akaki had some more stuff on his mind. He charged over like a wounded bull, with two of his arse-lickers in tow. Up close, he wasn't any prettier than he'd seemed from a distance. He was probably still in his thirties, but looked older, partly because any skin on his cheeks not covered by beard was badly pockmarked.

He raised one of his field labourer's fists and pushed the others out of the way to get to me. His eyes burned into mine.

His two arse-lickers demonstrated how hard they were by grabbing Nana and forcing her to translate as he went into another major-league rant.

'The murdering scum is telling you that he will kill the servants of the infidel crusaders as surely as we will kill their kings . . . He says he does this to avenge those of God's children they kill.'

Akaki prodded me so hard in the shoulder I reeled backwards.

'He says America has made many accusations against him; they have said that he is a man with a hidden fortune . . . These are infidel lies . . . He says that this is what he wants to say to the people of America.'

As I recovered my balance, I saw the screens in the Merc flicker into life again.

The two standing guard behind Akaki saw them too, and started gobbing off to their boss.

354

'Excellent.' Nana tried to look pleased. 'Charlie and Nick, help me with the camera and lights.'

I returned her smile. It wasn't all doom and gloom round here then. She was starting to call us by name.

3

Akaki sat, smoked and brooded as we helped Nana lug the camera and lighting gear over to the bench. Several AK muzzles tracked our every move.

The barn roof was no longer being pelted with rain, and the big red puddle around Koba's head was almost still. The sudden silence inside the barn only seemed to make it harder for Nana to ignore the bodies of Eduard and Nato. Her eyes kept straying back to them. I knew she felt responsible.

I glanced at them once or twice myself. They looked as though they'd been crucified. If the *Georgian Times* had thought Baz's body was grisly cargo, I couldn't wait to see what their headline writers would make of this.

I was pretty much resigned to the fact that, at this rate, we'd be joining them on the inside pages, dangling by the bollocks from a barn door. But there was still a chance. There was always a chance. When Nana's cavalry arrived, so would the mother of all gangfucks.

It wasn't long before everything was rigged, even with two of us on the job not really knowing what we were doing. It couldn't be helped. There's a limit to how much you can tear the arse out of a task before it's obvious you're doing fuck all, and on that front, at least, I was an expert. I'd been an infantryman for ten years.

Akaki groomed his beard with a gap-toothed plastic comb, preparing himself for TV stardom. There was a light either side of him and the camera right in front. He liked what he saw.

Nana fiddled about with the lens for a bit and altered the height of the tripod, but she knew as well as we did that she wouldn't be able to put this off for much longer. She stuck in an earpiece and plugged it into the camera.

Akaki handed his comb to one of his minions. It looked as though it had recently been dipped in goose fat. The expression on his face said he was ready, and ready right now.

But Nana wasn't, not quite yet, anyway. She moved to his side and murmured quietly in his ear. He looked at her and tugged thoughtfully at a handful of beard.

After a few more tugs, he started bellowing again, but this time Nana wasn't his target. Ponchos were going back on. AKs were being shouldered.

Charlie and I were busy looking busy, making needless adjustments to the kit. Nana came back over to us, pointing at the lights and conveying a series of highly technical instructions with her outstretched arms.

'I've told him that if this is to go out live to the US, I need to do a series of links to camera in English. These will be used as trails, to guarantee the biggest possible audience . . . I've also suggested he send some men to scout exterior locations, and round up enough locals for a crowd scene. He understands it's very important we get this right. We're going to meet them at the village hall once we've closed down the link.'

Three of the Taliwagons were already firing up as the guys clambered aboard.

Akaki was keeping just the two arse-lickers behind. They stood a few metres away, AKs trained on Charlie and me.

I watched the Taliwagons charge up the track, towards the houses nestled among the trees.

'Well done, lass.' Charlie put an avuncular hand on Nana's shoulder.

She smiled briefly then was back in control. She waved us away from the kit so Akaki could see what was happening. 'Nick, Charlie, go get in the van. I don't want him to see your faces when I go live. Go, please.'

She fired some more waffle at Akaki, and he was lapping it up. By the look on his face, he wasn't too far from suggesting the two of them got a slot together as Georgia's answer to Richard and Judy.

The lights burst into life as we made our way to the van, and the corner of the barn became Akaki's little slice of Hollywood.

4

Paata sat hunched in front of us, one earphone on, the other high on his head, ignoring everything but the image of Nana's face on the screens. We just watched and listened.

'Yep, that's OK, Paata. How am I for level? Did you get through? Are they coming? One, two, three, four, five . . .'

She took a deep breath and composed herself.

'Five seconds!' Paata kept his voice level. 'Yes, they are airborne. String it out.'

I caught Charlie's eye, and knew he was also thinking that we might still be able to keep our bollocks the right side of the barn door.

Nana just stared into the camera, nodding as the countdown crackled in her earpiece.

'Two . . . one . . . *On air* . . .'

'Standing right here next to me . . .' She turned to Akaki and gave him a deep, respectful bow, 'is a disgrace to mankind, the most despicable gangster ever to walk the blessed earth of Georgia.'

He nodded his acknowledgement then stared back into the camera.

'And within the last few minutes I have seen documentary evidence of his most appalling act of treachery to date . . .'

Her voice quavered and Akaki's brow furrowed.

'An abominable act . . . perpetrated by the murderer who sits before you . . .'

Akaki nodded his appreciation, not understanding a word. I hoped neither of the arse-lickers had taken a year out at Princeton.

Nana smiled and nodded back. 'Evidence so important that I have to relay it to our beloved nation right now, in case I do not live long enough to hand it over to the appropriate authorities . . .'

Nana swept her arm to embrace the whole valley, as if describing it as Akaki's domain.

'An affidavit was to have been sworn today by a member of parliament whose name I cannot mention because this monster beside me will recognize it . . .'

Her hand gripped the mike so tightly I could see her knuckles whiten.

'But, tragically, he cannot do that now. He is dead, murdered by Akaki's men, and others who did not want his evidence to see the light of day. Akaki now has possession of this document, but I have read it from cover to cover . . . and even if I wanted to, I could never forget the awfulness of what I have read . . .'

Paata muttered an acknowledgement to somebody into his mike and pressed a button. 'Five minutes, Nana. Keep going.'

She put a finger to her earpiece and nodded. 'The representative in question, a personal friend to many, known throughout this land as a man dedicated to fighting the corruption that stains our country, was murdered because he had proof that six members of our government are implicated in terrorist activities, in concert with the man you see before you—'

Paata hit the button again. 'Correction, Nana. It's ten, repeat ten minutes. Keep going, you're doing well. If he gets suspicious, cut the English and switch to the straight interview. OK?'

She fingered her earpiece again.

'Yes ... these six pillars of our establishment will greet President Bush when he arrives in our country this month ... and the hands they will extend to him in friendship are as bloodstained as that of the mass murderer, kidnapper, extortionist and drug trafficker they are in league with ...'

Charlie touched Paata's shoulder. 'This isn't actually going to the States, is it?'

He shook his head without looking round. We got the idea: shut the fuck up.

'It hardly bears thinking about, but the objective of this barbarity is to perpetuate the terrorist threat, so that the United States continues to send us aid; aid that doesn't find its way to feeding our hungry or repairing our hospitals, but lines the pockets of expensive, western-tailored suits ...'

Nana's voice cracked again. Akaki was starting to look concerned.

'Good news, Nana. It's four minutes, repeat, four – maybe less.'

'Unimaginable.' She nodded. 'But you must be told ...' She turned her head to Akaki and somehow managed a smile. 'This ... monster ... was paid one million American dollars by these politicians to plan and carry out the massacre of sixty women and children last month in the village of Kazbegi—'

She realized immediately that she'd fucked up. Akaki's head jerked round.

'*Sixty Minutes* ...' Nana did her best to smile, 'has the names of all six politicians, and the former FBI agent involved ...'

Akaki had smelled a rat. He muttered something to his arse-lickers.

'Three minutes, Nana. Hang on in there.'

'I am now going to expose those murdering and corrupt politicians to the people of Georgia . . .'

Her eyes flickered to the sky.

I hadn't heard anything inside the van, but the arse-lickers had; they ran outside and stared into the clouds.

Nana went for it. 'Gogi Shengelia . . . Mamuka Asly . . .'

Akaki was on his feet, his expression thunderous. He swept the camera aside and charged through the barn doors.

Nana kept on going.

'Giorgi Shenoy . . . Roman Tsereteli . . .'

The moment I stepped out of the van I could hear the beat of rotors. The helis must have stayed in dead ground until the last possible moment.

Akaki waved his arm and barked a sequence of orders. The arse-lickers tumbled into their Taliwagon. Akaki lifted his AK.

Nana was on autopilot.

'Kote Zhvania . . . Irakli Zemularia . . .'

The Hueys were virtually overhead. Akaki tried to bring his AK into his shoulder, only to be buffeted by the downwash.

The fourth Taliwagon screamed to a halt alongside him and the arse-lickers pulled him aboard. The heli dipped its nose and headed for the field just to the side of the barn.

Nana was shaking. 'There will be full exposure of all Zurab Bazgadze's allegations in a special edition of *60 Minutes* soon. Now back to the studio.'

She dropped the mike to her side. By the time Paata had wrapped her in his arms, her whole body was convulsed with sobs.

'Nana? We have to go.'

She looked over his shoulder at me. 'I'll help you, Nick. I'll help you with the police.'

I shook my head. 'No time for all that stuff. I'm taking Charlie home; there's something he's got to do.'

She shook her head, not understanding. 'What can be more important than wanting to prove your innocence?'

'Having the chance to die with your family around you . . .'

Charlie came up alongside me. 'See that treeline, lad?' He pointed to the slope behind the barn. 'Last one there buys the kebabs.'

5

I looked through the slats. Four Hueys were touching down in the field a hundred metres away. BDU-clad bodies leaped out and took up fire positions.

Paata was out of the van, dragging the camera from its mount, ripping out all the leads. He extended the small antenna that would maintain the link with the satellite dish and keep the feed live.

There was the rattle of automatic gunfire from the high ground to our right. Akaki's crew were putting down fire from the village.

The helis' engines roared and they lifted sharply. The guys on the ground spun around like headless chickens. It was like watching Kazbegi all over again.

One or two shots came from the field as the BDUs began to engage. I hoped they were aimed up at the village and not towards us.

Paata rushed outside, camera on his shoulder, Nana by his side.

I grabbed Charlie. 'Well?'

He looked at me but didn't answer.

I ran to the barn doors. 'Nana! Nana!'

She indicated to Paata what she wanted filmed.

'Nana!'

She turned back and I mimed the cut-away sign, finger across my throat.

The helis thundered overhead, eager to get out of the contact zone.

'Go!' she screamed. 'Go!'

She turned away and got on with her job.

I skirted round the side of the barn, Charlie following at a hobble.

We scrambled up to the treeline, using the building as cover, and then turned back towards the village, paralleling the road. We had a bird's-eye view of the chaos below us. BDUs milled around in the field, trying to take cover, not sure where. Maybe they hadn't got to page two of the textbook yet.

American voices tried in vain to command and control as one-in-four tracer burned down from the militants' light machine guns, thudding into the grass around their students.

One long burst arced down from the rooftops, scattering earth around the BDUs. They had no choice but to keep moving and get the fuck off the open ground.

Nana crouched against the woodpile outside the barn, talking to camera as the contact went on behind her. Paata panned across the sky as the whirl of rotor blades sounded from the high ground behind the barn.

The Huey was really close, coming in low, and swept over our heads, banking into a steep climb over the field then breaking right, towards the village. The crew were trying to get some kind of fix on the attackers.

Another burst of tracer forced the heli to bank sharp left and disappear back into the dead ground.

Charlie slowed. I grabbed his arm, hooked it over my shoulder, and dragged him along. I slipped in the mud, finally bringing both of us down.

365

Charlie landed on top of me. 'Any chance of a breather, lad?'

We lay where we had fallen, trying to catch our breath.

Another sustained burst from above us echoed around the valley. This time there was return fire; the boys in the field had finally got their act together.

Charlie shook his head. 'Why aren't those fuckers up there just running for it? Do they really want to take on the army? They all escaped from the same asylum as Koba?'

I dragged him to his feet. Before long, wooden houses began to appear alongside the road below us.

Charlie stopped. 'Listen, lad . . . No helis. Must have gone for reinforcements. Now's our chance.'

6

A tractor and an old Lada sat abandoned at the side of the track, but nothing that looked as though it might get our soaked arses out of here at any sort of speed, even if we could have dodged the militants to our right, and half the Georgian army down below us to our left.

The whole place fell eerily quiet.

'What about the Taliwagons?'

A burst of automatic echoed round the village before I could answer.

'Fuck it, let's go.' Charlie slid downhill and broke free of the treeline. I followed. He was making for a cluster of small wooden houses that hugged the main drag.

We edged into an unfenced yard and flattened ourselves against the back wall. All the shutters were closed. I heard a frightened child whimper behind them.

Squaddies at the bottom of the road loosed off with their AKs. From higher up, to our right, Akaki's men gave it back in spades. The barrels of their light machine guns must have been red hot.

A round ricocheted off the wall beside us and screamed up into the air.

I tugged Charlie's sleeve. 'Wait here, old one.'

Keeping low, I moved to the corner of the house. A dog started barking inside.

My hair was flat against my head. My trousers were caked in mud. My clothes stuck to me like clingfilm. I was just beginning to realize how hungry and thirsty I was.

I checked Baby-G. We had an hour and a bit until last light, maybe less, given the cloud cover.

I lay down on my stomach, and inched my way along the wall until I could see up and down the road. It was deserted. The villagers were keeping well out of this. I didn't blame them a bit.

The road stumbled uphill for about a hundred metres before disappearing. The militants' fire position must have been just beyond the bend. They'd chosen well. They had a clear line of fire all the way down into the valley where the helis had landed.

An American voice barked instructions about 200 to my left and BDUs darted around in response. Nana and Paata would probably be in among them as they pushed uphill, but we weren't going to stick around and find out.

I made my way back to Charlie. He had his leg elevated against the back wall, rain falling onto his face. 'The squaddies are getting close.' I held out a hand. He grabbed it and I pulled him up. 'I didn't see Akaki's crew, but they must be past the bend, a hundred up. We need to get up there and beyond their line. We'll stay behind the houses.'

'Well done, lad. So what are we hanging about for?'

I hooked his arm over my shoulder and we started to pick our way through a succession of unfenced back yards.

We'd gone another eighty or ninety metres when the houses veered left with the road. Another twenty or thirty and we'd be well beyond the line of fire.

We hit a fenced compound filled with pigs. It wasn't worth the effort of getting Charlie over the top. We doubled back up the slope and boxed around it. It all took time, and I didn't know how much of that we had to spare. The road might not be the squaddies' only axis of attack. The last thing we needed was to be caught in crossfire.

As we worked our way down again, the militants opened up with their light machine guns.

'Poor little buggers,' Charlie muttered. 'Talk about baptism of fire.'

'Shut up and get moving.'

I stopped, head up.

'Listen.'

The firing had come from behind us. We were beyond the contact.

All we had to do now was drop down into the village and see about hot-wiring ourselves some freedom.

7

We emerged beside what looked like the village hall. There must have been an election in the last year or so; the walls were plastered with fading campaign posters. A line of Zurab Bazgadzes beamed down at us.

'Our carriage awaits, lad.'

A Taliwagon sat just thirty metres away in the middle of the road. It was rusty and dented, but had four wheels and, with any luck, an engine. Best of all, there seemed to be no one with it.

'You ready, mate?'

He nodded.

I started running without checking he was behind me.

There was no movement, but the village was far from deserted. Shouts and a burst of automatic blazed from the other side of some buildings to my left, down towards the road.

I headed for the driver's side and flung open the door.

No keys.

I rummaged around in the glove compartment, the foot well, the door pockets. They were under the seat.

I jumped in and hit the ignition. The warm diesel fired first time.

I heard a shout to my right, and it wasn't Charlie.

An Akaki lookalike in a poncho glistening with rainwater was sheltering in a doorway no more than three metres away. His eyes were wide with shock. He came to his senses, dropped the handful of medical supplies he'd been holding, and went for his RPK.

The weapon swung up, almost in slow motion.

He looked beyond me and shouted again, but I shouted louder. 'Charlie!'

I hunched forward, praying that he'd bounce onto the back before I got sawn in half.

There was a blur of bodies and muzzle flash. The light machine gun jerked and sprayed a short burst into the air, then weapon and owner disappeared under Charlie's flailing body.

I leaped out and took a running kick at the militant's head.

My boot connected and Akaki's mate cried out.

Charlie rolled to one side and grabbed the weapon, and I kicked again. Charlie staggered to his feet and leaned over him, jamming the barrel into his chest. 'Get his mags, Nick! Get his mags!'

I lifted the poncho. The RPK was basically an AK-47 with a longer, heavier barrel and a non-detachable folding bipod mounted under the muzzle. It could be fed from special box or drum magazines, but also the familiar curved AK-type thirty-round mags. This boy had two of them in a chest harness. I pulled them free and we both legged it into the wagon.

I sawed at the wheel to aim the Taliwagon uphill, away from the square. The fuel gauge gave us just over half a tank.

Charlie pulled back on the cocking handle of the RPK to check there was a round in the chamber. Then he unclipped the mag and pressed his finger down on the top round to see how many were left.

'What you doing, lad?'

371

'Pointing us at Turkey.'

'No.' He put a hand on the wheel. 'Akaki first.'

'We don't have time for that.'

His hand didn't budge. 'Akaki.'

Fuck it. 'Just one pass, that's all you're getting.'

I threw the wagon into four-wheel and dropped the clutch, swinging us round until we faced the other way. My foot hit the floor.

The poncho had staggered to his feet but now had to dive back into the doorway to get out of the way.

I drove hard for the other side of the square before swinging the wheel right to head downhill. I squeezed the wagon into an alleyway and added a whole new set of dents to its already impressive collection.

We came out into the main drag like a cork from a bottle. The other Taliwagons had pulled in before the bend about 200 metres ahead of us. The militants were putting down a fearsome amount of fire against the BDUs below them. Three bodies lay motionless in the field where the Hueys had landed. The BDUs were still trying to fire and manoeuvre uphill, using the buildings as cover. Now they were closer, Akaki had better targets. Another body lay on the road between them, and I saw a couple of BDUs drag a wounded man into cover just beyond it.

I braked to a halt. Now we were here, I knew Charlie was right. But I wasn't going to tell him that.

I shoved the wagon into first. 'It's one pass, make the most of it.'

He turned his back to me and poked the weapon out of his window, wooden stock resting on the door, butt into his shoulder.

A few faces turned as we moved down the road, then went back to their war.

I accelerated.

Seconds later we were level with Akaki's crew and Charlie fired short, sharp bursts into anything that moved.

The noise inside the cab was deafening, even with both the windows open, and we were choking on cordite. I tried to keep the wagon as steady as I could. The rounds had to make their spots or we'd get a whole shitload in return.

The bodywork took a couple of crunching thuds as the militants got their act together.

Charlie re-cocked and got off two short bursts.

'Stop! Stop! *Stop!*'

I hit the brake and Charlie took aim at a cluster of three men, one of whom, unmistakably, was Akaki. He legged it while the two others tried to shield him.

Charlie's weapon fell silent.

'Stoppage!'

He changed mags, his eyes always on the target as it clambered into the back of a Taliwagon.

'Wait! Wait!'

He re-cocked and kept the bursts short and sharp. Akaki's wagon lurched forward and sped back the way we had come.

I braked hard and threw our Toyota into a three-point turn.

As we closed, their rear screen disintegrated and our windscreen took two rounds. The safety glass shattered but stayed intact.

'Keep going! Go, go, *go!*'

Charlie kicked out his side of the shattered windscreen. Shards of glass peppered my face, blown back by the wind. More rounds thudded into the wagon. Fuck it, there was nothing I could do but drive.

Charlie rearranged himself in his seat and shoved the RPK's muzzle through the hole in the screen. Its barrel sizzled in the rain. Charlie fought to keep the thing stable on its bipod and aimed as best he could, firing double taps to conserve rounds.

Akaki's wagon disappeared about fifty ahead of us.

'Go right, go right – cut him off!'

I swung the Toyota the way Charlie said, and found myself paralleling Akaki along a narrow mud track between two barns. Charlie held the weapon down to control it. 'Get your foot down! Get up there before him!'

I fought the wheel as the back of the wagon bucked like a rodeo horse.

We roared back up onto the high ground and passed the village square to our left. I threw the Toyota into a turn as Akaki's wagon broke out from the other side of the square. Charlie started firing before I'd even rammed on the brakes. 'Give me a platform. *Platform!*'

I held the wagon still as Charlie kept firing, short and sharp.

Mud kicked up around Akaki's wagon. It took hits but kept going.

Another burst.

'Stoppage!'

Akaki's wagon crashed straight into the side of the village hall, its wing ripped open. One body jumped out of the back; another fell. The driver stayed put, slumped over the wheel.

'Hold on!'

Ramming the gearshift into first, I aimed at the body running along the edge of the square.

Charlie worked frantically to change mags as we bounced and shuddered towards the runner. No mistaking who it was.

He turned, brought up his weapon, and fired.

I didn't know if we were taking hits or not, and I didn't care. I drove straight at him. 'Get that fucking thing loaded!'

The wind roared through the windscreen as Akaki turned and started to run again.

Too late; our wing caught him in the small of his back, catapulting him across the road.

I passed him; hit the brakes.

Charlie tried to get out.

'Stay!'

I threw the Toyota into reverse. The back wheel lifted over his body then came back down onto the road.

The front wheel followed.

I kept on reversing until Charlie could take aim. Two short, sharp bursts thudded into the body on the ground.

As we crested the hill away from the village, my foot never left the floor.

8

'One down, one to go.' Charlie had to shout to make himself heard over the wind rush.

'You pissed?' I kept my eyes on the road. We were only ten minutes out of the village and however much we needed them, I couldn't risk lights. What was left of the windscreen my side was shattered. The smashed glass and plastic safety layer protected me from the worst of the wind, but made it even harder to spot the puddles, or any deep hole that might swallow us up.

The firs covering the high ground to our right made our world darker still. The good news was, we were back on the pipeline, heading for Turkey and Crazy Dave. The five-metre-wide scar ran like a guide rail to our left.

I checked the rear-view. Still no pursuit. Fuck it; I switched on the headlights and put my foot down.

I'd just dropped down into two-wheel to try to eke out the fuel when the headlights picked out a static vehicle at the road-side. It was a rusting, lime-green Lada. The bonnet was up.

'Thank you, God.' Charlie reached down and pulled the RPK from the foot well.

I gripped the wheel. 'Come on, mate, I've got to get you home.'

'Fuck that, lad. We got the first bastard, now let's finish the job.'

'What's the point? He had at least an hour's head start. He might be in another vehicle by now, and halfway to Turkey.'

'So what? We check this out, and catch up with him then. I'm going for it. You in?'

As if I was going to leave him and drive on.

I stopped the Toyota and stuck it into first gear, ready to back him. As he climbed out, he pushed the safety lever on the left of the RPK down to the first click, single shot.

He walked around to the back of the Taliwagon, the big RPK in his shoulder, bipod folded up along the barrel.

Once he was level with me, we were ready.

'Come on then, let's do it.'

I lifted the clutch and crept forward as he limped beside me, using the wagon as cover. Why he'd got out, I didn't know. Then it dawned on me. He was enjoying this. He was doing it not only to get Bastard; he was doing it for himself. It was the last chance he'd ever have to do some soldiering, the thing that he was born for.

He stopped short of the Lada and so did I. I kept low in the seat. Bastard still had that Desert Eagle.

Charlie's eyes were fixed on the treeline, looking for trouble. 'Stay here, I'll check for sign.'

He hobbled forward, RPK at the ready.

He didn't go right up to the car; just circled it, checking the mud for tracks.

He tried the driver's door. The Lada was unlocked.

Charlie took a quick look inside, then moved slowly up the road, still casting around for sign.

Four or five metres ahead of the Lada, he turned and gave me a thumbs-up.

I rolled towards him and stopped.

He stuck his head through the passenger window. 'Flat shoes. Leading into the treeline.' He spoke very quietly, as if Bastard was within earshot. 'He can't have gone far; you saw how useless he was. We've got the fucker.'

He hobbled off without waiting to see if I was coming.

I killed the engine, grabbed the keys and got out.

9

We moved straight into the trees and started climbing.

Charlie was soon in trouble. I could hear his laboured breathing. He was carrying his injured ankle at a very unnatural angle.

I moved alongside him and put my mouth to his ear. 'Let's just do it until we can't see any more, OK? He could be anywhere.'

It wasn't as if there was any ground sign we could follow. The floor was covered with pine needles. He stopped and listened, mouth open, his head cocked to the left so his right ear faced dead ahead.

Finding our way back to the wagon again wouldn't be hard, even in the dark. All we'd have to do was drop downhill until we hit the road.

The rain battered its way through the canopy of firs, and the wind howled.

Charlie set off.

I stayed where I was. I'd be his ears while he moved about five paces ahead.

I drew level with him and he set off again. I wouldn't move

beyond him. I didn't have a weapon. He was going to be front man. It was the way he wanted it.

He took his time, weapon in the shoulder, forty-five degrees down but ready to swing up, safety still off all the way down to the second click.

He stopped after just one pace. It looked like his ankle had finally packed in on him. He crouched against a tree, looking up the hill.

I spoke into his ear. 'I'm getting knackered myself, mate. There's no way that fat bastard's going to climb any higher.'

Charlie pointed left, parallel to the road. His hand was shaking. He gave me a thumbs-up and adjusted the RPK, ready to move again.

I grabbed an arm before he could do so. 'You want me to take point?'

He held up a hand and we both watched it shake.

'Nah,' he said simply. 'He owes me, lad. And not just for a fucking bacon sandwich.'

He hobbled four paces to the left, weapon in the shoulder, following the contour of the slope.

I moved up to him again, keeping a bit of distance so our joint mass didn't present too easy a target.

He was silent for another few seconds, then dropped down into a waist-deep depression carved out by years of running water from the hilltop.

He froze almost immediately, reacting to a rustling noise in the dead ground.

There was a loud shout. 'Fuck you!'

Then a heavy-calibre shot and a falling body.

Charlie was down.

10

I ran into the dip.

Charlie wasn't moving, but Bastard was. He was out of sight, but I could hear him pushing deeper into the pines.

I grabbed the RPK and squeezed the bipod legs together to release them. I gave them a tug as I got to the top of the rise and they sprang apart. The barrel supported, I dropped to the ground, pushed safety fully down, and squeezed off a series of short sharp bursts in the direction of the noise. My ears were ringing when I stopped. Smoke curled from the muzzle.

No screams, no begging. Fuck him. I scrambled back down to where Charlie lay on his back in the mud and pine needles, so still he could have been sleeping. I knelt over him and cradled his head, and immediately felt warm liquid on my hands. He was making an ominous, slurping noise each time he drew breath.

I unzipped his Gore-Tex and tore at the hole in his shirt. Blood trickled down my hands. He had a sucking wound. The .357 round had drilled a hole in his chest, just below his right nipple. As he breathed in, oxygen had rushed to fill the vacuum in his thoracic cavity, and the pressure had collapsed his lungs. As he breathed out, air and blood were forced out like air and water from a whale's blowhole.

'Nearly stepped on the fucker . . .' Charlie coughed blood. 'I couldn't pull the trigger, Nick . . .' He tried to laugh. 'Fucking disco hands . . .'

His body twitched. He was in agony, but the crazy thing was, he was smiling.

But if he was talking, he was breathing – that was all that mattered.

I grabbed his hand and placed it over the entry site. 'Plug it, mate.'

He nodded. He wasn't that out of it yet; he understood what needed to be done. With his chest airtight, his lungs would inflate and normal breathing could resume.

'Got to check for exit wounds, mate. It's going to hurt.'

I rolled him onto his side, but there wasn't so much as a scratch on his back. The round must still be in him. A heavy round like that could only have been stopped by bone – maybe his shoulder blade – but a fracture was the least of his problems. We both knew he was in deep trouble.

Charlie began to groan. 'How's it look? How's it look?'

Over and over.

He'd be going into shock soon. I had to act fast, but what could I do? He needed fluids, he needed a chest drain, he needed the wound sealed; he needed the whole fucking cast of *ER* up here.

He groaned again.

Still no need to worry about his airway.

His hand had fallen from his chest. I put the heel of my mine over the hole to keep the seal. He coughed again, and the effort sent him into spasms of pain.

'How's it look? How's it look?'

His face contorted – another good sign. He could still feel it, his senses hadn't deserted him.

I needed to get him down to the wagon, and I needed to

keep the seal while I did so. I'd have to drive back to the village. The guy we'd lifted the RPK from had been standing in the doorway of what looked like a medical station – and the BDUs would have brought trauma packs.

We'd be arrested, but so what? I'd said I'd get the old fucker home, and I would.

'How's it look?'

'Shut up, and think life.'

There was nothing up here I could use to keep the seal, apart from my hand. How the fuck was I going to do that while I got him down the hill?

Bastard would be heading there too. He knew we hadn't come here by bus. But he wasn't going anywhere fast. I'd deal with him once Charlie was safe.

I looked down at Charlie's face. It was swelling like a football.

'Fuck, fuck, fuck!'

I lifted my hand.

There was a hiss, like air escaping from the valve of a car tyre, and a geyser of blood mist.

The round had certainly gone through one of his lungs, maybe both. Oxygen was being released into the chest cavity through any wounds. With me holding the seal, it had nowhere to go. The pressure in his chest had built so much that when he tried to breathe in, his lungs and heart had no way to expand.

I pulled him over onto his right side; blood that had pooled inside the lung poured out like milk from an overturned bottle.

I rolled him back and sealed the hole again.

He was losing consciousness.

11

I had to keep trying. 'It's OK, you can talk to me again, mate.'

There was no response. 'Oi, come on, speak to me, you old twat!' I pulled his sideburns. Still no response.

I lifted his eyelid.

So little dilation I could scarcely see it.

His breathing had become very rapid and shallow. His heart was working overtime to circulate what fluid was left around his body. There'd be more blood in his chest cavity now, pooling and killing him.

I listened to his breathing. 'Show me you hear me, mate . . . Show me . . .'

There was no reply.

'I'm going to move you, mate . . . not long now before we're out of here. Soon be on a plane, be back in Brisbane . . . OK, OK? Give me a sign, mate, show me you're alive.'

Nothing.

I lifted a lid, felt for a pulse.

None of those either.

I touched his face; the smile was still there. It was sign enough for me.

'Won't be long, you old fucker. Back soon.'

I picked up the RPK and lunged down the hill. I pulled off the mag as I ran, and pushed down. About ten left. I flicked safety to the first click. Every round had to count.

I checked left at the treeline, towards the wagons.

About 100 away, Bastard swayed from side to side as he stumbled along the road, arms flailing in an effort to maintain his balance.

Keeping in the trees, I followed.

He fell, and floundered for a moment like an upturned turtle.

I slowed almost to a walk, scanning ahead for a decent firing position.

He finally reached the Taliwagon. I watched him head for the driver's door and lean inside.

I put the weapon on the ground again, bipod in place, and eased myself down behind it.

The iron sights were on battle setting: 300 metres.

I felt surprisingly calm as I brought the butt into my shoulder, closed my left eye and took aim.

As I'd assumed, he was no big-time hot-wire man. He emerged from the cab and kicked the side panel in frustration before moving back to the Lada. A second or two later the engine turned over, but that was all it did.

Wet spark plugs. It must have been what had stopped him in the first place, and nothing had changed.

He persisted, but the battery was draining and it turned over slower and slower.

The wind took the sound and carried it away into the trees, but I watched him screaming out, punching the steering wheel with rage.

He climbed out and started towards the pipeline.

It didn't matter what his plans were; they weren't going to happen.

My eyes focused on his body mass. Left eye closed, I aimed low, into his gut.

I took first pressure on the trigger; breathed in, held it.

The foresight was sharp and Bastard was blurred.

Perfect.

I squeezed second pressure.

The weapon jolted in my shoulder and Bastard went down.

There was no movement at first, then his legs started to scrabble in the mud.

I got up. Weapon in the shoulder, bipod down, I moved towards him.

He was beginning to crawl over the pipeline scar, instinct dragging him away from danger. I doubted he even knew he was doing it.

He saw me coming.

He stopped, and curled on his side in the middle of the scar.

Dark, deoxygenated blood oozed from his gut and ran down the shiny chrome of the Desert Eagle in his belt.

Weapon in the shoulder, eyes on that .357.

I was only a couple of metres away when he held up a hand. He'd been saving his breath until he absolutely needed to speak.

'Nick, I'll split my half million with you . . . Chuck got his half mill . . .'

I just let him fill the gaps.

'I'm sorry about the cemetery thing, but I'd taken half his cash, man . . . I had to tidy up . . . Loose ends . . .'

His hand was still up, but more in supplication now than self-protection. 'You already got two-fifty, right? You said you'd split it down the middle. So I'll give you another two-fifty . . . That puts you ahead of us both . . .'

I heard the rattle of heli rotors in the distance. Bastard heard them too.

'Hey, Nick, tell you what – I'll give you it all . . . Get me back to Istanbul, I'll arrange the transfer. Come on, man.'

Hand still in the air, he pointed to his jacket pocket. 'I'll even give you the tape back. You're no fool, Nick. You know it's a good deal. Think about it. Chuck's gone. You gotta think of yourself now.'

This guy never gave up, did he?

I raised the RPK.

'Don't call him Chuck.'

I watched his face relax.

'Fuck you.' His hand dropped and went for Koba's weapon.

I pulled the trigger.

No need to check his pulse.

I dropped the RPK and turned and ran back into the treeline. I had to find Charlie again before it was too dark.

I needed to.

I'd promised Hazel I'd bring him home.

EPILOGUE

The farm
Three weeks later

It had been a simple funeral.

Hazel and Julie had thrown themselves into organizing every detail, even down to hiring the mini-JCB so Alan could scoop out Charlie's grave. I guessed it held the demons at bay for a while, kept the two of them in their bubble just a little bit longer.

There'd been no priest in charge yesterday, and no formal prayers. We all just stood round the coffin next to the hole, and everybody said their piece; then we lowered him into the ground, Hazel and Julie on one set of ropes, Alan and me on the other.

The whole thing was done economy, just the way a tight-arsed Yorkshireman would have wanted it. Silky was in charge of music. A couple of Charlie's favourite Abba songs blared out from the camper van nearby, and I wondered if his disco hands were behaving themselves when Boney M's 'Brown Girl In The Ring' followed shortly afterwards. That was when Hazel finally stopped holding herself together. The grandkids couldn't understand. They thought it was her favourite song.

Alan did the catering. The food was OK, but his kids said their dad's barbecue wasn't a patch on Granddad's.

Later that night, Alan had chucked in a DVD for them, but we'd all watched. We felt too numb to do much else, and ninety minutes of *Shrek* was as surreal a way as any of not brooding about absent friends.

By the time Alan and Hazel were putting them to bed, I was drained. I sat with Silky, watching disembodied images float across the screen, picking up the odd sentence here and there. It was current affairs time of night; President Bush had stopped by in Georgia on his way back from the VE celebrations in Moscow. The event had been covered for CNN by a local reporter, 'Emmy-nominated Nana Onani'.

I Googled her on Charlie's ageing PC before we turned in. The *60 Minutes* special had gone out; names had been named. Seismic changes were promised, but of course none had yet taken place. Two guys had been shifted sideways, and the other four had retired to their dachas to spend more time with their families.

Akaki threw up a few results, but nowhere near as many as Zurab Bazgadze. His state funeral had been a bit more lavish than Charlie's. I searched everywhere, but Jim D. 'Call Me Buster' Bastendorf didn't raise a dickie bird.

Now I was taking a final walk-past with Hazel. The plot was set among a clump of gum trees, with a low white fence round it. She'd thought it all out; made sure there'd be room for her as well, in due course.

It was last light and the sun was really low. Dust kicked up by the horses drifted across a blood-red skyline.

I started telling her how he'd been thinking of coming home when I caught up with him. 'But something stopped him, Hazel. I think I understand. I sort of missed it, too. You know, when you've done something for so long, it feels sort of . . . comfortable. I felt more at home out there with him than

392

I had for ages. I'm sorry; I didn't try hard enough to persuade him to bin it. I was selfish. I wanted to go along as shotgun.'

She smiled at me and shook her head. 'I knew the silly bugger wanted to die with his boots on. We've been together since we were at school. I knew him better than he knew himself. He thought he'd kept it hidden . . .'

She stopped to look out across the paddock at the dark silhouettes of the horses.

'Nick, I always understood what was going on in that thick head of his, and was prepared to live with it . . . If I couldn't make him stop, I wanted him concentrating on whatever he'd got himself involved with instead of worrying about me. That way he would stand a chance of coming home safe.' She smiled again as she headed towards the house. 'It worked pretty well for thirty years.'

She tucked her arm in mine. 'I know he wanted to do the right thing – you know, make sure me and the family were OK. But you know what, Nick? I'd trade it all for just a few more minutes with him.'

I stopped and looked up as her grandkids ran shrieking and giggling from the house a couple of hundred metres away and headed in our direction. 'You know what, Hazel? I think we'd all have liked a bit more time with Charlie . . . except for Charlie.'

The kids bounded up and hugged their grandmother, still not really sure what to make of things. Julie had told them Granddad had gone to teach the angels how to freefall, and they thought that was a great idea. But then they asked when he'd be coming home.

We reached the house. The VW was outside, all packed, ready to go. Well, sort of. The surfboard only had two bungees holding it down.

Silky came out onto the veranda, arm in arm with Julie. She came down the steps and gave Hazel a final hug, then jumped into the VW. With a bit of luck we'd be in the Whitsundays for breakfast.

Hazel kept her hand on my arm and pulled back to have a last look at me. Her eyes were brimming.

'Nick, if you see Crazy Dave, don't forget to thank him for what he's done for us. The money, getting you two back here – he's been absolutely wonderful.'

I kissed her cheek. 'He has, hasn't he?'

I climbed into the combi. Mother and daughter waved to us from the veranda as we turned down the track.

I leaned forward on the steering wheel, ready for a long night's drive, thinking about my best mate Crazy Dave.

I'd heaved Charlie into the Taliwagon and followed the pipeline as we'd planned, driving all night without lights, so the helis didn't see me. From that moment on, Crazy Dave had taken over. He got us picked up on the Georgian side of the border and driven into Turkey. He sorted passports, everything.

He'd got us flown back to Australia, me in Club Class and Charlie in cargo, and then he'd seen to it that Hazel was set up for life. But then, he hadn't had a whole lot of choice . . .

As I'd crawled along beside the pipeline that night, I'd mulled over what the fat fuck had said. Bastard's politico mates had given him a million for the job, but instead of spreading it around he'd skimmed off five hundred grand for his retirement plan.

Crazy Dave hadn't been far behind.

Charlie had only needed two hundred thousand, and the silly fucker had probably said he'd do anything for it.

So, I made a deal with Mr Good Guy of Bobblestock while waiting in the Club lounge at Istanbul. He'd give Hazel the whole five hundred thousand, telling her it was the agreed fee for the job. In return, I'd hold off telling the guys who knocked on his door how much mark-up he liked to take, or telling the companies that used him that he had a quality control problem – he didn't even check if the bayonets had disco hands.

The bit I'd enjoyed most was telling him that if he didn't get his finger out and have the cash in Hazel's account by the time me and Charlie arrived in Brisbane, I'd be on the next flight to Bobblestock, to come and separate his bony arse from his wheelchair.

Silky touched my arm. 'Why the smile, Nick Stein?'

I took my eyes off the track for a second, and grinned at her. 'Just thinking . . .'

I'd been thinking about her a lot – for 12,000 miles and plenty of time zones – and normally that would have been her short cut to a P45. I'd have left her in Brisbane, I'd have given her the van. I'd have cut away.

But this time, about 36,000 feet over the Pacific, I'd remembered something someone had once said to me in a car that stank of wet dogs.

'It's all about trying to hang on to the balance, lad . . . make any sense?'

I'd nodded to myself on the plane, and I nodded to myself again now.

'About what?'

'About how right you were. We are a good fit, aren't we?'

She laughed and leaned her head against my shoulder, and if that was what joining the human race was all about, I was up for it.

Something else I'd learned from the expert.

We passed the paddock where the old stallion had used to mope, but not any more. I'd fucked about with the JCB and dug a big hole in the corner of his field, and then I'd put Charlie's shotgun to his head and given it both barrels. I had an idea that the bay was smiling now as much as Charlie was.